DUCKS ON THE POND

DUCKS ON THE POND

AMY KLINGER

This is a work of fiction. Names, characters, places, and incidents either are the product of the author's imagination or are used fictitiously. Any resemblance to actual events, locales, organizations, or persons living or dead, is entirely coincidental and beyond the intent of either the author or the publisher.

The Story Plant
1270 Caroline Street
Suite D120-381
Atlanta, GA 30307

Copyright © 2024 by Amy Klinger
Cover illustration and design by Vance Kiviranna

The Library of Congress Cataloguing-in-Publication Data is available upon request.

Story Plant paperback ISBN-13: 978-1-61188-408-1
Story Plant e-book ISBN-13: 978-1-61188-422-7

Visit our website at www.TheStoryPlant.com

All rights reserved, which includes the right to reproduce this book or portions thereof in any form whatsoever except as provided by U.S. Copyright Law. For information, address The Story Plant.

First Story Plant Printing: February 2025
Printed in Turkey by Seagull Editions & Art Printing
0 9 8 7 6 5 4 3 2 1

For BB and Dos

Tracing its origin back to baseball announcer Arch McDonald in the 1930s, the expression "ducks on the pond" refers to the situation of having more than one runner on base and in scoring position.

> "You all think 'ducks on the pond' is just about how many runs can be scored in an at-bat. But I want you to think about it differently, okay? We're a team, so what you do at the plate—ground to third, bunt, blast a triple—that directly affects all our guys on the bases, whether they advance or get out. It's not just about you and your hit. So don't be stupid."
> — Coach Allen Bordo

PROLOGUE

Blame it on a stone. The flat and oblong kind. A water-worn stone, perhaps from when Lake Champlain had been an Ice Age inland sea covering this flat stretch of grassy ground, where a well-smacked ball getting past the right fielder could roll far and fast enough for an automatic home run.

Tucked into the laces of the catcher's right cleat, the stone was heavy enough to be noticed on impact, but not enough to say for sure it was deliberately flung, or so he thought. It was a trick Reuben learned in his high school years from Teddy Marks, the varsity catcher, who'd essentially taught Reuben how to play the position when he was just a freshman. Teddy had said, "Use it sparingly. You gotta save it for just the right moment, just the right asshole." Because every team has one: the guy who takes thirty practice swings before even stepping into the box. Hand held up to put the pitcher on hold as he digs, digs, digs at the dirt beside the plate, then takes yet more practice swings. Tall or short, but always on the stocky side, he's louder than everyone on the field. He throws his hands up at teammate errors and argues the close and not-close calls (never mind that, in this case, the ump is a local high school kid getting paid in snack bar vouchers).

And this time, it's not a he; it's a her. Dana Van Sykes. Clocking in at about five foot three, built solid and bow-legged like a bulldog with a bark to match. And this isn't a high school team, but a bunch of grown-ups playing in a competitive co-ed softball league in Orrsville, Vermont. At the top of the fifth, the game is scoreless, but the emotional stakes are high, amped up over things both related and unrelated to the game, things like past grudges and present grievances, "oil and water" personalities, and a community controversy that was imposing attention even on those who claimed they couldn't care less about it.

With a sudden buzz, the overhead lights kick on, their sensor set for dusk just as it becomes difficult for the players with middle-aged eyes to track the ball. The spotlights fade up to fully bright, heightening the drama as if the field is a stage.

The pitcher, Maddy, rolls her shoulders a couple times to loosen up, then she begins a complicated series of push-and-pull arm movements before windmill-whipping the pitch toward Reuben's outstretched mitt. An inside pitch that Dana chips up and out of play over the backstop.

The next pitch is nearly identical to the first, which allows Dana to recall and adjust, stepping just a hair back from the plate to catch the ball solidly, sending it soaring toward right field. But the hit sails sideward. Reuben lets out a relieved breath.

"Foul ball." The ump has the kind of flat-voiced underenthusiasm perfected by sixteen year olds. "Oh and two."

"Van Sykes," Reuben says, "didn't I once hear you say that actually, there *is* shame in going down swinging?"

Dana digs, twisting her cleat in the ditch. "I'll show you swinging—"

Reuben can tell by the focused power in her stance that Dana Van Sykes is spring-loaded to crush the next pitch. With his right hand, he carefully slides the stone from his shoe. The timing would need to be perfect. Reuben gives the signal to Maddy for a changeup. He can tell she is wary, both knowing that Dana is a sharp read, and the consequences of her catching a lob could be disastrous.

"C'mon, Mads. I got ya," Reuben assures.

The infielders chime in, too, "Alright, Maddy."

"Make her work, Mad Dog!"

The windup is a perfect deception, its full-speed motion revealing nothing of the flat, deadspin release. Maddy was right to worry as Dana had a calculation ready in her head if the changeup was served. She checks her swing for a split second and locks her target on the ball sailing toward her. But just before it comes in reach, Reuben flicks the stone at Dana's ankle. The distraction, coupled with the brainwork she is already channeling to adjust to the changeup, is simply too much. Dana Van Sykes swings and misses.

"Strike three, batter's ou—!"

Fortunately for everyone involved, Dana Van Sykes drops her bat before body slamming Reuben, who crashes back into the ump, the two of them domino falling into the backstop.

Like a match lit near a propane leak, the players explode into action. Joss, the shortstop—always the fastest runner—gets to Dana Van Sykes first, pulling the batter's shirt and spinning her around while Dana lets fly a few blind punches. The first-base coach tries to reach them, but instead gets sucked into a fast wave of players shoving and shouting, wrestling and fist-swinging. Reuben rolls off the flattened umpire. Peeling off his catcher's mask, he plunges into the fray, pulling people apart, which proves to be futile as a handful of spectators spring from the bleachers and add their bulk to the fight. The obscenities and condemnations fly.

"Cheaters!"

"Go back to where you belong!"

"God's gonna strike you down, Downes!"

This is not your typical brawl. Most of the players had never taken, much less thrown a punch, and so the chance of any injuries more serious than bruises and scrapes is small. Look left and you see Toren Abernathy, voted Washington County's Postal Delivery Person of the Year, grasping a fistful of organic farmer Aaron Reichert's beard. Marnie Colombe, mortgage lender and vocal PTA member, has Donny Scavutto in a headlock. The waitress swinging at the coffee roaster; the herbalist taunting the naturalist. And of course, Reuben, who is arguably the lightning rod in this situation, trying to defend himself against car-dealing twin brothers, Dwayne and Shane (*"Come see Dwayne and Shane—you'll never drive the same!"*).

If there is one cool head on the field, it is Patrice, who rushes in from right field to usher the stunned umpire off the field, insisting on giving the boy a ride home. The headlights of Patrice's car reverse out of the spotlighted scene—a chaos that could almost be described as gleeful. Or at least, a valve release on a pressure cooker whose force had been building all week and maybe even a couple of decades.

As the last of the sun slips behind the Adirondacks across the lake, a local patrol car pulls up, lights flashing. And just as quickly as it started, the brawl deflates. Players and fans, neighbors and friends, dust themselves off, wipe their bloodied noses, and blink at each other as if waking from a confused dream.

FIRST

"Don't get too comfortable with the batting order. Yeah, we want our leadoff to be a sure bet for getting on base and fast stealing. And number four is gonna be our power hitter. But there's something to be said for shaking things up, sometimes even midgame. A new order sets up fresh dynamics. Throws off the other team's pitcher. Restores confidence to a hitter in a slump. Change is good. Let's use it to our advantage."
— Coach Allen Bordo

CHAPTER 1

The rolling suitcase was like an obedient dog that slowed and paused with Reuben's gait as the innkeeper stopped along the hallway to show him and Hannah where they could find extra towels and blankets, then a few steps later pointing out a sepia photograph of the Schuyler Inn from the 1930s.

Hannah went up close to inspect, squinting into the details.

"The original part of the house was built in 1816 by Thomas Schuyler, one of the town's original settlers and owner of the lumber mill." Rosemary's voice was bright with the practiced tone of a tour guide. Full-figured in a floral dress, tan hose, and blocky shoes, the woman very nearly resembled one of the stuffed taffeta chairs in the sitting room they had just passed through.

"Ghosts?" Hannah asked.

Rosemary tilted her head questioningly.

Hannah slowly shifted her weight side to side so the floorboard creaked like a sound effect in a horror movie. "There's so much history here, I would imagine there's some energy of the lost hanging around."

"Energy of the lost?"

"Cold spots?"

"Only from drafty windows."

"Things gone missing?"

"When you're my age, you're certainly apt to misplace things."

"Doors inexplicably slamming?"

"Not that I've experienced, dear."

Hannah sighed. "Please tell me there's been at least one murder or suicide?"

Reuben shifted uncomfortably. It was a thing Hannah did, steering conversations into unexpected, sometimes off-putting directions, often—but not always—to do with the macabre. She had once told Reuben it was a trait she took on as a kid, a way of upending the kind of trite, small-talk exchanges that made her want to slice her ears off.

"No murders, no suicides. At least not on record." Rosemary added, "And I know the record." She stopped in front of the door to their room; the sign on it read *Sweet Birch Suite*. "I'm afraid you'll find the inn a little lacking in that kind of gothic romance. But I do have some pristine historical artifacts I'd be happy to show you, including a set of napkins that were hand embroidered by Mrs. Schuyler herself."

Rosemary's response was the kind of redirect that Reuben had used himself when he and Hannah were first dating, having met just over a year before at the Hartford Area Business Association's annual meeting. The two of them had been seated at the same breakout table, a discussion that was quickly dominated by Chuck, a personal business coach. During the "bio break," Hannah elbowed Reuben as he waited for a turn at the coffee table.

"That guy needs to be personally coached in shutting his piehole, am I right?"

"Sorry?" Reuben asked.

Hannah waved her hand dismissively. "You don't have to apologize. I'm not offended."

Hannah's eyes were swimming-pool blue, the kind painted on baby dolls. He said, "I meant. . . I wasn't sure what you were—"

"I'm Hannah Beck." She took Reuben's hand and shook it firmly.

"Right, Poppets," he said. "I remember from the intros." Hannah had told the group that her business was making hand-decorated cake pops designed to look like actual people, famous or otherwise.

"And you're Reuben Downes. I actually have one of your paintings."

"Wow, really?"

"But don't tell anyone because it's the one that used to hang in the waiting room at the Marlborough Chiropractic Center. I used to work reception there. The painting was always in my line of view, and it was kind of my escape on dull days. I used to imagine stepping into that lake. How cold the water would feel on my ankles. That green pine needle smell. Stuff like that. So when they laid off a few people, including yours truly, and didn't give us a single day's severance, I smuggled the painting out in what felt like a fair exchange."

This was a lot of information for Reuben to take in, and he wasn't sure if he should express appreciation that she liked the painting so much that she stole it or sympathy that she'd lost her job, so he chose to not comment on either. "That's quite a coincidence, then, that we ended up in the same breakout session."

"I actually, totally finagled it with my friend Constance who works in catering. I mean, once I saw your name was on the attendee list. 'Cause I thought, how cool would it be to meet you and tell you all that?"

9

The line for coffee was moving painfully slowly. Hannah must have noticed Reuben silently counting the number of people in front of him.

"Listen, there's an Italian bakery just a block from here. Their cappuccino is so good it brings tears to my eyes. Coach Chuck won't miss us. What do you say we ditch?"

In truth, Reuben had already decided to duck out of the rest of the meeting after he'd had some coffee to fortify him for the drive home. Normally, he would politely decline, but there was something about Hannah's unabashed openness that he was enjoying.

"You know," Reuben said, "that sounds great."

Once they were settled at a tiny table in Caffè Allegro, sipping what Reuben had to admit was an excellent cappuccino—something he wouldn't otherwise have ordered—he asked Hannah about Poppets.

"I'm very popular with the Bat Mitzvah set," she had told him. "And let's be real, it's not easy to capture the nuanced facial features of a thirteen year old. They don't let me put zits on them."

Reuben sipped, just enjoying hearing her talk. "Well, I'm sure most of your customers aren't expecting sophisticated portraits."

"Oh, no?" said Hannah. "You think a cake pop is any less of a canvas than what you paint your abstract impressionistic landscapes, or whatever you call them, on?"

"Yeah," Reuben laughed but saw Hannah was asking in earnest. "I mean, no. I don't actually know." He couldn't yet tell if this woman had a wickedly sharp sense of humor or was completely lacking in one. He tried to strike a more diplomatic tone: "I can imagine frosting isn't the most cooperative of mediums."

"It's fondant, not frosting. And you've never actually seen a truly skilled decorative cake pop, have you?"

"I'm not big into desserts."

"I'm not either," she said. "I just like making them." Without giving Reuben a chance to comment on the strangeness of being a baker who didn't like sweets, Hannah asked him, "Want to know why I named my business Poppets?"

It was like a verbal ping-pong match, and Reuben was on his heels but game to try to keep up. "Well, there's the obvious pun with cake pops," he answered. "And aren't poppets, like, dolls of some kind?"

Hannah explained that historically, poppets were a form of witchcraft—dolls carved from roots, clay, or even potatoes—to hex the person whose likeness they represented.

"Like voodoo dolls? You're some kind of baking witch?"

"Don't be ridiculous," she said. "I'm a businessperson. I make a huge margin on every cake pop. If my customers' hair started falling out, or their house burned down, or their girlfriend disappeared, or they lost a ton of money in the stock market, or their teeth turned black, or their hamster spontaneously combusted..." It was a lot of specificity. "That would be bad for business." She added. "You would have to be highly selective about who and when you hex."

"Huh." Reuben was still not sure to what degree she was or was not joking. "I've had clients I disliked but it hasn't quite risen to wanting to murder their pets."

"Oh my god, you're wondering if I'm serious!" She laughed so boisterously that an older couple on the other side of the cafe turned to look at them. Reuben smiled and gave them a little wave.

She lowered her voice and leaned in. "Relax. I'm only messing with you to seem more interesting than I actually am. I mean... you're like this tall, slightly-better-than-average looking, freaking amazing artist. And I'm just a college dropout who built her business around a trend that'll probably be dead in three years."

"I'm not any kind of big, amazing artist." But then, worrying that Hannah might start to feel underwhelmed by him, he added, "But you are correct that I was voted Most Slightly-Better-Than-Average Looking in my senior year."

Hannah let out that big, unselfconscious laugh again, and it was like a bright light switching on. Despite Reuben being over a foot taller than her, Hannah's way of inhabiting a space seemed so much bigger and fuller than his own—one which tended toward benign observation and a reticence to draw attention to himself. Even now in his midthirties, these survival byproducts of having grown up an only child who bounced around from school to school were still ingrained.

"Truthfully, I think you're above-average-adorable but a girl's gotta play a little hard to get."

Two months later, Hannah had moved into Reuben's loft apartment, the coveted top floor of an old sewing mill overlooking the Connecticut River. Within days, she'd claimed the sunny window seat as her morning coffee nook and cake pop "ideating space." It wasn't long before they hired a contractor to expand the kitchen to accommodate Hannah's baking business and bring it into compliance with Connecticut's cottage food laws. The renovation forced Reuben to shrink his painting area a little, but it meant that Hannah could sublet her kitchen rental space and use the savings to branch out into custom cookie portraits.

The trip to the Schuyler Inn was a short getaway during prime fall foliage season to celebrate the one-year anniversary of Reuben and Hannah's not-totally-serendipitous first meeting.

"Okay, then what about witches?" Hannah asked Rosemary.

"Hannah, I think—" Reuben tried to interrupt but Hannah kept on.

"I read somewhere that a lot of these old houses have 'witch windows' that go sideways, probably designed to keep witches out, but I like to imagine they were to let witches in so they could hide from the pitchfork-and-torch people."

For a moment, Reuben caught Rosemary's eye and gave a slightly pained smile, silently apologizing for his girlfriend's doggedness. Rosemary's good-natured chuckle seemed aimed at reassuring him. No doubt, as an innkeeper, the woman has encountered all kinds of odd ducks.

"That's certainly more interesting than the truth, my dear." She slipped a key into the lock. "Back in the day, windows were too expensive to make them custom sized, so people just used what they had on hand and tilted them sideways to fit the space. That's just the way Vermonters do."

Hannah turned to Reuben and discreetly mimed hanging herself in response to the innkeeper's mundane explanation.

On the far wall of the room was a tall canopy bed festooned with blue and yellow ruffled pillows. Nearer was a dresser set with a wide porcelain bowl that Reuben thought might have served as a chamber pot in its past life. There was a vase full of silk hydrangeas on one nightstand and a stack of leather-bound books on the other.

Nearly every surface, including the wooden hope chest at the foot of the bed, was covered in lace.

"Hope you'll be cozy," said Rosemary, setting the key on the dresser. "If you need anything between the hours of 8 a.m. and 7 p.m.," she rang a tinkling bell on a stand outside their door, "just jingle."

"Thanks very much, Rosemary," Reuben said.

Once he shut the door, Hannah hopped on the bed. "Firm. Not much bounce," she said. "I suppose that'll muffle the bed-knocking for the guests next door."

For precisely that reason, Reuben had tried to persuade Hannah to book a hotel instead. Inns inflicted a weird intimacy with strangers he was never at ease with. He didn't enjoy feeling like a guest, always keeping his best manners in place, trying to be quiet even when flushing the toilet in your own room.

He straightened a doily. "It's like someone's grandmother exploded in here."

"Well, I love it," Hannah told him. "And, we've got a perfect weekend ahead of us, starting with a wild game feast tonight, a gondola ride to the top of Mount Mansfield tomorrow morning, antiquing—duh—and a Ben & Jerry's factory tour. Then Sunday, there's this river gorge not too far away where, like, a hundred people have drowned since the 1950s. It's called the 'deadliest place in Vermont.'"

While Reuben didn't consider any of these things particularly "perfect" (he would have preferred a weekend in Boston, strolling the galleries and hitting a club or two for some live music), he recognized that this weekend wasn't about him. The getaway was meant to lift Hannah's spirits, coming out of a challenging month navigating a lawsuit threat from a bride whose party-favor cake pops, several guests pointed out, looked a lot like the groom and one of the bridesmaids—who'd apparently had a romantic attachment a decade earlier. Hannah's defense was that the two women wore the same midlength haircut with the same highlights, and passing them on the street, one would honestly have trouble distinguishing one from the other. Still, the bride claimed humiliation and emotional distress on the most important day of her life. Hannah was fully prepared to go to court, but Reuben and her lawyer persuaded her to settle, taking the high road for her business reputation's sake. As Reuben hoped, the trip planning had lifted Hannah's mood out of the angry funk she'd been in.

The first evening was more enjoyable than Reuben had been expecting, starting with the wild game dinner, which featured small plates of wild boar sausage, an elk chop, a rabbit skewer, and a duck taco. The sex later that night was an absurdly funny but ultimately unsuccessful exercise at keeping Hannah's more vocal expressions at a discreet level. To Reuben's mortification and Hannah's delight, the neighbors raised the volume of their television in response.

Waking after midnight with an arm stinging of pins and needles, Reuben lay listening. Even with the windows closed, the river beside the inn made for a cheerful background so different from the urban white noise at home, which was a constant stream of passing cars and intermittent train horns.

After breakfast the next morning in the cozy sunroom, Hannah was comparing itinerary notes with two couples that had traveled together from Doylestown, Pennsylvania. Reuben could feel their eyes bouncing back and forth between Hannah and him, the way strangers often sized them up as a couple, noting the contrast between her pretty petiteness and round-cheeked, rosy features, and his lanky frame topped by an unremarkable mop of brown hair. Reuben turned away, pretending to peruse the tourist literature rack.

Their day's plan followed exactly what Hannah had outlined, starting with a drive to the ski resort at the base of the state's largest peak. Behind the wheel, Reuben bent his neck low to get a full view of the mountains rolling by. The golds and oranges, flaming reds and evergreens, below a flawless blue sky felt otherworldly. Connecticut had fall but not quite the widespread color overload he was experiencing now. They passed a tall, white, steepled church tucked in among the foliage, so quintessential New England that it felt like a living postcard.

"We got a perfect ten of a day," Hannah said. "When my sister was here in July, it was nothing but fog and rain, rain, rain the whole time."

The resort's gondola ride to the top of Mount Mansfield was a little unnerving as Reuben and Hannah and a family of four were packed into a bubble-shaped car that traveled along a cable, rising two thousand feet, just short of the mountain top. They debarked and walked out among dozens of tourists, snapping photos of each other against the panorama of fall foliage.

Reuben and Hannah were quiet as they followed a hiking trail that was supposed to lead them to the peak's ridge line. As the terrain turned steep and more challenging, Hannah's flats offered no ankle support and even less traction. She slipped often and once lost a shoe that Reuben had to help her dislodge from a rock crevice.

"This is just nuts. Mountain goats hike stuff like this, not actual people," Hannah said as a lean, tanned woman practically ran past them. "Let's go back."

Reuben had been excited to see the promised sweeping 360-degree view. "Well," he hesitated, watching the woman rock-hop up the trail like Spider-Man, "I'd like to keep going. I can meet you in about an hour at the restaurant at the top of the gondola. Do you mind?"

Hannah's expression suggested she did, in fact, mind.

He tried again, "I just think it would be a shame to come all this way and not get to the very top."

She remained unmoved.

"I did tell you to wear sneakers..."

It had been a point of contention before they left the inn, but Hannah made it clear that sneakers weren't "cute."

"Fine." Hannah shrugged the bag off her back, more fashion accessory than backpack. "You might as well take these." She pulled a nearly bursting ziplock bag of trail mix and a squeezable water bottle.

"I have no place to put—" But Hannah accessed his jacket's outer pocket for the trail mix and slid the water bottle in his inside pocket.

"Please don't dillydally and daydream. We have a schedule."

Reuben would have preferred a little more flexibility in what was supposed to be a relaxing weekend, but he would take his small victory. As Hannah headed back down, he continued up, winding over rocky outcroppings and wide slabs that were tricky enough for him to realize that she had made the right decision for herself in turning back.

Though not in prime shape, Reuben maintained a steady, if a little winded, pace. When the trail finally reached the top of the ridge, he stood, eagerly taking in views in every direction for what must have been a hundred or more miles away. To the east, he could see Mount Washington in New Hampshire, and to the west, Lake Champlain laying low at the foot of the rugged

Adirondacks. Everything below him was ablaze with color while the alpine environment he stood on was lichen-covered rock and scraggly evergreens. He would have liked to continue hiking all the way to what the map called "The Chin," but there simply wasn't enough time to get there and back before needing to meet up with Hannah.

Moving aside for some hikers to pass, Reuben stepped onto a smooth rock face that seemed a good spot to sit and rest a moment. Now hungry, he was grateful that Hannah had foisted the trail mix and water on him.

The temperature alternated between sunny-warm and sharply chilly when strong, sudden gusts of wind kicked up and snatched at Reuben's jacket. As he snacked, a raven dipped and glided just overhead in a way that seemed like pure joy. Reuben was alert and attuned to everything around him. For years, he'd been working only in-studio, focused on abstract-style paintings that could best be described as "aesthetically pleasing" for the corporate environments in which they were hung. This natural, untamed setting felt like a much-needed jolt to the jadedness he had started to feel toward his work, as clients became ever more proscriptive with what they wanted from their commissioned pieces.

Reuben shifted his gaze from the wide macro view of the peak to the micro world by his feet: a fist-sized rock covered in green, black, and orange swirls of flaky lichen. Beside it was a little plant cluster whose spiked, green shoots more closely resembled sea vegetation than what Reuben had expected from high alpine flora. He reached down to a patch of moss to feel its cool, damp fur.

The quiet contemplation of the moment revived him, too. Living and working with Hannah in the same close quarters, there never seemed to be space to be alone for any kind of time. Had she continued the hike with him, even if she didn't fuss the entire way up, she would have provided running commentary, prodding him to respond when he wanted to simply admire the scenery.

He thought, *How can it be that the things I adore most about Hannah—her fearlessness, the way she talks without filtering, her vivid energy—are the same things that sometimes make me not want to be near her?*

◆

Seek & Find Antiques was one of several shops Hannah had researched. It was set back from the main tourist part of the town, down a well-maintained dirt road. It wasn't actually an antique store so much as a restored old barn that rented out space to individual dealers. Thus, the contents were relatively organized by themes, which allowed Hannah to seek out the stalls—some of them literal stalls—that specialized in old farmhouse kitchen goods, while Reuben gravitated to the rusty tools and farm equipment, and then eventually to an area stocked with baseball memorabilia. He picked up an old catcher's mitt, a massive slab of leather cinched together by a worn, knotted leather string. He thought about the mitt's original owner, imagining a stocky, eighteen-year-old Vermont farm boy, a catcher with a cannon of an arm who had dreams of playing in the minors. Though it felt a little like trespassing, Reuben slid his hand inside the glove, noticing how the splaying of the finger pockets, which had conformed to the owner's hand, felt just slightly off. A wider gap between the index and middle fingers, an awkward angle to the thumb. He thought about the sweat from the catcher's hand, soaked layers deep into the padding.

As an avid Little Leaguer and high school catcher himself, Reuben felt a warming of his thoughts as he recited in his head the names of his senior year teammates in their regular batting order: Crispin "Crispy" Mayer, Jimmy Deegan, Bobby Alfonso, Taylor Wade, Frank Gargiulo, Reuben, Denny Partridge ("C'mon get happy..." they would sing at him), Anton Bell, and Tiny Tim LaRoche.

"How old is this?" Reuben asked the vendor, a man his father's age with a thick salt-and-pepper mustache that seemed to animate when he talked.

"That'd be a Goldsmith Model 181. Circa 1925. This one's a Leather Front Khaki Back style. Look at that piping—it's beautifully intact," he ran his fingers along the edge to show. "For a well-used glove, this one was lovingly cared for. You won't see them in this good condition too often. Not the old ones, anyway. I could let her go for a hunner-twenty-five."

"Oh?" Reuben had not been intending to buy, and in fact, wouldn't have been able to say if he thought it was worth five dollars or five hundred dollars. In the moment, $125 seemed like a good deal for a mint condition, antique mitt. "Huh." Then, on pure impulse, he said, "Yeah. Okay. I'll take it. Visa good?"

"Visa good."

A couple stalls over, Hannah was eyeing a decorative muffin tin whose cups looked decidedly like six symmetrical breasts. When Reuben wandered over, she held it up to her chest and shimmied a little like a freak show stripper. He laughed then and lowered her hand to set it down when the proprietor scowled. Hannah pulled him to a side table with an assortment of metal instruments.

"Look at these cake decorating tools I found. Aren't they amazing?"

"They look like sadistic dentist tools to me. Is that a tiny saw?"

She turned to the woman who was now hovering nearby, "I'll give you thirty-five for the set."

"They're listed for fifty. I'd say I can't come down below forty-five."

"Thirty-eight. Otherwise, I'll just take the tiny saw."

The woman gave a wheezy sigh. "If you make it forty-five, I'll throw in this butter mold."

Hannah inspected the small wooden stamp, turning it over a few times. "Fair enough," she said and handed over the cash.

As they strolled through other sections, Reuben said, "How do you do that?"

Hannah looked up at him with a questioning expression. "Do what?"

"Bargain. I always feel so... not right about it."

"You didn't haggle over the price of that baseball relic?" Reuben shook his head. "That's part of the fun of it, not just for buyers, for the sellers, too. It's a dance of negotiation. Plus, these vendors probably don't even pay for half their stuff. They're the ones who show up just as garage sales are closing and take anything of interest for a steal because nobody wants to make a dump run for all the crap that didn't sell."

She stopped to pick up a blue bird made of blown glass. "So what'd you pay for it?"

"It's not important."

"Come on."

"Sixty," Reuben lied.

"I bet that guy paid ten bucks for it," Hannah said. "Don't feel bad. If it brings you joy, it's worth the hundred or more that you actually paid for it. Yeah, I see through your mistruths, mister."

She pinched his arm, not especially gently. And again, Reuben felt an unexpected tension between contentment that she knew him well enough to see through his lie and annoyance that she assumed he was utterly predictable. No matter that he clearly was.

They continued to wander the aisles, spotlighting for each other the more unusual finds. A taxidermied weasel with its pointy bared teeth; a collapsible top hat; a cigar box filled with buttons of all shapes, colors, and sizes.

As Reuben's pace slowed, his imagination sparked with ideas for assemblages and sculptures—a creative medium he had given up in art school when he chose to specialize in painting instead. But here, these fragments of the past were just calling out for new life. One moment Reuben was imagining building a tiny birdcage out of ornate keys, the next he was staring at a polished Underwood typewriter, running his fingers over the keys, admiring how precise their roundness was, how their elegant serif strokes were like tiny letter portraits.

Between the lift of the hike and this torrent of new ideas, Reuben had to admit that the financial success he enjoyed from producing commercial art was bad at feeding his creative soul. This acknowledgement lit something inside him that felt a lot like optimism.

"Hey," Hannah tugged his sleeve, jolting his mind back to the dusty antiques barn. "This is starting to feel like grocery shopping with my niece who stops to read every cereal box. Let's get going. You need a shower before we head to dinner."

Having eaten a giant waffle cone of Phish Food just a couple hours before, dinner was not an enticing prospect, but Reuben took Hannah's outstretched hand and reluctantly left the antiques behind.

That night, as Hannah was in bed reading a hardcover she picked up about funeral practices around the world, Reuben was restless.

"I think I'm going to take a quick walk around the property."

"Okay, but don't drown in the river. I just read that if it takes more than a day to find a body, it'll be totally bloated and that means no open casket."

"If that happens, you have my permission to cremate me."

Her eyes welled up with happiness. "You entrust me with your remains?"

"Let's hope it doesn't come to that any time soon."

Though his jacket was thin for the forty or so degrees outside, Reuben liked the bracing feeling it caused, keeping his muscles taught. In the quiet country night, he could tease out the sound of a single dry leaf flipping along the driveway on a breeze. He looked up to take in the clear sky of stars framed by the tops of the trees whose fading leaves filled the air with a musty sweetness. *There's a word for that smell*, Reuben thought, but he couldn't remember what it was. A car approached from up the road, getting louder, passing, and then fading. Reuben turned down a path that hugged the river, careful not to wander too close to the edge.

◆

"We should go out for breakfast," Reuben said.

Hannah had been up for nearly twenty minutes, twittering around the room, seemingly unable to stay still. Now she was wandering as she brushed her teeth, and it took a moment for her to return to the sink to spit and rinse before responding, "Why would we do that?"

Reuben had been thinking that he wanted to get out early to see how the morning light bent and stretched shadows out from the trees. He wanted to take real and mental pictures to bring home into the studio. "I don't know, there are probably some cool little historic towns we can explore. Maybe an old cemetery you can wander."

"While that's a fine idea for later," Hannah said, "I think there's a gap in your understanding of the '& Breakfast' part of this operation. Besides, I bet Rosemary has a collection of antique pancakes made by Mrs. Schuyler herself that she serves up for her favorite guests."

Hannah pulled out one of Reuben's shirts he didn't recall packing and smoothed it out at the foot of the bed. "I love this color on you," she said.

He knew she was trying to nudge him out of bed, but he didn't mind. He was feeling upbeat, had even had a change of heart while dozing off the night before, deciding that his conflicting feelings about Hannah were just the normal ebb and flow of being in a long-term relationship—his longest, in fact.

"Hand me some underwear?" he asked her.

She rifled through the suitcase. "I also brought these cords for you."

"I'll just wear the jeans from last night."

"I think these will be more comfortable."

"More comfortable than jeans?"

Hannah brought him the pants, underwear, and a wad of socks before going back to the mirror to apply lipstick.

"Seems a little dressy for antique pancakes."

She turned abruptly. "You and I spend all our days wearing baking or painting clothes. Is it too much to ask that, just occasionally, we resemble the mature, successful people we are?"

It was an unexpectedly strong reaction to attire, something she attended to for herself but almost never commented on for Reuben. "Okay, if it's that important to you." He started to dress. "Wow, you even ironed the shirt."

"I just thought it would be nice," Hannah said, watching his reflection in the mirror. "Besides, we have a big day ahead of us."

"We do?"

"Oh, I just mean, you know, making the most of our last day here."

In the dining room, sunlight reflected off the yellow and white tablecloths so brightly it took a moment for Reuben's eyes to adjust. The Pennsylvania travelers Hannah had chatted with the day before were already seated for breakfast. At another table was a young couple that looked barely out of college, noteworthy for the fact that their hands seemed fused together, so that efforts like spreading jam or pouring and stirring cream were impressively achieved single-handedly.

Rosemary, dressed in a buttery yellow cardigan that matched the room's decor, delivered Reuben and Hannah a couple glasses of freshly squeezed orange juice.

"I hope everyone slept well!"

"Like a corpse that was not murdered," Hannah said.

"How nice," said Rosemary, her grandmotherly smile not quite reaching her eyes.

After she returned to the kitchen, Reuben said to Hannah. "You did seem to sleep well. Better than you have in a while. Maybe getting away was just the thing to move on from the whole crazy bride thing."

"Oh that?" Hannah laughed lightly. "Yeah, she wasn't crazy."

"Not crazy. That's a poor choice of words, right? Paranoid. Maybe a little insecure about her groom's long-term fidelity?"

Hannah's big blue eyes searched his trying to suss out his meaning.

"Wait. What do you think... Oh! Oh my god, you thought... I thought you knew. This whole time, I thought you knew!" She pressed her fingers to her lips. "That's hilarious!"

"Knew what?"

She leaned in conspiratorially and whispered, "You thought it actually was a coincidence?"

"The bridesmaid thing?"

"Yeah."

"It wasn't?"

Hannah scrunched her face affectionately at him. "You must really love me to think that."

"What do you mean, Hannah?"

"You think I'm a better person than I actually am. That's really sweet."

Reuben opened his mouth to speak, closed it, and then said, "It was on purpose? You ruined that woman's wedding on purpose?"

"A: I didn't ruin it. It was a perfectly lovely wedding. And b: in every meeting, she was completely horrid to her mother, her sister, the caterer, me. As if everyone was there solely to please her."

"Well, it was her wedding."

She continued as if she hadn't heard Reuben. "And her husband was so lovely. He totally belonged with that bridesmaid instead. You're looking at me funny."

"How did you even know what she looked like?"

"Social media stalking, duh." She took in a giant mouthful of pancake and spoke around it. "Really, it's not a big deal. Even though I didn't think I should, I took your sound advice and settled. The end. She was compensated and will live happily ever after for the next year or so before her husband realizes she's a twat, and they get divorced."

"Here we are!" Rosemary delivered two plates, each arranged with two large pancakes topped with a melting pat of butter. On the side was a sausage patty and a cozy mound of sliced fresh fruit.

Hannah poured an absurd amount of maple syrup on her pancakes, her enthusiasm contrasting with the fact that she'd just confessed to acting with malicious intent and lying about it. Processing what he'd just learned, Reuben picked at the fruit pile, spearing a single grape and chewing it slowly and deliberately, followed by a pale-green melon ball.

Hannah was halfway finished with her plate when she observed, "You haven't touched your pancakes. Are you mad at me?"

Mad wasn't the right word but Reuben wasn't sure what was. "No, I'm not. I just think, maybe, even if she was a jerk, it doesn't mean you should have been, too."

Hannah squeezed her eyes shut, "Oh god. You're disappointed in me. That's so much worse than being pissed off." She took his two hands in hers and held them tightly. "You're right. It was a shitty thing to do. But maybe sometimes, Reuben, standing up for yourself is important, too. That bride was so dismissive. At every meeting, she looked right through me like I wasn't even there. And when she did talk to me it was loud and slow, like I was stupid—actually worse, like I was one of those automated phone systems. Made me feel so small." She loosened her grip but didn't let go. "The bridesmaid pop was just my little act of subversion. I swear, I didn't think anyone would notice."

This was a rare moment of quiet vulnerability for Hannah. Reuben knew if he let go of her hands, she would make some wisecrack that would undermine everything she'd just told him, and he just wanted to stay in this moment with this Hannah, so he gently rubbed her knuckles and said, "I guess I can understand that."

She took a relieved breath. "You are my love. I couldn't bear you thinking less of me."

Rosemary waltzed into the room with a pot held high. "Who wants more coffee?"

Cups around the dining room were raised as if in a toast to the coffee bearer. Hannah excused herself to head up to the bathroom, squeezing past Rosemary who was flitting from table to table filling cups like a human pollinator. Reuben took a few bites of pancake without really tasting it. His mind was lingering on the cake pop bride. He really did understand where Hannah was coming from; he'd worked with enough clients that behaved as if the people around them were the world's extras, whose presence was tolerated only for what momentary usefulness they offered. But what nagged at Reuben was an uneasy acknowledgment that he'd wholeheartedly believed Hannah's explanation, despite all the reasons he had to be at least a little skeptical.

When Hannah returned, Reuben was puzzled to find she had swapped her twill trousers for a calf-length, navy-blue dress he'd never seen her wear before.

"Is everything okay?" he asked her.

"Everything is wonderful." She smiled at him.

When Hannah got down on one knee beside him, Reuben broke out in a sudden, itchy sweat from scalp to armpits to the back of his knees. "Hannah, what are you doing?" He whispered as the ambient noise of chatter and clanking silverware suddenly silenced.

"Reuben Anthony Downes," she said with a quiet calm.

Oh no, no, no, no, Reuben thought—a record, stuck and skipping in his head; but out loud, all he said was "Shh, shhh, shhh," as if to quiet her so maybe no one in the room would hear what she had to say next, which was, of course, absurd because he could feel the intensity of everyone's stares, eager to be part of this public private moment. One of the women had even pulled out her phone to record.

Hannah held out an open velvet box, not with a ring but with a shiny silver men's watch. "Will you marry me?" Coming from Hannah, it did not feel like a question; it felt like a pronouncement: "You will marry me."

Her focus on their anniversary. The precisely planned weekend getaway. The strange behavior about his clothes. How had he not even had a whiff of this coming? His mind answered: because, until now, marrying Hannah hadn't even registered with Reuben. It was clear that even after a year living together, he was still puzzling—and struggling—with understanding this mostly wonderfully weird woman.

Could he marry her? He certainly could. Would he now, or a year from now, or five years? He didn't know. But perhaps the most important question was, should he?

Those swimming-pool eyes were enormous and pleading, ready to swallow him whole if he didn't say yes right that very second.

Reuben's slack jaw closed but offered no actual words. Hannah popped up, a sprung jack-in-the-box, and shouted to the room, "And . . . scene!" She took a little bow and spun to face everyone, a rigor mortis grin frozen on her face. "Hope you enjoyed our little piece of performance art."

Rosemary looked simultaneously concerned and dubious. A man with a silver crew cut started clapping lightly, which invited the others at his table to offer their tepid, confused clapping. More than anything, Reuben wanted to grab Hannah by the hand and pull her from the room, but she was determined to sit back down in her seat and pretend everything was fine.

Everything was not fine. Reuben could see a tempest roiling behind her smiling countenance, and it scared him.

"Hannah, I—"

"Don't."

"But I—"

"Still don't." She lifted her coffee mug and held it under her nose, blocking her words so only Reuben could hear them. "You just annihilated me."

He matched her discretion by fixing his elbows on the table and covering his mouth with his fists. "I had no idea you were going to do that."

"That's how it's done!" She shout-whispered at him. "It's supposed to be a surprise."

"We had never even talked about it."

"Do you not want to marry me?"

Reuben's hesitation was like a manifest presence, something pulsing with mass and heat. Finally, mercifully, he said, "I don't know."

Hannah closed her eyes a moment. He couldn't tell if she was fighting tears or trying to pretend she was somewhere else.

Reuben lowered his voice, stuttering with unease. "I—I just—I—I feel like maybe there are maybe some things I need to do."

"Things you need to do? Like things without me?"

Again, Reuben said, "I don't know," which, once said out loud, sounded painfully like "yes."

Her head started nodding tightly as if to a fast rhythm in her head. "You have things you need to do. I get it. I do. You have to do what you have to do. People have to do what people have to do, Reuben." And with those words, she lifted her fork and drove it straight down into Reuben's hand.

Reuben let out a howl of shocked pain. In an instant, one of the Pennsylvania men (an ex-Marine, it later turned out), crossed the room and caught Hannah in a bear hug before dragging her out of the room.

The fork was standing straight up, fully embedded in the fleshy part between the thumb and forefinger on the back of Reuben's left hand.

Reuben could feel the edges of his vision blur as someone, the college-looking guy (a nurse-in-training, it later turned out), held one hand firmly on his shoulder and the other on his forearm, telling him, "Hang on, you're okay. Rosemary went to get bandages."

"Where's Hannah?" Reuben asked.

"She's in another room. You're safe. She's not going to hurt—"

"I need to see her—"

"We have to take care of this first...what's your name?"

"It's Reuben," Rosemary said, briskly striding over with a big first aid box.

"Okay, Reuben, my name is George. I'd shake your hand, but..." He laughed nervously as Reuben's eyes teared from the pain. "Reuben, I'm going to need to remove the fork so we can get you fixed up."

It was surreal, both the image of the upright fork and the experience of looking down at his own hand as if it weren't really real.

"I think he's in shock," someone said.

"Looks like she forked him real good," someone else mumbled.

"On the count of three, Reuben."

George lied, quickly pulling the fork out after "one."

"Holy MOTHER of FUCK!"

There was surprisingly little blood coming from the fork's four neat punctures. George inspected the wound while Reuben took quick, shallow breaths.

"Reuben, do you know if she had eaten from the fork before she stabbed you?"

"I don't know. Yeah, yes, she was eating pancakes."

Someone asked indiscreetly, "Can you get maple syrup poisoning?"

Someone else a little louder said, "Wait, is this still performance art?"

George said, "You should probably get a tetanus shot."

In the meantime, Rosemary set his hand in a bowl of warm water. "There's some Castile soap in there, which is antibacterial."

"Isn't all soap antibacterial?" someone asked.

"Well, soap can be effective in getting rid of bacteria, but—"

"I need to see Hannah," Reuben said again, his voice croaking.

Rosemary nodded to a person behind him, and he heard the door open and close as they left the dining room.

"You'll want to see a doctor to make sure there's no nerve damage," said George.

Reuben's chest tightened and said, "It's my painting hand."

Rosemary's eyes softened in sympathy. "You'll be okay, hon." As she gently dried Reuben's hand, the door opened again. George's girlfriend spoke in a low voice to someone, but all Reuben heard was the word "gone."

"Wait, she left?" Reuben croaked.

"Yeah. She grabbed a bag and took off," George's girlfriend said. "She said she won't be back and doesn't want to see your . . . fucking fat face ever again. She told me to tell you that—I don't think your face is fat; it's actually kind of oblong. Anyway, Gary says he can call the police if you want to press charges."

"I'm not pressing charges."

Rosemary put a hand on his shoulder, "Maybe you want to take just a few minutes to think about—"

"I'm not pressing charges," Reuben said. He added, "I'm really sorry for the drama, everyone."

"Makes for a great story to tell people back home."

Reuben's hand was pounding cartoonishly. Stabbing pain, he thought, nearly laughing out loud. "Rosemary, can I trouble you for a glass of water? Also, I may need to stay a few more nights."

"Of course, you'll stay as long as you need."

George lightly secured a bandage with surgical tape. "Hell of a breakup, man," he said as he stood up.

I suppose it could have been worse, Reuben thought. Because somewhere deep in the tangle and turmoil of all the feelings he was experiencing—astonishment, regret, anger, worry, and pain, visceral pain—was the kind of thrill that comes from an ending about to become a beginning.

CHAPTER 2

After the aggressive silverware incident, as Rosemary dubbed it, Reuben spent a week convalescing in one of the bedrooms she almost never used for guests because it was only big enough to hold a pull-out couch and night table. Those first few days passed with Reuben's emotions pinballing wildly. He was raw and angry at Hannah one minute, not just for physically assaulting him, but also for proving how little she actually knew him in forcing him to make an on-the-spot, life-altering decision witnessed by a room full of strangers. But then he'd suddenly remember that out-loud, full-body laugh or the way the fringe of her dirty blonde, blunt haircut grazed her jawline, and his eyes would well up remembering the pain and panic he'd seen in her eyes when he had no words with which to answer her proposal.

Mostly, he stayed in the room, reading or streaming movies on his phone, only coming out for meals in the kitchen with Rosemary, and occasionally Guillaume, the on-premises landscaping and maintenance guy who spoke only French but seemed to understand English perfectly. Still, every day, at Rosemary's insistence, Reuben went out to walk along the river, and in those moments, he could again feel that breath of optimism despite the late autumn days getting shorter, darker, and decidedly colder. As his heavier feelings mellowed and the lighter ones expanded, Reuben worried that going back to Hartford too soon would allow him to slide back into the numbing comfort of his old life. Since he couldn't work anyway, he asked Rosemary if he could extend his stay.

"If you're going to be here a bit, that broom closet's too small for you," Rosemary said. "I have another option."

So for the past month and a half, Reuben had been renting out the mother-in-law apartment above Rosemary's garage and providing one-handed support with chores to offset the occasional meals she shared with him.

Even during the off-season, Rosemary could be found bustling around, tackling the upkeep she couldn't tend to when the guests were underfoot. Though she had help from Guillaume—Gui as she called him—it was Rosemary who handled all the clogged toilets, minor fix-its, laundry, grocery shopping, and cooking.

Reuben found her unflagging stamina and capacity for constant movement formidable, especially for a woman in her sixties. She waived it off as simply having been a fourth-grade teacher for twenty years.

"Teaching was like being on stage for a six-hour performance every day. It took a lot of energy to keep those buggers interested in learning something, let alone being decent to one another."

Performance, Reuben learned, was a skill Rosemary likewise tapped as an innkeeper. Because once all the tourists and wedding lodgers were checked out for the season, a different version of Rosemary showed up, one who traded out not just her attire, from flowered print dresses to fleece pullovers and jeans, but also her vocal intonation, posture, essentially her whole demeanor.

"The people who come to the Schuyler Inn want an experience that matches the idea they've created in their mind's eye," Rosemary told him. "They want grandmotherly comfort. They want blueberry muffins and hot cider, quilts and rocking chairs."

"Just seems...I don't know. Isn't it hard spending so much time acting like someone you're not?" Reuben had asked, thinking about how drained he always was after client meetings, being forced to present himself as buttoned-up and professional in ways that never felt genuine.

"Oh, it's still me under all the ruffles and aprons. And I really do enjoy my guests. Most of them, anyway. Maybe some of it's an act I play up, but a lot just comes down to 'On-season Rosemary' and 'Off-season Rosemary.' You and Gui are among the few who are privy to both sides." She was replacing a dead lightbulb in the basement while Reuben held the flashlight. "Besides, have you seen my online reviews? I'm booked all season. Means I can work my tush off from Easter to Halloween and then have a nice five-month vacation."

And that was Rosemary in a nutshell. She was pure pragmatism. You did A if you wanted to accomplish B. When her sciatica flared, she traded a midweek stay at the inn for a deep tissue massage. When a tree fell in a storm and shattered an upstairs window, she replaced all of the old windows with energy efficient ones, not because she cared so much about "being green" but because there was a tax break to do so.

"Between that and the reduced heating costs, the replacements will pay for themselves in two seasons," she said.

Reuben admired the approach and decided he would look for places to adopt it himself. But while much of Rosemary's Yankee spirit centered around economics, it often came down to an unwavering confidence that no one could do a job more competently than she could. Which is why a few years earlier, she had built the garage apartment Reuben was staying in for her sister, Ellie, who at the time needed care and support while recovering from an oxycodone dependency. As Rosemary told Reuben, she would never entrust Ellie's care to a rehab facility. A sister's love and 24/7 attention were what the complicated and delicate situation called for.

It was this personal history that later explained why, when Rosemary brought Reuben home from urgent care after the stabbing, she inspected the pain medication prescription he'd been given, and horrified him when she promptly tore it up, saying, "There's nothing a little Extra Strength Tylenol, an ice pack, and a cup of tea with honey and cayenne can't handle."

Rosemary attributed Ellie's recovery to her strength and resolve, but Reuben suspected much of the credit should go to Rosemary, whose openhearted care he'd also been sheltered under.

If anyone asked Reuben about the unexpectedly easy friendship that had evolved between the two of them, he'd chalk it up to sheer randomness. After all, had things not gone so spectacularly sideways with Hannah, Rosemary would have remained a colorful walk-on—an extra in the normally unremarkable drama that was his life. Instead, circumstances being what they ended up being, she gave him the gift of a temporary home and the space in which to figure out what he would do next.

Rosemary encouraged Reuben to focus on the basics. Getting up early and having a hearty breakfast. Staying off his phone, going out for longer walks or hikes so he could just be in his own head, and reading. While he tried to enjoy the history and biography books she enthusiastically plied him with, what he eventually connected most to were her cooking lessons.

At first, Reuben refused, saying he knew his way around the kitchen well enough to not have to eat out more than a couple times a week, and he made a mean stir fry if he did say so himself. So while he loved the food she served (and the few extra pounds he'd acquired were a testament to how much), her teaching him didn't seem like it would be a good use of time for either of them.

"Let me ask you something," Rosemary had said. "What is art?"

"Is this a trick question?"

"You're an artist. Define art."

Reuben thought a moment then cautiously answered, "It's an act of creation. Of communication. Connection. Taking something that's inside you and translating it with your mind and hands and heart to share with the world outside of yourself."

"By your own definition, cooking is art. So why not give it due respect if you're going to do it?" She was stirring a pot of risotto at the time. "Now I'm not talking about fussy or fancy. No sous vide or those dopey foams. Just taking the kind of care with ingredients and techniques that makes even a humble stew a work of culinary beauty." She stirred in a few grates of Parmesan, took a taste and added a couple more. "Besides, I've started thinking about what's next for you."

Just a few days before, they had talked about the possibility of Reuben staying in Vermont permanently.

Rosemary continued, "You need to know that I will be kicking you out when the time is right. Just like I did for Ellie once she was clean and strong again. I suspect that time for you is coming, probably just after the new year. And that means you'll be experiencing your first winter here alone." She dished out three bowls of risotto for herself, Gui, and Reuben. "From what I've seen, you haven't got a lot of self-reliance on account of the mollycoddled life you had back in that little city of yours."

"We have winters in Hartford."

"Honey, last January, we went twenty-three days without getting above zero. When it's negative fifteen, your nose hairs freeze up just walking to your car. The days are gray and short. And the nights are long and lonely without someone in your bed warming your toes and other parts." Rosemary tucked a loose curl behind her ear. "Confidentially, that's why I keep Gui around. Between you and me, he's a mediocre landscaper."

"Weren't we talking about cooking?"

"Sustenance, right," Rosemary said, pulling a dog-eared cookbook from the kitchen shelf. "Expanding your cooking repertoire in the right way will not only allow you to be well fed, it'll keep you from running back to that nutty cake popper." It became clear within his first week's stay that Rosemary had formed some strong opinions of Hannah the minute she walked in the door.

It wasn't wrong of Rosemary to think that in the dead of winter, Reuben might try to reunite with Hannah. He had already reached out twice. The first was the day after she left, in which he left a message letting her know that he would be staying put awhile, and she could stay in the loft until he knew what his plans were. A few days later Reuben's neighbor called, at Hannah's request, to let him know that she had cleared out all her things and was "burying the loft's keys in an unmarked grave." No doubt, Reuben thought, to exhume them on the next full moon for a cursing ceremony.

His second communication to Hannah was a whiskey-induced text that simply read:

> No, my hand is NOT fine, btw.

Twenty minutes later he received a reply from Hannah that said simply:

> Maybe it'll cause you to actually FEEL something.

His next message asking what the hell that was supposed to mean came back undeliverable.

And so Reuben agreed to Rosemary's cooking lessons, less because it kept him from having too much time to think about Hannah than because Rosemary's assertion that cooking—with its combination of techniques, chemistry, and improvisation—was another art form resonated with him in a way he'd never previously considered, and he was intrigued by the challenge.

Their first lesson was pasta.

"Doesn't matter what sauce you use, or whether it's spaghetti, bow ties, or *campanelle*, the most important step is to make sure the cooking water is ocean salty before you add the dry pasta. And don't ever forget to save a little of that starchy water to season your sauce."

Presented with a side-by-side comparison, Reuben had to admit there was, in fact, a real difference. These were the small but impactful tips that would elevate even the simplest dishes. Like buying whole spices and grinding them just when you needed them for fullest flavor.

"And if your spices are more than a year old, you're probably best off tossing them and buying new. For that, the bulk section at Rafferty's is your go-to."

Eventually, Reuben had enough skills to fully put them to work. On a chilly night in early December, he served Rosemary the first full meal he prepared on his own. Most notable was how he'd applied what she'd taught him about browning butter—how when you added it to anything from vegetables to fish to cookies to banana bread, it gave a richly satisfying layer of flavor, akin to toasted nuts.

He stood at the counter finishing off a late harvest of Brussels sprouts with the deep caramel-colored liquid and tossed everything with chopped hazelnuts and crumbled bacon. This was a side dish for the essential main course he was attempting to master: the salt & pepper roasted chicken.

"And here we are." Reuben set down a plate for each of them.

"Well, look how nicely browned those potato wedges are on the bottom. Patience paid off. You didn't flip them 'til the end, like I told you."

Reuben bowed his head humbly.

They ate in silence for a bit, assessing the results of his effort, until finally Rosemary declared it "Not perfect, but quite good." Like a teacher who never gave an A+, this was the woman's highest praise, and it gave Reuben a swell of pride.

"Now," she said, "I've been sitting on something since Thursday that I need to share with you."

"That sounds ominous."

"Ellie found you a house."

The news had caught him off guard.

"No. No, I told you, I'm not interested in a house. We talked about an apartment. Something easy, no maintenance, that I could rent and sublet if I need to move back." A house was too big. Too committed.

"Yes, you and I did discuss that. But just between you and me, Ellie's real estate business has been slow and struggling, and I wanted to help give her a little confidence boost. So I asked her just to keep an eye out for the right kind of property for someone such as yourself."

"*I* don't even know what I want, Rosie. How would you?"

She looked at him flatly.

"Okay, tell me then, what it is you think I want," he said.

She held up fingers counting off each of her proposed criteria beyond the rough budget he had discussed with her. "One: enough land for a little privacy, maybe two acres or more. Two: a decent sized kitchen now that you know your way around a frying pan. (Don't get cocky.) And three: two to three bedrooms since you're likely to have guests at some point. Or kids, you never know."

"Now you're being—"

"Four: not a fixer upper. Nobody needs a money pit unless they're going to flip it. And five: a big studio space in which to make and show your art."

That last one stung. Despite diligently following the exercises the physical therapist had prescribed, Reuben still had pain and strength issues with his thumb. Holding a pen, let alone a paint brush, was an angry, frustrating experience. And so, though he'd gone back to Connecticut to retrieve his truck and gather short-term essential belongings, he put his art supplies in boxes and just left them there, figuring that come January—when Rosemary assured him she would be booting him from the nest—he would move everything at once.

Reuben knew this rationalization might not be the whole truth. And the more he brooded about it, the more he wondered if what he was experiencing was a little of what pro athletes went through after an injury—a mental stumbling block of fear that they'll either re-tear that ACL and end their career, or fail to perform at their prior level, which he thought would feel even worse.

But instead of naming it as a kind of mental, with some physical, paralysis, Reuben decided to call it a "hiatus," and he took stock of his career, prodding deeper at the tenor of dissatisfaction with his commercial art business that had cropped up that weekend with Hannah.

He thought about his standout projects over the years, the ones where he had gotten lost in the pure joy of creating. One of the most memorable was an abstract mural painted on the bottom of an infinity pool, owned by the wealthy hedge fund brother of a former client.

As big and ostentatious as that project was, Reuben thought also about its opposite. One of his earliest creations as an eleven year old, the one that first lit up his artistic heart, a sculpture created from the inner parts of a disemboweled boombox. Green circuit boards, color-coded wires, tiny motors, ribbon cables, a handful of little blue pegs, LED lights, and a tuning gear that looked like a black, blood-shot eye. These were the pieces he glued and patched together to create an intricate cityscape featuring buildings of varying sizes—wires stretching between like clotheslines with little birds sitting on them, and that singular gear hanging above it all like a radiating black sun. He recalled how uncharacteristically enthusiastic his mother was, ensuring it was always one of the few decorative pieces they would carefully pack and bring to each new home they moved to when his father was inevitably transferred.

Now, wrestling with his artistic reentry, Reuben wondered if this original wellspring of inspiration could bring him back to his art in ways that were different. Maybe sculpture could be a distraction from the need to paint at the level he was used to.

A few days after the house conversation, Reuben dug out the business card he'd pocketed from the antiques collective and called to inquire if they still had the old typewriter. They had two, in fact. This time, though, having done some scouting on eBay, Reuben knew to offer the dealer thirty-five dollars less than what he was asking (it turned out haggling was not so hard when you were armed with knowledge, and it was the off-season for tourists). Buying both machines, Reuben felt a thrill from the absolute freedom to discover what new sculpture he could create with the bars, the platen knobs, and other raw materials available once he dismantled the typewriters.

He had slid them under the bed in the garage apartment, stowing them until he had proper space to work with them. A studio like the one Rosemary had described might just be what he needed.

The house sat at the top of a low, sloping hill. Built in the 1920s, its white front with double dormers resembled the face of a giant cat, crouched and ready to pounce. On the wide spindled porch, Ellie stood waiting for them, a dossier in her hand. Rosemary put the car in park and gave her sister a hearty wave, while Reuben stepped out, scoping the setting.

A stand of bare-branched trees flanked one side of the property, their lines darkly stark against a thick gray sky threatening snow. About a hundred feet to the left of the house was a low stone wall marking the property's edge, the other side of which was a well-traveled dirt road. He could detect an earthy, but not unpleasant, smell of loamy soil, wet leaves and wood smoke, a hint of hay and maybe manure.

"So good to finally meet you, Reuben," said Ellie, hand outstretched in a professional manner, her gaze confidently locked on Reuben's. He wasn't sure what he had been expecting, but at least superficially, he could find no trace of the troubled past Rosemary had described, not even in her eyes where the haunt of addiction still lived in Reuben's uncle who had gone through recovery. In fact, if anything, Ellie seemed more put together than Rosemary, whose coat he had noticed was missing a button.

"I'm glad I was able to get you in to see this place before it officially goes on the market," said Ellie. "It's crazy the number of people looking to buy, even at this time of year. My phone has been ringing off the hook."

"So glad to hear business is going well for you," Reuben looked flatly at Rosemary who just smiled sweetly.

Inside, the lights were on, warmly welcoming them. And there was a smell of freshly brewed coffee—a clever touch Reuben knew realtors used to make a house feel homey despite the minimal furnishings. Ellie offered him a cup, which warmed his hands as they strolled.

"The owners put in quite a remodeling effort in the five years they were here," Ellie explained. "Look at this stove. And the master bath has a gorgeous clawfoot tub. Though you might be a little too tall to fit comfortably in it. The couple had planned on raising a family here, but her job was transferred to Florida, poor thing, and she couldn't find any new work here. So when Rosie—"

"I told her about how you make your living—"

"Doing art—"

"From a home studio—"

It suddenly occurred to Reuben that Rosemary and Ellie weren't just sisters; they were twins. They didn't quite look the same, but they had an easy, fluid way of being together like the proverbial two sides of the same coin.

"These hardwood floors," said Rosemary.

"Walnut," said Ellie.

Their chatter faded to white noise behind Reuben as he wandered into the home's spaces. He noted the details as well as the big picture. The hand-forged hardware on the kitchen cabinetry. The dramatic indigo veins in the white marble countertops that gave the space a rustic, modern feel.

In the walk-in pantry, there was a blown-glass pendant light that cast a glow on the ample empty shelves. Way more storage than a bachelor—even one who could now cook—would need. In fact, it was all far more space than he would need. Though the asking price was roughly the same as what he paid for the loft four years ago, the house had much more square footage, including three bedrooms and two full baths. Who would fill those spaces now that Hannah was gone? What's more, how would he ever meet someone new living out here, isolated, where conveniences like a supermarket were a thirty-minute drive.

Reuben entered the living room where a stout wood stove had been set in the space that was once a fireplace. He reached out a finger and spun a little fan set on the soapstone surface. Rosemary kept a similar one on her wood stove, too, to help move the heat out and into the room. With an old house—one that perhaps still had some of the original windowpanes—the space was probably drafty and hard to heat.

There were bookshelves and cabinets built into the walls, all painted a cloudy light gray that contrasted against the white window frames. It was all very tastefully designed.

Reuben turned around to find the sisters' eyes on him, probing. He realized they were anticipating some kind of reaction.

"Look, I know you guys are really hoping to make a match here, and I get it. It's truly a beautiful home. I just don't need this kind of space. And I'm not sure I want to live this far out."

"Absolutely, Reuben," said Ellie. "I would never advise someone to buy the first house they looked at. That's a perfect recipe for buyer's remorse, and nobody wants that."

At the far end of the living room, there was a barn door hanging on rollers that caught his attention.

"What's behind door number three?" he asked.

"The owner used it as his home office, but it could function as any number of—"

Reuben slid the door sideways like a curtain, revealing a high-ceilinged, post-and-beam room. The outer wall, nearly all windows, gave a sweeping view of a meadow, and rising behind was a backdrop of rolling, receding layers of mountains, all shades of purple and gray. He crossed the room for a closer view. Down the outside steps was a garden, now empty but for a row of desiccated sunflowers shimmying in the wind. It was a raw, rough beauty—the perfect color palette. The embodiment of late November.

Nobody said anything as Reuben stood there for what must have been a solid couple of minutes.

"Well, I guess this is going to be my studio."

CHAPTER 3

The loft in Hartford sold within a week for fifteen thousand dollars over the asking price in a bidding war between two couples. Reuben spent a few days packing up and clearing out. A fresh start, he decided, required a ritual shedding of things, and so he put flyers under doors inviting the neighbors to come and take what they wanted from a collection that included an air conditioning unit; an ancient pair of roller blades; a boogie board; boxes of CDs, DVDs, and paperbacks; all but one pair of dress shoes; throw pillows that Hannah had left behind—in fact, all the bed clothes; a George Foreman Grill; a computer desk and its matching adjustable, ergonomic chair; art supplies he'd replaced with better ones; and an inexplicable number of chopsticks.

Anything that wasn't claimed, which wasn't much, Reuben delivered to Goodwill or trashed. He actually felt physically lighter as he tossed the last bag into the dumpster.

Before the final move to Vermont, Reuben spent a quiet evening with his parents in the house they had settled in when Reuben entered high school. The three of them exchanged belated Christmas gifts. Reuben had picked out a selection of jams for his mother, mustards for his father; and they gave him a twelve-pack of warm socks.

What Reuben had come to learn after he moved away for college was that the Downeses were more like a trio of people that cohabitated than a family. His father had been a workaholic consultant who thrived on rescuing failing manufacturing plants by transforming them into lean, safety-compliant environments. And it seemed to Reuben that, during those years of rootlessness, his mother adapted by throwing herself into bridge groups, volunteering in libraries and food pantries, and ferreting out acquaintances she got along well enough to spend time with but not enough to miss when the family moved on several months later. Not so with Reuben, who quickly learned that making friends meant leaving them behind, so it was easier to hold himself out of reach, and the kids at school generally left him alone. By the time he got to middle school, he had built up a reserve of resentment toward his father who would immediately shut down any whiff of protest when the subject of moving arose. Now as an adult, Reuben saw his parents just as people, piecing a life together just like everyone else. It may not have been a joyful childhood, but he turned out fine.

The visit was generally low stress and pleasant. They caught up on things like his father's new indoor tennis league, and a revival of *The King and I* his mother had recently seen on Broadway. But it wasn't long before the conversation turned to Reuben's move, which seemed to invite them to express their concern about living, as his father put it, "A hundred miles west of nowhere."

"Is this," his mother made a circling gesture toward the lower half of his face, "helping you blend in?"

"Are you referring to my beard?"

"It just hides your handsome face. And you used to have such nice shoes. What are those?" She pointed to the thick lug boots he'd left by the door.

"It snows, Ma."

His father asked, "That state doesn't have any pro sports teams, you know."

"No, they don't."

One thing Reuben insisted they not talk about was Hannah. When he'd first told them about the stabbing, a week after the breakup, his father said he was an idiot for not calling the police on her, and his mother all but begged him to get a restraining order. So over dinner, Hannah had only been referenced as one of the few benefits to Reuben's moving: he'd be far enough away from "that woman."

Full from the big lasagna meal, a bottle of wine, a box of Italian bakery cookies, and more time together than any of them had in years, Reuben and his parents called it an early night. He closed himself up in his old bedroom where the room's accumulated contents included his dad's fishing gear, a precarious tower of romance novels, an apocalypse-sized cache of toilet paper, and an assortment of memorabilia from Reuben's youth including a stationery box filled with unwritten postcards from all the various places they had lived—roughly a dozen spanning the country.

On a low bookshelf were Reuben's forgotten records and cassettes, including a couple of elaborately designed mixtapes from a short-lived high school girlfriend whose name was either Cara or Cora. His closet had never been cleared out, where Reuben found way more flannel shirts than he realized he'd owned. He sorted through a stack of neatly folded sweaters to see if there were any worth salvaging, and instead, found something he had forgotten he put there all those years ago: a Little League trophy, the batter frozen in its stance, perpetually awaiting his pitch. Taking the trophy out to look at it under the light, Reuben rubbed a thumb over the engraving to remove the dust: **1993 Third Place - Doha's Dry Cleaning & Tailor.**

He remembered the trophy, remembered how angry and deeply hurt he'd been at the time he buried it back there. First throwing it in the garbage, then retrieving it but not willing to have it on display where it would be a constant reminder of his first genuine friend, the one who had moved away the summer after that Little League season without a heads-up, not even so much as a goodbye, a forwarding address, or a card to let Reuben know where he and his family had moved to. Reuben hadn't thought about Paul in decades. He was as baffled now as to what had happened as he had been when he was thirteen and was even more surprised to admit that even after all those years, he still felt a bit of a sting.

Reuben set the trophy on the desk and decided to quit inventorying his room. He would be getting up early to avoid driving in the snow that was forecasted since he'd never gotten around to putting on winter tires as Rosemary insisted he must.

Early the next morning, the sound of sliding drawers and dishes being restacked in the cabinets woke Reuben, his neck painfully pinched having slept in his old twin bed folded up like a grasshopper in a matchbox. Over breakfast, Reuben preached to his parents the rewards of purging unneeded stuff, how he could box everything up before he left so they could donate or dump it.

His mother slid a couple of sunnyside eggs onto his plate. "It's not taking up space we need right now. Just leave it be."

"Honestly, Ma, there's nothing in there that I want to keep. Although I did nab an old Little League trophy. I seem to be in a bit of a baseball memorabilia phase. Dad, you'd appreciate this. I bought this cool antique catcher's mitt last fall. Just on a whim."

This was meant to be a conversational segue to the subject he wanted to bring up.

"How much you pay for it?" his father asked.

Why did people care so much about what you paid for things? "Not much. Just, like, fifty bucks."

His father scoffed. "Probably worth half that."

"Anyway, when I stumbled on that trophy, I got to thinking about that kid on the team I was friends with, Paul. Do you remember him?"

"Paul . . ." his mother said.

"Paul Brower," Reuben clarified. "His family lived over on Pernell Street. And then they just up and left that summer."

Reuben could just barely see her shoulders close in a little around her teacup. He could tell she knew who he meant.

"Well, you must have eventually heard what happened? I'm sure we told you when you were older?"

Reuben looked at his dad who just shook his head. "I never said anything."

"What? What happened to him?"

His mother still seemed hesitant to talk about it, so Reuben waited, leaving the question open between them.

"It was a hard story, Reuben. Not appropriate to share when you were a boy. But truthfully, we don't really know for sure. I don't know if anything untoward was ever confirmed."

"Mom, can you please explain what you're talking about?"

His father answered instead. "There were rumors that he was one of the priest cases."

"What do you mean?"

"You know," his dad said, "the pervert priests who molested all those kids."

It felt like a punch to the chest.

"That was such a long time ago," his mother said. "He's probably married with kids of his own now, and leading a normal, fulfilling life." She busied herself picking up dishes and carrying them to the sink.

For Reuben, it was like finding the piece of a jigsaw puzzle that had been missing for years. How had he not heard anything about it until now? Maybe because it had been the summer before the middle schoolers got swallowed up into the big regional high school, so anyone who knew Paul had put him into the "out of sight, out of mind" part of their brain. Because, like Reuben, Paul had been a bit of a misfit kid. Both were only children with a distinct lack of friends. Reuben because of being the new kid; Paul because... well, Reuben never really knew why Paul didn't have a circle of friends, other than the fact that his parents seemed a little antisocial and wouldn't allow him to have anyone over to their house. Still, Reuben remembered that first day of practice when he joined the Doha's team, and how Paul crashed through Reuben's self-imposed bubble by sliding over to him on the bench and splitting a pack of Twix with him. From there, the two fell easily into talk about Paul's new Dalmatian puppy and the superiority of Spider-Man over every other Marvel superhero.

It had been hard never knowing what had happened to Paul, but his father's explanation—if it were true—was so much worse to imagine.

◆

Reuben went outside to check that the contents of the trailer were secure before he left for the roughly four-hour drive back to Vermont. His mother followed him carrying an extra aluminum pan of lasagna plus a sealed bag of salad fixings.

"Ma, I don't have a cooler."

"It's January. Just put it in the trailer. Heat a slice when you get home and freeze the rest." She wedged the pan and salad securely between two boxes. "Better yet, cut it up into single servings, wrap them each in foil, and then freeze them."

He knew she was imagining him alone, huddled in the dark eating Hungry-Man dinners in front of the TV. "You know, I've actually become a pretty decent cook."

"I'm sure you have. And," she raised a narrow finger at him, "it's still nice to keep something handy in the freezer for a quick reheat."

"Fair enough. Thank you."

She tilted her head, giving him a concerned-mom face. "Are you sure about this, Reuben?" It was almost as if moving out of the area would make her miss him, even though they hardly saw each other when he lived only thirty minutes away.

"Vermont's not actually that far. You can come visit anytime."

"Maybe when the snow is gone."

Reuben's father had come out, a newspaper folded and secured in his armpit. It was that awkward moment of saying goodbye. "Safe trip, son." Reuben's father held out his hand for what Reuben knew would be a painfully firm handshake.

◆

Reuben had enlisted the help of Guillaume and Rosemary's neighbor's son, Liam, to unload the trailer in the late afternoon of his return. The steady snowfall hampered their speed a bit, but they finished moving the boxes and furniture into the appropriate rooms around dinnertime. Without much to say to each other, especially with Guillaume not speaking English, they quickly finished off the pizza Reuben promised them (plus one hundred dollars apiece) and headed out, leaving Reuben alone for his first night in the new house.

He started the Herculean task of unpacking, intent on getting most everything in its place that night so he could focus on setting up the studio the next day. But an hour into the effort, Reuben stopped and, instead, sat down on the bed and opened his laptop.

Throughout the drive from Connecticut, Reuben's thoughts kept returning to Paul Brower, wondering if Reuben could find anything about him on the internet. He decided to do just a quick search to see if Paul had a digital presence—where he lived and what he did for work. But there were dozens upon dozens of listings for Paul Brower. Reuben narrowed his search terms, making it clear what he really wanted to know: "paul brower priest abuse."

In the brief second before the search results appeared, Reuben made a silent wish that no legitimate matches would be found. That the rumor his parents had shared was just cruel gossip. But the first links that were served showed otherwise. There was, in fact, a Paul Brower named as part of a lawsuit brought against Robert Brinkman, a former priest who ran a boys' summer camp in one of the nearby towns from where they lived.

The allegations by four former campers, including Paul, were brutal and utterly devastating.

Skimming the details of one of the articles, Reuben clicked on a link leading to a video in which some of the victims had been interviewed. He moved the slider forward until he saw a face that looked familiar. The man wore wire glasses and had a deep crease between his eyebrows, but there was no mistaking the features of the boy Reuben had known.

"*You know, we were raised that priests were God's men. They were His messengers, and we had to show them the ultimate respect. And Brinkman knew it. He made you feel like you were special. Chosen for this sacred secret just between you and him.*" His voice was calm, but firm. "*All of that... mixed together with the pain and the shame. How is a twelve-year-old kid supposed to hold all that?*"

Reuben stopped the video, the question hanging, then settling in the empty room. He hadn't realized he'd been clenching his jaw until his teeth started to ache. He felt a heated sense of shame that he had spent the following years so angry with Paul, recoloring his memories to turn the sweet kid into some kind of two-faced jerk. How could Reuben's parents not have ever told him? And what about Paul's parents? Did leaving town the way they had mean they were somehow ashamed of what had happened?

But Reuben had no one to ask these questions or to help him process what he'd learned. Instead, he was alone in a big, strange house on a dusty dirt road where there weren't any traffic sounds and no streetlights and nighttime was darker than anywhere else he'd ever lived.

What had he done, choosing to be so isolated? Maybe his mother had been right that he was better off staying in familiar territory.

Reuben closed his laptop. As he sat watching the snowflakes collect in the corners of the window, he felt a sudden drive to make something—something that he could pour his emotions into in its creation. And he knew just the right starting point.

He moved room to room turning on every overhead light and opening box after box, determined to find it—the single-serve coffee maker Rosemary had given him just before he left for the closing on the new house.

"Why don't you want it?" he'd asked her, pressing the top of the brewer, its mechanical maw opening, demanding to be pod-fed. The appliance had clearly been used but was in good condition. "You could set it out in the living room for guests so they can have coffee or tea any time of day without having to bother you."

She took a deep breath in and slowly let it out as she did during the yoga practice they had tried to do together every other day. "Reuben, more than anything in the world, I loved teaching. I started that first September out of college, and until the day I retired at fifty-six, I always found new and exciting lessons, or at least other—hopefully better—ways of teaching. I worked hard to bring creative ideas into the classroom, not just relying on what worked in years past. Now, lots of teachers do that—for good reasons, of course—but that wouldn't have kept me happy.

"Over time, though, it became harder to do. Administration became more proscriptive with what had to be covered and how. Standardized test scores became my measure of success, not just for the kids. But taking the time to create a community where students helped each other? Where they could develop emotional, not just academic tools to put in their little toolboxes? That wasn't a priority anymore. I did it anyway, of course, but it wasn't easy to fit it in."

"I'm not quite making the connection to the coffee maker," Reuben said.

"It's a story, Reuben, you have to be patient. Would you like another tea?" She got up to refill the kettle.

"No. Thank you, this one'll do." (Disconcertingly, Reuben had noticed that he'd started picking up some of Rosemary's language tics.)

"Anyways, there was a little coffee shop three blocks away from Wheelock Elementary, my school. I would go in the morning, pick up a cup of their light roast and sometimes a pastry. I'd chat with Pria, the owner and baker, learn a little gossip, share a little gossip. But as my planning time got cut in order to fit more into the class schedule, I ended up skipping that visit and using the morning time for lesson plans and meeting with Gabrielle, my partner-teacher. Lovely woman, by the way, I could set you up if you're interested?"

Reuben shook his head.

Rosemary continued. "Well, I sorely missed my cafe time, but needed efficiency. And I needed coffee. So I bought this contraption. Looks like a little vampire, doesn't it?"

The teakettle shrieked in reply, a sound Reuben would not miss when he moved out.

Rosemary returned to the couch with a full cup for herself. "Coffee maker did its job. A fast cup of coffee, no mess to clean up—just toss that little plastic pod into the garbage. And so, for making the last three years of my teaching career just a little easier," she raised her cup toward the brewer, "I toast my tea to Bruce. I actually did name it that... Brew-ce. Get it?

"That's painful, Rosie."

"But every day, that cup of coffee was so utterly lacking in life and character, this poor little machine came to embody a system that was causing a bee's nest of angsty feelings that I kept pushing aside so I could focus on just getting through the day." She shrugged her shoulders as if to say "The end."

"So—I'm sorry—the coffee machine is why you retired early?" Reuben had recalled her mentioning at some point taking a hit on her retirement pension for not making it to age sixty.

Here, Rosemary hesitated. "Don't be ridiculous."

She seemed to sink deeper into the couch and didn't speak for a moment. Normally quick with a reply, she searched for the right words. "You know, over the years there have been so many situations." She paused again. "Bad people doing horrific things. Guns in schools, I'm talking about. We had drills and training, and it got to the point where I started asking myself . . . if it happened here, could I protect them? I hope to God I could. But what if I wasn't able to? How could I live with that?" She stood up and cleared the tea though she had barely taken a sip. "So it was time for me to go."

Reuben thought of his own elementary school teachers, most of them motherly women like Rosemary. It was unthinkable that protecting kids from getting killed had become part of their job requirements.

"So." Her tone bright again coming from the kitchen. "You'll be doing me a favor by taking Bruce. And there are a few not-terrible coffee brands I can steer you toward."

He had taken the brewer along with several other items she offered him, most of which he didn't really want, but didn't have the heart to say so.

Because the box with Rosemary's giveaways had been labeled *MISC*, Guillaume had deposited it in the laundry room. When Reuben finally found it, he dug around and freed the coffee maker.

Striding over to the studio, Reuben cradled the brewer in one arm and held a toolbox in the other, looking like a busy parent off to daycare drop off. With a socked foot, he slid open the studio's sliding barn door thinking *This will become a thing that I do: carrying stuff and opening the door with my foot.* New house. New habits.

The room that was to be his studio still gave him a thrill. The big glass windows overlooking the field seemed to invite the night to spill in, snowflakes and all. Reuben set the toolbox and the brewer on the tall drawing table they'd set up in the corner.

He set his music stream to shuffle Soul Coughing's discography and got to work dismantling Bruce, screw by tiny screw. Reuben set the iconic items—water tank, drip tray, brew button—in a pile of its own. Then he opened the brewer's guts, teasing apart wires from electronics like a surgeon.

The trippy jazz layered with Mike Doughty's percussive, nearly not-human vocals was a soundtrack behind the work as Reuben arranged and then rearranged black plastic molded parts, motherboards, pegs and clips and other bits. His mind was tunnel-visioned, channeling dark feelings about what he'd learned about Paul and helpless anger at a world where kids were put through active-shooter drills. The resulting sculpture was that of an ominous, industrial-looking building, perhaps a postmodern apartment complex, whose small windows revealed no people inside, just more scraps of technology living within.

A year later, when the piece was shown as part of an exhibit at Burlington City Arts, the local paper's reviewer had this to say:

> *Mr. Downes has created an indictment of America's consumer culture, literally building his sculpture from the discrete parts of a single-serve brewer—a product whose pods have produced so much landfill waste that they could wrap around the planet ten times. His structure is a hall of mirrors revealing humanity's own blasé soullessness.*

What the reviewer couldn't possibly know without dismantling the piece herself, was that hidden inside the sculpture, within a small plastic, cave-like piece, there was a little gold-plated baseball player, sawed off from a trophy honoring Doha's Dry Cleaning & Tailor for their third-place season in 1993.

CHAPTER 4

Despite being meticulously skilled at it, Reuben hated painting walls. Not so much the actual application of paint to plaster—that was freeing and almost meditative for him—but the taping and the drop-clothing, and after, the roller-soaking and the neatly putting of everything away. But the previous owners had colored the downstairs bathroom a gray-sage that was probably intended to be calming but just felt stale. Reuben had decided on a warm terra cotta that better shared hue and warmth with the oil-rubbed bronze fixtures.

He had just rolled his first strokes when he heard a clattering sound coming from outside. He tuned his ears for a moment and, hearing nothing further, decided it had been a car, probably hitting a pothole as it passed. But a couple of paint rolls later, Reuben heard the noise again, this time accompanied by something that sounded like a child laughing or crying, he wasn't sure which. Setting the roller securely in the pan, he took a rag to his hands as he headed to the window to investigate.

It took a moment's scan of the front yard to locate where the sound was coming from, but when he did, Reuben bolted to the front door and bounded down the stairs in just his socks. Having come from the wood stove's warmth inside, the cold hit him in a sharp blast.

There, standing on Reuben's truck like a giant hood ornament was a white goat, its wide, pink ears flicking in Reuben's direction. The two of them just looked at each other: Reuben baffled, the goat unfazed. He clapped his hands in the hopes of shooing it like you might a bird or a squirrel, but the goat simply continued to stare.

Are goats dangerous? Reuben wondered. He knew they kicked, but would they charge like a bull? Did they bite? And, perhaps what should have been the first question: why was a goat on top of his truck?

That's when he saw that across the road, behind a stone wall, there was a whole herd of goats watching, as curious and invested in the action as spectators at a golf tournament.

Reuben approached the goat on his truck cautiously, making kissing sounds to help it understand he wasn't a threat. The goat responded with a bleat that sounded like a laugh, so Reuben moved closer. But once he was about twenty feet away, he heard another noise, a kind of *whssht* sound. And then Reuben noticed someone was crouching down on the far side of the truck, their hand poking up, holding what appeared to be an apple as they tried to coax the goat down.

"Hello?" Reuben shouted. The hand dropped out of sight. "Is this your goat?" Dumb question—of course it was. But the person didn't reply.

"I can see your breath," Reuben said.

Still there was no response. He moved closer, again pausing at the thought of aggressive, biting goats, but this one with its upturned mouth and gold eyes seemed more amused than confrontational.

"I'm coming over," Reuben said to both the goat and the hiding person.

At that, a figure stood up, swept the goat into their arms and pulled it down roughly from the truck. Given the unwieldy nature of a four-legged animal with a mind of its own, this was neither a graceful nor fast effort. In fact, the man—for Reuben could now see it was clearly a man wearing an oversized army jacket and knit cap—struggled to avoid tumbling over backwards under the weight of the squirming goat. Once he regained balance, the man set the animal down and slipped a loose rope around its neck.

Reuben was frozen in place watching the action. The man gave a shrug and an embarrassed smile.

"Adios," he said as he led the goat away, turning up the road once they got to the bottom of the driveway. The herd across the way called after them until they, too, wandered off in the direction of their friends, exiting stage left, and leaving the field empty as if they hadn't really been there.

Reuben stood a moment more before realizing the cold flagstones had numbed his feet and his teeth were chattering. He gave a laugh. *Well, that wasn't your typical welcome wagon.*

SECOND

"Look around, boys. I guarantee at least one of the faces you see right here will be someone you carry with you as a friend for the rest of your life. That's just baseball."
— Coach Allen Bordo

CHAPTER 5

The relationship with Adrian started as professional in early February. Reuben had been comfortably settled in the house and was starting to produce work again. Feeling fully recovered physically, and mostly emotionally, from the injury to his hand, he had contacted a select number of galleries in northern New England, offering to bring some pieces to them for consideration. While he had garnered good interest from a handful, the most promising exchanges were with Adrian Ellison, whose Gallery Fifth was conveniently located in Burlington, roughly an hour away.

Their initial meeting was at Reuben's studio. He had invited her out to see the full range of his work, thinking that meeting face-to-face might make it more difficult for her to turn him down for representation, though it quickly became apparent that Adrian was efficient and clear in her decisions, and things like whether or not a prospective artist was a "nice guy" were not likely to sway her in any way.

As instructed, she followed the path to the studio's back entrance. Reuben met her at the door, offering a handshake that doubled as assistance stepping over the stoop, which had collected a slick, icy patch from snow melting off the roof.

"I hope you found the house okay?"

"Yes, thanks to a competent GPS." Adrian Ellison wore her hair in a loose braid over her shoulder and a flattering trench coat with jeans and low heels, a look that felt more Parisian than northern New England.

They eased into the meeting chatting about the stubborn winter temperatures and a mutual acquaintance in Hartford. As she strolled the room, she took in his work, asking about his process and experience with previous galleries and clients.

Reuben had set out a number of works including an unsold painting that had been featured in a gallery he sometimes worked with in Hartford. Others were pieces that he hadn't shown before, and one—a particular favorite of Hannah's—had hung in the studio living room. These were some of his noncommissioned works, the ones that had a little more edge and unexpected elements to them. He had no new completed paintings to show. Having followed the inspiration sparked by his work with the deconstructed brewer, Reuben's artistic reboot had centered around sculpture, starting with dismantling the antique typewriters and transforming them into a three-foot metal crow built from the parts.

"How did you end up in Orrville of all places?" Adrian asked. "It's pretty isolated compared to where you were. Compared to most places, in fact."

Reuben kicked himself for not anticipating the question and preparing an intelligent answer that didn't involve getting stabbed and stranded. What he said came out bland and vague. "I came for a long weekend and ended up feeling like I could stay."

"Change of scenery, that kind of thing?" Adrian stopped in front of the largest of the paintings and seemed to be assessing it as she listened to Reuben.

"Sort of. I'm still figuring things out. How this environment influences my work and, you know, stuff like that." Reuben was distracted listening to and judging his own words, which made him feel inarticulate, which made him self-conscious, which made him actually inarticulate.

Adrian moved to the corner of the workbench where he had set the crow. "And this?"

He pulled the sculpture forward to give her a closer look at the bird's outstretched wings made from tarnished silver letter bars. "Yeah. I've recently found myself engaging with, I don't know what you'd call it, recycled art, junk sculpture—"

"Don't ever call it that. It devalues what you do." She ran a thin finger the length of the bird's back. "A bit rustic, rough. It's very different from your paintings. Not incompatible. Are there more?"

"Sculptures? I have some stuff in progress, out in the barn. I could show you."

Reuben had set up the old barn with shelves and bins to organize the items he had started collecting from the classifieds and the "Freecycle Zone" at the town's solid waste drop-off station. These were not items for which he had specific plans; they were just raw materials he would keep on hand to pick up and see what creative thoughts they inspired.

"I have a cataloging system," he said, pulling a clipboard holding a printed spreadsheet he'd enjoyed geeking out on. "Small appliances and electronics are over here. There's a toaster, an iPod, an iron." He guided her along the dusty barn. "Over there are musical instruments, garden tools, kitchen utensils, things like that." He held up an old eggbeater and turned the handle to make the gear work, but succeeded only in grinding out a crumble of rust.

"That'll lend a little grittiness to your project," Adrian said, the first bit of humor she'd shown.

Her half smile disarmed him, and for a moment, Reuben lost his train of thought. "Yeah, so... when I have an idea I want to explore, I pull pieces aside and add them to this crate."

He showed her a collection of circle- and star-shaped parts: cogs, flywheels, spur gears—taken from deconstructed bicycles, a push mower, and a couple of fishing rods. "These are part of a work in progress." Adrian leaned in for closer inspection but didn't say anything.

"I don't usually show what I'm working on. It's still in the earliest stages and could change direction at any—"

"I understand you're in the exploration phase with this new medium." She started walking toward the door. "I am interested in representing your paintings. The sculptures, we'll see over time."

She selected three paintings for their initial agreement. Reuben delivered them a week and a half later, allowing her time to transition one of her former artists out of the gallery.

Gallery Fifth felt like a good fit for Reuben, and not just because of the allure of its owner. The space was neither too big nor too small, and the artists were a thoughtfully curated collection that complemented each other's tone and style without feeling like a mishmash.

As he waited for Adrian to wrap up a phone call, Reuben noticed her voice had an even, soothing quality, like listening to classical music. When she leaned over to write something on a scrap of paper, his eyes went right to the loose V-neck of her blouse, catching a glimpse of pale-gray bra lace before he forced himself to turn and look out at the passing pedestrians. His only company these last months had been Rosemary and, by proximity though not direct conversation, Guillaume. *I really need to make some new connections*, he thought.

Apologizing for keeping him waiting, Adrian walked him over to the space. They spent a little over an hour installing the paintings. When they were finished, Reuben was about to leave and then turned back to her. "Hey, I don't know many people around here yet. I wonder, since it's almost dinner—I mean, yes, in an early bird special kind of way—I wonder if you might like to join me . . .?"

Her facial expression didn't change, and Reuben immediately wished he could rewind the words that had spilled out on total impulse. "Please don't answer that, Adrian. I don't know what came over me. It was totally inappropriate."

"Give me ten minutes to wrap up a few things," she said as if it had been a perfectly matter-of-fact thing to ask.

A few weeks later, just as decisive as Adrian had been in forging a professional alliance with Reuben, she suggested they try adding a personal one, as well, to which he heartily agreed.

Where Hannah had been a modulating mood ring of colors, Adrian was a study in cool hues. She was blue glacial lakes and sharp, granite peaks. She was the other side of the pendulum from Hannah in other ways, too. Reserved and calm, she was content to spend time with Reuben when it was convenient for her and clear in letting him know when and why she couldn't. Initially, he worried she was second-guessing their involvement and finding reasons to break away gently—an insecurity that caused him to say things like "only if you want to" and "it's okay if you already have plans" immediately following any suggestions he made for getting together. Finally, Adrian sat him down and said, "I like you Reuben, a lot.

No buts or howevers. You can relax." Her words were an immediate lift for Reuben, like setting down a rock he hadn't realized he'd been carrying.

Reuben's first sale in the gallery, Adrian insisted, was cause for a celebration. Instead of an expensive dinner out, Reuben decided to prepare a four-course meal for the two of them, planning and happily prepping a menu that pushed his budding culinary skills to the limit.

It was a thoughtfully orchestrated dinner that included wild mushroom bruschetta, antipasto salad, and a pork tenderloin stuffed with prosciutto and pistachios. He'd left the cheese and wine selections to Adrian whose prior training as a sommelier lent her a more sophisticated palette for pairing.

No longer strangers, there was an easy joy in the two of them moving through the house, always with a glass of wine in hand, as the smells of raw and simmering ingredients filled the downstairs. Their soundtrack was a Nina Simone concert brought so alive by the combined acoustics of the tall-beamed ceiling and the indulgently high-end stereo Reuben had bought when he moved in, that it seemed as if she were actually performing from the living room.

"Painter, sculptor, and a skilled culinary artist. I could get used to you having me around," Adrian had said finishing off the last fig with a sliver of aged Manchego.

"I could get used to having you get around me." He wagged his eyebrows suggestively.

Adrian snort-laughed in the most un-Adrian way, shocking herself and setting them both to laughing even harder.

"Reuben Downes, is that a clumsy, drunken attempt to move this party upstairs?"

◆

The collateral damage of pots, pans, dishes, glasses, and silverware would remain untouched until the next day. The same with the cheese board remnants and a mostly empty bottle of vintage port which would end up leaving a crescent-shaped stain on the coffee table. Reuben and Adrian planned to luxuriate in bed the next morning, knowing neither had any commitments to tend to, and that Adrian's seventeen-year-old daughter was more than happy to have her mother's house to herself.

Deep-sleeping off their indulgences, they were naked under a fluffy down comforter, only their faces exposed to the air, when the honking in the driveway started. Not quite asleep or awake, Reuben dreamt that the neighbor's goat had returned, had somehow gotten inside his truck, and was head butting the horn.

Reuben pried open his eyes, scratchy and dry as sandpaper. The horn sounded again, this time in a more insistent, seemingly irritated, sustained note.

"What the hell?" Reuben said.

"Make it stop," Adrian groaned next to him.

Sliding out from under Adrian's dead-weight arm, Reuben begrudgingly left the bed's cocoon. The floor was bitingly cold, their having forgotten to load the wood stove before coming up to bed. He quickly slid on socks, jeans, and a sweatshirt and scuttled down the stairs hoping, but failing, to pre-empt another honk.

Wrenching open the front door, Reuben blinked against the sunlight, finding Rosemary, standing outside a mud-splattered truck, her torso leaning in through the driver's side window about to hit the horn again.

"Stop it!"

"Oh, hello there!" She reinforced the greeting with a high and hearty wave.

Reuben's head felt axe-split open. "What the bloody hell? What time is it?" He rubbed a speck of grit from his eye, feeling unfocused and off-kilter.

Rosemary consulted an imaginary watch. "Lunchtime." She pointed her chin at the black Audi parked beside his truck, her expression knowing and teasing. "You get yourself a fancy new car?"

"No."

"Oh, you have a visitor?"

"I do."

"I see," Rosemary said folding her arms over her chest and nodding approvingly.

"What?"

"Mind you don't keep any sharp objects lying around."

"Still too soon, Rosie." Reuben tugged on his second boot and a parka. "What are you doing here? Whose truck is this?"

"You said you were running low on firewood." He could see now that the back of the truck was loaded with a tree trunk that had been cut into big round pieces. "Beech came down the other day, right across the backyard. So Gui and Roddy cut it up and loaded it in Roddy's truck for me to bring to you. Where do you want me to dump it?"

Once he'd moved into the new house, Reuben found that Rosemary had an uncanny sense for when to give him the space to settle in and when to pop up with support. Most of the time he didn't even know he needed help until she had already stepped in to provide it. This time, her presence felt like she'd missed the mark, and Reuben had to tamp down a little testiness by reminding himself that on a normal Sunday, he would have been awake for hours and appreciate the thoughtful gesture.

"Wow, I know that's not a small amount of work. I'm—" Reuben tried to choose his words carefully, not wanting to seem ungrateful, "Thank you. But I'm thinking I've probably got enough wood to close out the season. And I heard it's supposed to hit sixty this week."

"Oh, this stuff is too green to use now. I'm just getting you a jump on next season."

"Next season? That's, what, five months away? Probably more advanced planning than I need. Besides, this isn't even firewood. It's giant logs. What am I supposed to do with them?"

"She means for you to cut them," Adrian said from the porch. She was wrapped in the big couch blanket.

"Hello there!" Rosemary greeted her. "You must be..."

"Adrian."

"I'm Rosemary."

"Adrian runs the local gallery I'm working with."

"Ohhh. A business meeting," she said, and Adrian laughed.

Reuben sometimes wondered how his strange friendship with Rosemary would look to others, so he hadn't said much to Adrian about her other than to say he had rented her apartment, and she had been an enormous help in making the transition to Vermont.

"Anyway, about the wood," he pointed to the truck. "I don't think I can—"

"It's free wood, Reuben." said Rosemary. "Turning it down would be like hitting a deer on the road and not taking it home to eat." He knew she was both serious and poking fun at him. "It's high BTU. A cord of this quality'd cost you about three hundred fifty bucks."

"Yeah, but if it's going to take me a month just to make the wood usable, I'd be happy to pay that much." He let out a white cloud of breath. "It's freezing. Why don't you come in for some coffee?" Then he remembered the mess in the kitchen. And the living room.

"No, but thanks. I had my coffee four hours ago. You enjoy your leisurely day. I'll take this back and make use of it myself." She got back in the truck and shut the door.

"Rosie, wait." He walked over and leaned toward the driver's window. "I'm just not that guy. I don't chainsaw things."

"There are less useful skills you could learn than how to use a chainsaw. But anyway, it was just a thought," she said, though he knew it was more than just a thought to break up, load, and deliver nearly an entire tree. And he sensed that he'd hurt her feelings. Being helpful to people was an essential part of who Rosemary was.

"I suppose I can stack it behind the barn until I learn how to cut it up," he said.

Adrian chimed in, "You might post on the B3 to see if anyone has a log splitter you can rent."

As Reuben had learned, each town in Vermont had its own B3—Backyard Bulletin Board—a daily email where people posted items for sale, announced events, complained about vandals, reunited lost pets with their distraught owners, and posted any other messages and opinions deemed worthy of sharing with their fellow neighbors.

"Ah! Speaking of the B3, I almost forgot." Rosemary grabbed a sheet of paper lying on the passenger seat and handed it to Reuben. "In case you missed it."

Rosemary had circled one of the posts.

Backyard Bulletin Board

**Orrville Neighborhood Forum No. 3542
Coleslaw Softball League Tryouts
Wayne Radko, WayneR@STREETMAIL.
com, Nathan Lane, Orrville**

On Saturday, March 28th, from 11 a.m.-1 p.m. at Sunset Field, the Edison County Mallards will be holding tryouts for our upcoming season in the Coed Fastpitch Softball League for Adults in Western Vermont, aka COFSLAW VT, aka The Coleslaw League. This is a coed league of experienced, fast-pitch players. It is NOT your father's beer league (though you must be over 21 as we do enjoy a post-game brew or two). If you can't succinctly explain the infield fly rule without the Google, let us kindly direct you instead to the Washington Trout. Tell Vince that Wayne sent you.

"Coleslaw League? What am I reading here?" Reuben asked.

"Thought you might like to oil up that musty mitt you bought."

"I haven't played since—"

"You know what's the infield fly rule?" She demanded.

"Of course."

"And we know you like a good beer, so no harm in stopping by. Might do you some good to get out and meet folks—you know, folks that you don't do 'business' with."

CHAPTER 6

The feeling was a familiar one, like all those first days at a new school when stepping out meant a crowd of eyes turned toward Reuben, curious and sizing him up. He sat in his truck scouting the handful of players unloading gear and taking a jog to the far end of the field and back. Back behind the outfield was a thick forest. It wasn't hard to imagine a homer getting past the left fielder and disappearing altogether. The chain-link backstop was solid and seemed relatively new, which was not the case for the faded, rickety-looking benches on either side of home plate or the rusted bleachers along the third base flank. It was a scrappy, rural field—what you'd expect from a town named Orrville—except for the fact that there were overhead lights that looked powerful and nearly new.

A quick knock on his window jolted Reuben's heart. He looked up to see a Black man with a warm smile giving him a little wave. Reuben opened the window.

"I see the mitt in your lap. But you're not leaving your driver's seat. Maybe you change your mind? I wasn't sure, either. But my friend, Joss, she insisted that I come even though this is not the sport I play."

Reuben took a moment to process his words while also instinctively trying to place his accent.

"I am Patrice. Come, let us go together." He was open and encouraging the way teachers at his new schools had often been.

"Hi. Yeah, I'm Reuben. Let me just grab my sweatshirt."

So what if he hadn't played, even for fun, in a dozen or more years, or that he was out of shape? The group that was warming up seemed to represent a wide range in age and fitness level.

One of the players raised a hand to Patrice and broke into a jog, quickly closing the distance between them. "You made it!" She had shaggy, long bangs in front and a buzzcut around the rest of her head. She was short and wiry, and looked no more than sixteen, though the post had indicated that all the players were at least twenty-one.

"Yes, and I have now bought a mitt." He held it out to her like an offering, then pointed to Reuben. "This is my new friend, Reuben, who also came to do the trial. Reuben, this is Joss. She is a short stop," he said, giving both words equal emphasis. "Is this correct?"

"Yep. But it's just one word smushed together: shortstop." She smiled.

"Short stop," he said and high-fived her.

Joss side-eyed Reuben, giving a single chin-lift head nod. "Come on over." They arrived at the benches as three more players approached the field from the opposite direction.

"Why don't you guys take a warm-up lap? Then toss the ball around while the team figures things out. First day's always a fustercluck."

The air was damp, and a light but steady wind seemed to cut right through the weave of Reuben's sweatshirt. In Hartford, by the start of April, spring would already have a solid foothold with buds swelling on the branches and the first purple and yellow crocuses brightening the sidewalks. By contrast, Vermont seemed to be straddling the two seasons with one foot more solidly in winter. But apart from the shadiest north-facing spots, the snow was essentially gone, and the daytime temperatures had been slowly warming.

Despite the spongy ground, Reuben's knees jolted uncomfortably with every jogging step. He would need to get out for some runs or hikes in the coming weeks to get his body used to moving again. Grabbing a dirty softball from a pile on the ground, Reuben walked about fifteen feet away from Patrice before turning and sending over a light overhand toss, careful to slowly warm up his rotator cuff.

"How do you and—what's her name, Joss—know each other?" Reuben asked.

"Sometimes we work together." He tossed the ball back, also without much force, but Reuben could tell Patrice knew how to throw. "I am a counselor at the Lakeshore High School. Some of my students participate in a youth program she helps run."

"She looks like a high schooler herself," Reuben said. He took a step back and put a little more speed behind his throw.

"Don't judge her book by the cover. She is fierce in many ways."

This time Patrice's return throw had some heat, and the ball smacked hard in Reuben's glove, waking up the nerves in his hand. He still had some lingering achiness and decided to add some padding to his old high school glove, a bit of foam like he used to use. He briefly considered using the antique glove, which was hearty and thick, but for the money he paid—a fact that continued to nag at him—he opted to keep it in its mint condition.

Patrice asked him, "And how did you end up being here today?"

"I moved to the area in January. Don't know too many people yet, so a friend of mine who knew I used to play, she suggested I stop by."

Reuben was curious to ask how Patrice, a Black man with an unfamiliar accent, ended up as a high school counselor in what was known to be one of the Whitest states in the country. But what he'd learned from Hannah was that asking, "Where are you from?" was maybe not the best way to get to know someone's background, the implication being that they're outsiders, foreigners who aren't part of the community. "It's rude," she had said, "and, most of the time, it's racist." So instead, Reuben took another hard smack to the hand and said, "For someone who doesn't play the sport, you sure have a solid throw."

"I used to play a lot of handball. Joss thinks this will make me a good out fielder." Reuben's return throw tipped the top of Patrice's glove, and the ball landed and rolled behind him. "But because of this mitt, I am not so sure." He let out a hearty, unselfconscious laugh.

A man's voice behind Reuben shouted, "Okay. Let's get everybody in."

There were seven people taking seats on the bleachers including Patrice and Reuben. The guy standing and pacing in front of them seemed to be in charge. He was probably in his late fifties, stocky and sporting a navy-blue tracksuit.

"For those that don't know me," he turned to Patrice and Reuben, "my name's Wayne. I started this league nineteen years ago with Donny over here, and Kip next to him." Donny and Kip held up their hands in welcoming waves. Wayne continued, "Seems that my forum post about tryouts was viewed by *some* as being a little *off-putting*, and maybe we didn't get the turnout we hoped for. What can I say, it's been a long time since we've had to recruit, so . . ." He picked up a bat, gripped it as if to take a swing and then set the tip down in the dirt, leaning on it like a cane. "Anyways, you two are the only newbies." He pointed to Reuben and Patrice. "So congratulations, you made the team. Let's do the intros and get down to practice."

Reuben wasn't sure how he felt about that. Sitting in the car, he found himself almost hoping he wouldn't make the team, which would have given him credit with Rosemary for trying without having to actually go through with the commitment.

Paying extra attention to remember the other players, Reuben repeated their names and positions over in his head, hoping to make them stick. Wayne with the big voice and bat prop was coach and catcher. Donny, who had a janitor's worth of keys hooked to his belt loop, was team manager and first baseman; and Kip, with his Cubs hat, was centerfield. Joss, as Reuben already knew, was shortstop. She seemed chummy with the young guy next to her, the left fielder named Cameron. Their pitcher was Maddy with the ponytail. Reuben was informed, their third and second basemen—a married couple the team referred to as "the Erins" on account of them being Aaron and Erin respectively—were working at their sugarhouse for the Maple Open House Weekend.

That left Patrice and Reuben to introduce themselves.

"Patrice," Wayne said, "Joss tells me you've got a *hell* of an arm, but don't actually know how to *play* the game." He put emphasis on particular words and had that loud, no-nonsense way of speaking like every gym teacher Reuben ever encountered.

"This is correct," Patrice said.

"I don't know how that's going to work, but she *assures* me she'll onboard you fast. There's only three weeks before our first game, so Joss, that's on you. And maybe the rest of you can work with Patrice on skills and drills during breaks. Meet up before practice when you can." Wayne now lifted the bat to his shoulder.

"Reuben. What's your deal?"

"I played Little League and some varsity baseball. Intramural softball in college." He didn't want to set expectations too high. "Haven't picked up a glove since then, so I'm sure I'm pretty rusty."

"Nonsense. Like riding a bike. Just don't *injure* yourself going too hard too fast. That goes for all of you." He focused back on Reuben. "What's your position?"

"I played catcher, but I can be wherever you need me."

"Let's get you at third until the Erins are back, and then we'll figure out where to put you. That leaves Patrice in right field today. We can work with that. There's more to say—practices, schedule, blah-blah, but let's get out and play some ball."

Wayne was clearly a cut-to-the-chase kind of guy. Not unfriendly or harsh, just efficient, the way Reuben supposed a coach should be, even if he thought the "everybody hustle" tone might be a bit much for a team of adults.

Still, the players reacted quickly, windmilling arms and twisting torsos as they took the field, while Wayne continued to shout directions. "Let's start with some *infield* practice. Maddy, we'll get some pitching in later, but for now, play the position. And, Kip, you and Cameron work with Patrice in the outfield before we start hucking flies at you. We'll leave second open for now."

Reuben was surprised at how good it felt to be back on the ball field. It was a unique kind of time machine, stepping fully into muscle memory. He relished the flow and feel of scooping up a fast grounder, rising and launching into a perfectly executed throw to first. It felt like a long dormant spring had been tapped, and all the physics of force and motion imprinted from hours upon hours of drills came rushing back into his body. He wanted more. More line drives, more hard-hit grounders, more over-the-shoulder pop flies.

The others seemed to feel it, too. There was an energy in the air, a joy in being outside and moving the body after the long hibernation. Wayne was the quintessential coach, chattering and chiding the team as he peppered hits, directly to the players at first, then making them work harder to field the play. Joss, fast and low to the ground, let nothing past her. Donny, though packing a few extra pounds, was flexible, able to do a decent stretch split to capture the short throws. In the outfield, there was a lot of laughter coming from Kip, Cameron, and Patrice. The only one who seemed less than enthused was Maddy, who had no trouble fielding but would pick up stones at her feet and hurl them to the sideline between plays.

"Don't mind her. She's just itching to pitch," Joss said, as if reading Reuben's thoughts.

"Yeah, sure," Reuben said, remembering the handful of pitchers he caught for in high school, how they were like show dogs in a field of mutts, eager to step into the spotlight on the mound and show off what they were trained to do. He asked Joss, "Is the league really fast pitch?"

"For sure. Sometimes a team that's short on players has to scrub, but that's a last resort. Lobbers get creamed in this league."

Reuben nodded at Maddy. "She good?"

"Great speed. Hard pitch. Sometimes wild. Last season, she fractured a guy's ankle."

Maddy turned sharply, mitt poised on her hip. "Batters get hit by pitches all the time!"

"She has really good hearing, too," Joss said.

Maddy aimed her words at Reuben. "The guy was trying to draw a walk to bring in the tying run. If he'd just stepped out of the box, he wouldn't have gotten hit."

Donny chimed in, "He actually tried to get her to pay his ER bill."

"Wow, this league's no joke," Reuben said.

Wayne shouted, "Outfielders! Come in and hit. Except Kip, you take second. Maddy grab a bag of balls and go warm up against the net. Patrice and Cam, let's go twelve swings each."

The trio of outfielders jogged in. When he reached the pitcher's circle, Cameron said to Wayne, "I wish you wouldn't call me Cam."

Joss shouted to Reuben. "Yeah, don't be surprised if he starts calling you Rube, which is kind of an insult, isn't it?"

"Or Ruby?" said Maddy.

"Ruby Slippers, maybe," Donny laughed.

"Ruby Tuesday," said Cameron.

"Like the restaurant," shouted Joss.

Kip groaned, and Cameron turned around, saying, "Please tell me you're joking."

"Fuck off, it is, too, a restaurant."

Wayne cut in. "If you ladies are done gabbing, it would be awful nice to get some batting practice in."

"Wayne, I'm sure you don't mean it unkindly," said Cameron, "but the implication that women just sit around making idle chat is not only insulting to Joss and

Maddy, it also fails to recognize that we men are likewise social creatures, and verbal communication is something we really should be doing more of, not less."

Wayne's expression didn't change apart from his blinking eyes, which seemed to show an internal struggle between irritation and forced patience. When he spoke, his voice was measured. "And *that* is all well and good, when you're at the hairdresser's—or barber shop, if you prefer. But *we* are *here* to play softball. So let's please prioritize that, *Cameron*."

Cameron folded his arms in response, and when none of the rest of the team moved into position, Wayne took a breath and said, "Nevertheless, I shall be more mindful about..." he hesitated to determine the right words, "...de-genderizing my colloquialisms."

"Thank you." Cameron pulled a pair of batting gloves from his pocket and slid them over his hands. "Joss says you're too old to learn new tricks, but I continue to have faith in you, Wayne."

"Nah, I'm with Joss," said Kip.

As someone who spent so much time alone, Reuben had forgotten the cadence and easy play of camaraderie. He exchanged a smile with Patrice as if to confirm that, yes, they would enjoy becoming part of this team.

Wayne wasn't technically a pitcher, but he could consistently put the ball across the plate, giving the batters something to swing at nearly every time. Apart from Cameron and Joss, who apparently liked to go to the batting cages together, it was a slow refresh for the players. The practice was filled with a lot of infield pop-ups and piddly grounders. Even Reuben's timing was off, and he failed to connect solidly with all but a couple pitches. And for Patrice, hitting was an altogether new experience, "not like the wiffle ball very much."

When Maddy was warmed up enough to pitch, they batted around again, this time with even less success given her fast windmill and lapses in accuracy—some pitches flew wildly over the backstop, others were driven hard enough into the ground to leave a dent in the dirt. When he first got up to bat, Reuben felt a certain preoccupation with protecting his ankles, but once he adjusted to Maddy's speed and sharpened his reflexes to react to pitches that were disarmingly close to his body, he managed to connect a few.

The last to bat was Wayne, who had come in from the outfield collecting the few hard-hit runaway balls. Approaching the plate, he took a few practice swings. When the infielders took several steps back to the edge of the grass, Reuben suspected that pounding the ball with all his might was Wayne's specialty.

"Put a little cayenne on," he told Maddy.

About half of Wayne's hits went so far over the players' heads they didn't even try to snag them. They just turned and jogged to retrieve balls that fell shy of the woods' edge. When Reuben went to relay for Cameron, Wayne just said, "Leave it. Play to second." And the next hit was a hard grounder that Reuben smoothly fielded to Kip covering the base.

"Last one!" Wayne yelled. "Live play. I'm a runner."

The pitch came in just outside, and Wayne smacked it hard and fast up the middle, practically grazing the top of Maddy's head. Having positioned himself too far back, Kip ran in to field the ball; Joss went to cover second anticipating that's where the play would be. But halfway to first, Wayne went down. Reuben didn't know if he'd tripped or collapsed but he was rolling on his side, holding his hamstring and howling in pain.

Donny squatted beside him while the others gathered around. "Did you feel a pop?" he asked.

Wayne, biting his bottom lip, nodded.

"Cameron, help me get him up." Donny and Cameron each took one of Wayne's arms over their shoulders and lifted so he could hop on one leg to the bench where Maddy was waiting with a cold pack. "I'll get him home," Donny said. "Kip, you pack up the gear and take it to your place?"

"Course."

"I hope you will be feeling better soon, Wayne," said Patrice.

"Yeah, Wayne," others mumbled.

Kip collected the balls from the backstop while Maddy went to retrieve the bases. Reuben and Patrice gathered the bats and helmets and started putting them in the bag.

Once Donny pulled out of the parking lot, Joss asked, "Seriously? Again?" She tossed her glove down and sat on the bench to untie her cleats. Cameron just shook his head.

"You're what, twenty-six, Joss?" asked Kip. "It's not easy getting old. Guys like Wayne, their brain thinks they can still move like they did thirty years ago."

"This is the third year in a row he's gotten injured and left us short."

"We'll just have to pull out the sub list again."

Maddy chimed in, "There's no way Larry's coming back. Not after Wayne told him snakes had better arms than he had. Who the hell is going to catch?"

"Reuben said he was a catcher," Cameron said. "You game?"

"Yeah, of course," Reuben said. "But it could just be a pull, right? He'll probably be back."

Kip looked at him and just shook his head. "Not likely."

◆

It was Sunday morning, and Reuben was vaguely aware that Adrian had been up for an hour or so, stoking the wood stove, brewing some coffee. They had both nodded off early the night before in the middle of a documentary about people who gave up plastic for a year. But Reuben was still heavy with sleep and dozed a bit longer before calling down to her. He had expected to be a little sore from the practice, but it was bone deep in nearly every square inch of his body.

She came back to the bedroom, dropping her robe on a chair before sliding under the covers and climbing on top of him.

"I'm not sure I can move," he said.

"It's okay, I can do the moving." When he looked dubious, she sighed, "Roll over, you baby."

Reuben lay on his stomach, a pillow propped beneath his chest as Adrian, now straddling his rear, kneaded his shoulders, adjusting her pressure according to the level of flinching and sharp inhales coming from him.

"Jesus, even my armpits hurt."

She slid her hands there and tickled him.

He jolted hard and then groaned at the sudden movement, "Mother of God, are you trying to kill me?"

"I'm definitely not the Mother of God."

As Adrian worked his back, Reuben talked about the softball practice and what he'd learned from Kip after the two of them loaded the gear into his car. Kip offered Reuben some of the six-pack he had been planning to enjoy with Wayne and Donny after practice.

"What makes you so sure Wayne is gone for the season?" Reuben asked.

The late afternoon sun offered a weak but steady warmth. "Oh, he's not gone. He'll still coach and he'll hit. That's how he did last year. With Cameron pinch running. Now that kid's got a set of wheels."

"Every at-bat? Is that even allowed?"

"We make the rules. Plus no one's going to say when the old-timers have to quit. We play serious, but we still have heart. Besides, Wayne built this league. Makes me wonder if it'll go belly-up once he quits for good."

Kip had a bit of an accent that Reuben was starting to recognize in people who grew up in the state. It had shades of rural Maine, but was tighter, with a tendency to clip consonants at the end of words. Like Rosemary who said "Vermahn" instead of Vermont, and Kip who said "harh" instead of "heart."

"You and Wayne and Donny—you guys were raised here?" Reuben asked.

"Wayne and Donny are friends since grade school. I met them when I was working at the lumber yard in my twenties. Wayne's a handyman and Donny works for a construction company, so I'd see 'em around." He kicked a stone away from his foot. "That field was Donny's big idea. He and his brother inherited the land when their dad died—twenty acres apiece. Brother wanted to sell to a developer who would only buy if he could get the whole lot. Donny said no fuckin' way would he let the land turn into a strip mall. So he and Wayne 'borrowed' a bulldozer in the middle of the night—there might have been some tequila involved—and they set to making the field to honor Donny's dad who was a giant Red Sox fan. That, and so they could start the league."

"No kidding?"

"Course, Donny's brother never spoke to him again. But I'm not sure they spoke much anyways."

They sipped at their beer and watched a chipmunk rummage around for seeds in a nearby patch of grass. "And the others on the team? What's their connection?"

"The game," Kip said simply. "We all just love the game."

Reuben could see that. He'd had no idea how much he missed playing—or even that he missed it at all—until that first grounder of the day came firing at him.

"So where does the coleslaw come in?" Adrian asked.

"Just an easy way to pronounce the league acronym, I guess. Although Kip did say, there was a woman who used to hand out paper cups of coleslaw during the seventh inning stretch as a gag. Until one game, more than half the spectators ended up getting E. coli. Sounds like that immediately put an end to the tradition."

Reuben continued to tell Adrian about the team, the few details Kip had shared about the players. Like how Joss and Cameron were super tight friends—just friends—from their University of Vermont days, and that Cameron sometimes sang in a band. That when Maddy turned thirty last season, Wayne brought his grill to the field, and they had a post-game barbecue with the other team. That the Erins ran a small farm and would sometimes bring everyone vegetables.

Reuben stopped talking and tried to relax under Adrian's skilled hands. Though the second-guessing he'd had early in their relationship had quieted considerably, and most of the time he was at ease around her, there were times when he found himself trying to analyze her silences. Sometimes she seemed to not have anything to say; other times it felt like she was thinking about something else entirely or was simply bored with the conversation and had mentally moved on. He thought this might be one of those times, so after a moment, he said, "Your massage skills are truly prodigious."

"At least you're not jumping out of your skin anymore." She wound her way down to Reuben's lower back and gently kissed the base of his spine. "Think you're able to move yet?"

"I think some parts are quite moved, actually."

"Let's hurry up and give them some attention. I have to be at the gallery by eleven."

CHAPTER 7

The tall rectangular facades of Endicott's Hardware and the building to the left of it were reminiscent of an old spaghetti Western set, the backdrop of a twenty-pace, turn-and-draw shootout between outlaw and sheriff. The interpretive sign out front indicated the two structures had, in fact, been built in 1832, forty years after the village of Orrville had been established by Thomas Orr, a former military officer in the Revolutionary War.

Reuben scanned the brief history display that detailed how the main building had originally been a hotel providing lodging to the lumberjacks who worked in the region. But at the turn of the century, Albert Endicott converted the space to a feed mill and hardware store. Since then, four generations of Endicotts have run the store. In 1993, they expanded to include the neighboring sandwich shop as a way of encouraging loyalty to the local store when a "certain megacorporation retailer added a hot dog stand to its cheap and cheaply made home improvement offerings." Reuben felt a guilty twinge, having done all his new home shopping at the implied retailer, and decided to shift his business to Endicott's when it was time to get yard tools for the spring cleanup. For now, he had stopped by on his way to softball practice for supplies to replace the caulk in the downstairs shower, as well as some nuts and bolts for a new sculpture he was working on.

The entry to the store was like stepping into a different time. Front and center was a glass cabinet featuring jars of old-time penny candy brands like Mary Jane and Necco Wafer as well as more ubiquitous ones like Snickers and Twizzlers. On top of the cabinet was the store's original register, its golden brass shining and lovingly restored like an ancient Egyptian sarcophagus. All around, the walls were cluttered with antique Pepsi Cola and Esso Gas signs—originals, Reuben assumed, not replicas—plus enormous old logging and farming tools.

Stepping just beyond the front part of the shop, he hit a jarring juxtaposition, where bright fluorescents lit up the conveniences of a modern hardware store including a dozen or so aisles organized in a way that wasn't entirely clear. Gardening and painting supplies were obvious enough but kitchen goods like paper towels and lightbulbs were shelved beside a selection of carpentry tools, and pest control and pet food were shelved together in a subsection within concrete and masonry supplies.

Reuben kept an ear tuned to the conversation by the checkout counter where a group of four men ranging in age from twenties to fifties were gathered. Three of them appeared to be customers, or at least not employees. Reuben got the feeling the group had been eyeing him through the window as he read the history sign. But when he entered the store, they talked among themselves, avoiding eye contact with him.

"Garvey's gonna have to dig the trench deeper. That new house those Philly people put up changed the whole water flow on his property. They won't even help pay for it."

The youngest of the group chuffed and said, "You see the sign at their driveway? '24-Hour Video Surveillance.' What's that for? In case there's bears or something?"

"You know of any bears that can read, dumbass?"

"I'd pay Garvey fifty bucks to do a naked junk run 'crost their patio. That'll give 'em something to surveil."

"He'd do it for ten."

"You know, those people hired a lawn guy?"

"Somebody ought to have told them to move up to Burlin'tn."

"Yeah, nice thing about Burlin'tn is it's so close to Vermahn."

Reuben added a selection of fasteners to the basket that already held caulk, a caulk gun, and a new utility knife. On his way to the checkout, he also picked up a box of trash bags and some work gloves.

"Excuse me," Reuben said to a guy with a long, scraggly beard who was blocking the path to the register. The man didn't say anything in return but took a step aside.

Reuben set the basket on the counter. A man about his age started to scan the items. Reuben had noted that he'd been quiet but was clearly listening and nodding along with the conversation around him.

"Fixing a tub?" he asked Reuben. He was a big guy, taller than Reuben and broad-chested in a forest green polo shirt whose cuffs strained against the chiseled bulk of his biceps. His wide-set eyes bore an unquestionable resemblance to one of the men pictured in the history display. An Endicott, Reuben suspected.

"Shower stall," Reuben corrected. "But yeah, the old caulk is disintegrating."

"Silicone'll give you a stronger seal, but latex is easier to work with for people who haven't done it before."

The particular angle of the guy's words seemed to suggest he assumed Reuben was in the latter category, which was true, but there was no way he was going to own up to it now. "Thanks. Good to know I picked the stronger seal."

"Got mineral spirits? Might want to have some on hand for cleanup."

His words felt less like an upsell and more that, again, Reuben had been sized up and assumed to be an inexperienced do-it-yourselfer, like he was the underdog contestant on a home improvement reality show.

"I actually do have a can of mineral spirits at home."

The register beeped as the rest of the items were scanned.

"You local?" Asked one of the older men leaning on the counter.

Reuben wasn't sure how, or even if, he should answer, so he said, "Is that...does that...uh—"

"In case you want to join the store's rewards program."

This felt like another test of some kind. "Okay, sure, that would come in handy."

The man behind the counter said, "Just need your name, phone, and address to sign up."

"It's Reuben—R-e-u-b-e-n Downes with an e-s at the end. 860-466-3417. Address is 3231 Popple Hill Road."

"The old Chambers farm?"

The youngest of the men said to the others, "Last owners of that house hired Kath to do a big remodel. They didn't last long."

Reuben felt oddly compelled to defend the previous owners of his house, people he'd never actually met. "The wife's job was transferred to Florida, actually. Otherwise, I believe they wanted to stay."

"Where you from?" Asked the fourth guy, the shortest of the three. "Eight-six-oh's not an in-state area code." Four pairs of eyes were on Reuben waiting for his reply.

"I believe I just told you," said Reuben. "The house on Popple Hill."

◆

"I'm not sure if they meant it," said Reuben to Kip as they warmed up their arms with some throwing, "but the whole exchange felt a little unwelcoming."

"Oh, they meant it," said Kip.

"What, why?"

"Eh, you know, it's an outsiders thing. New people coming in, changing how we do here. Not saying everyone feels that way, but there're some."

"So what, I was supposed to own up to being a novice and switch to latex caulk so they could totally emasculate me?" Reuben overthrew to Kip who had to jog to chase down the ball.

Donny, throwing next to them with Cameron, had been listening and said, "You're not wrong. Jackson Endicott likes everyone to know he's the biggest cock in the coop."

"For a business that wants people to buy local, you'd think he'd be a little friendlier," said Reuben. "I happen to like the hot dogs at Home Depot."

"I wouldn't take it personally, Reuben," Donny said. "Sounds to me like Garvey's got some shitbird new neighbors, and that maybe the guys lumped you in a 'newcomers' box along with them."

"For all they know, I could be a third-generation Vermonter."

At this, Donny and Kip burst out laughing. Cameron just slowly shook his head.

"What?" Reuben demanded. "Just because I don't have a Vermont accent—"

"No such thing," scoffed Donny.

"There very much is," Reuben insisted.

Cameron said to Donny, "Well, you do pronounce some words a little weird."

"Harsh," said Kip.

"Like what?" asked Donny, firing off a hard grounder.

Reuben pointed the ball in his hand at Kip. "Like Kip saying 'harsh' like it's 'hearse' with an 'sh' at the end."

"And you say 'loike' instead of like," Cameron pointed out to Donny.

At that, Kip and Donny went on the offensive about Reuben's jeans—not just the brand but the way he wore them—as being a telltale sign of being "from away." Their laughter was good-natured, thankfully a different tone than what Reuben had experienced at the store.

Their throws were becoming erratic as quick gusts of wind came through, tossing around the just-barely budding branches on the trees. A weather front was moving in fast. They could see it in the clouds rolling in overhead, but Wayne's hope was that they could get a couple hours of practice in since the forecast for the next several days was looking wet.

Joss was in the outfield teaching Patrice how to drop step and get in place to catch the fly balls hit behind him. Handball seemed to have given him a solid instinct for reading where the pop fly would come down, but keeping the ball in his glove once he'd caught it was a skill that needed a little work. Reuben made a note to bring glove oil next time and help work out some of the stiffness in Patrice's new mitt.

Earlier during practice, Reuben had met the Erins. The young couple arrived with a sleeping baby named

Cedar strapped in a car seat. With their matching fresh-faced apple cheeks and golden hair, they couldn't have been more perfectly cast for the role of "Young American Farm Family" if a Hollywood agent had done it. Aaron was warmly welcoming to Patrice and Reuben, inviting them out to the farm for a free pint of syrup and a greenhouse tour.

Wayne, having self-diagnosed a hamstring tear, had returned to coach practice with the support of a single crutch that was clearly too short for him. He barked orders for setting up drills and directed the team on plays they were already in position to make. Reuben knew this was the catcher's job, but suspected it would remain in Wayne's purview even when Reuben strapped on the gear and stepped in behind the plate. In the meantime, he and Maddy pulled off to the side to get in some pitching time.

Apart from just barely meeting the Erins, Maddy was the only player Reuben couldn't really get a read on, mostly because she was both serious and quiet. She had a natural kind of prettiness, Reuben thought, but in a way also held a subtle harshness, like a pioneer woman who had gone through periods of hunger. She was intense, he could tell that. When her pitch was dialed in, it had a force behind it that seemed personal, his mitt a particular target in her mind.

"Where did you learn to pitch?" he asked her.

Maddy shrugged as if it were obvious. "High school."

"Good coach?"

"Yeah."

"I had a bunch myself, from ages seven through seventeen. Only one, though, Coach Bordo, really taught me to appreciate the grace of the game. Others knew how to build skills and train, but—"

Maddy's pitch, a perfect knee-high strike, smacked his mitt painfully, hard enough to be felt through the extra cushion Reuben had taped around his hand.

"Damn, woman," Reuben said. Maddy lowered her eyes but failed to totally stifle a satisfied smile.

The next pitch, though, went so far over Reuben's head that, leaping up, he wasn't even able to tip it. The ball flew off, deep into the parking lot. "We'll get that one after practice," he said.

Practice, however, was cut suddenly short when the clouds let loose with a downpour that sent the players scrambling. Everyone was soaked by the time the bases and gear were finally loaded into Donny's truck.

As they retreated to the shelter of their cars, Wayne yelled, "Keep an eye out for a text with the upcoming schedule. First game is next Saturday against the Trout!"

CHAPTER 8

The rain carried on for days, sometimes just a fine mist, other times, a soaking, heavy downpour, even a burst of wet snowflakes on one of the colder mornings. With the perpetual dampness, Reuben truly wouldn't have been surprised if surfaces around the house—including his own skin—started to sprout a coat of moss.

He spent much of those days in the studio, sometimes working on smaller sculptures, testing out new techniques and ideas he had for bigger projects. Those explorations had started veering away from small electronics and appliances, gravitating instead toward the old tools and farm equipment Reuben was keener on collecting. His artistic tone had shifted, too, beginning to fall squarely in the kind of rough steampunk aesthetic he'd first explored with the typewriter crow.

Adrian was still a little lukewarm about the sculptures, suggesting that they were a little "off-brand" for Reuben Downes the painter, a phrase that struck an odd note, and when he jokingly said that kind of language sounded "off-brand" for Adrian Ellison, she patiently explained that inconsistencies in tone and style could make it harder for her to build a buying audience for him. Reuben wasn't convinced, but agreed to dedicate most of his studio time to painting.

Though it was the seventh straight day of rain, the warming temperatures had brought the landscape to life with bursting buds and shimmering yellow-greens of new foliage. Taking his lunch in the studio, Reuben sat watching the moody sky swirl and dissipate above mountains. Nearer in the garden and beyond it in the field, the birds were busy. Not just the chickadees and house sparrows that had loitered through the winter, but hermit thrushes and a few red-winged blackbirds bobbing on the tall grasses.

Reuben loved these meditative moments in what still felt like his new home. It was a pause to clear and calm his mind after a morning focusing on a newly commissioned painting for a patron's summer home on the New York side of Lake Champlain. He felt good about his progress, which left the rest of the afternoon to work on a horse sculpture whose layers of scrap metal were shaped to capture the animal's moving muscles. The next step was selecting, clipping, and buffing out a collection of rusted chains he would use for the mane and tail.

Contrasting with the morning's classical piano playlist, the afternoon soundtrack was a mix of industrial Nine Inch Nails and trip-hoppy Portishead. The electronic textures and DJ samples were gritty auditory texture for the tactile work he was doing. Reuben was so deeply engaged with the work that he completely lost track of time. When the text from Adrian came, telling him to pick her up at six thirty, he had only an hour to shower and be out the door.

This was to be their first public appearance together as a couple, attending another artist's opening reception at Burlington City Arts. Adrian was an invited guest and would be working the room. She mentioned he should likewise make connections there, maybe chat with other artists, a suggestion that reminded him of how his mother used to encourage him to put in a little effort to make new friends.

In the day's fading light, Reuben's GPS guided him to an affluent-looking neighborhood in the town of Valoir, pronounced "Veloor" by the locals. The manicured homes were a showcase of the area's nineteenth-century history, a town whose location on the Deertail River made it a prime spot for the old sawmill and metalwork operations. Adrian's house, she had told him, was on the historic registry, built by a shipbuilder named Edmund Peckham in 1876. It was a solid, stoic-looking home made of brick with a double row of gray shutter-framed windows.

Carrying an oversized umbrella against the steady drizzle, Reuben reached the doorstep as Adrian was coming out. Dressed in a black, off-the-shoulder dress and strappy sandals, she exuded a modest elegance, the light application of makeup making her even more radiant.

"You are lovely," he whispered as he side-kissed her cheek. "My luck is just so dumb."

She fluttered her hand, waving aside the compliment. Reaching out to straighten his collar she said, "I like this color on you."

He looked down at his slate-blue shirt, filing the compliment away for future clothing purchases.

"So I'm a touch early," he said. "Should I come in for a drink?" In the few months they'd been a couple, Adrian had never invited him into her home. Though she hadn't said as much, he suspected she wasn't ready for him to meet her daughter, Leila. Glancing in the window, he could barely make out the top of the girl's head above the couch.

Adrian slid her arm in his, "The lot is likely to fill up quickly, so it's probably good for us to get there a little early."

The reception was for a photographer named Bettina Hess. Her exhibit, *What We Hide*, was a series of images taken on a cross-country trip during which she knocked on peoples' doors and asked to photograph the contents of their closets. It was a hybrid project: part photography, part performance art. In the introduction, she talked about how the initial concept was to explore the ways in which all lives are, in one way or another, "in the closet." The photographs displayed exquisite skill for composition and lighting while also capturing an impressive range of subjects that included the mundane (a lineup of gray and navy suit jackets) and the unexpected (a life-size, fully inflated Easter bunny). There was the obsessively organized (color-coded cubbies) and the delightfully chaotic (an avalanche of sports equipment). There were explorations of cultural differences as well: drag queen platform heels contrasted with rugged cowboy boots contrasted with trendy basketball shoes... statements all their own.

Bettina had stationed herself near an oversized print of a survivalist's pantry filled to capacity with canned goods and cereal boxes. There was a crowd around her, and she seemed to revel in the experience of being the center of attention in a way Reuben had never felt at ease, though he'd learned to fake it under the right circumstances.

Reuben waited his turn then approached Bettina. "It's a really impressive undertaking. And your eye captures so much depth within the frame, visual and obviously metaphoric," he said, hoping to convey how he appreciated her work.

"Thank you. I think it became a bit of an obsession for me. I almost didn't know when to quit and come home."

Following Adrian's advice to engage with the other local artists, Reuben offered what he thought would be a good conversation opener. "I'm curious, what was the most surprising aspect of the project?"

Bettina didn't hesitate in responding. "Without a doubt, it was how—not just willing—but enthusiastic people were to let a complete stranger into their home. Literally opening doors for me." She took a sip of wine. "Out of forty requests—we're talking cold-call-weirdo-lady knocking on their doors—thirty-one of them agreed. It was as if the simple act of being asked was all anyone needed to be willing to share their world. Speaking of, who are you?"

Reuben was about to answer, but their conversation was interrupted by the center's director pulling Bettina aside and whispering in her ear, and she thanked Reuben before stepping away to meet someone. Reuben had turned to search the room for Adrian when a voice from behind startled him.

"Reuben Downes." Reuben turned to find a large man with a full head of swooping silver hair. "I understand I should introduce myself to you." His outstretched handshake was just inches away from Reuben's abdomen. "John Eastlake, real estate developer. I appreciate some of your work."

There seemed to be a lean on the word 'some.'

"Oh? That's terrific to hear," Reuben said. "Thank you."

"Adrian and I go a-ways back. I was an investor in Gallery Fifth. Between you and me," he leaned in conspiratorially, "she's done far better than I was expecting."

"She's a smart woman."

"Clearly. She snatched you up."

Reuben couldn't tell if he meant professionally or romantically. Either way, the man's demeanor suggested that he was someone who thought he was the important person in the room, despite it being an event for someone else.

Though Reuben would have liked to prematurely end this conversation, Adrian had sent John Eastlake over for a reason. Reuben shifted the conversation back to the gallery and some of the projects he was working on. "I don't know if Adrian has mentioned but I've been exploring some new directions with sculpture, using repurposed tools and materials. I'm hoping to add a couple to the gallery soon."

"Reuben, I'm a real estate developer. I know a profitable, repeatable formula when I see one. You've got a good thing going with the paintings, why mess with that? People appreciate sculptures in a museum. They don't buy them. It's indulgent, impractical."

Here was something Reuben could dig in on, the first interesting part of the conversation, "I have to disagree, John—" But he didn't get in a further word on the subject.

"Here's my card," said Eastlake. "Let's talk next week about commissioning a couple pieces for one of the complexes I'm about to open."

Reuben took the proffered card as John Eastlake shifted his focus and lobbed a wink and a wave at someone across the room. "You'll excuse me, Reuben."

The bar was mercifully empty, and Reuben ordered a glass of red. Adrian came over and purred in his ear, "I hear you're an *arrr*-tist."

But Reuben had a residue of irritation from his exchange with Eastlake. "That guy you sent over to me." He couldn't suppress a look of distaste.

"Oh, John's just a lot of bluster."

"With an ego the size of Montana."

"He said he has a commission for you."

"I have no interest in doing work for him."

"He's a good person to have in your corner."

"Oh yeah, he mentioned he helped finance the gallery startup."

Now Adrian was the one who seemed irritated. She took a breath in and let it out slowly. "Yeah. Twelve years past, and he still makes sure he gets credit for it." She took a sip from Reuben's glass of wine. "In any case, the gallery has already accepted the commission on your behalf." Reuben started to protest. "Don't worry, he's hands off on stuff like that. He'll tell you what general size and color theme he needs and give you a reference he likes from something you've already produced. The rest is artistically open to you. Seriously, it's a good gig that I have no doubt will lead to work with other clients."

"He just seems like such a giant turd. And that's from a ten-minute conversation."

"He can be. But not with this. I promise. I wouldn't set you up for a headache."

Reuben believed her. Or at least believed that *she* believed she wouldn't. "Okay," he said. "But can we get out of here soon? I'm meeting some of the Mallards after this."

Adrian gave his arm a squeeze. "I have one more person to talk to, then we can go."

To reach the indoor batting cages at the Fun Zone Family Center, Reuben had to pass through a minigolf course, a gymnasium filled with giant inflatable slides, and a ninja warrior obstacle course. The noise and freewheeling activity on a Friday evening rivaled some of the shows Reuben had been to in his twenties. Here, families unleashed their children, letting them ricochet throughout the space, exhausting themselves, some to the point of nuclear-level meltdowns.

Reaching the locker room to stash his jacket and keys was like entering the eye of a hurricane, and Reuben just sat on a bench for a couple minutes to reset his equilibrium before heading inside to meet Joss, Cameron, and Patrice.

At the far end of the Fun Zone was a lineup of three batting cages, all of them occupied. The sounds were familiar: the *thwunk* of the automatic pitching machine, the subsequent *ping* of a hit, all echoing under the high ceiling and stadium-bright lights. Reuben could see Patrice was at bat in the middle lane. Joss was standing to the side giving him tips as Reuben approached.

"Remember to bend your knees a little. That's too much. Better. As the pitch comes in, and you start swinging, you're going to shift that weight from your back leg to your front." She pantomimed a swing in slow motion, exaggerating the moves. "That's how the energy moves from you through the bat to the ball."

Earlier that day, Patrice's text message simply said, *"Joss is helping me at the Fun Zone batting cages after dinner. You should join us."*

Reuben met Cameron on the bench behind a protective net. "Have you guys been here long?"

"About forty minutes," Cameron said. "I already took a turn."

"Cameron, can you slow down the pitch a little?" Joss asked.

He got up and pressed some buttons on a panel. When the next pitch came in, it was slower with a higher arc. Patrice connected with it.

"YES! You rock star!" Joss shouted.

"She gets so jazzed seeing him put the pieces together. She would really make a great coach."

Cameron was looking at Joss with the kind of wistful affection that Reuben recognized as being the unrequited variety, mostly because he suspected Joss was gay and treated Cameron like a favorite brother.

Patrice brightened and bounced with energy as he started to make contact with the ball more consistently, even launching a solid line drive that winged the pitching machine.

"See? The key really is watching the ball right out of the pitcher's hand," Joss said. "Cameron, crank the speed up a notch."

"No, thank you. I am getting blisters." Patrice held up one of his hands. He parted the net and came through. "Reuben, you are here."

"Looking good, Patrice!"

"Come, take my place."

Joss head-nodded a greeting at Reuben. "Bats are over there."

Before deciding to come, Reuben wondered if Joss and Cameron might think he was too old and uncool to hang out with. If they did, they didn't show it, and truthfully, Reuben had no idea how old Patrice was. He had such a buoyant personality that he could as easily have passed for twenty-three as for forty-three.

Reuben took a few dozen swings, having Cameron increase the speed a couple times to better match, and then exceed, Maddy's. It was a relief to feel himself returning to form, relying on the consistency of the pitching machine for getting lots of swings in. Still, he knew there was really no substitute for hitting against a live pitcher, getting a read on their arm mechanics and timing idiosyncrasies. When he finished, he said as much to Patrice.

"Don't feel discouraged if you find it harder to get a solid hit off Wayne or Maddy in practice. And an opposing team's pitcher will actually try to throw you off, changing things up. Assuming they have the skill."

"Some of them do," Cameron said.

"You'll be fine," Joss said to Patrice. "Just remember the building blocks we worked on today and keep your eyes on the pitch."

Cameron started changing out of his athletic sneakers for a pair of casual street ones.

"With handball," Patrice said, "it is just you and the ball. You are not weighted down by equipment. No mitt, no bat or helmet. It is a purer sport."

"Hey now—" said Joss.

"Don't get her started," said Cameron.

Reuben had often waxed poetic about baseball to Hannah the few times they'd sat down to watch a Mets game. And though he knew that only the die-hard fans truly understood the beauty of the sport, it didn't stop him from trying to explain to Patrice.

"Think of baseball—softball in this case—as a more choreographed sport. It's action and reaction. Yeah, the structure is more artificial than handball or basketball or soccer, but it's a subtler game that honors patience and attention to detail."

Patrice was unmoved by Reuben's admittedly abstract explanation. "But it is a sport. It should be energy and athleticism on display," Patrice clenched his fists to emphasize the point. "This is what people want to see. Who wants to watch patience? This is not rewarding."

"He has a point," Cameron said.

Joss threw her batting glove at him. "You're dead to me."

Cameron said, "I'm ready for a beer. How about you guys?"

"Not for me," said Patrice. "Some of the families here are from the school. I don't want them to see me having any alcohol."

"So come and have a Coke—" Joss started.

"As they say, it is not a good look. Parents who see me in a bar may decide I am not good to guide their children."

Joss seemed to think he was being too sensitive, but Reuben wondered if Patrice might feel the need to tread more carefully than others in his profession just by virtue of his accent and the color of his skin.

Patrice wished them a good weekend and navigated his way toward the exit. Joss, Cameron, and Reuben stepped around caroming children who were oblivious to all but the biggest obstacles. The Fun Zone's Fun Foam Bar was filled with parents whose expressions seemed to reflect a weary relief at having made it to the end of the week, their beer and grown-up conversation only occasionally interrupted by their progeny demanding more money. There was a twangy country song playing from a speaker above the one empty table available to them. As Cameron, Joss, and Reuben settled into their seats, a waiter came to take their order for three pints of Bitter Wolcott, a local IPA, and a basket of onion rings to share.

After he left, Reuben opened the conversation. "Cameron, I hear you're in a band?"

Cameron looked down, pulled a cardboard coaster toward him and flipped it a few times. "Kind of. No, I mean, yeah, that's true. We haven't played for anyone yet except the drummer's wife, so it's not totally a thing."

"Don't buy this modesty act," Joss said. "I've heard a couple recordings. They're really good. They've got a great, hard blues sound. And this guy," she smacked his hand playfully, "tough to believe it, but he can actually sing."

Cameron just shook his head uncomfortably as the waiter returned with a tray of beers and an enormous basket of golden onion rings.

"These are the best," Joss said, digging in. "I don't know what the fuck they put in their sauce, but I would lick it straight off my fingers if you guys weren't here."

"You mean if Reuben weren't here," Cameron corrected. "You do stuff like that all the time around me. Frankly, it's gross."

"Uh, you mean endearing," Joss said.

Curtailing an argument over what was or was not gross, Reuben asked, "So is that what you do for work, Cameron, make music?"

Cameron seemed to think the suggestion absurd, "Pff, no. I make coffee. I mean, not like pots of coffee. I work at the roasting plant."

"He gets, like, five pounds free every month if you ever want any," Joss chimed in.

Joss and Cameron's rapport was just as Kip described it. Over the evening, Reuben got to hear the story of how they had met on the first day of UVM's freshman class orientation. Now at twenty-five, they had traveled the kind of emotional terrain that marked the tail end of the teen years into young adulthood, and it showed in the way they were completely at ease around each other, unrequited love notwithstanding. Because it really seemed clear that Cameron had a thing for Joss who was not only oblivious to the fact, but she seemed to most value the platonic aspects of their relationship. "We tell each other everything," she said at one point. "Even dating stuff."

Cameron quickly changed the subject. "What about you, Reuben? What do you do for work?"

Without consciously realizing he was doing it until later, Reuben talked only superficially about his work, toning down the more esoteric parts of being artistic, and instead grounding it in the pragmatic world of art that paid the bills: the paintings he produced for hotels, medical facilities, and the like. Coming so quickly from the art opening was a kind of whiplash between worlds, and in the moment, it felt like selling art to wealthy clients was somehow less real than roasting coffee or working as a handyman or being a school counselor. He decided to change the subject.

"I have to say, Joss, you're doing a great job with Patrice. It's hard to believe he's never played before."

She splayed her hands out on the table. "I adore Patrice. He has this beautiful goodness about him that just puts people at ease." Reuben knew what she meant. "You should see him with the kids. I mean really troubled kids, some of them. Poverty, parents in jail or on drugs, you name it. And he calms them, he makes them laugh." She took a couple sips of beer. The bar's music and chatter filled the space when she stopped talking.

"Is it okay if I ask what his story is?" Reuben said. "How did he end up here?" Reuben knew it was just a different way of asking where Patrice was from, but he was genuinely curious about what part of the world Patrice had grown up in.

"Yeah, I don't know a lot of details, but he was part of a resettlement program for people from Congo. From what I heard, he was high school age when he arrived in Burlington with his brother and an aunt. I don't know what happened to the rest of his family but he had spent a few years abroad in a refugee camp before coming here."

"Oh," said Reuben. It wasn't at all what he was expecting to hear, having wrongly imagined Patrice's journey was the result of self-determination, not war. "Does he ever talk about it?"

"No," Joss said. "But it's hard to know if that's because he doesn't want to talk about it, or if people just aren't comfortable asking. I know I'm not."

◆

Getting ready for bed that night, Reuben was thinking about what it must have been like for teenage Patrice, landing in a place so foreign, not just in its climate and landscape, but its language and culture, the technology and media. And now, Patrice was on the other side, a man who was generous in spirit and enthusiasm, who was, as Joss described, a point of light for students experiencing their own difficulties at home or in school.

The thought led him back to Paul Brower, and Reuben wondered if he'd had someone like Patrice helping him navigate his trauma all those years ago, maybe he wouldn't have moved away. Given Reuben's own experiences with school counselors back then, it seemed unlikely they were trained, or even equipped, to deal with that kind of abuse experience.

Realizing his mind was too occupied to sleep, Reuben headed down to the kitchen to make some tea, a habit he'd carried on after his stay with Rosemary. He sat at the table and opened his laptop, determined to see if he could learn more about present-day Paul. But general searches only brought up references to the abuse story and a different Paul Brower who was the retired CEO of a home security company. So Reuben moved to social media where he eventually found a listing for "his" Paul

Brower, whose photo showed a grown man wearing practically the same gold wire glasses he'd had as a kid. The profile was sparsely populated with pictures of pretty sunsets over an ocean, some tropical looking plants, and a photo of a woman in a straw hat that Reuben immediately recognized as the now-aged version of Paul's mother.

Reuben clicked on the message app and added Paul's name in the addressee box. The message sat empty for several minutes, cursor blinking. Reuben's fingers hovered just above the keyboard, composing in his head what would even make sense to say. Twice he clicked away and scrolled the news feed, seeing updates from other artists and friends in Hartford whose kids were maturing at lightning speed. When he returned to start the message, he haltingly typed.

> Paul, I'm not sure you'll remember me from our time in Little League back in '92.

Reuben stopped there. He got up to set the kettle back on for another cup, then sat back down to type.

> But I remember you used to love watermelon Jolly Ranchers. That smell always reminds me of summer.

He deleted those sentences and typed again.

> I didn't learn until a few months ago about what happened to you. I didn't learn until a few months ago about what that monster did to you. I didn't learn until a few months ago about the abuse you suffered.

He got rid of all of it but the opening sentence. The words were stilted and weird, and what kind of idiot opens a message by saying, "Sorry, I didn't know you got molested"?

> Paul, I'm not sure you'll remember me from our time in Little League back in '92. I hope this doesn't come across as weird after all these years, but I stumbled across your profile and thought I would reach out and say hi.

Before he gave himself a chance to delete the message and go back to bed, Reuben clicked send. Paul might not be active on social media anymore or even read the message if he was.

Feeling stupid and embarrassed, wishing he could recall the message, Reuben washed the mug and set it in the dish rack, then gave the counter a quick wipe down. When he turned to put the laptop to sleep, he saw a reply from Paul Brower.

> Sure, I remember you. You made the error that allowed the tying run to get on base in our last game. Kidding. I mean it's true, you did bobble that grounder, but I also remember we used to hang out a lot.

The immediacy of texting and messaging amazed Reuben to this day, perhaps even more than a phone call which literally brought someone's voice to your ear from far away. He was so excited to have gotten an immediate response from Paul that he took his laptop upstairs to jot off a reply.

> Come on, we lost that game because of the monster hit that kid got off Frank Gargiulo's changeup! Saw you're living in CA, how's that treating you?
>
> It's mostly fine. I like how my part of the state has a no-snow policy. You still in CT?
>
> I was living in Hartford but moved to rural VT last fall (still figuring out if that was a good idea). I actually just joined a fast-pitch softball team, and it brought back a lot of memories.

Reuben had gotten into bed and propped himself up with a couple of pillows. The laptop was the only light in the bedroom.

> I bet.

The short reply left a lull in the exchange, an awkward electronic pause. Reuben's fingers hovered over the keyboard, unsure if he should type what was on his mind or simply say goodnight. But the blinking cursor between them seemed to speak what hadn't yet been spoken.

> I didn't actually stumble upon your profile. I tried to find you.
>
> Yeah, I figured.

Reuben paused in his typing, again trying to find the right words for an impossible topic.

> When I was visiting my parents in Jan, they told me what I never knew about why your family left town. I hoped it wasn't true.

The program showed no indication of Paul typing a reply.

> I wish there was something helpful I could say other than I'm so sorry.

On the screen, he could see that Paul was typing a reply, longish—or heavily edited like Reuben's own—given the time it was taking.

> I appreciate your thoughts. It hasn't been easy but I'm ok.

As Reuben tried to think of a thoughtful reply, Paul messaged again.

> I have good and bad days. Probably wouldn't be here if not for a LOT of therapy. Got enough baggage to sink a cruise ship. And I still get pretty uneasy in social settings, but I was also a weird kid (you may have noticed, ha-ha) so maybe some of that's just me amplified. Yeah so it's a downer of a story but at least it doesn't end there. I've got a good life here. I get to work from home doing programming work. I'd ask about your life but it's after midnight in VT and I don't think you signed up for a marathon pen pal session.

Reuben sent a last message for the night, giving a brief rundown of his own life in art—this time talking both about his commercial and noncommercial work—and expressing a hope that they could stay in touch. Paul said he would like that and thanked him for reaching out.

> I remember being really happy those months before. We had a lot of fun together. You were a good friend.

> I remember it that way too. Let's talk again soon.

Shutting down the computer, Reuben lay in bed feeling deeply glad that he'd reached out, and even more that Paul wanted to keep in touch.

Over the years, Reuben had only tepidly engaged in social media, finding it a bit distasteful the way it shined a light on people's neediness for attention. *What's so bad about living your life in private?* But every so often he would catch something that genuinely moved him. And now, the medium he looked down on had made it possible to recover a part of his past that had felt like something trapped in amber—sharply visible in his memory, but stuck, frozen. And now, for the first time, Reuben wasn't remembering backwards; he was thinking forward, imagining a sunny, early summer day that would be perfect for him and Paul to someday take in a baseball game together.

CHAPTER 9

The rain stopped Saturday morning. No tapering drizzle, it was just done like a shut-off hose. Within twenty minutes the sky was wide open and blue. To Reuben, it felt like being able to breathe again. He took his coffee out to the porch and just stood there, sipping, taking in the view. The sodden grass, almost painfully green, seemed to be quivering in the sunlight, growing right before his eyes. He would need to get a lawnmower soon. Across the road, the goats wandered over and were grazing on some dandelions that had popped up near the fence. Reuben noticed a couple of babies running and tossing their bodies into the air, thrilled at being newly alive. Spring had indeed sprung.

There was still enough morning chill in the air to not want to be outside long if you weren't moving around, so Reuben headed to the kitchen for breakfast. As he prepped some peppers and onions for an omelet, his thoughts returned to the previous night's exchange with Paul. Looking back as an adult, Reuben thought it was a double tragedy, not only had Paul suffered terrible abuse, but his parents chose to uproot him from everything he'd known, a total world change.

Lost in his thoughts, Reuben overcooked the omelet. Even now, he could hear Rosemary in his head, "Nobody likes tough eggs." If not for the ping of an incoming message, he might have burned the toast, too. It was a group text from Wayne showing a picture of two mallards floating in what appeared to be center field.

> In case you were wondering, game's canceled.

Another text quickly followed:

> Anyone who's got time, come lend a hand at Donny's whose backyard had a mudslide last night. Big mess. Barb says she'll make chili.

The replies came in quickly. Kip would be there. Joss and Cameron would join. The Erins wished they could, but they had flooding of their own; thankfully, they had a big family and neighbors already at work with them. Patrice would come after the babysitter arrived. Maddy would make it. Reuben chimed in that he, too, would be happy to help.

Mudslides. He thought they only happened in Central America and California, but he guessed that with enough rain, any hillside could give up against gravity.

As Reuben dressed in his work clothes, a new text chimed in, this one from Donny.

> Thanks all. We're at 62 Rodney Road. Bring shovel/rake/gloves. Ruby, can u stop at Endicott's? Need an axle bracket for the wheelbarrow.

He sent a photo for reference.

Reuben wouldn't put it past Donny to be setting him up for another uncomfortable encounter with Jackson Endicott, but given the situation, it seemed likely the need was legitimate.

On the heels of Donny's text, another came in. This one from Adrian.

> Cook me dinner tonight ? Also, reminder to call John E.

Reuben was less than keen to speak again with John Eastlake, and he had planned on "forgetting" to do so. Which is why it irked him that Adrian put the request officially on record, knowing he'd have no excuse now.

He texted back:

> K

He hoped the brevity conveyed a kind of passive aggressive annoyance that *OK* or *Will do* wouldn't have. Then he set a reminder on his calendar: *Call Dick.*

◆

The parking lot at Endicott's was full enough for Reuben to have to park at the far end of the deli. It seemed Donny's wasn't the only yard with rain damage as two women on the sidewalk discussed a stream overflow that washed out a portion of their road.

As Reuben headed to the store, he glanced at the truck beside his. Recognizing the knit cap, Reuben realized the man waiting in the passenger seat was the guy who had recovered the goat from the hood of Reuben's truck. He was about to say something, an acknowledgment, but the man looked away, reaching down for something by his feet. Reuben turned to go and nearly collided with the driver of the truck, a guy whose baseball cap was pulled so low over his face that Reuben, being significantly taller, could only see a thick, dark mustache beneath the brim.

"Sorry, excuse me," Reuben said. As he continued to the store, behind him, he heard a short, quiet exchange in Spanish. He wondered if the goat farm across the street was a business or family operation.

The jangling bell over the door seemed loud enough to alert everyone within three miles that Reuben had entered the store. From the painting section, he heard Jackson Endicott's voice explaining, as if to a child, the difference between gloss and semi-gloss. Reuben went the opposite direction, trial and erroring his way down the aisles until he found a wheelbarrow on display and the replacement parts beside it. Finding just one axle bracket option, he grabbed on and went straight to the checkout.

There was no one handling the register, so Reuben waited. Glancing around the immediate area for an employee, he only saw a young mother wearing her baby in a hammock kind of contraption. On the counter was a bellhop bell positioned behind a sign that read:

Hit me if no one's here.

Reuben continued to wait. Not because he felt particularly patient, but because he was imagining that Jackson Endicott and the other clerks were secretly waiting him out to see if the new guy would ring the bell.

Reuben's inner dialogue went something like this:
You know you're being absurd?
Yes, and I still refuse to ring that bell.
So you're going to wait here for how long?

Five minutes? Ten? All day, idiot?

Reuben looked around one more time, then gently nudged the bell's pin which let out a half-assed ring that he was sure no one heard but him. He hit it again with more force.

"I heard you the first time." Jackson Endicott said from one of the side aisles. He came over and took up position behind the counter. "Well, good morning, Mr. Popple Hill Road."

"Do you memorize the addresses of all your customers?"

"Just the do-it-yourselfers in case I have to make a house call." He winked at Reuben. "Speaking of which, how'd your little caulking project go?"

In truth, Reuben had ended up with a sticky mess that he had to remove so he could start over. He would need to get more caulk but there was no way in hell he was going to get it at Endicott's. "All good, sealed up tight."

"See now, I told the guys you weren't as all-thumbsey as you looked." He scanned the sticker on the bracket. "This comes to a whopping seven twenty-eight with tax."

Reuben handed him his credit card.

"No can do." Jackson pointed to a sign on the front of the register. "Ten dollar minimum for credit card purchases."

Reuben opened his wallet and silently cursed to find just four single dollars. He looked over to the display of impulse items near the checkout area to bump up to ten and grabbed a beeswax lip balm. "I could actually use this, too."

Jackson scanned the item. "Oooh, close, but it only brought you to nine-oh-eight."

Reuben grabbed another beeswax lip balm and slapped it on the counter.

"You're gonna have fresh lips for months, Mr. Popple Hill Road. Hey, since we're pals now, mind if I just call you Popple?"

◆

It turned out the mudslide was more of an underground stream that had become an overground stream that had become a river for a few hours the night before. The rushing water collapsed part of the hillside behind Donny and Barb's house, taking with it entire trees and a bear-sized boulder. The deposit of mud and stone was massive, and there was still water flowing in pockets.

When Reuben arrived with his work gloves, shovel, rake, and the procured fastener, everyone was already hard at work and covered in dirt. They paused briefly to give waves and "Hey, Reubens."

Just beside the slide, Cameron and Joss were digging a trench to lead any remaining stream water away from the house and into a natural drainage toward the edge of the property. On account of his hamstring, Wayne had commandeered a bulldozing Bobcat and was making quick work of the deepest debris piles while Donny was directing him where to unload. Meanwhile, Patrice and Kip were sorting larger stones into a pile that Maddy would then load into the one working wheelbarrow. The other one was lying on its side like a wounded animal. Reuben headed over to make the repair.

"Oh good," Maddy said. "We can use that other wheelbarrow. And the extra hands." She passed an arm across her forehead, swiping away sweat and adding a streak of dirt. Adding one last rock the size of a watermelon to the stack, she picked up the handles to wheel away the pile.

"Where are you headed with those?"

"I'm bringing them out front so we can line the culvert at the end of the driveway. Kip says that'll get the rocks out of the way and keep the weeds at bay in the summer."

"Ah, the old two birds, many stones approach." Reuben said.

Maddy regarded him.

"Like two birds, one stone, but . . . you have a lot of stones there . . ."

"Yeah, no, I got it," she said and then continued to the front of the house.

Reuben watched her wheel off, thinking that as pitcher and catcher, they should have at least some kind of rapport. Though clearly, dumb jokes weren't going to be the bridge. He turned to the job at hand, affixing the new bracket before righting the wheelbarrow.

Donny approached him. "Thanks for stopping to pick that up. How much do I owe you?"

Twelve dollars and forty-six cents including two lip balms he didn't need. "It's nothing, I got it."

"Appreciate it. Was Jackson less Jackson-y today?"

"Not especially, no."

Donny laughed and clapped a muddy hand on Reuben's shoulder. "He must like you, then."

The group worked the cleanup for several hours, taking occasional breaks for iced tea and pretzels that had been set out on the back deck. Once Wayne had cleared the thickest mud deposits, he took a seat on the front loader and barked orders for raking up and leveling out the ground. Patrice carried a canvas bag over his shoulder and sprinkled grass seed over the areas that had been prepped. Reuben joined Kip and Joss in breaking up the bales of hay, covering the seeds to hold them in place, in case—no one dared say it aloud—it started to rain again.

After the backyard was tidied and set up for regrowth, the team went to the front of the house to help set the stones in the freshly cleared culvert.

Reuben joined the lineup of people passing down the stones that Maddy had piled. It felt like a kind of historic reenactment, that gesture of moving stones from one pair of hands to the next, all the way down the line, the way the original settlers had likely done when they first farmed the area.

But when Cameron started setting the stones in chaotic disorder on the floor of the culvert, Reuben decided here was a place he could be most of use. "Switch with me, Cameron." All eyes turned to Reuben. "Just trust me."

He stepped down into the ditch and rotated one of the stones Cameron had just placed. Reuben then took the stone Cameron was holding, dug a pocket in the mud for it and set it firmly beside the two already in place, adjusting the angle for a more aesthetic fit. The group leaned in, tilting heads assessing the new placement.

"That looks better," Donny said.

"Reuben's an artist," Cameron said.

Maddy scrunched her face skeptically, "I wouldn't go that far. It's just rocks."

"No," Joss said. "He actually is. That's what he does. For work."

And suddenly feeling like a zoo animal, Reuben shrank a little under their curious stares.

"Funny, you don't look like an artist," said Kip.

Reuben smiled, "It's not like we go around wearing berets and squaring our fingers at people."

"Let's see, Picasso," Donny said, "show us how it's done." He took a stone from Patrice and held it up beside the one already in his hand, posing like a gameshow hostess offering two prizes to choose from. After a second's assessment, Reuben pointed to the one on the left.

"Mind you," said Reuben, "rocks are not my medium." He rolled the stone in his hands a couple times to get the mud off, spending a little extra time cleaning the smoother, more rectangular side. Setting this one in place beside the far left one, he then saw a better alignment where the respective edges would form a nearly parallel line, and relocated the stone just south of the trio, pressing it down, then kneeling on it to help it sink into the soft dirt and make the arrangement level. Reuben stepped back to give everyone a better view. Donny nodded in approval.

"I don't know much about design, but I like it. Barb'll be pleased. She's always tackling some new landscape project to make the yard look better."

Wayne, who had been off to the side, leaning on a shovel said, "Do we really have time to work up a masterpiece? I don't know about you all, but I'm pretty beat."

Kip laughed, "Yer arm must be all kinds of sore from shifting that Bobcat, Wayne."

"Reuben, you're in charge on this one," said Donny, "Cameron, back of the line."

So Reuben collected a selection of stones at his feet and placed each one as quickly but aesthetically as possible. The group continued to work together on the culvert, while Wayne went to help Barb set up the food table and beer cooler, which was important work, too, he stressed.

As the team worked, they peppered Reuben with questions like he was the career day guest in a classroom of elementary students.

"So are you, like, a museum artist?"

"I've done a few gallery shows, but no, you won't find my work at The Met."

"Oil or watercolor?"

"Oil, and lately, sculpture."

"Clay sculptures?"

"No, I make them from recycled materials."

"Like soda cans?"

"More like machine parts and old tools—junkyard things."

"Do people actually buy your art?" This was Donny's question. "You can make a living at it?"

"Sometimes collectors will buy. But I make most of my income from large-format paintings for corporate clients. Hospitals, hotels. Things like that."

"Any of them around here that we've seen?" Maddy asked.

"Not yet. Those installations are mostly in the Hartford and Boston area, a couple in New York. But I have had some interest this week from a real estate developer in Burlington. Supposedly a bigwig by Vermont standards."

"Eastlake," Donny said.

"That's him. John Eastlake. You know him?"

"Yeah, I was part of a construction team on a project of his. Can't say a whole lot of nice things about him, so I won't."

This didn't surprise Reuben. Still, he had to reluctantly acknowledge that Adrian was right. It really was time to build the pipeline for new projects, and Eastlake, with all his properties, had the potential to offer a steady stream, which instead of sidelining him the way it had in the past, got Reuben to imagine the financial cushion would allow him to pursue his more creative projects.

When the group had finally run out of mud to shovel, ditches to dig, seeds to sow, and stones to place, the work crew wandered back to the deck where a crockpot was tethered to the house via an extension cord like an astronaut to the mothership. On one side was a stack of bowls, a mug filled with silverware, and a neat pile of folded cloth napkins; on the other was a collection of small dishes filled with shredded cheese, sour cream, and chopped scallions.

"There's soap and a towel on the upside-down bucket over by the hose here. You're welcome to use the facilities inside. Barb just asks you to remove your shoes first. Your socks too, by the look of them."

The deck was fully lit with afternoon sun, adding some warmth that helped dry the mud on everyone's work clothes so it cracked and flaked off when they moved. Reuben sat down beside Kip on a picnic bench, while others, holding their steaming bowls of chili, formed a semicircle with their folding chairs.

"It's cool, that you make art for a living," Kip said to Reuben.

"I feel pretty lucky to be able to do it."

"I have a day job doing IT for a company, but my side gig is sound."

"Like for a recording studio?"

"No, not like that. I record sounds like a photographer takes pictures."

This wasn't something Reuben had ever imagined. "I don't even . . . wow, that's very cool. How did you get into that?"

"I started it in my teens. My mom was a naturalist. When her arthritis kept her from getting out in the woods anymore, I went out and recorded the birds and chipmunks, sounds of the stream or the wind in the trees, and brought them home to her."

"That's really sweet."

"Over time, I got some good equipment and branched out, collecting audio clips of things like door knocks and checkout registers and restaurant noises. I made a whole library of everyday sound effects that I eventually sold to this movie production house. That was a decade or more ago. Now they just buy from cheap stock audio sites but sometimes I'll get a request for something unique, like a woman screaming in a particularly shaped tunnel. That one ended up in the movie *Bloodbathers*. I don't recommend watching it."

"How often do those kinds of requests come in?"

Kip laughed. "'Most never, anymore. But I still take out the equipment a dozen or so times a year. I like to capture sounds with context." Kip paused as if to check that Reuben was still interested. Reuben nodded to encourage him on. "By that I mean, it's not just recording pigeons in a barn loft. It's pigeons in the old Cody Farm barn loft, just at dusk as they settle down for the night." Kip plucked a soggy leaf up from his feet and twirled it in his fingers. "I'm not sure it's much interesting to anyone but me."

"No, it makes total sense that there's quality to sound like there's quality to light."

Just then the back screen door swung open. As a woman backed her way outside, her bright-red potholder mittens carrying a baking dish, Donny shouted, "Ah, here's my bride now!"

Reuben asked Kip, "Oh, are they newlyweds?"

"For the last twenty-two years."

Barb smiled adoringly at Donny. Her face was shaped like an upside-down heart, with a well-defined widow's pointy hairline above her wide forehead, full cheeks leading down to a deeply dimpled chin. "And here's some cornbread just out of the oven," she said to the group.

Donny introduced Patrice and Reuben as the newcomers to the team. "Well, it is wonderful to meet you both, and thank you for helping us out," she said. "You are all just amazing. I don't know what we would have done without you."

Donny popped a beer and raised it. "A hearty thanks to the Mallards!"

Cans were raised. "Cheers!" and "Go, Mallards!" they said.

As the team set upon the food, small side conversations sprang up. Maddy leaned in to ask Kip how his dog was doing with her heart medication; Reuben gathered Maddy worked at the vet's office where Bianca the Basset Hound had recently been seen. Cameron and Joss were locked in a discussion about whether a new pizza place was authentically Chicago-style. Wayne was telling Barb about his own cornbread recipe with cheddar and diced hot chiles.

Reuben turned to Patrice and said, "You mentioned a babysitter. How old are your children?"

Patrice nodded as he finished a mouthful of chili. "I have one son. He is almost three years old. My wife, she works at the nursing home and sometimes has to be there for the weekend."

"That's really generous of you to come out today."

"When help is needed, it is important to provide what we are able. This I believe very much."

"Yeah. That's really true." Reuben had to admit, he surprisingly enjoyed doing this kind of hands-on, good neighbor work. Back in Hartford, the word "community" took on a different hue, referring instead to Reuben's circle of fellow artists and gallery owners, simply a group of people within a geographic region that had a common vocation or interests. Support among that group looked different, too. When Riga Lufkin's studio had a fire three years prior, there had been a great deal of head-shaking among her friends and colleagues, and a small

GoFundMe campaign was set up to help pay for losses insurance didn't cover. But the rebuilding was handled by professional contractors.

"Patrice, Joss told me a little about how you came here from Congo. I can't even imagine what you went through."

He nodded and seemed open, not at all reluctant to talk about it. "Yes, I was fifteen years old when I came here. I don't know how much you know about the fighting in the Republic of the Congo—"

The talk around them quieted down as the group tuned in to hear Patrice's story. He shifted his attention outward, welcoming their interest.

"There was a civil war, and my parents were lost in the fighting. My father's sister took over the care for me and my younger brother, and we three went to a camp in Botswana." He spoke as if explaining a normal story of migration. "But that was not a safe place either, and so we applied to be resettled to the United States. We got very, very lucky to be accepted, as there were not many who were." He paused to take a forkful of chili, and others did the same.

Barb chimed in, "And so they sent you to Vermont from Africa? That must have been quite a shock to you all!"

Patrice laughed out loud. "They warned us about the cold and snow, but I tell you, I would wear three jackets and still be shivering! I was sure my blood was turning to ice. But," he continued, his eyes getting large, "I always remember when we saw snow for the first time. My brother and I, we went outside in just our pajamas and danced until we were soaking wet and totally freezing."

It was a beautiful image, young brothers from a faraway, war-torn world discovering the simple joy of falling snow.

Barb encouraged him to tell them more, so Patrice talked about how completely foreign everything had been, starting as soon as they landed at JFK. "You call it a restroom, which is very confusing to someone who is looking to use a toilet—I told them, I am not looking for a place to rest!" And about high school, where he and his brother were among barely a handful of other Black students, their skin so dark, their clothes charity-supplied. "There were many times when people looked at me as if I were an alien from outer space."

"It's why Patrice is so good at his work," Joss interrupted. "All teens feel like aliens at some point."

Maddy said, "There's a big difference between fleeing war and not having the latest iPhone all your friends have."

"It is different, yes," said Patrice. "And sometimes, that is the drama we see, but most of the time, I work with teenagers that have real problems. The ones that feel alone. I decided to do this work so I could be the kind of counselor for them that I needed when I was their age."

It was easy to understand Joss's affection for Patrice. He was someone you wanted to be around.

Looking at the assortment of people gathered on the deck, sharing a meal after a dirty day's work, Reuben came to a realization that felt both obvious and unexpected: these are my friends now. Patrice and Kip, Donny, Joss, and Cameron. He wasn't entirely sure about Maddy or Wayne yet, but given time, it seemed feasible. And Rosemary, of course. Friends of circumstance, not selection like they had been in college and later, as part of the arts community. Apart from the Erins and Joss and Cameron, the Mallards were a collection of people who wouldn't otherwise have had reason to spend time together, their connections happily random.

Reuben's phone vibrated in his shirt pocket. Adrian texted:

> Timing on dinner?

Crap, he thought and quickly typed back,

> Sorry, day got away! Rain check for tomorrow?

She replied, tossing back the same shorthand he'd sent to her.

> ☹ K

The sun was just sinking behind the tree line, taking any lingering warmth with it and giving the team incentive to start gathering plates and bowls onto the tray.

"Just leave it," Barb said. "You've all done enough today!"

"Except you," Donny said, elbowing Wayne hard in the ribs.

As the group wandered back to their cars, Reuben caught up to Kip.

"I would really love to know more about your audio work, maybe even give a listen to some recordings."

"Why, Reuben Downes, are you asking me on a date?" Kip said, acting the genteel Southern belle.

As an artist, Reuben had been hit on by enough men that he had become skilled at picking up the vibe and heading it off before it happened. Had he missed those signals with Kip? "Oh, I didn't...I wasn't. I have a girlfriend—"

Kip burst out laughing, "Don't look so traumatized, Reuben. I'm strictly a hetero bromance kind of guy."

CHAPTER 10

Poking through the bins in the barn left Reuben feeling flat. He'd used most of the interesting pieces, and what was left was more suited for the scrap pile's scrap pile located in a big barrel in the corner of the barn. He had the afternoon to do some scavenging, but the dump was closed on Tuesdays.

Reuben tapped Rosemary's number into his phone.

"I'm sorry I don't recognize this number. Who is calling, please?"

"I've been busy. You were the one who told me to join the softball league."

After the rainouts, the league had to make up games whenever they could, sometimes adding a doubleheader. Even with their tight roster and Wayne limited to batting, the Mallards had the best record, followed by the Blue Jays in a close second place. Reuben ended up contributing solidly to the team as both catcher and hitter, and it felt good.

"So I did. Wayne treating you okay?"

"Yeah, actually. It's a good time. Good people."

"Now's where you say, 'Thank you, Rosie, you always know what's good for me.'"

"Someday I hope to get better at knowing for myself."

"What can I do for you?"

"I was wondering if you had any, I don't know, old stuff lying around."

"Reuben, all my stuff is old."

"I mean things I can recycle for a sculpture I'm working on."

She was quiet for a moment, thinking. "I keep a pretty lean space. I only hold on to what I use. But you're in luck. An old-timer friend of Gui's just died."

"That doesn't sound lucky at all."

"Not for him, for you. The guy's son, David, is having to clear out the family's storage barn. It's filled to the gills with old junk, some of which I'm sure you can use. I picked up a couple of quilts there last week that I aim to restore. I can give him a heads up if you want to trek north. He's up by the border."

Reuben had been to a couple barn sales in recent weeks. He enjoyed the experience, a patient treasure hunt where you never knew what would turn up. In rare moments, he felt like Indiana Jones, hands itching when he found those dusty gems, like the apple crate filled with old model trains he'd brought home for ten bucks or the pristinely packed trunk of Bavarian china that Adrian fell in love with. Those he negotiated a fair price for.

It took a solid two and a half hours to get there, the GPS guiding the way along back roads that alternated between rolling fields and tight, tall woods. There was no mistaking the property when he arrived, it being the only house within what felt like a couple of miles. The old farmhouse was built just a few steps from the road, the exterior recently painted a scrambled egg yellow with white trim.

Reuben shook hands with David, the middle-aged, third-generation son of a French-Canadian family that had migrated to Morgan in 1925. David told Reuben a little about the family as they walked the dirt path to the barn.

"The biggest disappointment was when my uncle left farming to become a doctor. Imagine that, huh?" David said.

The barn, propped up by three long, angled logs, was leaning so precariously sideways, it seemed a huff and a puff could blow the whole thing down around them. But the setting inside wasn't as scattershot as Rosemary had led Reuben to believe.

Taking a few of the galvanized sap buckets was a given. Reuben dropped them in the center footpath where he would leave the pieces he wanted to take. The barbed wire coils would be useful at some point, he was sure.

"That's a beauty," Reuben said, pulling a crosscut saw from a nail on the wall. He took a swipe at the dust and cobwebs with his shirt sleeve.

"Got a whole cabinet of canning jars on the shelf here," said David a few feet ahead. "The antique kind with the metal clamp lids." Reuben nodded noncommittally as he wandered, the sunlit dust motes parting and swirling around him.

He pulled tractor chains, an iron triple hook for hanging deer, and a stack of wooden planks that David said belonged to a cow pen they recently took down.

But then, in the back corner, something completely unexpected caught his eye.

David followed his gaze. "Oh yeah, there's that."

A giant crucifix was humbly leaning askew against a wheelbarrow full of crumbling bags of mulch. The nearly life-size carving of Jesus was casting a mournful expression at the wall.

"Mind the rake," said David just as Reuben tripped over its upturned teeth. "My grandfather was a deacon in the church. Gone maybe twenty years, now."

"Your grandfather or the church?"

"Both." David started pulling disintegrating boxes away from the base of the cross. "One of the parishioners carved it by hand."

Together, they lifted the wooden relic and propped it up against the back wall. It was a good eight feet tall. Finding it under any circumstances would have been startling. Coming so closely on the heels of what he learned about Paul felt like a kind of dark, cosmic joke. Reuben just stood, rubbing a hand over his beard.

"What they would do, my granddad told me, is put it up in the church yard at the start of Lent to remind the parish to stick with giving up the things they were giving up. Then at the crack of dawn on Easter, the groundskeeper..." David wrapped his arms around Jesus's knees and lifted up, releasing the figure from hooks on the cross, "...would take old Jesus down and put a purple sash in his place. Resurrection and such."

Up close, the craftsmanship was beautifully imperfect in the way of folk art. Reuben's mind was tugged away from Paul, thinking instead of the person who'd made the piece, the painstaking, loving patience with which the details had been carved. Curved fingers. Ribcage. A pair of hollowed out cheekbones. The crown with thorns honed sharp enough to cut.

"Do you know anything about the person who made it?"

"Nope. Probably just some parishioner."

His words gave Reuben a pang. A passionate creator whose name was gone to the world and whose skilled work was cast aside like the obsolete rusty tools and broken motors strewn around it.

Reuben turned to David. "You don't want it?"

"What the hell would I want with a giant crucifix?" Then he said, "What the hell would you want with a giant crucifix?"

"I don't know just yet."

They wrapped the figure of Jesus in a moving blanket and secured it in the bottom of the truck bed with the rest of the items Reuben had collected. The cross was too tall to lie flat, so David helped Reuben strap it in, top down with the bottom and one half of the horizontal beam sticking out above the truck sides.

The interested looks of drivers as they passed Reuben's truck on the highway back suggested that it must have been a curious sight. It would be tough to mistake the structure for anything but a giant cross, and yet the idea was so unlikely, he seemed to get the benefit of the doubt even driving past a state police car clocking for speeders.

Once home, Reuben set the boxes of collected items beside the bins and then cleared a space in the rear of the barn to keep the crucifix out of sight, stashed behind an old water-damaged armoire that the previous owners had left.

Back at the truck, having released the straps, Reuben was then confronted with how to transport the cross to the barn. The simplest answer was to carry it on his shoulders but even Reuben had the sense to pause at that, looking up at the sky and wondering about the possibility of a spontaneous lightning strike. Instead, he brought over a large yard cart and again strapped down the unwieldy cross before hauling it, and eventually, the Jesus figure, to their new home.

CHAPTER 11

If there were no clouds, the glare could be tough for a catcher in the late afternoon, the sun high enough in the sky for an inning or two before it ducked behind the distant ridge line. Luckily, the Mallards were still finishing their pregame, having taken the field after the visiting Muskrats had finished their batting practice. Unlike the last couple of weeks, the Mallards had a full roster for the Coleslaw League's season ender. Wayne had recovered enough to play again and would be alternating innings with Erin at second base, each of them taking turns minding Cedar from the dugout. Wayne, it turned out, was good at mesmerizing the baby with an endless supply of clownish faces.

Reuben lowered the forehead pad of the catcher's mask trying to shade some of the sun, but he still wasn't really able to see Kip's pitch until it was a split second away from reaching the plate. It was an exercise in paying extra close attention as Aaron took a few practice hits. He popped to left field, grounded to third, and then hit a clean one-hopper to Joss at short. *An Al D hop*, was the thought that popped into his head, though it took him a second to recall the reference.

Al D. was one of two Als from the Little League team—there was Al Merchant and Al D'Attoli. Al M. was a naturally gifted athlete, fast and fluid at any position. Al D., by contrast, was one of those kids whose father signed him up year after year despite his son's utter lack of coordination, let alone interest, in the sport. The kid was hopeless, as if his mitt had a force field around it that deflected every grounder or pop fly that came near him. And their coach, Mr. Batista, was the kind that believed in giving every kid equal play time even if it meant losing a three-run lead because the other team could place their hits. And they always aimed for Al D.

The Al D hop, Reuben now remembered, was actually coined by Paul at one of their early-season games. Dressed in polyester gray pants, Doha's Dry Cleaning & Tailor t-shirts tucked (a Little League law), socks and stirrups pulled tight (also law), cleats double knotted, the two were walking from the snack shed to the field having retrieved a box of orange wedges for the teams. The boys each had a Laffy Taffy in hand that Reuben had bought with a laundered, rolled up dollar bill he'd found in his pocket. They would need to finish the candy before getting to the bench, because if they didn't have a piece for every member of the team, Mr. Batista would make them spit it in the garbage.

"I swear, if he puts Al D. in for the last inning, and we lose today, I'm walking off," Reuben said.

"Man, that kid can't even catch a cold!" Paul said.

"I've only seen him make one play before. Like ever. Even in practice."

"That one-hopper when he was at second!"

"That play's so easy, even Al D. can make it. They should name it after him," Reuben said.

Paul shoved the last of the taffy in his mouth and tried his best to chomp it down to a manageable size. "The *Al D hop*!" His words were barely comprehensible through a fat wad of taffy, his enthusiasm launching purple saliva out of his mouth and down his chin. This cracked the boys up so hard, tears streamed down their cheeks, and they had to set down the oranges to keep from spilling them. For the rest of the season, The *Al D hop* stuck. An inside joke between friends who imagined they had all the time in the world, or at least a few more seasons, through which to keep it running.

Reuben made a note to remind Paul about the *Al D hop* the next time he checked in. They had stayed in touch, messaging a couple times a month with Reuben telling him about his art projects and the softball season. They even met via video once so Paul could introduce Joey, his new black lab puppy.

Aaron foul tipped a pitch into the backstop. Retrieving the ball, Reuben saw Rosemary and Guillaume in the bleachers, a small snack cooler set between them. Reuben waved, and Guillaume responded with his signature double thumbs up.

Adrian, he could see, had just walked in from the parking lot, dressed casually in jeans and a heather gray tee that was snug in all the right places. Even dressed down, Adrian was a woman for whom the words "put together" always seemed to apply. She was a natural beauty, and Reuben felt a swell of pride knowing she was coming home with him after the game. She smiled at him and set a foldable camping chair beside Rosemary.

Adrian had only missed two of the eleven games the Mallards had played, even lingering during a couple of rainy ones before they got called due to thunder rumbles. Having never otherwise been to a live sporting event of any kind, she had been hooked by what she called the "earnestness" of the league. He overheard her talking with another artist saying she loved the "simple beauty of this community contest, stripped bare of the noise and hustle of modern life." This despite the fact that her attention was often diverted to her phone, even during close games. She said her favorite moments were when a runner got caught in a pickle between the third baseman and the catcher trying to either force the player to make a break or retreat. She spoke in awe of the players that could skillfully slide during a close play and leverage their momentum to pop up, hands free, standing on the base as if they'd always been there, minus the telltale cloud of dirt hanging in the air around them. But what Adrian especially appreciated was watching Maddy pitch, taking down the other teams.

"How does a whip-skinny girl like that have so much power?"

"Speaking as someone on the receiving end of her pitches, she just puts her whole-body force behind it." It was true; Maddy's windup was like a medieval trebuchet launching a stone hard enough to crush a wall. But it wasn't just that. "With Maddy, I feel like there's also a mental thing. I don't know if she's imagining someone from her past that's wronged her, but there are times when she pitches, that it feels...I don't know...personal, especially with some of the big guys."

Adrian had nodded pensively, "I get that."

"Meaning?"

"Just that, as a woman, there are times when—no offense—you want to pummel the men around you."

"Um, anyone specific?" He said, pointing hesitantly at his own face.

Adrian waved her hands around. "Just your species in general. It's not your fault. You were born with a chromosome that happens to embody all the barriers and bad behavior women endure. Evolution is slow. A lady's memory is long."

This seemed wholly unreasonable. Nearly all the men he knew were good guys. The exception, of course, was John Eastlake, whose general way of being hadn't, in any way, altered Reuben's knee-jerk dislike of him at the art opening, even now that he was a client. A big fish in a little pond, Eastlake was a man who relished using his wealth and influence not so much as a club but as a screwdriver twisting just enough to secure people to him. Like Reuben, under contract for three large-format paintings, whose overall direction was far more directive than Adrian had led Reuben to believe it would be. But the money was good, and the work had high visibility, so he put his head down and painted.

Still, Adrian's relationship with Eastlake remained a bit of a mystery, and she wasn't forthcoming with details. After six months, Reuben had learned that the things Adrian held back were almost never oversights or omissions; they represented boundaries, and so he didn't push. But it had been on his mind lately, that it might be time to talk to her about letting him in a little more, particularly regarding her daughter, Leila, whom he'd only briefly met once in a chance encounter at a Fourth of July parade. He was ready to argue that if Adrian's affection was genuine (as it certainly was for Reuben), it shouldn't be an issue to deepen their relationship.

"Bring it in!" Wayne yelled from the backstop where he had been catching Maddy's warm up. The team jogged to the dugout.

The Muskrats were a clumsy, somewhat slow team, but they had a lot of fun together. Their second baseman, a guy named Jeffrey, was always cracking jokes between batters. ("Man, you guys. I was on an elevator earlier today, and I swear, this guy let out the biggest rip of a fart." Their pitcher, who was accustomed to his shtick paused to allow for Jeffrey's punchline delivery, "It was wrong on so many levels.") Since Wayne made the schedule, Kip said, the Muskrats were almost always the last game of the season for that very reason. The play was lighthearted, and the win was typically easy.

It was the last day of August. The field grass seemed tired, a shade faded, even from the week before. The leaves were also losing their luster, some yellowed and falling from their branches. On the higher elevation peaks, fall had already started to show in scattered pops of orange and red.

The bleacher crowd was larger on this early Friday evening, a mix of supporters for both teams celebrating the end of the summer season. The following week, the gear would be stowed in the shed and the field would be turned over to the middle school soccer team for their daily practices.

In addition to spectators like Rosemary, Guillaume, and Adrian, there were the regulars, including Barb; Wayne's wife, Ming, and their twelve-year-old son, Connor; Linda Child, the town clerk, and her husband, Carlton, who were both friends of Donny's; and a handful of others Reuben had met but whose names he couldn't recall. These were the steadfast spectators, the ones who treated the weekly games like neighborly barbecues with hot dogs and chips from the snack bar and BYO beverages for those who wanted something stronger than a warmish can of soda. When he was catching, Reuben would hear snippets of their conversations. How someone's garden had caught "late blight" on their tomatoes and another's that had promising contenders for the giant pumpkin contest. There were updates on who was divorcing whom, whose cat had been hit by a car, and which kid might have been responsible.

But most of the time, when he was behind the plate, Reuben concentrated on the game, tag teaming with Wayne on calling the plays before they happened.

"Got two down. Play's to one!"

"Be ready to get your wheels on, Patrice!"

"Maddy, if it comes to you, I'm right here at home."

"Check and chuck infield, check and chuck."

The experience of playing was so different from the rest of Reuben's days, which were mostly solitary and inwardly focused. In the studio, his environment was compact and tightly controlled, a tightrope of sorts stretched between his mind and the canvas. And though the sculptures added a little more complexity with various tools, all that work was still Reuben, alone. He never imagined how much the game would become, not just a physical, but a mental relief, a release allowing his concentration to turn outward to the people around him, things that were outside his control: every batter, every pitch, his teammates' moods, the dryness or moisture in the soil, the direction or lack of wind. He could take all the circumstantial information in and try to anticipate what would happen, but ultimately, once the pitch left Maddy's hand and the play was set in motion, all he could do was think on his feet and react. And it felt good.

As Reuben stepped into the batter's box for what would likely be his last at-bat of the season, a determined V of honking geese caused everyone to pause and watch as they traversed the sky toward the sunset. They wouldn't practice together again until next spring. Reuben thought, *I'm really going to miss being out here.*

The crowd at The Peatbog was a mix of college kids, late twentysomethings, and the well-over-forty crowd, owing to the fact that the band, Hippo Campus, was made up of players representing the same age groups. The drummer didn't appear to be legally able to drink; the bass player and guitarist were middle aged with balding heads and graying beards; and Cameron, on vocals, was right in between.

The Mallards had planted themselves at a center left table where they would have a good view of the stage (which was essentially a platform tucked in the corner) where Hippo Campus was setting up and checking mics. The opening act had been a folk duo called Pelly & Pock who were dressed in flower child bell bottoms and leather fringe. After the pair's final song, Pelly (or Pock?) invited the crowd to visit the side table where they would be selling t-shirts and macramé plant hammocks. The room applauded supportively as they left the stage.

Reuben weaved through bar patrons to join his teammates. Though the group had socialized a few times over the season, it had always been right after a game either in the field parking lot with Donny's portable grill or at the nearby Alewife, a local watering hole. No one ever changed into "civilian" clothes in between, so it was a little jarring to see everyone cleaned up—hat-free, wearing nonsporty shirts and jeans. Donny was clean-shaven. Maddy's straight hair was loose around her shoulders. It even seemed possible that Joss was wearing lipstick. Wayne was the only one whose going-out wear looked pretty much the same as his hitting-the-field wear.

It had been Wayne who decided the league would hold the end-of-the-season party at The Peatbog when Joss announced that Cameron's band's debut coincided with the last game. As the league's self-described "headmaster," Wayne put out a message to all the teams to meet there around eight, shortly before the band was scheduled to take the stage. Though Cameron was reluctant at first, given it was Hippo Campus's first show, Wayne and Joss argued that the league would provide a decent crowd, making the bar happy and probably earning the band a few fans. In an aside to Reuben, Wayne had said, "They better not suck, or I'm never going to hear the end of it."

The team had ordered a smorgasbord of bar food: two loaded mounds of nachos, baskets of mozzarella sticks, Buffalo wings, and a pile of soft pretzels with cheese dip on the side. And of course, there were pitchers of beer stationed within everyone's reach. All paid for by the league's annual dues.

Patrice moved over to let Reuben fit a chair in.

"You guys all clean up pretty good," Reuben said, taking a seat. He'd consciously kept his eyes from landing on Maddy when he said it. It had been about a week since Reuben had a dream about her, and he had felt awkward and self-conscious when she was near. Not during the games—it was easy when their exchanges were focused on the plays, the mindless cheers and chatter. But beforehand, when the team was setting up the field, or after, during the cookouts, Reuben avoided talking to her directly, feeling that somehow, she would look at him and just know.

"What kind of dream?" Kip had asked, eyebrows wagging Groucho Marx-style.

"It wasn't a sex dream. We were just swimming in a lake together."

"That sounds literally like a sex dream."

"It was just swimming. No touching. No one naked." He took a swallow of beer. "I don't even think of her in that way."

"She's pretty cute."

"Why, have you thought of her in that way?"

"I haven't not thought of her in that way." Divorced now for two years, Kip had told Reuben that he was still settling into the idea of being single, but that come fall, he "probably... might possibly, would maybe consider" trying to date again.

"You should test the waters," Reuben said. "Tell Maddy you're thinking of getting a hamster, and that maybe she could talk you out of it over coffee."

"Oh no, Maddy's too intense for me. Besides, you went and got dream dibs."

"Things are going well with Adrian, so I'm off the shelf. And just because someone has a dream about a person, doesn't mean they're attracted to them. It could just be that they want to have a closer relationship. Platonic."

Reuben was sure this was the subconscious explanation behind the dream. Because after a full season, Maddy continued to keep him at arm's length. Even in this end-of-season celebration, off the field in a bar, she barely looked at him.

"Hold onto your pretzels, folks," Donny said, pointing his chin at the door. "Looks like the Jays just landed on The Peatbog."

"Nemesis" would be a strong word to use for a rival recreational softball team, but there was a clear existential tension between the Blue Jays and the Mallards that went back to the earliest years of the league, and actually, even farther. The story, as it was told to Reuben by Donny, went like this.

Wayne had been an all-star catcher in high school—not just a skilled defender behind the plate and a powerhouse hitter, but an all-around smart ball player and team leader. Pepper Danberry, who became the Blue Jay's team manager when the rec league started, had been captain of the other regional high school's team. Pepper was good, but he wasn't quite at Wayne's level. Their senior year, the two teams were just about equal in their respective records, the difference being that Wayne's talent elevated his team's abilities, while Pepper's team elevated his—at least according to Donny who played left field at the time.

Midseason, word got around that a talent scout from Boston University was on tour of some of the Northeast high schools and would be stopping by a game between the two teams. Wayne's family didn't have a lot of money, and his grades weren't much to hang his ball cap on. So college would mean needing a scholarship, and everyone thought this scout might be the ticket.

It was early in the second inning, Pepper was on third and taking risky leads, just egging Wayne to make a play. But Wayne was cool, patient, just kept pushing Pepper back, focusing on the batter. On a 2-2 count, a wild pitch came in that Wayne managed to block cleanly. That should have turned Pepper back. But in what appeared to be a suicide mission, Pepper made a break for it, maybe figuring if he barreled into Wayne hard enough, the ball would get knocked loose. Because that's exactly what happened.

Wayne was just a couple beats behind in realizing there was a freight train coming at him. Just as he turned to make the play, he and Pepper collided at the plate. Wayne's mask went flying and he took an elbow to the jaw, dislocating it, which ended the game and what remained of the season for Wayne.

"Was it a legitimate play? Yeah. Ballsy, but it was legit," Donny had said. "Was Pepper's hit illegal in any way? Not really, he came in feet first. He'd just held off on the slide long enough to have maximum speed and force behind him." So there had been plausible deniability that Pepper had done anything to deliberately sabotage Wayne's chances at catching that scout's eye, but it left a major 'I coulda been a contender' chip on Wayne's shoulder anytime Pepper's name was mentioned. "Though off the record," Donny said, "I've always wondered if Wayne was secretly a little relieved, having expressed on more than one occasion that maybe he wasn't college material to begin with."

Years later, when Wayne and Donny were starting the league, they knew they would need some seed starters from nearby towns. At the time, Pepper was working in the governor's office and knew a lot of people, so Wayne invited him to pull together a team. Picking up right where they left off in high school, their competitive natures kicked in, this time radiating outward to each other's teammates. The ongoing rivalry—sometimes friendly, sometimes less-than-friendly—became a permanent league fixture, even years after Pepper stopped playing, and his team continued without him.

For the last two years, the Blue Jays team manager was number seven, shortstop Dana Van Sykes, one of two women on the team, which was the minimum number required on the field to avoid a forfeit. The Mallards all knew Dana Van Sykes. Even Patrice had a less than warm opinion of her. "She makes me think maybe she did not have very good role models growing up."

A trucker-style baseball hat resting on top of her dense, frizzy blonde hair, Dana was first of the Jays to enter The Peatbog followed by three teammates, their eyes scanning the crowd for seats.

"It's good Kip got here early to grab a table," said Joss turning aside to take a drag off a vape pen. Now that the season was over, she had resumed the vice despite Cameron's obvious distaste for it.

Kip had brought some of his audio equipment, aiming to record the band's first live concert as well as some ambient bar noise that he would sell to a stock sound effects company he occasionally freelanced for. He sat closest to the stage, headsets on, enveloped in his own world as he toyed with buttons and knobs, adjusting levels while the band tuned and did their test riffs and Cameron spoke into the mic, "Check one, two. Check, check."

A few minutes later, prompted by a fast *tap-tap-tap* of the drumsticks, Hippo Campus launched into their first song. It had a gritty, vintage rock sound, distorted guitars, and a driving beat. Cameron's vocals, shaky at first, but quickly gaining confidence, seemed to channel Chris Martin, Bono, and Jim Morrison all at once. What was most surprising—seemingly to all the Mallards—was what a good frontman he turned out to be. The stooped awkwardness that normally hovered about his shoulders seemed to have fallen away, and Cameron the performer was like someone they were meeting for the first time. Even Joss seemed rapt to see him in the spotlight, pushing the energy of the music from the stage outward to the audience, his gaze settling on a pretty girl timed with just the right lyrics. Cameron faced off playfully with the other guitar player. He closed his eyes to lyrics expressing the depth of his yearning for "more life out of life." This charismatic performer was and wasn't the Cameron they knew. Living between Boston and New York City, Reuben had seen many bands perform at various stages of their careers, and it was clear this one had something real going for it. Three songs in, you could feel the crowd sensed it, too.

That was, except for a cluster of people at the bar who were more interested in what they had to say to each other than the music. In a small bar, the impact of their raucous laughter and numerous toasts was not insignificant. A man at the next table, whose floppy brown hair and sharply angled nose strongly suggested he was Cameron's father, kept turning to the bar, hoping someone would notice the eye-daggers he was sending their way.

"Fuckin' Blue Jays," said Wayne. "I'm going to go shut them up."

Donny fired a look of alarm to Joss, their unspoken exchange suggesting that it would be unwise for Wayne to approach the Jays.

"I'll go," Reuben said. "It's okay, Wayne. I'm closer to them anyway."

Hippo Campus rolled into a slower, ballad-type song. As Reuben moved in the direction opposite the stage, he was struck again by how engaged the audience seemed to be, their eyes focused, their heads nodding slowly to the beat.

It wasn't just the Blue Jays at the bar. Reuben recognized a few players from the Muskrats gesturing with their Switchback bottles as he approached. He saw Dana notice him when he got close enough, her eyes narrowing at him.

"How's it going, Van Sykes?"

"It's going."

"Hey, uh, just thought I'd come over to ask that maybe you and the gang here could turn the volume down a notch." Reuben spoke so the others nearby could hear, and he noticed them shift their weight in response.

"It's a bar, Downes." Dana said, "People talk in a bar."

"It's just that it's Cameron's band up there—their first show ever. And they're actually pretty good if you listen."

One of the other Jays, a big guy named Jim or Tim or Tom chimed in, "Yeah, we're not the ones who insisted on having the end-season party here. It's a stupid idea if you don't want people to talk."

"Look, the band's just doing a thirty-minute set. They're probably halfway through—" Reuben could see other nearby patrons turning, irritated. "Or there's another bar two doors down—"

"You're going to kick us out of our own party?" Dana said, her voice getting louder, further drawing the crowd's attention.

Change your tactics, Downes. "How about this. There's—" he counted, "seven of you? I got your next round. Just keep it down for another fifteen minutes is all I'm asking." He pulled out his wallet and set a fifty-dollar bill on the bar, leaning in to the bartender. "These guys here—their next beers are on me." The bartender nodded.

Reuben turned back to Dana and the players, "Thank you. It's much appreciated." Disappointed that he missed nearly the entire song, he walked away not waiting for a response.

The incentive seemed to work. Joss raised her mug to him when Reuben sat down again. Wayne asked, "What'd you do to shut them up?"

Suddenly unsure as to whether the team would approve of bribing the Blue Jays, Reuben said, "I just talked to them respectfully. That's all."

Donny's expression called bullshit, but before he could press for the real story, Cameron spoke into the microphone. "Okay, we've got two more songs to play for you tonight. This next one is the story of a castaway who one day discovers that he's not the only one living on his desert island."

"Doesn't he mean deserted?" Donny asked. "A deserted island hasn't got people. A desert island hasn't got water, but an island is surrounded by water so it can't be a desert."

"Would you shut the fuck up?" Joss asked. She was leaning forward, keen to hear the lyrics.

The song opened with a quick solo by the bassist and then it kicked into an ear-friendly reggae style. Cameron lit up the stage again, bopping his head to the beat and sharing the chorus with the rest of the band. A trio of young women pushed their way to the front and danced, their drinks held high above their heads. They started singing along with the ending refrain, "*Build a fire. Build a fire. We'll build a fire together!*" so Cameron flipped the mic down to them and gestured for everyone to sing along. A surprising number of audience members did, some drunker than others. Three Mallards—Patrice, Donny, and Maddy—shyly mumbled along; the rest, including Reuben who'd never been a sing-along kind of guy, simply nodded along to the beat. Joss, Reuben noticed, was simply staring up at the stage, as if trying to recognize "her" Cameron.

By the time Hippo Campus had finished their final song—a high-octane rocker—the collective mood in the bar was one of good-feeling energy.

"Thanks to The Peatbog for letting us do our thing. And thanks to all of you—it's been a blast. Give it up for Pelly & Pock!" The duo held up peace signs in response. Cameron closed the performance with "We are Hippo Campus, and we hope to see you again soon!" There was a swell of cheers and an ear-piercing whistle in response.

After the set, as the band wrapped cords and set their instruments back in their cases, strangers broached the stage to offer compliments. The older couple seated close by gave enthusiastic hugs to Cameron, all but confirming they were his parents.

Kip finished packing his equipment and rejoined the group. "Man, those guys were tight! When they hit it big, they're going to be glad I got a recording of their first show."

"As if," said Joss. "Vermont bands don't make it any farther than Rutland."

"Except for...what was that band name again? Rhymes with fish," Kip said.

Cameron broke away from his bandmates and sat down at the table as his teammates delivered literal pats on the back. And just like that, the spell was broken. Here was Cameron again, shoulders slightly rounded, head tilted down. His onstage bravado had evaporated as he smiled bashfully taking in their praise and enthusiasm.

Joss had hung back a little, noticeable enough for Cameron to directly ask her, "What'd you think?"

She took another vape drag before answering, "Yeah, solid, solid. Seems like you guys are even good enough to land a few groupies." She gestured to the three dancing women who were hovering behind Cameron, waiting for an opening.

Maddy asked Cameron, "This is your first show? Sure doesn't seem like it."

"We spent a year writing and practicing. Our drummer's a perfectionist. He wouldn't allow us out in public until everything was buttoned up super tight."

"Hey, man, you guys sounded good," said a voice, and the various Mallards seemed to collectively raise their eyebrows when they saw the words had come from Dana Van Sykes, who was standing there with Jim-Tim-Tom.

Wayne lifted his mug in response to Dana's uncharacteristic graciousness, "Here's to another good season, Blue Jays." Everyone raised their bottles in return, "Good season!"

"Yup, see you all in the spring," she said and started to walk away. But as she passed Reuben, she leaned into him. "You can shove your money up your ass." She put a hand on his chest and discreetly slid the folded fifty in his breast pocket. Then the two Blue Jays rejoined their flock.

"Your words were effective, Reuben," Patrice said, "You are a worthy ambassador."

Reuben smiled uneasily, "I guess sometimes people just need to be encouraged to do the right thing."

THIRD

"Let me be clear. On game day, you will, each and every one of you, arrive at the ball field in a clean uniform. Your shirt will be tucked in. Your socks pulled up. Your cap will be on, and it will most definitely be turned bill facing front. Do not test me on this. I will bench you in a heartbeat if you do not follow these simple rules.

"Why is this so important? First, it shows you actually care about being here. Second, the other team is going to size us up and judge whether we're a competitor or a joke, just on appearances. And my friends, we are definitely not a joke."
—Coach Allen Bordo

CHAPTER 12

While not entirely a hibernation, winter passed mostly indoors for Reuben with only occasional outdoor attempts to acclimate to being a four-season Vermonter. Like the time he'd asked Kip to take him downhill skiing. Though Kip had grown up within forty-five minutes of some of the state's best-known resorts, he was a minimally experienced skier, a fact that Reuben should have been tipped off to when Kip said not to worry about snow pants, they could just ski in "long johns and jeans." So when the chair lift spit them out at the top of an intermediate slope rather than the bunny trail—because "you need steeps to get speed"—and Reuben watched Kip simply point his skis and bomb straight down the trail, causing other skiers to dodge and scramble out of his way, Reuben took off his own skis on the spot and asked the lift attendant if he could get a ride back down the mountain.

The cross-country skiing outing with Adrian was more successful, but not without a hard fall that left Reuben's elbow swollen and bruised for more than a week. Rosemary gave him a pair of snowshoes from her guest stash that she no longer needed since she'd mostly stopped hosting in winter. Those hit the sweet spot for

Reuben, allowing him to get out and move in the snow without having to concern himself with balance issues.

The other addition Rosemary provided that winter was a cat, a feral beast with part of its tail missing who was so ornery and aggressive when you got near it that Guillaume called him *le loup-garou,* which means werewolf in French. The scrawny black-and-white cat had shown up on Rosemary's property during an especially cold stretch and, knowing Reuben had complained about the mice getting into his bins in the barn, she delivered the cat in a Havahart trap, saying that it was Reuben's turn to take in a stray and give it a place to stay in his barn. Lou Garoo, as Reuben called him, would growl and hiss whenever Reuben came into the barn to refill the food and water bowls, but the cat stuck around. He did turn out to be a formidable predator, leaving the stiff and broken bodies of mice like sacrificial offerings at the barn's entrance and once at the back door of the studio.

It wasn't until mid-March that Reuben received a group text from Wayne asking who would be returning for the 2016 season. Reuben didn't hesitate, being the first of the team to respond that yes, he was in. The others all chimed in one by one that they, too, would be back.

> Great. See you all at the field next thurs for some spring clean up. Five sharp.

Apart from get-togethers with Kip, Reuben hadn't had any contact with the Mallards since the end of last season's gathering at The Peatbog. The in-between time seemed both long and short, a time lapse that revealed both small and significant changes when the team reunited at the field to rake up the goose turds, pull weed sprouts, and wipe down the benches and bleachers.

Wayne looked exceptionally tanned, having just returned from a family vacation in Cancun. Donny had new sneakers so white, they hurt your eyes to look at. Patrice shared pictures of his new baby girl, Kali, which he said meant "energetic" as she proved to be even in utero. Maddy told them about the condo she had bought the next town over, "It's nothing fancy, but I really like that it's mine." Joss had thinned and was lean and muscular in her form-fitting CrossFit tee. Cameron's buzzed hair and stubbled chin made him look, if not tougher, at least less like a teenager.

The clean-up effort only took a couple of hours, at which point people peeled off to head home, it being a "school night," but Kip and Reuben decided to hit the Alewife.

On a normal Thursday at the bar, Jackson Endicott and his crew would take over the dart board in a league they created just for themselves. Those nights, Kip and Reuben would be content with sitting at one of the high-top tables, tuning out the nearby hoots and high fives and tuning in to whatever sporting event was showing on the big screen behind the bar. But tonight, Endicott's Hardware was celebrating its 110th anniversary with an in-store party, which meant Kip and Reuben could play as many games of darts as they liked, regardless of how mediocre they were at it.

As Kip kicked off the third game, he started telling Reuben about a project he had been working on the last three springs. It was a quest of sorts to capture the sound of the very first drop of the season's sap run. The effort required careful tracking of temperatures, snow and rainfall amounts, daily cloud cover, all combined with everything that's uncontrollable and unknowable about nature. He had been scouting his spot every day that week.

"Keeping an eye on the weather, but if the forecast is right, the run is going to start sometime in the next few days, maybe even tomorrow."

"Interesting," said Reuben. "Why the first drip? Does it sound different? It must sound different as the first drop in an empty bucket."

Kip rocked his head side to side as if to agree but also disagree. "It's less about the actual sound. You probably wouldn't notice much difference between the first and the fourth drop. I would, but that's me." He landed a dart just outside the bullseye.

"Then why?"

Kip thought for a moment and was about to say something but then shrugged it off. Reuben had learned that if he stayed quiet, Kip would eventually say what was on his mind.

He took a couple sips to finish off his beer before speaking. "After Piper left, I kept going back over in my mind, asking myself: When did it happen? Was it a specific morning when she woke up and thought, *I don't want to be married anymore*? I get it's never that simple. Probably just a gradual thing."

As Reuben stepped up to take his throws, Kip continued, "So I got to thinking about how we almost never get those clear markers. You know, those exact points in time that mark a change. Birth and death are the biggies, for sure. But all those smaller moments are vague and ongoing, and they just roll by so's you don't even notice.

"Course, the sugaring season builds over time. There's all kinds of sciencey stuff going on inside that tree all winter long. But there is a single first drop. Maybe it's not the beginning, but it's a beginning. And that sound can be captured."

It was an interesting concept to Reuben. If a photograph aimed to preserve a specific moment in time, why couldn't a sound recording? "So you've got the perfect sound clip, now what? You can't frame it and hang it on a wall. You wouldn't play it over and over, unless you layered it into music or some other sound collage. That audio company doesn't care if it's the first drip or the four hundredth, assuming they'd even want a recording of sap drips."

Kip took a long sip of beer and wiped the foam from his lip with a sleeve. "Why's it need a reason?"

"Well, because..." Reuben had no answer. And so he continued to gnaw on it, trying to tease out some kind of artistic meaning from the determination to capture the specific sound quality of a particular moment.

Kip ended up taking the dart match two games to one. They rotated the barstools around to the other side of the table to keep an eye on the Celtics game. Janice, the only waitress they knew by name, took their order for another round and a plate of poutine.

Reuben asked Kip, "This might sound weird and out of the blue, but what do you think about creative collaboration?"

Kip didn't hesitate. "You mean like Martha and Snoop? Definitely a case where the parts are better than the sum of the whole. Or some of the parts are better than some of the whole?"

"I'm serious."

"I don't know what it is you're being serious about."

"That first drop of the sugaring season you're after. What if I painted it—or better yet, constructed a scene—combined with your audio? Kind of an interactive experience. I could ask Adrian to give us some gallery space."

Kip squinted at him with mild distaste. "Eh, I don't know about that..."

"Why not?" Reuben asked.

"Sounds too much like art."

"I hate to break it to you, but the way you just described what you're trying to do...that's art."

"Okay, but then it's my art. For me."

The waitress returned with the beers and a big bowl of fries smothered in gravy and knobs of melting cheese curds.

"Thanks, Janice." After she left, Reuben said to Kip, "At least think about it?"

"I don't even know why you would be interested."

Reuben hadn't considered his own motivations; he just followed his own creative impulse. "I guess..." He carefully pulled a gravy-soaked fry from the stack. "I think there's something meaningful in the way you talk about it. It makes me feel intrigued. Maybe capturing or re-creating an exact moment in this way forces people to pause and pay attention. And that doesn't happen very often these days, even in an art gallery where mostly people just stroll past."

In the silence that followed, he imagined Kip's mental wheels turning.

"I dunno. Maybe," Kip said. "Maybe."

"Yeah?"

"You can come with me to the woods tomorrow. No promises, though, about *creative collaboration*."

CHAPTER 13

The lengthening days meant a brighter early-morning sky, which led Reuben to wake sooner than he otherwise would have liked. But it also meant he could linger in bed savoring moments like these when Adrian's warm shoulders and backside were pressed against his. She was his mirror image, the soles of their feet just offset so her toes curved comfortably against his arches, a slow pulse beating there that he wasn't sure was his or hers.

Sensing he was awake, Adrian rolled over, sliding her arm around his ribcage and nudging her always-cold nose against his spine and said, "Ehhggggs," the way a zombie would say, "Braaains."

"Oh, that's so nice of you to offer. I'd love some." Reuben said, pulling her arm tighter around him. Now that Leila was at college, Adrian stayed over most nights.

"Nooo, you. Too tired."

"Tired? You just woke up."

"Eh, I didn't sleep much. I went downstairs so I wouldn't keep you awake."

He vaguely remembered her sliding back into bed in the predawn.

"You worried about the gallery? Things will pick up again once the weather warms."

"Oh, I know that."

Reuben rolled onto his back to look at her. The lack of sleep didn't show; she was pink cheeked and clear eyed.

"Just stuff on my mind," she said. Before he could ask, she flipped the covers aside. Sliding into his bathrobe, she padded off to the bathroom.

"You want bacon, too?" Reuben called once the toilet had finished its flush.

Adrian popped back out the door. With her bright eyes and her mouth foamy with toothpaste, she looked like a rabid puppy. She garbled, "Is that an actual question?"

Once Adrian had gone downstairs to stoke the wood stove, Reuben got up to wash. Their toothbrushes in the holder by the sink caught his attention—how they leaned on each other like a couple affectionately growing old together. He smiled at the thought and the image it planted in his mind.

By the time Reuben came downstairs, Adrian was emptying the dishwasher and had set up the kettle for coffee. Though the kitchen was compact, they had worked out a natural cadence of movement whereby Adrian seemed simply able to sense when she needed to give Reuben a clear path between the island and the refrigerator or the pantry.

As he got to work peeling strips of bacon apart and laying them on a baking sheet, Reuben couldn't help but feel something hanging in the air between them like a cartoon thought bubble waiting for the words to be written in it. The feeling persisted as he gently pushed at the eggs and tipped the pan to set them. During breakfast, the conversation was simple small talk and polite requests to pass the butter.

After a notable silence, Reuben said, "I feel like you're waiting to tell me something. Did I do something wrong?"

She immediately sought his hand to reassure him, "No. God no, everything's terrific between us. I'm really content." But then she backtracked, "Well, maybe content isn't the exact word—"

Reuben put his fork down, bracing himself for how she would explain. "Things are 'terrific,' but you're not content?"

"I'm not discontent, there's no worry there. And also, I don't think I'm really ready to talk about it."

"We're already in the middle of talking about it."

Adrian reached for the French press and topped off their mugs, still not sharing her thoughts.

"Ade . . ."

She wiped the corner of her mouth with a napkin then looked out the window, pensive for a moment as Reuben waited. "It's just, I miss Leila so much. I don't think it really hit me until last week when she said she won't be coming home for spring break. I get that she's ready to make her way in the world, but it kind of broke my heart. She's been my sidekick from the time I was twenty-one, and it feels like a part of me has been cut out."

"You don't have to feel weird about telling me that. It's perfectly normal."

"Except that's not the part I didn't want to tell you." Adrian took a last bite of bacon. After she washed it down with some orange juice, she said almost casually, "I think it's that maybe, I might want another . . . baby."

Reuben watched the steam rising from their mugs. He felt knocked sideways, a complete about-face from everything Adrian had been saying both in the lead-up to Leila leaving for Syracuse and in the weeks that followed. How, having gotten pregnant just before she graduated college, Adrian was excited to finally live just for herself as an adult, a woman relieved of the daily responsibility of keeping track of where Leila was, who she was with, what she was doing. And now, at thirty-nine Adrian wanted to start all over?

He chose his words carefully. "That's a little unexpected."

"I know," she said. "I know it's out of whack with what I thought I wanted. But—" she squeezed his hand tighter, "I think I may have just been trying to convince myself that I was supposed to feel happy and free, when all along, maybe I was feeling a little . . . empty."

It was hard not to feel stung. Just past a year into their relationship, Reuben had felt things were better than ever between them. They went to concerts and the theater, engaged in the occasional outdoor adventure. Reuben made dinners and Adrian made reservations. They had managed to keep a clear boundary between their personal and professional relationships. Everything had felt easygoing and fun.

He took his plate to the sink and let the running hot water rinse the toast crumbs before he spoke again, knowing she was eager to hear his response.

"Adrian, I certainly don't want to presume anything, so let me clearly ask. Are you saying you'd like us to have a child together?"

"I don't know for sure. Which is why I really didn't want to have this conversation yet."

"I'm not hearing anything about marriage. In this scenario you're contemplating, would we not be married?"

There was a long (*pregnant*, he thought) pause before she answered, articulating her words slowly. "Reuben, I'm not sure I'm cut out for marriage. But co-parenting—obviously, with benefits—could be really great."

Reuben couldn't look at her. His mind was reeling from how, in an instant, the coziest, most pleasant of mornings had turned into a baffling, existential moment not just for them as a couple, but also himself. In Reuben's mind, there was a natural order to things: you met someone, you built a relationship, maybe you broke up, or maybe you got married, then maybe you had kids. Co-parenting sounded like a job, not a life.

This is exactly what blindsided means, Reuben thought. The word immediately called up an image burned in his memory of Hannah on one knee, looking up at him full of eagerness and hope. While the situation with Adrian was entirely different, the alarm he was feeling suggested that responding the wrong way could have disastrous consequences, though it seemed doubtful they would be violent ones.

And yet, at the same time, Reuben felt hurt. This wasn't something that cropped up just last night. Adrian could have talked to him at any point that she was feeling, as she put it, "empty."

Reuben silently left the kitchen. Reaching his studio, he slid the rolling barn door firmly closed behind him, cursing the stupid structure's utter inability to be slammed for effect. From the kitchen came the sound of a chair sliding on the floor followed by Adrian's footsteps.

"Please don't shut yourself in the studio. You wanted to have this conversation!"

Reuben yelled through the door, "This is definitely not the conversation I wanted to have."

"Can I open the d—"

"I just don't get you, Adrian. You kept total control of our relationship when Leila was home. Now that she's away, and I'm finally feeling like things are comfortable between us, you go and yank the reins again."

"All I said was that I thought I might want to have another child." A pause, then she said, "It's not like I have the luxury of waiting much longer."

Reuben was pacing the length of the barn door. "Do I factor into this equation for you? I mean, besides contributing my DNA?"

"Did you not hear what I said about co-parenting?"

"Fucking hell, Adrian. Co-parenting? I just want some time for us to be us. Just us."

He opened the sliding door and found her standing, her hands pulled into her sleeves, her arms folded over her chest, a posture that made her look vulnerable.

Reuben took a breath in and let it out very slowly. In his mind, he heard one of Rosemary's mantras, "One foot in front," which was her shorthand for saying you don't just show up at your destination, you have to take the steps to get there.

"Move in with me. Then we can talk about a baby."

◆

Reuben was imprinting in his mind the cast of light in order to recall it later in the studio. It was late morning, so the shadows were short, huddling close to the bases of tree trunks, stumps, and stones. In places where the sun didn't reach, there were still patches of dirty snow, full of ice crystals slowly turning to water as the March temperatures inched higher.

Kip was just ahead with Bianca the Basset Hound lumbering behind him, her ears brushing the ground, her nose on constant alert for unexpected scents that led her deeper into the woods and back again. The men weren't speaking so that the recording equipment could just focus on the sounds of their footsteps crunching the dead leaves. Kip stopped at the foot of a craggy slope where a stream trickled from above over mossy juts of rock and last fall's matted ferns. Now still, Reuben paid attention to what was being recorded. The chatter of the stream, like language, cheerfully interrupted by an occasional *Chicka-dee-dee-dee-dee-deet*. A breeze made the high branches rock lightly.

Kip confidently rock-stepped across the stream. He pointed to the destination, which was just beyond by a strand of thick-waisted trees, three of which had galvanized steel sap buckets tacked to the lower part of their trunks. The tented triangle rain lids over the buckets made them look otherworldly, like quaint houses for forest gnomes.

Moving from tree to tree, Kip said, "We're in time." As he sat down and arranged the equipment, he chattered. "I missed it last year. Waited almost all day, hanging around with Bianca and a book. When I left in the late afternoon, it hadn't started running, the bucket was dry. Come back the next morning, and there's about a teaspoon of sap in the bottom, just sitting there flipping me the bird. That's why, this year, I tapped three trees with three different degrees of light exposure."

"All day, you say?" Reuben said. He should have thought to ask. It wouldn't be easy to lose a full day's work as he was coming up on a deadline to finish a project for a friend of Eastlake's. And then there was Adrian to consider. They agreed to wait a day before re-engaging the conversation about her moving in.

"Course, no reason it couldn't happen soon. On a warm day like today, all depends on the cloud cover."

High thirties did not necessarily feel "warm" to Reuben. He looked skyward through the jagged branches and could see swatches of blue between the wispy, white clouds. Might as well settle in, he thought, and unstrapped Adrian's camp chair he'd attached to a pack stuffed with a water bottle and some snacks. Meanwhile,

Bianca sprawled herself over a pile of leaves, let out a hefty sigh, and instantly started dozing.

Once the mics were in position, Kip laid a flannel blanket over a flat rock and sat down. The forest was airy and open, much more so than among the tightly packed trees in the woods beside Reuben's house. Even with the pre-spring's muted, muddy colors, the spot was truly idyllic. The peeling paper bark of a yellow birch caught Reuben's eye as it was lit shiny gold by a break of sunlight. The tree's roots clutched like ancient fingers to a crumbling, lichen-covered boulder.

Realizing there was no official parking area or even a trail leading to this spot, Reuben asked, "It's a really beautiful spot. How'd you find it?"

Kip shrugged his shoulders. Reuben waited.

"My mom and I used to picnic here when I was a kid. She called it her sanctuary."

"I can see why. So it's your family's property?"

Kip laughed a little, "No. We could barely afford a house back then."

"So it's public land."

"I wouldn't say that."

"A friend's?"

"Also no."

"Then how'd you get permission to tap the trees?"

Kip squinted his eyes a little. "When I was a kid, the property was owned by one of the old Endicott brothers, but his kids sold it to some holding company in Massachusetts. They've been sitting on a few hundred acres in this area for about a decade. My thinking is it's not exactly right to keep all these woods off-limits to people who actually live here."

As a teen, Reuben had a few run-ins with trespassing on people's property, including one where a woman fired a shotgun in the air when the high school kids he was hanging with were caught drinking in the woods behind her house. The experience had left a certain heightened sensitivity to property concerns.

"Yeah, but tapping trees..."

Kip said, "I'm a staunch adherent to leaving no trace. Once my work is done, no one ever knows I've been here."

"I guess they would have put up No Trespassing signs if they really wanted to keep people out." Reuben cracked open a can of seltzer and took a swig. "I've been thinking about doing that myself at the edge of the yard. I'm going to be moving some of the sculptures outside once it warms up, and I don't want anyone messing with them."

"Don't be putting up signs."

Reuben recalled the conversation he overheard on that first visit to Endicott's Hardware when the guys mocked the surveillance camera warnings by the new neighbors. "Oh, I don't care what Jackson Endicott and his buddies think."

"It's not that. It's just if someone hurts themself on your property—step on a nail or break an ankle—they can sue you."

"So then it makes sense to put up a couple No Trespassing signs."

"No, that does not make sense."

Reuben rewound the conversation in his mind. He spoke slowly trying to help Kip understand the lack of logic, "So if someone sees my No Trespassing sign, chooses to ignore it, gets injured on my property despite having been warned not to trespass, I am liable."

"Bingo."

"I think you've got that backwards."

"Suit yourself. Or maybe I should say 'Sue yourself,' 'cause that's what'll happen."

The conversation had a whiff of the old "Who's on first?" routine, and Reuben thought that maybe it was best to drop it. They were quiet. A bug flew near Reuben's nose, and he swatted it away. He was still thinking about what Kip was saying— it couldn't be right. "It just doesn't make sense, Kip."

"Look, if everybody who owned land in this state tried to keep people off it, there'd be no access. No hiking, swimming, or skiing. The way of the world is to buy up and own stuff. People with big money, like these Massachusetts clowns, they can own it all, and you and I would never be able to sit here and enjoy it. So the state powers decided there should be a disincentive to shutting out riffraff like us. I, for one, approve."

Reuben had to admit there was convoluted logic in it, though it didn't make him feel any better about moving his artwork outside. Though really, who would want to trespass on his property? It was just a field and beyond it, a stretch of woods that someone else owned. Their problem, not his.

Kip stood up and pressed a palm to one of the maple trees that had been enjoying a steady stretch of sunlight. He checked a weather app on his phone. "It should be today. Might be soon if the clouds hold off."

Over the next hour, the two chatted about nothing in particular—engine-light issues, how to keep bats out of the roof.

The morning's exchange with Adrian kept creeping to the front of Reuben's mind. He wasn't sure he wanted to talk specifically about it with Kip yet, especially not before he had a sense of where Adrian was going to land—she had agreed to think about it, but Reuben wasn't optimistic. It even seemed possible that she would be breaking up with him that very evening.

"Things with you and Piper. What did she say? How did she end things?"

"One of those it's-not-you-it's-me things." He picked up a stick and started breaking it into small, evenly sized pieces. "She kept saying I hadn't done anything wrong. That I was, quote, extremely likable."

"Ouch."

"Yeah, then she corrected herself and said I was 'lovable, even.' Which pretty much put me on par with Bianca the Basset Hound." The dozing dog responded with a satisfied, wheezy sigh. Kip neatly lined the small stick pieces on the rock, like a raft for a mouse.

"Were you wrecked when she left you?"

Kip made a quick swipe scattering the sticks to his feet. "Not really. I just kind of thought, okay, that chapter is now over. I figure if I couldn't disagree with her falling out of love with me, then she was probably right to do it." He stood with a groan and an overhead stretch. "Why're you asking? Something up with you and Adrian?"

"Yeah. No, nothing. Things are good, actually. Steady, comfortable."

"But?"

"I think we're just trying to figure out what's next."

"Well now, let me get comfortable in my therapist hat—" He tugged his Cubs cap down over his ears and spoke, "Tell me, Reuben, why do you zuppose you asked about zee end of zee relazionzhip rather zhan zee beginning?"

"I suppose if you're prepared for the worst, anything else is a pleasant surprise, right?"

Kip regarded him sympathetically. "At least *these* skies are blue, right?"

Reuben followed Kip's eyes skyward. It was a flawless robin's egg dome above them, and the sun had raised the temperature enough to make Reuben lower his jacket zipper.

"We'll be needing to hush up now," Kip said. "I think we're in the window."

But they were not in the window.

Down from the north, a gusty wind came in like a moving company shoving a pile of dense gray clouds overhead and parking them there. Without the sun's radiating warmth, the air temperature dropped several degrees. Kip was determined to wait it out.

"This was definitely not in the forecast," he said.

Later that afternoon, Reuben was back in the studio making some progress on a birdhouse condo he was constructing for the backyard. With The Clash blasting on the speakers and his concentration absorbed in placing tiny roof shingles, he didn't notice Adrian had entered the studio until she slid her arms around his torso. Jolted, he sent the long tweezers clattering to the floor.

"Jesus, Ade!"

She turned down the volume on Joe Strummer telling everyone to "Know Your Rights," then said, "You'd better get used to it."

"To you scaring the crap out of me?" He stooped to pick up the tool.

"To having me around. All. The. Time." She was smiling.

It took a beat for Reuben to process. "Really?"

"Really."

"Really-really?"

"Mostly really."

Reuben deflated a little.

"No. I mean, yes, really-really. I just—" She looked at him squarely, "You need to know, I'm not ready to sell my house. And I wouldn't ask you to move there and leave your studio. I talked to a friend who's wanted to move closer to Burlington, and she's going to rent it starting next month. That also gives Leila her home base to stay at when she comes home. If she comes home, I should say," Adrian said, sounding a little sad. But then she brightened. "So as of this moment..." She pointed to the doorway where a big box labeled BATHROOM sat, "You officially have a new housemate."

"A cardboard box filled with expensive hair care products—count me in!"

"And it comes with a real-live girlfriend with fabulous hair!"

He pulled her close. "Your hair is actually fabulous. We're really doing this?"

"Really-really really." She rested her chin on his shoulder, speaking quietly into his ear, "And you're right. We need to table all the talk about babies and just be you and me for a while."

Until that moment, Reuben hadn't realized how much he'd been bracing himself, shoring up his defenses and perhaps, in some ways, already seeing the relationship in a mental rearview mirror. Now, the relief felt physical, like sandbags had fallen from his shoulders. He was nearly overwhelmed, "Be careful, if you keep telling me I'm right, I might end up falling in love with you."

"I'm not worried," she said. "About you being right, I mean."

That evening, they celebrated over a giant bowl of pasta tossed with garlicky, red pepper shrimp and a bottle of 2007 Chateau Haut-Brion Blanc that Adrian had been gifted by the vintner's nephew. Without a doubt, it was the most expensive wine Reuben had ever tasted. And while he couldn't tell much difference between a good twenty-dollar bottle of wine and a very good forty-dollar bottle, this wine was clearly in a class of its own. They took their time savoring it as Adrian coached him in wine tasting, encouraging him to focus on the senses and trying to put words to the experience. The aroma, he said: "Fruit, but not just one kind, like pear *and* apricot." The body: "Almost 'thick' in a way that other white wines feel lighter."

Maybe it was the wine or the satisfying meal. Or the green daffodil shoots promising new blooms in the garden beds. Or the boost of late light from springing the clocks ahead. Or maybe it was that all Adrian's shoes—and there were many—were neatly soldiered in a closet that had previously been empty. For all of it, and more, Reuben was experiencing something that felt awfully close to joy.

The following night, an email came in from Kip. No subject line, no message, just a link to download a file. If it were anyone other than Kip, Reuben might have assumed the message was a hack attempt, but Kip was always sending links and attachments without explanation, as if the things he selectively shared just spoke for themselves. In this case, it did. A twelve-second digital recording. Near silence, then the percussive ping of a drop of liquid striking a metal surface, followed by a barely perceptible, fading ring of reverberation. "Zoomed in" was the only way Reuben could think of to describe the experience of that concentrated moment of sound.

The recording did exactly what Reuben suggested it might: force the listener to pause and pay attention, to truly listen. He imagined sound waves like rings radiating out from a stone thrown in a pond, picturing the waves bouncing back off the encircling wall of the pail and colliding with each other until they faded away. Reuben played the recording again and again, each time noticing something subtle, but new. It was meditative.

Reuben thought, *When I build the sculpture for it (because there was no question now about whether he would), I'll need to capture a sense of continual shift and fleetingness. Maybe he would create subtle changes in light, mimicking the sun's migration in the sky that day, and the way that wall of cloud rolled in, eclipsing the light and warmth. The display, he decided, might loop, but it could never stay static.*

He was jotting some notes on a junk mail envelope when an incoming video call interrupted his thoughts. Reuben assumed it was his parents, who he was overdue checking in on, but was surprised to see Paul's name and thumbnail photo in the pop-up window.

"Hey, man," Reuben said when the camera stabilized. He wasn't used to seeing Paul without the thick, owlish glasses, and his eyes looked small and vulnerable.

"My mom died today."

Reuben sighed. "I'm so sorry, Paul."

"She wasn't even sick. We had lunch last week."

Paul's dog Joey, no longer a small puppy, jumped into his lap, utterly delighted to be sitting there, panting and grinning in happy contrast to his owner's choked-back tears.

"Oh, damn, that's so hard. I know you were close with her."

Adrian came halfway down the stairs, her head towel-turban wrapped after her shower. Reuben had nearly forgotten she was there—that now, she would always be there, and he felt a flush of happiness that he had to set aside to keep his attention on Paul.

Adrian mouthed, "Are you coming to bed?" Reuben just perceptibly shook his head no, and she turned and went back up.

"You know what the worst part is? Well, not the worst because, you know, she died..." Paul started biting at the nail on his index finger, a gesture Reuben remembered from when they were kids because Paul's mother had put clear polish on his nails, thinking the bad taste would break the habit. He said, "I don't know what I'm supposed to do. For her funeral, I mean."

"I'm sure there's someone who can help."

"For about the last year and a half, she'd started going back to church. This small one out in Loomis. It made me so mad. We argued about it a lot. I just couldn't understand why she would go back to the Church—any church—ever again. You know what she said? She said she thought maybe it was a test. Maybe what I went through, what the family went through, was a test of her faith. That's what she said."

Reuben was appalled. "Paul, you know that's not—"

"What am I supposed to do with her 'faith' now that she's gone? The one time I tried to walk into a church for a friend's wedding, I was so stressed, I threw up in the bushes."

Reuben carried the laptop to the kitchen for a glass of water.

"Sorry. I don't mean to dump this on you. You've got things to do."

"No, I'm here for you, Paul. I'm glad you called."

"Well, my therapist is in Turks and Caicos. And I tried talking to Joey, but she just wants her butt scratched."

Paul pushed the dog off his lap and reached for a box of tissues. Without siblings and now both parents deceased, Reuben imagined the world suddenly felt very lonely for Paul. Reuben was no therapist, but he could at least keep his friend company. And so they talked until nearly two in the morning. First, about ways to handle the funeral. Reuben suggested asking if the church would hold a funeral mass for Paul's mother without him needing to be present, and then have them turn the body over for cremation so Paul could put her ashes to rest privately outside the church. Paul laughed, saying he wasn't sure the Catholic Church was all that flexible, but he would look into it.

Then they spent time googling some of their former teammates, laughing at how Robbie Ellis had grown up to be a bouncer at a bar at the Jersey Shore, and how Pat Quinn's Bozo the Clown head of red hair had all but disappeared. Reuben told Paul about Kip's sound project, and his own thoughts about how to bring the experience to life artistically—what materials he would need to seek out, what lighting effects.

When the conversation quieted, Paul said, "I know it's not my fault, but it will always feel like my fault."

"What will?"

"Crushing my mother's faith."

"Paul, you can't..."

"Most days, I'm okay. My brain knows it's Brinkman and the fuckers that chose to protect him. But then there are days when I can say the words, 'It wasn't my fault.' over and over like a prayer, but it feels empty. And then I think about all the kinds of detours I could have taken back then that could have avoided him altogether."

"I hear you and I can understand why you feel that way. But I'm going to be one more voice reminding you that you were just a kid. And I knew you then." Reuben tried to find the right words. "We weren't equipped to even imagine that stuff could happen to kids like us, let alone know how to avoid it. That's not on you. That'll never be on you. I don't pretend to know anything about your mom or her relationship with her God, but I have to believe she never, not once, saw you as responsible for what happened."

Paul simply dropped his head into his forearms and sobbed.

◆

Having spent the few remaining hours of the night on the couch so as not to awaken Adrian, Reuben woke with his back achy and pinched. He would need to start doing some stretching and jogging to get ready for the start of the softball season since practice was picking up the following week.

Reuben's mind was also sluggish from an early wake-up as Adrian was getting ready for a meeting in Stowe with an artist that was new to the area.

"What was up last night? Who were you talking to?" She was all speed and energy in the kitchen, a hummingbird flitting from refrigerator to cabinet to toaster and back again. Reuben simply sat in a heavy heap at the table.

"My friend, Paul. His mother died, and he needed some company." Reuben had only talked superficially to Adrian about Paul, saying that he was a close childhood friend Reuben had only recently reconnected with.

"Ah, that's so tough." Adrian came over and kissed the top of Reuben's head. "You're a good friend for staying up with him." She sat down with a bowl of yogurt and blueberries, adding a zigzag of honey on top. "So what are you working on today?"

"That's right, I didn't get to talk to you. Kip and I are collaborating on a project, sound and visuals. I'm going to start doing some idea sketches."

"Oh, I thought you might be focused on the Teshima painting."

"That...too. Yeah, I'll make some progress on that. I've just got my brain firing on this new conceptual piece." He told her about the proposed installation, the interactive scene of an early sap run. "In fact, I thought maybe tonight, you and I can look at the calendar to see when we can reserve some space in the gallery, maybe early winter?"

Adrian shook her head, "We don't do maple."

"What does that mean—you don't do maple?"

She looked at him as if she didn't understand what he didn't understand, the two of them locked in a staring standoff. Finally, she said, "Vermont. Maple. We're not interested in cliches."

It was the second time she used the word "we" in reference to the gallery.

"Ade, I'm not talking maple leaf-shaped sugar candy. It's not gift baskets with cheese. This is capturing the essence of a moment—"

"It's the subject matter—"

"It's heritage—"

"I don't care if it's Andy Warhol painting pints of Cherry Garcia. It's cliche. If we're going to be taken seriously, the gallery's reputation has to transcend its location. We get dismissed all the time as being provincial. I'm not going to have one exhibit undermine all the work we've done to change that." Adrian's tone softened, and she covered his hand with hers in a motherly way.

"I'm sorry, Reuben. I have no doubt it will be a splendid exhibit, just not at Fifth." She stood abruptly and deposited the bowl in the sink. "I bet MASS MoCA would be all over it though."

Adrian poured hot water into a travel mug, then snapped the lid on the tail of a tea bag hanging over the rim. She stopped before leaving the kitchen. "Oh, when you get the chance, could you please run a laundry today?"

And just like that, they had become domestic partners.

CHAPTER 14

Planting garlic, Rosemary had said back in the fall, is an expression of optimism. "Each clove," she held one up to her eye like a gemstone, "is a seed that'll eventually grow into a clone of its mother. Plant them just two or three inches deep before the ground hardens in October. If the chipmunks don't dig them up, and if a harsh winter doesn't kill them, they'll be some of the first sprouts you'll see come spring."

Sure enough, out of the twenty-four cloves they had planted, twenty-three green, finger-like shoots had emerged in the raised bed Rosemary had helped Reuben construct. He decided to keep the previous owners' sunflower patch where it was, which still left a good portion of the sunny backyard open for growing a variety of vegetables, something he was equal parts excited and intimidated by.

Now late April, Rosemary had come back to help jumpstart the garden. She squatted down to inspect the sprouts. "Not bad at all. They're good and healthy. But I brought some compost to give it a boost."

It was a perfect spring day, breezy and comfortable with the sun warming Reuben's forearms. It had been over a month since he'd seen Rosemary, when she had hosted Reuben and Adrian and her neighbors for dinner, so this visit was both garden tutorial and social catch-up.

Reuben had set a pot of soup to simmer while they were out back, working the soil and sowing plants that liked the cooler spring temperatures: green and red leaf lettuces, spinach, peas, and radishes. The seeds were tiny specks that Reuben could barely handle with his fingertips as he tried to plant one at a time.

"Don't be so precious," Rosemary said, generously sprinkling spinach seeds like pepper. "When you get extra sprouts, you just pull them out. Show no mercy."

She had also brought ten tomato seedlings plus two pepper plants, an eggplant sprout, and some herb sprigs in various yogurt and sour cream containers. These would need to be kept in the studio window until it was warm enough to plant them outside. Reuben wasn't sure he could handle the pressure of keeping all those plants alive, but Rosemary assured him he just needed to not over- or under-water them, which pretty much guaranteed he would do one and then the other.

Rosemary stood up, straightening her spine slowly. The physical labor of running the B&B and all its chores creeping up on her. Slapping her hands on her jeans to remove the loose dirt, she glanced over at a flat, wooden tray stand Reuben had set out filled with birdseed. A bright red cardinal landed, chasing away the smaller sparrows that had been jockeying for position at the perch. "Well now, there's a great way to attract a bear."

Adrian had warned the same, but he loved watching the birds—the demure and clever ones, the loud and bullying ones. Even the squirrels added their entertainment, finding ways to acrobat up and over the lip, crowning themselves feeder champions as they daintily nibbled whole sunflower seeds like teatime sandwiches. It was all a welcome distraction when Reuben's commissioned work was stuttering or sluggish, which it had been lately, particularly with one piece on which he was running dangerously close to the deadline.

Instead, his inspiration and enthusiasm were engaged with the forest sculpture, which Reuben told Rosemary about as they sat on the patio savoring the soup and surveying their work.

"It took a little nudging, but Kip agreed to work together on it. Ironically, I think what brought him around was the fact that Adrian had shot down the idea of us exhibiting at the gallery."

"Why's that, do you suppose?" Rosemary asked.

"I think he's uncomfortable considering what he does as art, but to hear him talk about it—"

"I meant Adrian."

"Oh. She just didn't think it was a good fit for the gallery."

Rosemary just nodded thoughtfully then asked, "Then what's the plan for putting it out in the world?"

"We'll be constructing it in the barn. From there, I guess we'll figure it out when the time is right."

While he was tempted to risk a bear encounter just to see that big, wild power up close, Reuben reluctantly removed the feeder that evening. So it was infuriating when the next morning, he found the resident birds had turned their attention to the next best food source: the garden with its freshly planted vegetable seeds. There were about a dozen little birds scratching at the dirt, cocking and bobbing their heads, literally consuming his and Rosemary's labor with their greedy little beaks.

Reuben, in his pajama bottoms and bare feet, came running out, waving his arms to scare them away. But the damage had already been done.

"You look like a madman." Adrian, also in her pajamas, was leaning on the studio door frame.

"Greedy birds." Reuben stood, hands on hips, as if daring them to come back. "I've got to plant all over again."

"They'll just come back. This is their all-you-can-eat buffet now."

"I can't have that. We worked too hard. I'm going to set that bird seed tray out again."

"My Uncle Otto always puts up a few scarecrows when he plants seeds."

"Does that work?"

She shrugged, "Maybe? Probably not. I don't actually know."

Reuben thought for a moment. "It can't hurt, right?"

He started off to the barn for supplies, then stopped and turned back to the house. "I'll need pants. And a shirt."

"Yeah, you're not exactly dressed for yard work."

"For the scarecrow, I mean."

◆

It turned out Reuben wouldn't need to divert any of the lumber he'd collected for the scarecrow. He didn't have to sew a fake burlap head or get a bale of hay from Endicott's to stuff into an old pair of jeans. Reuben had a ready-made fixture that would make quick, easy work of the installation.

He had just finished securing the post at the far end of the garden when Adrian startled him by opening the studio door and leading Kip out to the patio. He was in the middle of saying, "Thought I'd drop them off. . ." His words trailed off as he and Adrian stood blinking in the sunlight, trying to determine what precisely they were looking at.

"Good lord," said Adrian.

"In the flesh," said Kip.

Reuben had been so engrossed in the effort, he hadn't taken time to figure out how he was going to explain the backyard presence of an eight-foot-tall crucifix with its life-size Jesus dressed as a scarecrow.

"Reuben, what—" Adrian started, "What is . . . where did you get that?"

In the moment, sticking to facts seemed to be the best course of action. "I brought it home a couple months ago along with a bunch of supplies from a barn out in Morgan," he said. "Not the clothes, those are mine."

Squinting a little, Adrian said, "Is that really the best use of—"

"Oh, it's okay, I was taking them to Goodwill anyway."

"I'm talking about the crucifix, Reuben." She tucked her chin and gave a long, critical look at the scarecrow. "I get the idea of provocative art—"

"Oh. No. That's not what this is. That's not what I'm doing here. I'm just trying to scare away the birds."

Or at least that was his original intent. But then things got complicated.

After he'd left Adrian to go rifle through the barn for the supplies he would need for the scarecrow, it was—dare he say—a revelation that the crucifix would fill the need perfectly. It was the right height, it had a spike on the bottom to easily secure it to the ground. Most significantly, it came with a detachable, human sized figure with outstretched arms. And so, a project that would have taken several hours to construct would be done in less than one.

And everything had gone as practically as that until Reuben was sliding the well-worn sleeve of an old flannel shirt over Jesus's outstretched left arm. When the edge of the cuff revealed the roughly carved hand, a spike head protruding grotesquely from the palm, Reuben thought, *What am I doing?*

Growing up, Reuben had never had any religious instruction. His parents were devout atheists who disabused their son at an early age of the notion that there was anything divine or magical about the way in which the world worked; it worked through random occurrences giving way to the laws of science. No God, no Santa, no menorah miracles.

Once, at a reunion for his mother's family, an aunt pulled fourteen-year-old Reuben aside and handed him a Holy Bible, saying she'd bought it just for him, hoping it would bring his soul as much joy as it had hers. Like a contraband copy of *Playboy*, he'd hidden the Bible from his parents beneath his mattress, and in the subsequent weeks, he'd tried, truly, to give it a read, but the passages simply didn't connect in his brain. For Reuben, reading the stilted words felt like trying to grasp meaning from the warbled words of Charlie Brown's teacher.

In most of the towns Reuben's family moved to, the churches were never a significant part of the culture. In fact, it surprised Reuben, as he paused, hovering over the carved palm, to realize that the first and only kid he'd ever known who regularly attended CCD classes and Sunday church was Paul. And the thought, once articulated, was an unsettling door cracking open.

Reuben had no patience for people who tried to argue that "things happen for a reason," a suggestion he found repugnant in the way it tried to put a balm, a Band-Aid, over difficulty or pain. In this, Reuben agreed with his parents: there was no higher plan. Life simply moved forward and sometimes good things happened, sometimes bad. Most of the time, the world existed in between.

And yet—perhaps it was the artist in him—Reuben did believe there was something almost magical about finding patterns. Recalling how he'd nearly laughed out loud when he'd first seen the crucifix in the barn, the irony of encountering it so close to his reuniting with Paul. That uncanny intersection looked an awful lot like a connection, if not a pattern.

A new crackling tension emerged in Reuben's mind. He looked up from the statue's hand to its sorrowful face and felt a welling of anger for what had happened to Paul. For the way it changed the course of that particular boy's life, not to mention so many others, forever.

He thought back to Hannah, how she'd told him that the bridesmaid cake pop was meant to be an act of protest in response to her client's bad behavior, Hannah's personal version of subversion. It was just unfortunate that she actually was really good at creating confectionary likenesses.

Starting at the bottom, he secured the shirt. With each button he silently repeated in his head like a mantra: *He was just a kid. He was just a kid. He was just a kid.* Reuben stopped when he reached Jesus's lowered chin. Grabbing the threadbare jeans from the ground, he roughly tugged the right pant leg over the statue's crossed, spiked feet. The left side he would leave loose to comically flap in the wind. An extra deterrent to shoo the birds, which, after all, remained his original objective, despite this new upheaval of emotions.

When he'd finished, Reuben propped the scarecrow in the corner and sat down on the dirty floor, tired. There was a memory that he had tucked away of one of the last times he and Paul had spent together before Paul left for that fateful camp. Even now, it remained vividly clear because Reuben would sometimes close his eyes and play it like a movie in his mind just so he could keep the details alive.

It had been the town's Fourth of July celebration, and Paul's father had dropped the two of them at the park just before sunset. Having attended the fair with his family every year since he was able to walk, Paul was excited to steer Reuben through the festivities. They strolled past the big grills sending meaty smoke from hot dogs, hamburgers, and sausages into the air. On the opposite side were the slushie and cotton candy stalls where kids clutching sweaty dollar bills lined up as they waited impatiently for their treats.

Paul and Reuben wandered along taking fast glimpses at the girls in spaghetti-strap sundresses and wedge-heel sandals, while any that glanced back instantly dismissed the two boys, as if maturity level was something they could discern within seconds. And their assessments were mostly accurate because, really, Reuben and Paul were more interested in demolition derbying around the bounce house where they sent a preschooler sobbing to her mother before the attendant kicked them out. The boys moved on to games, throwing darts at balloons and winning a wooden paddleball toy. Then they sat in the grass, shoveling whole handfuls of kettle corn into their mouths as they watched a troupe of dancing dogs perform.

Reuben had a moment where he thought, *This is what normal summer is.* Fairs and fireworks, the town pool and the skate park. Not being slumped in the back seat of the car, the songs on the portable CD player a soundtrack to the rolling miles leading to yet another new town. This time, his dad had promised him—no more transfers, no more new schools. A bedroom he could settle into and claim as his own. And now, best of all, a friend who liked all the same movies he did, who he could be goofy and kid-like with in all the ways he'd never really let himself before.

That's why it hit Reuben's heart so hard when he'd learned that Paul had gone. It felt like betrayal, leaving Reuben humiliated and questioning if he even knew what friendship looked like. His mother had told him to stop moping. At his age, friendships came and went. Reuben would find his clique once school started again, and why didn't he strike up a friendship with the kids who lived next door? *Because they're at least three fucking years younger than I am!* Reuben shouted at her in his mind.

Eventually, his mother proved to be right. He did settle in with a small group of friends, a mix of guys and girls who were good, but not great students—all generally nice, often funny kids. And during baseball seasons, Reuben would become tight with a second baseman named Gavin, but once the season was over, they drifted back to their regular hang-out crews, simply nodding and high-fiving each other in the halls when they passed. Casual, social, these were the words that came to mind when Reuben thought back on his friendships after Paul. But that pure happiness of spending time with a good friend remained elusive.

How could he explain all that to Adrian and Kip?

Instead, he held to his story. "It is literally the shape of a scarecrow." Reuben held his arms straight out from his shoulders mimicking the figure.

"Wait, hold that pose," Kip nodded slowly. "You know, I kind of see a resemblance. The shaggy hair, beard. You're not quite that skinny. And I've never seen such a tragic expression on your face, but maybe the birds'll think they've really let you down this time."

"Betrayed you, even," Adrian chimed in.

"The Judas of Sparrows," Kip turned to her, "He should totally cast them out of the garden."

"That's Old Testament," she said. "Get your Bible straight, mister."

"And you guys accuse *me* of being insensitive," said Reuben.

◆

Later that night, Reuben sent a photo of the scarecrow to Paul, telling him about the installation and some of what was going through Reuben's mind in the process. Paul replied within minutes:

> Apart from my lawyer sending Brinkman to jail, that's the best thing anyone's ever done to stick up for me. 😂

Coming to bed, smoothing jasmine-scented lotion over her hands and elbows, Adrian said, "At least you didn't put it on the front lawn. I suppose it's only the squirrels' sensibilities that will be offended." She slid in under the covers. "But if it doesn't work with the birds, we can take it down? I don't want to feel judged every time I sit on the patio with my beach reads."

He grunted an acknowledgment, not ready to make that promise. Before he fell asleep, Reuben hatched a plan to hedge his bets and make sure he could keep the scarecrow up.

The next morning when Adrian was cleaning the breakfast dishes, Reuben pretended to replant the vegetable seeds, squatting low and making a charade of scattering and covering them up with soil. Then, when she left to run some errands, he tossed handfuls of birdseed on the grassy ground on the other side of the barn far away from the garden, diverting the birds, thereby providing "proof" that the scarecrow was working, and should remain right where it stood, at least through the growing season.

After a few days of training the birds to find their food source elsewhere (complete with Jackson Endicott offering his unsolicited two cents regarding the economy-sized bag of birdseed Reuben was purchasing), Reuben planted actual vegetable seeds in the garden just as Rosemary had shown him. He'd also taken to rising early those first few days to stand vigil on the patio until the seeds had finally started to sprout, all the while managing to keep Adrian under the impression that Reuben's scarecrow seemed to work better than her uncle's had against the crows in the cornfield.

"Crows being smarter, I guess," she said.

"Sparrows being more God-fearing, maybe," Reuben said with a nervous laugh.

By mid-May, the lettuces were baby ruffles, the peas were tiny green shoots, and the radishes had sprouted a pair of heart-shaped leaves. Reuben found himself fascinated by their determination to thrive, standing themselves back up after a hard rain, each day doing their singular job of converting sunlight and water, growing seemingly before his eyes.

Having managed to also keep Rosemary's potted seedlings alive in the studio window past what was forecast to be the last hard frost, he was now able to relocate the plants directly in the dirt where they could stretch and spread their roots. While it was a relief to have them out of his workspace, their presence lingered in his subconscious, infiltrating an oversized abstract painting with the curled shapes he'd discovered in the fuzzy tomato leaves and the tiny bells of pepper plant blossoms.

The piece was for yet another of John Eastlake's contacts, a woman who owned a summer retreat on Lake Memphremagog. Reuben was grateful for the steady work, but he also couldn't help feeling an undercurrent of unease in the way he was beholden to Eastlake, even in this small way. Given the man's multifaceted business and personal tentacles, the likelihood of getting tangled up at some point seemed plausible, if not inevitable.

CHAPTER 15

Reuben had just one leg in his sweatpants when Patrice popped by the truck window. He was carrying his young son who was peering in at Reuben half in his underwear.

"I have brought my boy today, Reuben!"

"I can see that, Patrice."

"Naomi is coming, too, with the baby," he pointed behind him where a woman had a sling wrapped around her, presumably with little Kali tucked inside.

Then, a pounding on the roof of the passenger side startled Reuben anew. "Shake a leg, Ruby!" said Joss. "But put your pants on first."

Just an hour before, Reuben was delivering a painting that he'd managed to finish just under the wire a day before the bank's ribbon cutting. Days when the art and softball worlds pressed up against each other in this way, Reuben experienced a kind of mental shift that required a few moments to adjust his general way of being and interacting with people, and so he had no quick comeback for Joss, who was briskly striding away, bat slung over her shoulder like one of the seven dwarfs heigh-hoeing off to work.

When he got to the dugout, the Blue Jays were already on the field taking their warm-up. Dana Van Sykes was at bat, her booming voice calling every play before the pitch.

Seeing Reuben take note of her, Wayne said, "I got here ninety minutes early, and they were already doing BP. On our field."

Donny gave Wayne a slap on the back, "They're just trying to psych us out *'cause they know they can't beat us playing straight,*" he shouted the last part loud enough for the other team to hear.

Wayne wandered over to the backstop, "Hey, Van Sykes, can you guys wrap it up so we can get time on *our* field?"

Dana continued to face the pitcher, wagging her bat over her shoulder and said, "Oh, did you-all's team finally make it? Thought we were going to have to lend you one of our players." She took one last swing, a cannon-shot line drive over the shortstop's outstretched mitt. "Blue Jays, bring it in! The Mallards have decided to play today."

As she passed Wayne, she said, "Don't know if you noticed, but we've got a new guy in left field. Well, not new. He used to play for the Trout. Your pitcher should remember him. She broke his ankle a couple years back. He's looking to even the score." She paused for effect. "But I'm just talking runs, of course, not breaking bones."

Reuben overheard the conversation as he tightened his laces. He looked around to see if Maddy had heard, too, but found that she was over by the bleachers, digging a cleat at the dirt as she chatted with a crew-cut, burly looking guy who was holding a supersize cup in both hands. "Who's that guy?" he asked Cameron who was pulling a few balls from the bag.

"It's a German name. Something that reminded me I was hungry when he introduced himself."

"Wurst?" Joss chimed in. She used her teeth to pull a leather strap tight on her mitt.

"No."

"Schpaetchzle?" She exaggerated the pronunciation.

"Dude, I didn't say it was German food." Cameron snapped his fingers and pointed. "Berger! That's it. His name's Berger."

"Hamburgers are German," said Joss. "They come from Hamburg."

"The guy is not named for a patty of grilled meat."

"Of course not, Patty would be from Ireland, not Germany."

The two continued their banter as they split off to shortstop and left field, respectively.

Maddy, still back at the bleachers, released her ponytail, then smoothed and resecured it as she continued talking with the guy.

"Hey, Maddy," Reuben shouted to her. "You ready to warm up?"

She said something to Berger, and he held up his hand for a fist bump, which she returned before jogging over to Reuben. "Yep, let's get to it," she said, catching a glance at the Blue Jays left fielder. "What's *that* guy doing here?"

Reuben could see she was miffed by his presence. "Hey," he said. When she continued to watch the guy snag a high pop fly, Reuben said, "Hey, Maddy. Look at me."

He put his hands on Maddy's elbow to get her attention, which he instantly removed when she flinched as if his hand were made of fire. "What?"

"You don't need to worry about him. He's just a guy, same as all the other players you pitch to. You've got this. Okay?"

She nodded. "Okay."

The first inning was short with a rapid series of outs in both the top and bottom. In the Jays next at bat, the center fielder was at the top of the order, taking practice swings. Dana Van Sykes made a special point to tell everyone on the field and in the bleachers that, "It's payback time, Frankie. Go get 'er."

Frank took position at home plate, squinting and kicking the dirt like a bull. He was a big guy, about six feet tall, probably over two hundred pounds. Though he was a right-handed batter, the protective brace was on his back ankle, which meant the pitch likely caught him in a vulnerable spot as he tried to jump out of the way.

Reuben couldn't resist getting under the guy's skin a little. "I gotta warn you, her warm-up was potent. Pitches are coming in super hot," Reuben said just loud enough for Frank to hear.

"Whatever, man," Frank replied, intent on concentrating.

The teenaged ump's voice cracked a little on the shout: "Okay, batter up!"

"Maybe you've just got delicate bones," Reuben said.

Frank held the bat up one handed and slid the other behind his thigh giving Reuben the finger.

Maddy's expression was focused as the team cheered her on.

"Hey now, Mad Maddy!"

"You got this, Madster!"

"Just over the plate."

"Just pitch-to-glove, pitch-to-glove, Maddy." Reuben said. She nodded as if clearing her head.

When the pitch came in, it was deep inside, causing Frank to curve his belly inward and freeze for a moment in a Michael Jackson toe stand.

"Ball!"

Frank stepped out of the batter's box as Maddy walked off the rubber to catch the return throw. She walked a tiny circle before getting back to position. When the second pitch came in, Frank had to duck to avoid getting clocked in the head, which drew boos from the Blue Jays bench.

"Ball two!"

"What the hell!" Frank shouted at her. "You got something personal?"

Maddy pressed her lips in a tight line as the team rallied behind her, willing her to pitch a strike, or at least not a heat-seeking missile of a pitch. Even Berger gave a shout of encouragement from the sidelines.

"He's not even there, Maddy," Reuben said to her. "It's just you and me. I gotcha." He gave her the signal for a pitch high and outside, hoping the direction might rein in her focus.

She gave him a tight half smile, and for a split second, the teams and the fans seemed to fade, and it really was just the two of them, a connection he hadn't felt before. Maddy nodded, she was ready.

Her windup was perfect; the release and wrist-snap follow-through were textbook. But somehow, the pitch sank hard and fast, colliding with Frank's other ankle, the one not protected by a brace. Howls of injustice erupted from the Jays as he crumpled like a marionette, shouting, "Son of a bitch!"

"Oh, no no no no," Maddy came running over. "Frank, I'm so sorry, I didn't mean . . . I was trying so hard not to—"

Two of Frank's teammates rushed to his aid, one leveling a glare at Maddy as they shouldered him off the field. Reuben tried to talk to Maddy, saying it wasn't her fault, but she shrugged him off and left the field. Wayne was already on his way over to sub in to pitch.

The Jays' big hitters drooled over themselves seeing the fat lobs Wayne sent over the plate. But being big hitters, they became so determined to crush the ball that Cameron and Kip made relatively easy work of catching their outfield flies, even Patrice nabbed an ice cream cone of a catch. "Put some sprinkles on it!" Wayne shouted to him.

Still, the Mallards infield saw more action than normal, and by the bottom of the seventh, the teams were even with six runs apiece. Donny, determined not to go into extra innings as it was his and Barb's anniversary, took a hearty swing at the first pitch, and sent a hard and low line drive that bounced once in fair territory and took off like a shot past the third basemen, where it rolled far and away, driving home Aaron, who had been on first, and handing Dana Van Sykes and the Blue Jays yet another squeaker of a loss.

CHAPTER 16

Adrian had spent the week visiting Leila in New York. It was the longest Reuben and she had been apart since they started living together, so her return later that afternoon seemed cause for a mini homecoming celebration that would include lobster risotto and a fresh-from-the-garden spinach salad. He'd also bought ingredients for a cherry dessert to be named later as well as some other staples they had been running low on. And so, coming up the walkway with two overstuffed grocery bags eclipsing his view, Reuben nearly upended everything when a dog on his porch let loose a string of deep-throated barks. He set the bags down roughly in the grass, assessing his safety, determining whether he needed to flee back to the truck. The dog was leashed but agitated enough by Reuben's presence to be roughly jostling the woman trying to restrain it.

"Can I help you?" he shouted to her.

"Do you live here?"

Reuben paused, not knowing if he should answer. But the groceries and the keys poised in his hand seemed clear indicators that, yes, it was his home.

"Yeah, I do."

The dog, a large mutt that seemed at least part German shepherd, continued to bark at him. "Romulus, hush! Settle!" She palmed a treat, which Romulus took before obediently sitting down, though he remained on heightened alert. Reuben felt much the same.

"Are you aware that you have a crucifix dressed as a scarecrow in your backyard?"

"I'm sorry," Reuben asked, "who are you?"

"Joy. I'm Joy. Is that your scarecrow?"

Reuben tried to make his brain work faster so he could respond appropriately. The trouble was, he didn't know how to define "appropriate" for this situation. Should he play it off that someone else put up the scarecrow as a joke? Or be indignant that Joy and Romulus were trespassing?

Instead, he asked, "Would you please remove yourself and your dog from my porch? I'd like to get the ice cream in the freezer."

"You're not answering my question."

"What were you doing in my backyard?"

Joy seemed prepared for this question, "I was walking Romulus, and we had stopped to look at the goats. There was a cat in the bushes that startled him, and he took off after it, chasing it into your garden."

"Oh, crap." Reuben set down the groceries and bounded to the back of the house. He squatted down beside the raised bed finding his seedlings trampled, bent and broken like battleground soldiers. In the space between the plants, the freshly watered soil showed deep, frantic paw prints belonging to Romulus and, likely, Lou Garoo.

Joy had followed Reuben to the back. She was tug-of-warring with the dog who was huffing and straining against his harness, trying his best to pull her over to the barn instead.

"Your dog decimated my garden," Reuben said flatly. He did a quick triage on an uprooted jalapeño plant that had just started bearing fruit.

Giving one forceful tug to get Romulus to follow, Joy said, "Well, it was the cat who ran this way. Romulus was just following."

"Chasing."

"But what about that?" She pointed to the scarecrow.

Reuben looked at Joy, her pristine white visor and expensive-looking power-walking shoes, a fanny pack girding her waist. He brushed the dirt from his fingers as he stood. "What about it?"

"You've turned Jesus Christ into a clown!"

Her total lack of accountability was infuriating, and Reuben's response came out unchecked, "I'm sorry your Christian sensibilities were offended when you traipsed through the privacy of my backyard."

"I'm Jewish!" Joy said, punctuating each word as if it should have been obvious.

"Then what's your—" Reuben stopped himself short of asking what her expletive problem was. He just wanted Joy and her stupid dog off his property so he could salvage some of the garden. And now that he looked more closely, he could see blood on the wooden frame of the raised bed. "Can you please just take your dog and leave, so I can put away my groceries and see if the cat needs medical attention."

Joy looked at him, her jaw indignantly set. "Fine." Thankfully, she turned and speed-walked back down the driveway without further words.

Reuben turned to the scarecrow, trying to imagine it through the eyes of someone stumbling upon it unexpectedly. He had become a little blind to it in the weeks since he'd put it up. Seeing the scarecrow anew, he had to admit the sight was jarring, not just in its convergence of the sacred and profane but in its sheer size and imposing presence. Still, what right did she have to judge him, on his own property, for something she knew nothing about? It wasn't even her religion. She was simply offended by proxy.

In the barn, Reuben tugged a string attached to a bare ceiling lightbulb. The space flooded with light, but not enough to see in the corner crevices. He whistled. "Hey, Lou. Lou Garoo. Where are you, buddy?"

Reuben finally spotted the cat tucked in a defensive ball high up on a shelf. If possible, he looked even more bedraggled than usual as a part of his ear had been bitten and was bleeding. Dragging a stepladder over, Reuben climbed up and reached for the animal, aiming to bring him down to get a better look at the injuries. But the cat had no intention of being handled and instead let out a low warning growl before he swatted viciously at Reuben's hand, delivering a single deep slash, and emphasizing the point with a foul-smelling hiss.

Using garden gloves produced no better results as Lou Garoo again went on the offensive, then retreated even farther to a nook, putting himself squarely out of reach behind the intersection of two beams.

"Idiot cat." Reuben shut the light off and left the barn but knew he wouldn't be able to just leave the animal to suffer or potentially die from his injuries. Between Lou Garoo and the garden mess, Reuben's day was now officially hijacked, and he felt angry all over again.

He pulled out his phone, searched the Mallards' group text, and singled out Maddy's number.

Hey, it's Reuben. Do you make house calls?

...

She seemed to be typing, pausing, maybe erasing, and then typing again.

...

Um, what?

Sorry, aren't you a vet?

Vet tech

Oh, that works, too, I think? My cat got in a fight with dog. Bleeding but not letting me near. Don't know how bad he's injured. Help?

...

...

What's your address?

While Reuben waited for Maddy to arrive, he quickly unpacked the groceries (the vanilla bean ice cream having turned to soup), then he went back to see how many plants he could resuscitate. Resurrect, he thought with a small nod to Jesus. Some of the seedlings would bounce back, but others, including an heirloom tomato plant, would be lost for the season, its stem having broken too far down. Reuben could trace the path the fracas took, mowing down three areas of the garden like a tornado cutting through a swath of land.

After nearly twenty minutes, Reuben heard a car come up the driveway. He went to meet Maddy out front, aiming to prevent her from wandering to the backyard and having to explain more than just the animal brawl.

Maddy was dressed in a pair of cutoffs and a loose t-shirt from a local take-out place with a tagline For pizza's sake! written across the chest, which he read as quickly as possible, making sure his eyes didn't linger. But when he looked away, his attention was then drawn to the curve of her calf, following it down to where a delicate gold chain was draped around her left ankle. *She has runner's legs*, a thought he immediately squashed and grounded his focus on the canvas bag she carried over her shoulder.

"So where's this cat?"

"Right. He's a barn cat, so in the barn." He led the way. "I really appreciate you coming out here. I didn't know what else to do."

"It's cool. Like I said, I'm just a tech, so I'm a little limited. If the injuries are serious, you'll need to take him to a vet."

"He's not really a pet, just a stray that's living in the barn."

"Do you give him food and water?"

Reuben nodded.

She smiled as she let herself into the barn, "Hate to break it to you, but that means he's a pet."

The daylight outside slipped in through the gaps in the barn's wood walls. Maddy looked around the dimness and seemed to take in the neat stacks of labeled bins, the clean workbench, the yard tools hanging on individual hooks. She veered off a little and nearly tripped over the coiled snake of an electric cord. Reuben reflexively lurched forward to brace her arm, but she waved him off. "All good," she said.

As he pulled the lightbulb string, she said, "You're very organized."

He couldn't tell if it was a compliment or if she thought he might be compulsive. "Without a system, I'm just a few cardboard boxes away from being featured on *Hoarders*."

Reuben used the flashlight on his phone to locate the cat, still in the tight corner, his eyes reflecting like a monster's. Maddy gently called to him as she slipped on a pair of surgical gloves. "Hey, buddy, hey, big kitty . . . What's his name?"

"Lou Garoo."

"Werewolf? You speak French?"

"He was named by a Quebecois friend."

Lou Garoo eyed Maddy suspiciously as she climbed the stepladder, cooing and saying soothing words as she went. But once her slow-moving hand got within two feet of him, he began that distant thunder of a growl. When she reached her open palm toward him, he swatted at her and hissed. Maddy backed down the ladder. "He's going to need some incentive. Given his name, I'm going to guess he can be a little ornery, even when he's not injured?"

"He's a barn cat. I've never had any reason to see if he's cuddly." Maddy pulled a shower-sized towel from the bag and a small, tube-like packet. Reuben continued, "I actually don't like cats. But I'm returning a favor, and he earns his supper keeping the mice in check."

"Well, I hate to tell you, but this guy is going to need some TLC. I don't think he'll have to get stitches but that ear's a little mangled." She climbed back up the ladder, leading with the packet.

Reuben could see Lou Garoo's nose twitching, catching a whiff of something that interested him. Maddy kept it just out of reach so that he had to come closer if he wanted to find out what she held. It was a back-and-forth game of drawing the cat out, then seeing him retreat when Maddy got too close. Eventually, she gave him a small taste of what was in the tube, and that was it. Any skittishness was overcome by a determination to get more of the treat. Once he emerged from the corner onto the shelf, she set the packet down and let him lick at the contents. With impressive speed, she cinched the towel around him, wrapping him up in a tight burrito that kept his legs pinned, leaving the cat raging but immobilized, hissing and howling at having been duped.

Once they were down on the ground, Maddy had Reuben hold the straitjacketed cat as she syringed a fishy-smelling sedative into his mouth. As they waited for the drug to mellow him out, she gave Lou Garoo the rest of the treat and was eventually able to clean his bloodied ear.

"Doesn't look like he's missing any flesh, but it's a big gash." She gently rubbed the cat on his nose which made him close his eyes. In her professional capacity, Maddy became quite chatty. "Do you have a room you can keep him in for about a week? I brought a cone but it's not safe for him to be outside with it on. No doubt you have some predators out here. And without it, he'll just irritate that ear to infection. Also, has he had a rabies shot?"

This was becoming more complicated than Reuben signed up for. And he knew keeping a cat anywhere in the house would not please Adrian. "Maybe you know someone who would want to adopt a mean, mangy barn cat?"

Maddy laughed as if he were joking. Reuben laughed, too, as if he had been.

By the time they moved the cat and his food and water dishes into the laundry room and laid down an old fleece blanket for a bed, Lou Garoo was sighing deeply and bearing the lazy eyes of a drunkard. Maddy was able to examine him, finding just one other bite on his foot and treating it with a topical antibiotic.

"He's neutered, so that's good." Lying on his side, the plastic cone of shame encircling his doped-out head, the once-feisty, fierce-hunting werewolf was now literally, an emasculated, stoner house cat.

Reuben closed the door on the makeshift infirmary. "Can I write you a check or something? You've given an awful lot of time and supplies to help my nonpet of a pet."

"Don't be silly. I have a soft spot for the ones with a bad attitude."

"Well then, what about dinner? Why don't you stay for dinner?" Reuben asked, immediately cursing his stupid mouth for saying the words before he remembered the romantic evening he'd planned for Adrian.

"That's really sweet, but I have plans."

"Oh, with Berger?"

She looked at him, surprised, "A group of friends. But yeah, Berger's one of them."

"How about a glass of iced tea, then? At least let me offer that on a hot day."

They sat on the porch, a pitcher of iced tea with mint sprigs and big floating ice cubes on the table between them. It was the first time Reuben and Maddy had been alone together. Their conversation was stilted and halting, particularly now that the cat was settled in the house.

"Your property is beautiful."

"Yeah, I got lucky in finding this house. Actually, my friend Rosemary found it—you know her, she's the woman in the bleachers who sometimes brings the mini-muffins for everyone."

Maddy nodded, "Yeah, she's a hoot. She cheers really loud when you're up to bat. It's super cute."

She looked out toward the woods. "Must be nice not to have neighbors right on top of you. I love my condo but there are zero secrets with the people upstairs." She made a mortified face and took a sip from her glass. "So where do you do your art?"

"The studio's out back."

"Oh, can I see?"

After the run-in with Joy, Reuben did not want Maddy to see Jesus in the backyard. "It's wall-to-wall work in progress, so I can't show you."

"You don't have to be embarrassed. It'd be really cool to see how you go about your work."

"I would but it's a confidentiality thing. With clients. A contract stipulation. They want the element of surprise and all that."

"Oh. That would never have occurred to me, but I guess it makes sense."

There was a lull in the conversation as a car drove along the road kicking up a cloud of dust behind it. Reuben reached to refill her glass.

Maddy said, "I have to tell you, I feel like such an idiot about that last game."

"The Jays?" Reuben waved it off. "Don't give it a thought."

"I don't know what it is about that guy. It's like he's a refrigerator and every pitch I send is a magnet."

"It's just part of the game. Injuries happen. At least nothing broke this time." Then he added, "I wish I'd done a better job helping you ignore him."

Maddy shook her head, "No, no, it's just me. You were great and are actually pretty good at getting me to focus. When Wayne's behind the plate, he's all, 'Where'd you pull that pitch from?' and 'Try to keep it in the backstop next time' which just makes me tense. If Wayne's a stick, you're a carrot." She scrunched her eyebrows. "That came out weird."

"No, I get it, meaning, like, you're a mule." Reuben shook his head. "Wow, leave it to me to make weird even weirder."

Maybe it was the warmth of the sun, but he thought Maddy might have blushed. She had such a clean-scrubbed, natural prettiness that was different from Adrian's sculpted beauty. Realizing these were not thoughts he should be thinking, Reuben deflected the conversation. "Did you ever notice that Wayne has that Captain Kirk way of talking? 'Don't . . . forget, you gotta *check* the runner before you *chuck* . . . to first.'" Maddy lit up with a grin and followed his lead.

"'Maddy, I keep *tellin'* ya . . . you gotta . . . *bring* the heat!'"

They were laughing hard, continuing to sling Wayne-isms when Adrian pulled in the driveway, behind Maddy's hatchback.

Reuben, still laughing, swiped a knuckle at the corner of his eye, and Maddy settled her own laughter behind her hand as Adrian arrived at the porch steps, a compact suitcase rolling behind her.

"Hey there," Reuben said, "How was the trip?"

Adrian nodded, "It was lovely. There was a lot of shopping and eating. Leila sends her hellos."

"Oh, hey, you remember Maddy, from softball?"

"I do."

"We were just having tea on the porch," said Maddy, stating the obvious.

"You're like a couple of Southerners," Adrian said.

Reuben could see Adrian was making calculations behind her eyes. He jumped up to give her a quick kiss before taking the suitcase and delivering it just inside the doorway.

Maddy picked up the conversation, "There was an incident with your cat. I came by to help."

"Maddy's a vet tech." Reuben said as he returned. "Also, just a heads up, Lou Garoo is in the laundry room, recovering." He could see all this random information was not what she expected to come home to. "Why don't you take my seat, Ade? Can I get you a glass?"

She declined the tea but took the seat, so Reuben half sat, half leaned on the porch railing as he told a much-abridged version of the altercation between Lou Garoo and Romulus.

"But once the sedative wears off," Adrian said, "he'll go back to the barn."

"I don't recommend that," Maddy said. "The wounds aren't deep enough to require stitches, but he still needs time to heal in a clean environment. Plus there's the cone."

"Cone." Adrian repeated.

Just then, Reuben saw both women's attention shift to something behind him, followed by the sound of a vehicle pulling into the driveway. He hoped it might be Kip popping by.

But it wasn't Kip. The car was a shiny red MINI Cooper convertible. There was a woman behind the wheel who looked like a Hollywood starlet dressed incognito with her head wrapped in a silk scarf and her eyes covered by dark, blocky sunglasses. She turned off the engine, but remained in the driver's seat while Reuben, Adrian, and

Maddy all held still, staring for nearly a minute as they waited for something to happen.

Eventually, the woman, dressed in a crepey sundress, stepped out of the car and walked cautiously as a crane toward the house. She untied the scarf, releasing an angular blonde bob.

Reuben said, "Hannah?"

Hannah had decided it was best not to call first in case Reuben refused to see her. "You really shouldn't have your home address on your studio website," she said. "You never know who's going to just show up in your driveway."

"Clearly," he said.

The introductions among Reuben's ex-girlfriend, his current girlfriend, and his just plain friend were awkward, but everyone offered up hellos and smiled politely. Nobody said, *I've heard so much about you.* In fact, Reuben hadn't really told Adrian much about his time with Hannah beyond it having ended with the fork stabbing, mostly because Adrian never asked about her. Maddy, who essentially knew nothing, seemed to sense the strain of the situation and used Hannah's arrival as an opening to take immediate leave. Immediate being relative, because in order for Maddy to get out, the three women had to shuffle their cars, backing out of the driveway one by one as Reuben stood on the grass, his hand raised, shading his eyes in what looked like a salute against the late afternoon sun.

After Maddy drove off, Adrian idled in the road for a moment before zooming back up the driveway, parking roughly beside Reuben's truck near the barn. Hannah's jellybean of a car followed, the bottom scraping noisily on the high-centered part of the dirt driveway.

Before any further pleasantries could be exchanged, Hannah, her impossibly large blue eyes fixed on Adrian, said, "Don't worry, I'm not here to steal Reuben back or anything." She leaned over to Adrian, who just perceptibly leaned away, and said in a fake loud-whispered aside, "I totally dodged a bullet when we split." Then, to both of them, she said, "I'm actually here for the weekend with my fiancé, Asher. Oh, but we're totally staying at a hotel this time—a chichi place right by Lake Champagne." Her nervous chatter felt so familiar to Reuben.

"Plain. Champlain," he corrected.

A bit of fluffy pollen landed on Adrian's shoulder. She plucked and released it, watching it float away as she said, "It would be lovely to chat more, but I just returned from a trip myself, so I have some unpacking to do. And I'm sure you two have things to catch up on. Enjoy your visit, Hannah."

Everything felt off-kilter to Reuben, like he was on an amusement park ride where things unexpected and a little scary jumped out as you moved through a darkened tunnel. Adrian's presence, now in the house, felt particularly charged as if he'd done something wrong.

"Why don't we go for a walk," he suggested to Hannah. "It's a quiet road, hardly any cars come through."

They walked side by side in silence to the end of the driveway, as if they needed distance from the house before speaking. Across the street, a single goat lifted its head, the lower jaw working in rhythmic circles as it stared, flatly unimpressed by Reuben and Hannah's presence. Farther out in the field, someone in a wide-brimmed hat—perhaps the guy from the truck at the hardware store—was walking among the rest of the herd as if through a waist-high flood. The person looked up, but quickly turned away before Reuben could toss a wave, as he had gotten in the habit of doing when encountering the rare person along the road.

"Adrian seems nice," Hannah said. And then, "Actually, that's not honest. She seems kind of cold. Nothing personal."

"Well, you did kind of catch us by surprise."

"Even still, you know I can read people. But I get it. She's not at all like me. She might even be good for you. I've ended up with a guy who's a one-eighty from you. He's funny and outgoing. Total optimist despite being a forensic investigator—which, how cool is that? And oh. He. Is. Gorgeous." She tilted her head at Reuben as if trying to figure something out. "Your hair's long. And that beard. Kind of got a Jesus thing going on."

For this observation and everything else that had occurred that day, Reuben's patience had frayed to a thread. "Why are you here, Hannah?"

Hannah took the kind of long slow breath he knew that she used to settle and focus her mind. When they came, her words were carefully enunciated, as if scripted. "I wanted to see you so I could apologize for stabbing you. I was not my best self in that moment."

Reuben's fingers wandered to the scars on his left hand, feeling the four small indentations there. The gesture brought him back to those dark, foggy days, wallowing and recovering in the tiny room. He felt a flash of anger. "I certainly hope the bar for being 'your best self' is a little higher than not stabbing people. You could have ended my career. Do you know that? It took three months before I could even pick up a brush."

"I know," Hannah said quietly, even a little shamed. "It was terrible." She corrected herself, "I was terrible. All I can say for myself is that you ripped my heart out, barehanded, and held it pulsing and spurting blood all over that lacy, white tablecloth—"

"I get the metaphor."

"But what I have since learned, with the help of a counselor and a low-dose prescription medication is that I only saw you how I wanted to see you. Not how you actually were."

"And how was I actually?"

"I don't know. Honestly, I don't think you knew either. So I filled in the blanks for you."

"Not exactly blanks—" But in a way, this made sense to Reuben, how from the beginning, he often felt like Hannah was dragging him by the wrist rather than him traveling beside her.

"Back then, if someone asked me to describe you, I would talk about what you do. 'Reuben does art. Reuben goes with me to shows. Reuben sings in the shower.'"

"I never sing in the shower."

She rolled her eyes. "I'm trying to make the point that if I had to tell someone what you cared about. What made you excited or really mad—not just 'I-asked-for-no-mayo mad'—I would hear crickets in my brain. And if I didn't know the answers after living together and screwing together and doing laundry and day-tripping and watching movies together, maybe you didn't know either." She paused to take a breath. "So even though I thought it was the thing that could most bring us together, getting married would have been a huge mistake. Like pairing an exotic mango with a plain old parsnip."

"This is what your counselor told you?"

"Not a direct quote."

Reuben kicked a rock at his feet and watched it veer off into a ditch.

"I guess your counselor isn't totally wrong." And it was satisfying to know that building his life here seemed to have given him a better sense of the things that mattered to him—his friends and lover, his sculptures, his home and the garden. "Well then, I'm glad you found someone who is more pineapple than parsnip."

"Oh gawd, me too. Plus I'm so much calmer now!" Reuben must have raised an eyebrow, not seeing that particular change. "Maybe not on the outside, but my inner dialogues... they used to be so vicious. You don't know, but I carried a lot of anger back then. And jealousy of other people's happiness. I worked hard to cover it up, but I was like a super-dark, bitter-chocolate cake pop covered in a thick layer of pretty pink fondant. It's why I reacted the way I did when you dumped me. All those eyes, looking at me, silently deciding for themselves why you wouldn't want to marry me."

"You have to admit, proposing in public probably wasn't the best approach."

Hannah shrugged. "Better for you though. Without witnesses, your injuries would have been much more serious."

Reuben laughed until he saw the grave look on her face.

She slapped him hard on the arm. "Bah-hahaha! You're still so easy to get!"

CHAPTER 17

Throughout his career, Reuben had often been asked how he could tell when a piece was "done." There were other artists he knew who struggled with this, always seeing something they could add or change, the ones who really had to force themselves to step away to break the loop of endless revisions. While Reuben might make tiny corrections here or there before turning over the finished work, he almost always knew when a piece was complete. Putting the feeling into words people could relate to, he would say it was like reading the last sentence of a book, how that period means there's no more story left to read, even if the feelings may resonate well after you close the cover.

And so, that Sunday at 10:36 a.m., Reuben officially set down his brush on a painting for Ellie's real estate office. He was generally happy with the outcome—an engaging, pleasing-to-look-at design created around the gold-and-blue-toned color palette she'd requested. It wasn't going to awe anyone, but it wasn't supposed to.

Reuben found himself thinking that this moment of completion was a kind of conceptual counterpart to Kip's idea of the starting moment. What he'd said was true: beginnings and endings happen all the time, and we almost never acknowledge, let alone notice them. Reuben took a few steps back, and was still, letting the moment settle over him. He thought maybe this pause, this acknowledgement should be a new ritual.

A light knock interrupted Reuben's thoughts. "Yeah?" he asked.

"There's something...going on," Adrian said through the door.

"That sounds concerning." Reuben slid the door open.

"I've been on the porch reading for the last forty-five minutes, and in that time, five cars have turned onto the road, slowed down to the point of stopping in front of the house, and then drove off. I thought maybe there's a party somewhere in the neighborhood, and people are looking for the address. But then, you got this text from Rosemary." She handed Reuben his phone.

> I sure hope Joy Adams got it wrong and there's some other artist from CT who put up a Jesus scarecrow.

Adrian asked, "Is Joy the woman with the dog from yesterday?"

Reuben grunted in response. "What, did she go door-to-door telling people?"

But Adrian already knew how word had gotten around and was pulling it up on her own phone. "It's the B3."

Orrville Neighborhood Forum No. 3560
Shocking Discovery

JOY ADAMS, ADAMSFAMILYVT@YAHOO.COM, CHEESE FACTORY ROAD, ORRVILLE

As former Treasurer of the Orrville Select Board, I feel it is my responsibility to inform the community about a disturbing sight at 3231 Popple Hill Road. The owner, who I understand is a newly arrived so-called artist from Connecticut, has put up a life-size statue of Jesus Christ dressed as a scarecrow. I don't know what community standards are like where he comes from, but around here, this kind of offensive art has no place. Whatever the motivation or statement he's trying to make, it is extremely offensive and should be taken down immediately.

Adrian let out a hefty sigh. "At least she didn't mention you by name. Can you please take that thing down now?"

Reuben took a moment to process the situation. Not only had he been "outed" publicly for something he'd done privately, now his house was being gawked at.

"Come with me." He took Adrian by the wrist.

They went out the studio's back door and headed down the driveway to the road. Starting thirty feet to the left, they walked slowly, Reuben keeping his eyes trained on the house to see if—and if so, where—the scarecrow could be seen. It wasn't until well past the driveway and the mailbox, but before the swath of ferns, that they could see a sliver of a view. But it would be hard to make out the scarecrow if you didn't know what you were looking for.

"This is what's riling people up? It's ridiculous."

Just then, a car slow-rolled up behind them, its driver leaned out the window craning his neck. "Hey, is that the Jesus scarecrow?"

Reuben turned and shouted at him, "It's nobody's business!"

Chastened, the man slowly pulled his elbow back in and continued on his way. Reuben took long strides back up to the house. Adrian jogged to catch him. "What did you expect, Reuben?"

"I'll say it again. It's nobody's business."

"Except it is." She tugged the hem of his t-shirt and made him stop to look at her. "It's my business. If this turns into a thing and becomes associated with your name...as your gallery representative, it is literally my business."

His defensive posture eased a little as the truth of her words sunk in.

Adrian said more gently, "It's just a garden. Why does this even matter to you?"

Reuben could hear another car turn onto the road and slow down by the house. Without turning around he said, "Let's go inside and talk."

◆

They sat facing each other on the couch, Reuben holding a throw pillow against his chest. "You remember my friend Paul?"

Adrian squinted her eyes, "The one whose mother passed away?"

"We lost touch when he moved away suddenly. I only found out why recently." Reuben told her about what happened, the priest's abuse, the diocese cover-up, and the devastating and permanent effect it had on Paul's family.

"He's a grown man, living a functional adult life, but those scars are never going away. He couldn't even stomach going to a church for his own mother's funeral. I know it was decades ago, but now that he's a friend again—even from this distance—hearing about it and talking with him, it made everything real and personal." He played absently with the pillow's zipper, opening and closing it a few times before speaking again. "I didn't consciously set out to make a statement about sex abuse or religious hypocrisy. I didn't intend to create some kind of symbolic solidarity with Paul. But at a certain point, it might have become those things."

Adrian reached out and held his hand. Her expression was open and empathetic. She pulled him over to her, and he laid down lightly on her chest. She said, "We'll keep it up. As long as you want it there, we'll keep it up."

CHAPTER 18

Orrville Neighborhood Forum No. 3561
Regarding Scarecrow

GIANNA AGOSTO, NANAGIANNA8@GMAIL.COM, FASCINATION STREET, ORRVILLE

I second Joy Adams's insistence that the crucifix dressed as a scarecrow be taken down immediately. Other people's sacred objects should never be ridiculed. It's practically hate speech, and I believe the Select Board should take action against this individual if he doesn't comply.

Not Shocked by Shocking Discovery

CARLTON ELLIS, CJELLIS@VTTIME.BUS, TRASH BEAR RD, ORRVILLE

Prompted by Joy Adams's post, I went to see the Jesus scarecrow on Popple Hill. Set back as it is from the road in the owner's backyard, I had to work pretty hard to find it. Which is a useful reminder that not only does the First Amendment apply to everyone, it's especially protected when exercised on one's private property. You don't like the display? Look across the street. There's a charming herd of goats that I'm sure won't offend.

Freedom Of Religion Also Means From It

DARBY ECCLES, DECCLES@STREETMAIL.COM, COTTONWOOD CIRCLE, ORRVILLE

I haven't made my way to see the Jesus dressed as a scarecrow yet, but I have no objection to the point the artist, Reuben Downes, seems to be making—that religion shouldn't take itself so seriously.

Instead, I'd like to use this moment to reignite a conversation started three years ago when the Committee for Inclusion & Equality recommended that the town either represent all faiths throughout the year or decline to display any religiously inspired holiday decorations. As a lifelong atheist, I supported the latter proposal and am dismayed that it has been disregarded every year as the town hall continues to host its annual tree-lighting and Christmas carol-singing event. When our town government privileges the rights of one religion over another's, including nonbelievers', it makes a joke of the idea of the separation of church and state.

Therefore, I will be bringing this issue up at our next Select Board meeting and encourage others to join me in speaking up, once again, to advocate for change.

Scarecrow Jesus

OLIN HASTINGS, ROLLINOLIN@STREETMAIL.COM, BARBARA JEAN RD, ORRVILLE

Seven years ago, clear as day, I saw Jesus working as a tollbooth taker on the New Jersey Turnpike. He wished me a radiant day. Point being, they say God walks among us, and I tend to agree. Maybe He's just doing His part to ensure a good corn harvest?

Tuesday's game against the Muskrats had been canceled on account of a thunderstorm that the weather radar showed would hit in the first inning. The jaw-rattling storm rolled in hard and fast with fierce wind, lightning strikes, and heavy rain. It raged for no more than forty-five minutes and then moved east, but not before leaving behind broken branches that pulled down power lines and caused a handful of outages, including one at Reuben's house—not his first, so he had a ready supply of candles, headlamps, an antique hurricane lantern, and a couple of camping lights from which someone had removed and repurposed the batteries.

Adrian had work to do and decided she might as well go back to the gallery until the electricity was restored, so Reuben sat on the porch, a cold beer in his hand, reveling in the breeze that tailed the storm, a merciful break from the high heat and humidity of the past few days. Lou Garoo napped in a tight ball at his feet. His bitten ear now scabbed over and mostly healed, both the cat and Adrian insisted he be released from the confines of the laundry room. But just that short time of bonding over food and litter box cleaning had caused the cat to develop a cautious tolerance to Reuben's presence, and it moved him to think that the smallest amount of care gave Lou Garoo some interest in being less solitary.

If there was an upside to the power being out, it was that Reuben was forced to delay seeing the evening's B3 until he had a chance to charge the low battery on his phone. Far from winding down, the posts just continued, sparking offshoot bickering between residents about freedom and blasphemy and definitions of art. Several people seemed particularly agitated by the fact that Reuben hadn't responded to explain or defend his actions, which was even less likely now that people were insisting on it.

The evening was a beautiful pause from controversy, from work. There was nothing but this moment of calm. He could still hear the occasional low rumble from over the mountain, but the sky, now clear of fat thunderheads, was turning a dark slate blue. The lightning bugs had started to appear in the last few days, their intermittent signals flashing across the yard's vastness. There were sounds, too, low whirs and whistles of toads, the scritches of katydids.

Right here, Reuben thought, *this is all I need.*

But his reverie was broken when an extra-wide pickup truck, its high beams bouncing, came firing down the road. When it made a sharp turn into Reuben's driveway and came up toward the house, Reuben instinctively grabbed the baseball bat from the gear bag he'd set on the porch earlier that day.

The truck came to a stop just before the walkway began. The driver's door popped open. Reuben couldn't see the figure clearly, but could tell it was a big, broad-shouldered man. Reuben lifted the bat, propping the barrel in his left hand, trying to look menacing, like an old-timey union thug.

"Man, put that thing away, Popple. You're gonna hurt yourself."

"Jackson?" Reuben let the bat drop. "What the hell?"

Jackson Endicott lumbered toward the house. He was holding something in his right hand. "Didn't mean to alarm you. Mind if I come up?"

"The power's out. It's not really a good time."

"Y'know, I can get you a good price on a generator."

"You came out here to give me a sales pitch?"

Jackson laughed. "Heck, no. I came to lend a little moral support. Course, Joy Adams might call it immoral support." When Reuben didn't crack a smile, Jackson said, "Jesus H. Christmas, lighten up. I'm on your side."

"That's surprising."

"Popple, I'm full of surprises." The steps creaked under Jackson's substantial weight as he stepped up onto the porch. Lou Garoo lifted his head sharply, then bolted away toward the barn. Now, up close, Reuben could see Jackson was carrying a bottle of whiskey—he held it up like a rabbit he'd just killed with his bare hands. "You got a couple glasses?"

Reuben considered saying that he preferred to be left alone in the dark to admire the fireflies, but it was just the kind of thing Jackson Endicott would turn against him on his next visit to the hardware store: *Over here in the kiddie section, we got some bug cages. Or maybe an ant farm is more your thing?* Besides, the man brought whiskey. What's more, Reuben realized he was genuinely curious to hear what Jackson had to say.

"Yeah. I'll go get 'em."

"Before you do...can I see it? Scarecrow Jesus, I mean. No jokes, I promise."

"At this point, I'm not really hiding it." Reuben reached for the matches and lit the red hurricane lantern. The smell of burning kerosene filled the air as he led the way along the path to the backyard. "Watch your step. Some of the flagstones are loose."

Reuben stopped at the crucifix and held the lantern up like a Scooby Doo specter. "Jackson...Jesus. Jesus...Jackson. Maybe you're already acquainted."

Jackson nodded his head slowly as he approached. "It's bigger'n I was expecting. Never thought of it before, but it makes sense as a scarecrow, the arms being out and all."

"That's what I said! I have to believe I'm not the first person to do this."

"Not sure many people can get their hands on an eight-foot-tall crucifix."

Reuben explained where he'd gotten it, and what David said about how it had been used. Jackson recalled a similar Easter holiday display at a church in the town his cousin grew up in.

"I remember passing that purple sash every year when we'd go over for the egg hunt," he said. He kept talking as they walked back toward the porch. "And anyway, it's not like you can just toss something like that in the landfill or add it to the burn pile when it's no longer wanted. The B3's server would explode over that. Plus, I'm a big believer in upcycling. Waste not, want not 'n all. My wife's friend, she makes mittens out of old sweaters—they're the warmest."

Having only interacted with him through intimidating retail transactions, Reuben was surprised at what a talker Jackson was. But there was still the question of why he'd stopped by. Reuben went inside to retrieve some glasses. He returned a few minutes later, also carrying a bowl of pretzels.

They sat in the porch chairs, and Jackson poured a rough dram for each of them. Then he lifted his glass and said, "*I will do nothing because of public opinion, but everything because of conscience.*" When Reuben looked at him uncomprehendingly, Jackson said, "Seneca the Younger."

"You weren't kidding when you said you were full of surprises. And apparently, random quotes."

"Look, public opinion is almost always about people sticking their noses where they don't belong. What I'm trying to say is, noses don't belong in your backyard."

"You're not curious as to why I put it up?"

"Irrelevant."

"So you think I should just leave it?"

"You're not hearing our friend Seneca. You're the captain of your ship, Popple. You're the one who should decide how and where to steer it. Well, and maybe that pretty gallery lady you live with since it's her home, too."

Reuben's face must have expressed surprise that Jackson knew about Adrian.

"Word gets around. As you now know." He smirked, taking a bite of a pretzel.

"I can't figure you out, Jackson."

"Well, you're not the first."

"I mean, from day one, you were needling me, making me feel like a complete idiot. There were times when I drove fifteen miles out of my way to get something I knew you had in the store. Is that what you want?"

"Course not. But I don't blame you." Jackson swirled the whiskey around in his glass. "I don't always have a good barometer for when funny's not funny for everyone."

They sat for a moment just looking out at the yard, nature's summer party scene teeming with bugs and amphibians and bats flapping erratically overhead. A scene of sex and death.

"This Seneca guy," Reuben said, "he a hero of yours or something?"

"Let's just say I'm well-read on the Stoics."

"Now there's something you don't hear every day."

"Philosophy is a hobby of mine. I started my degree in it, but when my dad's health started failing, I left school to take over the store so my melon-head brother wouldn't run it into the ground." He poured them both another splash of whiskey. "That was almost twenty years ago." He seemed surprised by the number. "As for the Stoics, they believed that worrying about events that aren't in your control creates unnecessary grief. That always made sense to me."

"I'm not going to lie, Jackson, I'm still not putting the pieces together as to why you came out here tonight."

He nodded. "I don't know where you grew up—and don't take this the wrong way—but I suspect you're not especially experienced with the vagaries of small-town living."

Go figure, Reuben thought. "Yeah, I moved around a lot as a kid. And then it was suburbs and city living until I landed here."

"So here's one way to understand it. Imagine a fish tank, one of those twenty-gallon rectangle things with the sunken ship, plastic sea plants, and that bubbly treasure chest. When the tank is filled with a couple dozen fish—all kinds of fish—swimming this way and that, they go about their business, eating, shitting, and staying alive. They don't notice much when a new fish is added to the tank because there's so many that as long as it doesn't get up in their business, it's just another fish. That's city living. Now keep that same tank but have maybe six or seven fish floating around in it, they're gonna be more attentive to changes in their space. And when a new fish is introduced, they might get a little territorial. You see what I'm getting at?"

"I'm the new fish."

"Mind you, most folks will just see you as a curiosity, nothing more. But a handful are going to project their fears of 'the Other' onto you. You can read some Hegel regarding that topic. Or Sartre. Or Simone de Beauvoir for a feminist perspective."

"Now you're just showing off."

There was a sudden buzz-click from inside the house as the electricity kicked back on. The light was jarring, like closing time at the bar when the blinking patrons adjust their eyes to really see the people they've been hitting on all night.

Reuben drained the last of the whiskey in his glass, feeling a little buzzed. "You're making it hard to keep disliking you, Endicott."

"Don't you worry. You'll still get plenty of crap when you come into the store. I have a reputation to maintain." He handed Reuben the half-empty bottle. "It'll take some time, but the brouhaha will settle whether you take the scarecrow down or leave it up. But I meant what I said.

Let it be on your terms, not Joy's or Patton's, or anyone else's."

"Wait, who's Patton?"

Jackson just laughed and walked down the steps to his truck. He held up a hand as he reversed out the driveway, lights bouncing backward like a fast rewind of when he first showed up.

CHAPTER 19

VERMONT INDEPENDENT WEEKLY
Crucifixation! "Scarecrow Jesus" Has the Orrville Community Up in Arms

By Patton Papadopoulos, published July 15, 2016

When Joy Adams's dog snapped his leash and chased a cat into her nearby neighbor Reuben Downes's backyard, Adams had no idea she would make a discovery that would spark a townwide debate about free speech and blasphemy. Then again, when the 42-year-old Orrville resident took to the town's Backyard Bulletin Board, raising her concern about the nearly life-size crucifix featuring Jesus Christ dressed as a scarecrow presiding over a vegetable garden, controversy seemed likely to ensue.

Downes, who made Orrville his home over a year ago, may be familiar to those in the local arts scene as a talented abstract painter whose commercial work can be seen in environments as diverse as The Hotel Champlain, Alastor Wine Bar, and the Capitol Medical Center. His collector pieces, often shown at Gallery Fifth in Burlington, include smaller, more intimate paintings and the occasional whimsical, sculpture made from repurposed scrap metals, antique tools, hardware, and the like.

So is the installation—now dubbed "Scarecrow Jesus"—intended as a sculpture? Performance art? Political statement? Downes is keeping mum on the matter and declined to respond to the paper's outreach efforts. In fact, Adams is the only concerned party that has been able to speak with him about the display. "He provided no explanation whatsoever and completely dismissed my concerns when I confronted him. The man was more worried about his melting ice cream than he was about causing distress to his neighbors." Along with Adams, other community members' demands for the crucifix's removal have been ignored.

While some residents have speculated Downes has an axe to grind with the

Catholic Church, others see a more spiritual motivation, including Reverend Claire Beaudry, senior minister of Burlington's First Unitarian Universalist Society.

"What could be more human than asking the Divine to protect our crops and provide a healthy, bountiful harvest? Corinthians 9:10 says, 'For God is the one who provides seed for the farmer and then bread to eat.'" Beaudry continued, "Without an artist's statement, we should assume good intent. In this way, we send positive rather than negative energy out to the world, compassion rather than aggression."

And indeed, this range of public opinion may be precisely the objective behind Reuben Downes's silence, as people project their own experiences and beliefs onto Scarecrow Jesus. Still, the fact that the installation is squarely in the artist's rural backyard, difficult for anyone to view without trespassing, makes it seem plausible that the crucifix was never intended to be seen. Meanwhile, the community's free-speech advocates have publicly urged Downes to move Scarecrow Jesus to the front yard, in full view, to reinforce the point that this expression is protected by the First Amendment—and not simply because it is on the artist's private property.

For now, it seems Scarecrow Jesus is staying put even as the controversy continues to swirl in the community. Some, including Adams herself, have suggested the Select Board take up the issue by establishing community standards—a process that could take several months, at which point Vermont's growing season will have been put to bed. Will Halloween see Scarecrow Jesus donning spookier duds? God—or perhaps, Reuben Downes—only knows.

It was true, Patton Papadopoulos had tried to reach Reuben three times before the Wednesday morning publication, each message urging him to "take control of the narrative" by giving a statement, written or verbal, that could be included in the article. Reuben's "narrative" was simply that he wanted to be left alone.

It seemed that Patton Papadopoulos, in his hunt for an Orrville source that wasn't on the Select Board, had reached out to Jackson, representative of the town's oldest family and community commerce center, which, in turn, had prompted Jackson's visit.

The newspaper's statewide circulation meant the story had now officially spilled beyond Orrville, and Reuben's "no comment" stance was going to become increasingly difficult to maintain. In fact, when Reuben arrived at the field for practice that evening, he could see most of the Mallards were gathered around Donny, some standing, some sitting on the bench, as he read to them from what must have been the article. Reuben could feel his stomach twist, not sure what he was going to say to everyone once he finally reached the dugout.

"Here's the man of the week himself," Wayne chuckled. "Kicked up quite the hornet's nest, Downes."

Reuben set his gear on the ground. "Yeah. I, um . . . I don't want to go into a whole explanation or anything. I just don't really want to talk about it. I hope you guys know it's never my intent to hurt anyone."

Maddy chuffed. "That's a whole lot of not-answers." She snapped a ball hard into her mitt a few times, leaving Reuben to wonder what kind of answers she had been expecting.

Kip was amused. Patrice seemed pensive. The Erins were doing farm things at the farm. Joss and Cameron elbowed each other in the ribs which turned into hard, playful shoving before they took to the field. It was practice time, and thankfully the team had more important things to do. Tomorrow's game was against the Jays, and the Mallards would need to be in top form to beat them.

"Reuben, you run the infield, and I'll catch Maddy's bullpen," said Wayne.

Patrice approached Reuben and spoke quietly. "People get very charged about their gods, I know. I also trust that your heart has its reasons." He squeezed Reuben's shoulder and then jogged off. Reuben pulled his bat from the gear bag thinking about how different Patrice was from his own high school guidance counselor whose most frequent advice to him was, "Try harder to fit in."

As Maddy walked off toward the sideline, Reuben tried to catch up to her for a quick update on the cat, but she was moving too quickly, seemingly intent on not engaging with him. Her back turned to him felt like an unexpected wall. He decided not to follow her and instead went to retrieve the bag of balls.

Kip was on the bench switching over to his cleats. "Not exactly the ideal way to get your name in the papers."

"This really shouldn't have been a thing. I figured it would just die down. But it keeps getting weirder. A couple nights ago Jackson Endicott showed up on my doorstep, spouting philosophy like some weird love child of Yoda and The Rock."

"Can't unsee that in my mind, thanks."

Reuben pointed his chin in Maddy's direction. "Hey, does she seem off to you today?"

"Hard saying not knowing."

"What does that mean?"

"It means people have their days."

"Okay, but do you think it's something personal? Like, with me?"

"What makes you ask that?"

Reuben realized Kip didn't have the context behind Reuben's question, specifically, that he and Maddy had enjoyed a fun and friendly time together the week before when she'd come over to help with Lou Garoo. "No, just, you know, I thought she and I were building a pitcher-catcher rapport, that's all. Nothing more than that."

"I will say that in seasons past—before you came along—Joss nicknamed her 'Moody' on account of how she'd sometimes not talk to anyone at practice or in a game. Not a single word. She'd just do her pitching thing and head home right after."

"What do you mean, before I came along?"

Kip looked at Reuben with a sardonic expression, "I think you know what I mean." He got up and headed toward the field.

His words echoed in Reuben's head. "What? No, I don't." He chased Kip down and leaned in close, whispering. "Are you suggesting Maddy might . . . might . . . what?"

Kip regarded him again with a sly smile in the corner of his eyes. "Maybe you don't see the way she looks at you, but I sure do."

On reflex, Reuben turned to Maddy off on the sidelines where she was saying something to Wayne as she stretched her arm sideways across her chest. "No way." Reuben said. "It's your imagination. Besides, from what I experienced just now, she's not interested in even being near me."

"Well, she grew up in a cult. That's what Joss said, anyway. So you never know."

"Kip, I can't even piece together all the things you're saying right now."

"Downes!" Wayne shouted. "You holding a press conference or something? Get a move!"

Adrian was on the porch when Reuben got home in the early evening. Her eyes followed him up the walkway. She had an energy that seemed to suggest she'd been waiting for him; he assumed he knew why. Reuben dropped his gear bag and sat in the chair beside her. There was no way she hadn't seen the *Weekly*. And yet, it wasn't the first thing she chose to talk about.

"Did you have dinner?" she asked. "I brought home some Thai takeout. I'll reheat it for you."

"That's okay, I had a sandwich before practice."

"How'd it go?" Her tone was upbeat. "Are you guys pumped for the Jays?" She flexed in a body builder's pose. "They're going to come out swingin' tomorrow."

"Punny, yes."

Maddy had been on fire during practice. Fast and hard enough to bruise Reuben's hand. And he could tell she was pitching to spots and hitting them, following a deliberate order, something he hadn't seen her do before: low inside, low outside, high inside, high outside, and then smack down the middle. But the Mallards' practice was uncharacteristically sloppy. Grounders were missed. "Hey, Joss, you got cement in your shoes?" Plays to first were overthrown. And underthrown. "Is there a fucking force field around me?" Hitting was lackluster. "Damn, Kipper, you deserve two strikes for that sissy swing."

"If we play like today's practice, they're going to slaughter us." Reuben settled back in the chair, but not too comfortably, as he was still wondering what she would say about the article. "At least it's not a playoff game. You know, if they win, they win."

"Yeah, but it'll wreck Wayne for days if you lose. Are all his various and sundry injuries healed these days?"

"More or less. I swear that guy has a brace on every joint. Still, he's out there in the field and pounding the crap out of pitches."

The front yard scene wasn't quite as magical as it had been the other night after the storm, but the lightning bugs were firing up again, and the frogs just starting to trill.

Reuben decided to throw open the conversation. "Did you see it? The article?"

Adrian nodded.

"Any fallout yet?"

She flinched just the slightest bit. "Not exactly. But I have some different news to share with you."

Please don't tell me you're pregnant, he thought. In an instant, his mind became a runaway train imagining that her birth control had failed (or she stopped taking it?), and what kind of father would he be with his own lousy father as a role model? Not to mention childcare was scarce and ridiculously expensive—would he have to become a stay-at-home dad?

"Reuben, are you even listening to me?" Adrian was watching, waiting for him to say something about whatever she had just told him.

He tried to buy time. "I'm processing."

"What's to process? It's an amazing opportunity. The gallery is in an up-and-coming neighborhood in Montreal, and the exposure for your work will be fantastic."

The mental train tracks took an abrupt turn. "I'm confused, Ade. Why would a gallery in Montreal have any interest in me?"

"Because I told them about you."

Lou Garoo appeared suddenly like a phantom. The cat threaded figure eights between Reuben's ankles, ingratiatingly reminding him that the food bowl needed filling. Reuben nudged him away, wanting instead to put together the pieces behind Adrian's news.

"Why would you do that?"

Her hesitation was palpable, and she seemed to choose her words carefully.

"It just seemed that, given everything going on, it might be a good time to take steps toward decoupling our personal and professional worlds a bit."

Reuben leaned forward, elbows on his knees. He prodded the tender bruise on his catching hand. The pain brought into focus what Adrian was telling him. "You're kicking me out of the gallery?"

"It's not like that."

"Don't you think we should have talked about it? That I might have an interest in the direction of my own career? You just went ahead and pimped me out to some unknown gallery owner?"

"That's a bit dramatic. And he's not unknown. He's a friend of John's." Adrian immediately realized her mistake.

"Eastlake? This is him pulling strings."

"No, Reuben. It's me. I'm making the call. And frankly, it's something we should have done when we first decided to live together. Instead, I've been on my heels trying to put out a public relations fire before it becomes one. And now, with the gallery named in that article, it's too late."

"You said to keep it up." He pointed toward the back yard. "Keep it up as long as I needed to."

"And I'm honoring that by finding you a new gallery—"

"In Canada!"

"—a better gallery!"

"Without any input from me."

"You know, if you and I weren't together, I would have just cut you loose, no soft landing."

Reuben stood, sending Lou Garoo scrambling for the bushes. "But we are together. We're domestic and business partners." And then at the word "partner," a thought occurred to Reuben. "Does he get a cut?"

"What?"

"Eastlake. Does he get a cut of your sales?"

"What is your obsession with John?"

"Does he?"

"I don't know how this conversation went so sideways. I was just trying to—"

"Is John Eastlake still your business partner?" He enunciated each word.

"Gallery Fifth is my business, my name on the lease."

"You're still avoiding the question."

Adrian seemed furious. Nostrils flared, her eyes sharp. "Fine. Yes. As an initial investor, our contract stipulates that he gets a percentage of every sale. And yes, John was concerned that this controversy was going to blow back on the gallery." Reuben started to speak, but Adrian cut him off. "I agreed with him, so he gave me some names to reach out to. This was the first one I called. Are you happy now?"

"Are *you* happy? That he gets to tell you what to do with your business?"

Reuben could see he struck a nerve. She stood now, looking at him eye to eye. "You think you're different from him? When you first started talking about your project with Kip, do you remember what you said to me? You said, 'Let's look at the calendar and see when we can do an exhibit.' You didn't ask if it was something I would consider. You didn't wonder if your 'maple syrup' display was appropriate for the gallery or our clientele. You didn't care that the space you'd need would have squeezed out another artist."

"That's completely not the same thing, and you know it."

"It comes from the same place, Reuben. You. John. You all think you know how to run my business better than me." She held up a business card so Reuben could see it, then placed it on the side table. "Talk to the guy in Montreal or don't. It's your choice. But I can't represent you anymore."

She went inside, letting the screen door swing and slam behind her.

◆

They didn't speak again that evening. Adrian staked her claim to the bedroom, while Reuben hunkered down in the studio. He started a new canvas, letting the emotions express themselves in stormy charcoal and orange flares. But it felt too obvious, a sloppy art vomit, and so he tossed his brushes aside and collapsed into the couch. He popped on his headphones and fed his ears a gritty, garage punk playlist kicking off with "Goofy's Concern" and all the things Gibby Haynes doesn't give a fuck about. The songs were ideal company, a crew of rowdy friends encouraging and justifying his indignant mood.

Reuben had no idea how long he'd lost himself in the music but by the time he turned his attention back outward, the near-full moon was casting a milky hue over the garden and grass. Set against the darker woods and distant mountains, the scene—complete with a looming Scarecrow Jesus—looked like a film negative. A breeze coming in from the open windows seemed to hint at fall, still weeks away, but already Reuben had noticed earlier that day, the vibrant ridgeline greens were starting to fade just a touch.

Picking up his phone, Reuben saw it was just past eleven. He checked email—skipping over the B3—then opened a browser and typed the name of the gallery from the card Adrian had given him: Gallerie la Genèse. The site that came up was well designed, clean and modern, but with a playful tone and energy. He toggled the site for English translation.

There were some impressive pieces based on what he could tell from digital photos. Reuben could see an affinity between his work and theirs, though each was distinctly different: a range of mediums, diversity of styles. The closest to Reuben's sculpture work was an artist that went simply by the name Sandrine who made elegant dresses—hoop skirts, bustles, corset tops—from hardware pieces, metal sheets, and fragments, *Cotte des Mailles Feminine/Women's Chainmail*, she called it. The gallery appeared to be housed in a restored factory with high open ceilings featuring a maze of duct work, the industrial tubes and elbows offering their own ambient display. The gallery owner was Marc Barthelme, a man roughly Reuben's age, whose photo seemed warm and unpretentious. From what could be garnered from the site, the gallery was a substantially large space, one that offered big city exposure.

His adrenaline now calmed, Reuben had to admit it was, without a doubt, a lucky leapfrog of a career move. No, not lucky. Orchestrated, he reminded himself. Still, the disgust he felt for John Eastlake didn't rise again. Maybe Reuben was tired. Or maybe deep down, he understood that, although he wished she'd talked to him first, Adrian's intent had come from a reasonable place.

It was tempting to quietly climb the stairs and slide into bed with her, but Reuben wasn't yet feeling magnanimous enough to say he was sorry. Instead, he decided to keep some space, and in the morning, he would get up early to cook scrambled eggs with fresh herbs and cherry tomatoes from the garden. An apology in gesture, if not words.

Reuben changed the music to Coltrane and stretched out fully on the couch, sinking into its surprisingly comfortable, if a little short, embrace. Not quite ready to doze off, his mind was tugged back to softball practice and Kip's suggestion that Maddy had feelings for him. Reuben had chalked up his own benign attraction to Maddy simply to the fact that she was, well, attractive. Even if Kip was right, her interest was probably just as superficial. And yet, he seemed to suggest it might be more. Could it be more? Could Reuben's own feelings potentially be something more?

This line of thinking was neither good nor appropriate—an unexpected smoke bomb that made things suddenly confusing and hard to see. But eventually, the air would clear, and the world would go back to what it was. Maddy would move past whatever was troubling her during practice, and the next evening, the Mallards and the Jays would have a tough but ultimately fun game. One team would win, one would lose.

As for Adrian, Reuben could now see that untethering their professional ties would give them a chance to reset and bring a new clarity to their relationship, maybe even a first step toward something deeper and more committed.

Reuben decided that over breakfast the next morning, he would share his newfound enthusiasm for ending their gallery contract, and together they would draft a carefully worded joint statement to stem any Scarecrow Jesus related fallout for Gallery Fifth. The two of them would make an appointment to meet Marc Barthelme together. They could book a room at a boutique hotel in the city, spend a couple days visiting the food markets, shopping the bohemian neighborhoods, taking in the street performers, eating exquisitely rich French food, and maybe hitting a late-night jazz club. Reuben liked this plan, and for the first time all day, he felt settled, drifting off to the upbeat riffs and runs of a quartet playing in his ears.

CHAPTER 20

The next morning, Reuben woke to the smell of brewing coffee. He blinked away the blurriness and unfolded his body from a mediocre but not terrible night's sleep. He slid open the studio door and followed his nose to the kitchen. Adrian was seated with a steaming cup in front of her. When she saw him, she poured coffee into an empty mug at his place. Reuben smiled, drawing in a deep breath of coffee aroma and sighing out a swell of affection.

He leaned over to deliver a good morning, make-up kiss but stopped when he saw the stuffed duffel bag by her ankle. His heart flopped in his chest, a gasping fish in the bottom of a boat.

"Oh, come on, don't do this," sadness soaking his words.

Her eyes were glassy, he could tell. She said, "Sit with me."

Reuben urgently needed to reel the situation back. "No, wait. Just listen. I spent a lot of time thinking last night, and you're right. Ending the gallery contract is the best thing. It'll allow us to start fresh and just be a couple for once. Let's just try that. We'll take it one month at a time. No pressure."

She looked down at her mug as if into a deep well. "You know, I was so young when I had Leila. The father was a guy I barely knew who wanted nothing to do with us. I was just out of college and terrified, but determined I would never move back in with my mother. And that meant it was all on me to care for this baby. To find work and someplace to live, to shop and pay the bills. It was hard. God, it was so hard. But it also made me really proud." She took a sip and held the cup, warming her hands. "Those early years shaped who I am. And I know it sounds selfish and rigid, but I don't like sharing decisions. The hard truth that I now understand is that I don't want to intertwine my life with yours, Reuben. Or anyone's. I love you, I do. But I like myself so much better on my own."

What could he say to that? Reuben knew Adrian well enough to recognize that these were the missing puzzle pieces that fit. It cut deeply to hear her say it, but her words made sense. When people described Adrian as "aloof" or "cool," what that really meant was that she was comfortably detached.

"But you were right about something, too," she said. "I need to cut those ties with John. He took a chance on me when no one else would, and I felt indebted to him. But a lot of time has passed, and I've not only repaid that debt, I've given him a healthy profit. So today, I have an appointment at the bank to get a loan to buy the building outright."

Reuben nodded, too distracted by their breakup to feel any satisfaction in the news that she was also giving Eastlake the boot.

Adrian slid a sheet of paper over to him. "It's not an official document, but I printed something up for us to sign in case the bank has concerns about boycotts or anything directed at the gallery. It just says we've terminated . . ." She was clamping down hard on her emotions, her jaw tight and unmovable.

For the briefest moment, Reuben thought about pushing the printout back at her unsigned. He could reach out to a lawyer and pursue a breach of contract. But he knew enough to recognize that his impulse came from a place of raw hurt and a desire to hurt back.

"I'm sorry, Reuben," Adrian said.

He gnawed at the inside of his lip a moment before taking the pen from her and, without reading, Reuben signed his name and dated it, July 17, 2016. An ending—firm, unequivocal. He stood up. The fired artist, jilted lover in his slept-in boxers and t-shirt. Reuben rejected the coffee she had poured for him and left the room without another word.

Reuben wanted to be the kind of guy who stiff-upper-lipped it, so that two weeks later when someone asked about Adrian, he would say, "Yeah, it didn't work out. We decided to just be friends." Instead, later that day, he sent a text to Rosemary.

> Adrian ended things. No stab wounds.

Rosemary responded right away.

> That's too bad. The dumping part, I mean.

A couple seconds later, she sent:

> Gonna drop off blondies for the team since I can't make the game. Be by in an hour.

The cookie bars were still warm when Rosemary arrived. Their sweet, butterscotch aroma escaping through the foil made Reuben want to take them under his arm, lock himself in the studio and eat the entire batch by himself. Rosemary looked at him hard. He was unshowered, wearing the same rumpled t-shirt (though he did manage to put on shorts); his eyes were puffy and tired, his shoulders sunken forward.

"She for-good gone? You sure about it?"

"She took a bag of stuff back to her house. Going to come by tonight to pack up the rest while I'm at the game." Reuben let out a dramatic sigh. "It's not much for her to pack though. I feel like, maybe, she always had one foot out the door."

Rosemary patted him hard on the upper arm. "Some people just aren't cut out for the long haul. That doesn't make her a bad person," she said. "You go put those in the kitchen." She repositioned the straps of a canvas bag over her shoulder. "Then meet me out back."

"What for?"

"Dirt therapy."

Under the outstretched arms of Scarecrow Jesus, they sweated in the garden, Rosemary in her giant sunhat and garden clogs, Reuben reapplying sunblock to his sticky neck and forearms. They mercilessly pulled weeds, hacked at the dandelions and tough-rooted crabgrass. There was good satisfaction in taming the wild tangles competing for sunlight and nutrients against the domesticated carrots and pole bean vines. Rosemary scolded Reuben for failing to hill the potatoes, saying, "Nobody likes green potatoes." She had him uproot the lettuces and spinach plants that had "bolted" and were now too bitter to enjoy.

The small heads of young sunflowers were like curious spectators watching them work. But beyond the bits of affectionate needling, Rosemary and Reuben spoke little. By design, Reuben thought, remembering how after Hannah left, Rosemary had kept him busy with chores around the inn, how she believed there was healing in the meditative aspects of work.

But then, Rosemary opened a conversation, "So what are you doing about this guy?" She nodded her head toward the crucifix.

"Seriously, you too?"

"Well, you pissed off Joy Adams. You landed yourself in the newspaper. You lost your girlfriend. I figure you must have a good reason for keeping it up, let alone installing it in the first place."

Reuben stabbed the trowel into the dirt and snapped, "What if I don't? What if I put it up as a joke because I'm an asshole who hates religion and neighbors and girlfriends?"

Leaning on the long-handled hoe, Rosemary laughed, "Well, I suppose it's better to be an asshole with a cause than just a regular old asshole."

A chickadee landed on the outstretched arm of Scarecrow Jesus. It combed a tiny beak through its chest feathers, then tilted its head, as if it, too, expected a response. Reuben stood, brushing the dirt from his hands and slowly rolled up to standing.

While he knew Rosemary would be an open, if not entirely sympathetic ear, he just didn't feel inclined to talk about it. Instead, he said, "What I can tell you is this. I put up the scarecrow for reasons that, at the time, seemed less complicated than they became. And what was supposed to be a private, personal expression has been blown far out of context. Now, every day, people I don't even know feel like they're owed an explanation. And the more they push, the more I simply want to tell them to fuck the fuck off."

Rosemary tugged off her gloves indicating their work in the garden was done, or at least hers was. "You know, as a teacher for many years, I saw it all the time when one of my kiddos did something they knew they were responsible for—usually it was breaking something or being careless with someone's feelings—and rather than owning it, they dug their heels in deeper, making the situation worse and harder to come back from."

"I'm not an eight year old, Rosie."

"No, m'dear, you're not."

There was always an invigorating energy on game nights, even with those teams that appreciated the post-game keg more than the play time. But the Blue Jays being the Blue Jays, everything was amplified, like a pair of crackling, static-charged wool socks. If the competitive nature between the Mallards and Jays was always right at the surface, tonight it was edged with something else, something nearly hostile—which was not totally unexpected from Dana Van Sykes, but the rest of the team's typical trash talk seemed more biting. What's more, the Jays fans in the bleachers outnumbered the sprinkling of Mallard fans, and they had already taken to heckling the Mallard infield during warm-up.

Wayne had noticed the vibe, too. "The *bug* up their *butts* seems particularly hairy tonight," he said as the team gathered for the pregame pep talk.

Kip was leaning against the backstop. "When I was over getting their lineup, Dana made sure I heard her say she'd recruited a few warm bodies for the bleachers—some townspeople who weren't too pleased with the..." He glanced a moment at Reuben and put his fingers up in air quotes, "*'disrespect'* a particular member of our team had shown the *'Good Lord.'*"

"Bullshit," said Donny. "I've known Dana Van Sykes since she was fifteen. I remember when she got caught shoplifting a bunch of stuff from the church bazaar. Good Lord, my ass."

Maddy aimed a sharp look at Donny.

Wayne chimed in. "Yeah, and I know some of the guys she dragged out to the stands. They're as devout as a flock of pigeons. About as smart, too. Mostly they don't pass up a chance to act like jerks. Van Sykes thinks a bigger, louder crowd will be the tipping point they need to pull out a win. But we're not going to give them an inch. We just keep our heads down, ignore the idiots, play our game. Same as we always do." He poked a stout finger into Reuben's chest protector, "That goes *double* for you, Downes. Personally, I couldn't care a *fig* what you put up on your property. *Until* it becomes an issue on the field. *Don't* let it."

"I hear you, Wayne," Reuben said. The truth was, the sting from the breakup was front of mind, and Reuben had no patience for Dana Van Sykes's bizarre aggression.

Reuben pulled the catcher's helmet on, leaving the face mask raised so he could check in with Maddy. Most games, they would do a quick meet before she took to the mound. Today though, he had to jog to catch her. "Hey, Maddy." She turned with a flat expression. He tried to lighten her mood. "I don't see what's-his-name here today. That's good, right?"

"Frank. And no, it's not good because he ended up with a hairline fracture from when I hit him last game. And he sent me another x-ray bill. But thanks for reminding me."

She paced the mound until Reuben got the message that he had been dismissed by yet another woman. He walked back to home plate and hunkered down in front of the ump.

The first two innings were a battle of wills, neither team wanting to give up so much as a base. When Reuben stepped into the batter's box in the bottom of the fourth, the score remained 0-0 with no outs. Aaron had just singled and was standing on the base chatting with Joss, who was first-base coach. The bleacher crowd was loud, timing their shouts to break Reuben's concentration. When he swung and missed the first pitch, they broke into a fresh set of jeers.

Focus, Downes.

Settling his breath, Reuben tapped an old trick he'd learned from Coach Bordo. It was centered around the idea that every pitch was hittable until it wasn't. Unless the batter was deliberately not swinging, he needed to have absolute confidence that the next pitch was going to be a hit. While it seemed obvious, the simple act of watching the ball from the pitcher's hand and thinking *"yes, yes, yes..."* to the incoming pitch focused the batter's attention on the moment-by-moment action as the ball approached. The very second a pitch went off course, the *yes* turned to *no*, and the batter backed away.

So as the Jays pitcher finished her windup, Reuben zeroed in completely on the ball as it left her fingertips. That *"yes, yes, yes"* become a mantra that tuned out everything else. As if in slow motion, he could see that the arc would cross the plate a little outside and about knee-height. Reuben's instinct kicked in. He adjusted, swung, and caught the pitch right in the sweet spot, and the ball sailed over the leaping second baseman's outstretched mitt. Reuben sprinted to first and rounded the base to see their center fielder had thrown hard to home, enabling Reuben to cruise into second. The call at the plate was close but the catcher had just nipped Aaron on the slide, tagging him out. The ump was a tall but quiet teen named Jasper who couldn't always be counted on to make the right calls, but he seemed to have gotten it right this time since neither Aaron nor Wayne protested.

The raucous cheering from the Jays fans nearly drowned out the Mallard players saying, "Good try, Aaron" consolations to Aaron and "Nice hit, Reuben."

As Jasper brushed up a cloud of dirt from the plate, Dana Van Sykes lingered at second base beside Reuben. "So," she said, "you think it's a joke to mess with people's faith?"

Was she really doing this now?

"You know, if someone's faith is undermined by anything I do, they're not especially faithful."

Dana kicked at a clump of dirt. "You think you're so much smarter than everyone else, don't you?"

"I don't get what your problem is, Van Sykes—"

The pitcher, now facing them, cleared her throat. Dana shrugged and walked back into position, but as she did, she turned her head and mumbled just loud enough for Reuben to hear, "Why don't you go the fuck back where you came from?"

Reuben felt his face heat up. Dana Van Sykes's disdain for him may have found a new target with Scarecrow Jesus, but it had started before then, even as far back as the end of last season's gathering at the bar with Cameron's band.

He shouted after her, "Are you kidding me? Is that what you're pissed at? Because I wasn't born here? Or is it because I offered to pay your tab last season so you and your crew would stop being a bunch of rude assholes?"

She just smiled and shook her head smugly, but the bleacher crowd took note of the exchange and taunted Reuben, "Leave her alone!" and "Just play the game, trash man!"

The entire exchange sideswiped Reuben's attention so much that when Patrice sent a pop fly to center field, Reuben missed tagging up and got caught out in a double play by their second baseman.

The Jays fans erupted with whoops and whistles. Reuben tugged the batting helmet from his head, annoyed at himself but especially irritated that Dana Van Sykes had gotten under his skin.

Jogging back to the bench, Reuben could see the disappointment his teammates were trying to hide as they busied themselves examining their mitts and retying cleats before taking the field. Wayne just shook his head in disgust. Certainly, a rookie mistake like the one Reuben had just made in a scoreless game against their biggest rival didn't endear him to anyone, but he also knew his teammates were now feeling the amplified tension with the Blue Jays.

Reuben felt on edge as if there were a bunch of wasps hovering, humming around his head, threatening to sting. It wasn't only the rude fans and his teammates' disappointment that was getting to him, it was an ache just below the surface from knowing that at that very moment, Adrian was packing up and removing all traces of her presence from his house. Earlier, on the drive over, he'd made a conscious decision to put the breakup in a mental box and shelve it for the duration of the game;

there would be enough time to feel her absence when he got home. But the lid on that box was seriously close to being dislodged.

He blamed Dana Van Sykes.

As Reuben fiddled with the damned rusty hook on his shin guard, something small, round and shiny like a coin caught his attention. It was a flat stone with smooth, silvery veins of mica reflecting the overhead lights. It reminded him of Teddy Marks, the varsity catcher who'd essentially taught Reuben how to play the position, and the sly trick he'd passed along. *Every team has an asshole*, Reuben echoed the catcher's words.

Setting up the chest protector so it blocked any view from the Jays bench, Reuben took the stone and tucked it neatly into the laces of his right cleat. He then headed over to Maddy in the pitcher's circle.

"Hey." He approached her and spoke quickly and quietly before she could send him away. "I know you and I are a little off, and maybe we can talk after the game?" She opened her mouth to respond but he interrupted, "That's not why I'm here, though. I need to ask...do you think you could throw a changeup if the situation presented itself?"

She shrugged. "I guess."

"Good. Keep an eye out. If I give you devil's horns pointing down, like this," Reuben gestured close to his waist so no one else could see, "we'll give it a try."

Maddy nodded, "Okay, got it."

The crowd in the bleachers had been getting progressively louder—and no doubt, beer-emboldened—to the point where one of the Mallard fans—Donny's brother, maybe—shouted at them, "Pipe down! We can't hear the damn calls!" When Reuben and Joss made a picture-perfect play, tagging out a fast-running Jay on a steal to second, there were boos, and a guy in a tight red tank top threw an open can onto the field. The Mallard fans howled at the bad behavior, and the ump had to pause the game while Cameron removed the can, shouting, "Cut the bullshit, dickface!"

A couple plays later, when Dana Van Sykes came up in the batting order, the Jays runners were in scoring position on first and second. From the bench, the Jays third baseman yelled out, "You got two ducks on the pond, DVS! Bring 'em home and show these losers how it's done!"

"Oh look, it's Dana Van Psycho."

"Do you ever shut up, Downes?"

Entering the batter's box, Dana held her hand up at Maddy like a traffic cop as she dug a trench beside home plate. It was a tactic, Reuben knew, not just to break Maddy's cadence but to make Dana's compact strike zone even smaller.

Maddy looked like she would rather be anywhere else. The first pitch was in-the-dirt wild so that Reuben had to block it with his whole body to keep from letting the Jays runner take third. Walking Dana (or worse, hitting her with a pitch) right before their cleanup hitter would put the Mallards in a tough position. Reuben needed to bring Maddy into the moment.

"Hey now, Maddy. You gotta *focus*. Tough it *out*, girlie," Reuben said, doing his best Wayne imitation. She didn't crack a smile, but he could see the inside joke hit its mark as she shook her head a little. The warming effect on Reuben was immediate, like he just won a blue ribbon. The exchange felt private and personal, leaving him momentarily distracted until Maddy nodded at Reuben, letting him know that she was ready, and he should get back into position.

The next pitch was outside. Dana fouled it up and over the backstop.

"It's just you and me here, Maddy." Again, his own words seemed to take on a more intimate tone than he intended. And again, Reuben reminded himself, *Focus*.

He turned his attention to Dana, an easy way to bring him back to game stakes. She had stepped out of the box yet again, swinging at pretend pitches, once, twice, thrice, four and five times.

"Van Sykes has got nothing. It's why she takes so many practice swings."

Dana stepped up to the plate and said, "Tell your outfielders to get their wheels on. I'm gonna send it clear to Canada."

"Seeing as we're facing south, that'd be quite a foul ball."

The next pitch also cut outside, but this time Dana was ready for it. She caught the ball solidly, and for an instant, Reuben thought it was a goner over Patrice's head in right field, but mercifully, it peeled off and away.

"Foul ball," said Jasper flatly. "One and two."

"Hey, Van Sykes. Didn't I once hear you say that, actually, there is shame in going down swinging?"

"I'll show you swinging..."

It was a now or never moment. Reuben had riled Dana up enough to know that the next pitch would be the critical one. He flashed the downward devil horns to Maddy. He could tell she wasn't happy, both knowing that Dana was a sharp read, and the consequences could be disastrous.

"Don't worry, Maddy, I've got you." Would every encouragement now feel like it had a creepy subtext?

With his right hand, Reuben freed the stone from his laces. It had heft without being heavy, and a smooth, cool feel in his fingers. Like a worry stone he'd had when he was a kid, Reuben rubbed it clockwise three times. His timing would need to be perfect.

From her windup, Reuben couldn't tell if Maddy would actually go through with the changeup; her powerful motions were consistent right up until the very last second when her hand, positioned backwards, choked off the force, releasing the ball lower and with a backwards spin.

Dana must have caught onto the speed change as she held back her swing and spring-loaded to crush the pitch. It was right then that Reuben flicked the stone, bouncing it perfectly off Dana's flexed ankle.

The distraction worked. Dana Van Sykes swung and missed the ball that smacked right into the pocket of Reuben's glove. Reuben caught a flash of Maddy's open, gleeful smile. She raised her arms high overhead in triumph.

"Strike three, the batter's ou—"

"You son of a bitch!" Dana shouted just before she body-slammed Reuben backwards into the ump. The two of them crashed hard to the backstop. As Reuben shook the shock away, he saw Joss drag Dana backward as players from the Jays bench swarmed the field.

"You okay?" Reuben asked the kid-ump who simply nodded, his jaw hanging open as he watched the brawl explode in front of home plate. Reuben glanced quickly around for Maddy and was relieved to see she had simply walked off the field and was stuffing her backpack to leave.

The infield was a mess of shoving and shouting, slaps, and swinging, but mostly missing, fists. Wayne and the Jays catcher were trying to pull people apart. Reuben peeled off his mask and entered the fray to help do the same. If they could just get the teams on opposite sides, he thought they could calm things down. But then, a new wave hit as the rowdier fans from the bleachers shoved their way, elbows first, into the fracas, one of them grabbing Reuben by the chest protector straps and hauling him sideways. Reuben crashed into the guy, and they tumbled together to the ground.

Scrambling to his feet, Reuben could see a few people hurrying away from the scene, including Patrice who was ushering the ump to the parking lot. Off to his left, Reuben heard Donny yell, "Get the hell off me!" as he spun in circles trying to shake loose a woman who had leapt onto his back.

Notably for Reuben, there were swears aimed at the "flatlander," the one who "hates Jesus." At that last comment, someone delivered his best imitation of a kung-fu kick catching Reuben's chest protector and knocking the wind out of him before the guy's own momentum crashed him into Joss who flung him into Cameron.

The scene had an almost gleeful frenzy about it, a sense that, despite whatever bad feelings had broken the dam, no one was getting seriously hurt. Wayne had managed to get physically between one of the drunken spectators and Kip, who was much smaller and likely one wisecrack away from getting his neck wrung. But the more Wayne tried to calm the situation, the more ramped up the guy became, now shifting his adrenaline from Kip to Wayne, sending angry, cutting words at him.

"You're broken, Wayne! You always were, you little pussy." Wayne turned his head to the side to avoid getting drunken spittle on him. His arms were raised like an unarmed man showing he was not a threat. But the guy kept coming at him. "Just keep running your little pickup league. Your team is a bunch of cheating losers. Just. Like. You."

It was too much, watching Wayne stand there taking that kind of verbal assault. Reuben took three furious strides toward them and took a swing at the guy. The strike landed more like a hard chin-push than a punch, but it was enough to knock the guy off-balance, and he fell into Dana Van Sykes, who staggered like a wobbling bowling pin that did not fall.

That's when the flashing blue-and-red police lights swept over the field, settling on the dirty, scraped-up faces of the players and fans, everyone blinking and shaking their heads, embarrassed and wondering what the hell had just happened.

◆

No arrests were made, mostly because there were only two cops to about twenty perpetrators, and a lot of "he did-she did" explanations of what had happened—Dana telling anyone who would listen how Reuben sabotaged what was about to be a game-changing hit, and Reuben claiming he'd done nothing to provoke that kind of response from Dana. Regardless, Officer Lempke, the lead police officer on the scene, made it clear she would be recommending to the town's Select Board that the rest of the season—what amounted to two more games for every team—be canceled, and the league reevaluated the following year.

Beyond the scrapes and bruises, what nagged at Reuben the most when he finally arrived home was how quiet Wayne had been, simply nodding to the police, owning responsibility for everyone else's bad behavior. Reuben sat a moment in the driveway thinking about where one's accountability ended, and another's began. Everyone who joined the brawl made a choice to fight versus those who walked away. Dana body-slamming Reuben was a result of Reuben sabotaging her swing, which had been prompted by Dana insulting him, which seemed to have stemmed from a gesture at a bar nearly a year ago.

Action. Reaction.

What was done was past. But making things right, Reuben could hear Rosemary say, could start anytime. Tomorrow, he would take down Scarecrow Jesus, bag the faded clothes and toss them in the trash. He wasn't sure what he should ultimately do with the crucifix, but it had gathered dust for over a decade in someone else's barn, so it wasn't unreasonable to store it until he found a home for it. It would certainly make for an unusual classified ad.

Adrian had left the porch light on for him, its warm glow suggesting for a moment that she was waiting for him, just putting the teapot on the stove, eager to hear game highlights. But of course, the house was empty. He could feel it as soon as he came inside. The air seemed thinner, and there was a faint echo as he set his gear down in the hall.

Averting his eyes from the absence of her things on the shelves, the vacant spots left by her curated wall art, he headed to the shower, ready to be rid of the sweat and the dirt and the grass stains. In the bathroom, the counter had been cleared of all her moisturizers—once a source of amusement as she gave him a tutorial highlighting the unique benefits that each one provided to her face and various parts of her body, which of course led to his attentive exploration of those parts. Her natural deodorant, eye liner pencil, and eyebrow brush, the suite of hair-care products that made her smell like almonds and honey, all gone. But the real ice-pick stab to his chest came when he saw the canted angle of his now-bachelor toothbrush in its holder, how strangely dejected it looked compared to several months ago when he first asked Adrian to move in.

Suddenly, Reuben no longer wanted a shower. In fact, he didn't even want to be in their once-shared space. The Alewife was closed at that time of night. He called Kip to invite him over so Reuben could share the news about the breakup, and the two of them could piece together a fuller picture of the softball brawl. But the phone went to voicemail, which was unusual, making Reuben wonder if Kip, and likely the team, wanted to put some space between them for a while. Reuben hung up without leaving a message.

Downstairs, he opened the narrow closet where they—*I*, Reuben corrected himself—kept the wine and liquor. Reuben reached for the half-empty bottle of Jameson's that Jackson Endicott had left behind and carried it outside.

In the barn, the phone's flashlight reflected a pair of gold-green, predatory eyes, sending a jolt of adrenaline through Reuben before he realized it was Lou Garoo, hunkering down on one of the crates. The cat, equally startled, let out a warning hiss.

"Quit your spitting, cat. I'm not here for you."

Reuben pulled the overhead light string and lit up the barn. He poured a glass of whiskey and took a full swig before setting bottle and glass within reach on the workbench. It had been a couple weeks since he'd gone to the storage bins, as evidenced by the lawnmower parked in front of them. Rolling it aside, he reached the barrel filled with scrap metal pieces. It was heavier than Reuben had expected as he dragged it to the center of the barn and spilled out the contents, which clattered loudly on the cement floor, sending the cat scrambling to a far corner of the barn. These pieces, he decided, would be the ones he would use to create the forest floor in the sugaring sculpture. Whether Kip would still be willing to collaborate, Reuben didn't know, but selecting the pieces seemed like a good project when you needed something to quiet your mind and occupy your hands.

He sorted the pieces into piles, mentally identifying them as *Use*, *Store*, and *Dump*. The *Use* pile included scraps that featured cool oxidation colors and designs, while others had textures and patterns that would lend themselves well to being cut into leaves with the shear tool. He would mine the other barrels later in the week, sourcing rebar to bend into rugged roots, and reclaimed wood pieces to be given a second life as constructed trees.

Though he'd sipped slowly, the whiskey had mellowed Reuben enough to think it was a good idea to text Adrian, just a brief message letting her know that he was home, that he supported her decision, and he was focused on moving forward.

Instead, what he sent was:

Please change your mind.

Her reply was quick and unambiguous.

No, I'm sorry.

Reuben grabbed the whiskey bottle by the neck and snapped off the light, leaving behind the semi-sorted scrap piles.

The moon was officially full, again flooding the backyard with an otherworldly glow.

"Reflected light of reflected light. Everything is reflected light," Reuben said aloud, imagining it sounded profound, as if there were a metaphor somewhere just beyond the capacity of his whiskey-soaked brain, which he was continuing to drown.

He wandered over to the garden where Scarecrow Jesus was spotlighted, center stage. The hat had slipped forward, channeling more "Bob Fosse dancer" than "Lord and Savior." In that context, it was easy to personify the statue as a silent companion, especially when you were sullen, alone, and moderately inebriated.

"I'm not falling for it." Reuben pointed an accusing finger at the crucifix. "You're just an upcycled tree."

At its essence, this was true: that anonymous artist had taken a raw-form log and used hands and tools to create a statue. As far as Reuben's beliefs went, there was nothing inherently divine imbued in the grain. No commandment that said, "Thou shalt not enrobe this work in flannel."

As if acting on a dare to double down on his blasphemy, Reuben picked up a fallen tomato and winged it at the crucifix. Not only did he miss by a good two feet, his drunken imbalance sent him careening into the cucumber trellis, knocking it over and getting himself tangled in the vines.

"Jesus Christ!" he said out loud. And then laughed, "Not you. I mean, technically, you, but not actually you."

The sunflower heads twittered in the breeze like a sitcom audience.

"Thank you. Thank you, friends, I'm here seven nights a week."

Reuben sat down in the dirt to slow the spinning in his head. He was being disingenuous, and he knew it. Because as an artist, Reuben was highly attuned to the fact that humans ascribe meaning. That's art: the communication of ideas or emotion from creator (not the Creator) to viewer. Scarecrow Jesus may have been a private backyard display, but it was, in truth, an outward expression of anger and hurt.

And now, whether he liked it or not, it mattered to other people both within and beyond his circle.

"Enjoy the stars tonight, Scarecrow Jesus. You're headed back to storage tomorrow."

Whether because of his reluctance to sleep in an empty bed or simply a drunken need to collapse on the nearest furniture alternative, Reuben spent a second night on the couch in the studio. It seemed likely that his own snoring had woken him in the predawn—4:16 a.m. according to his phone. His mouth was sandpaper-parched, and his eyes heavy as billiard balls. He decided that if he was going to make a trip to the kitchen to guzzle a gallon of water, he might as well head upstairs to steal a few hours of more comfortable sleep.

Every body part, including his scalp, seemed to pinch and wince as Reuben rose slowly from the couch. Fully standing, he stretched to full height, then stopped abruptly, noticing a light in the garden. He leaned left then right to see if it was just a trick of his eyes. But the light remained, an upward glow starting from the base of the crucifix.

Reuben's hangover fog cleared instantly, and he thought, *Is this literally one of those "I've seen the light" moments? Is this the proverbial message from God?* He didn't feel any different. There were no voices in his head, no sense of calm or inner peace. Quite the opposite:

Reuben's heart was hammering, and he felt himself break out in an uneasy sweat. He kept staring at the light, thinking it would move, lift from the ground in some way. As his mind cleared, *divine visitation* dropped on the list of possibilities just under *vegetable thieves*. Maybe it was Joy Adams or one of the thug spectators from the game coming to vandalize, or maybe steal, the crucifix. Either way, Reuben would need to scare them off.

He felt his way to the worktable, his hand landing on a jar that held a small collection of art tools. He found the X-Acto knife and removed its protective cap. Not much of a weapon, but in the dark, it could seem somewhat threatening. He slid the door open, nearly silently in its track so that as he stepped out into the warm air, he could hear faint whispering.

With the element of surprise in his favor, Reuben flipped on the outdoor light and yelled, "Hey!" Three heads popped up just above the summer squash plant. One of the trespassers grabbed the light and bolted off toward the woods with the second. The third, a man whose thick mustache Reuben recognized from the sidewalk outside the hardware store, swept a small child onto his back and ran off the way the other two had gone.

Reuben didn't chase them; he simply stood on the back stoop and watched the flashlight bounce among the trees, getting farther away until it disappeared entirely.

This was a new wrinkle.

CHAPTER 21

The jangling bell at the entry to Endicott's was drowned out by the whining, grinding sound of a key being made. Reuben could see Jackson in the corner of the store. He was wearing a pair of safety goggles, concentrating on the machine. The customer was a tall teenaged girl whose face was locked on her phone as she speed-typed with one hand. Once he was finished, Jackson polished the key with a rag and held it out, but didn't let go when the girl tried to take it.

He said, "If I ever catch you using *that* thing," he gestured to the phone, "when you're behind the wheel, I will take this back."

The girl looked at him with big, nervous eyes and simply nodded. She met him at the register and paid as Reuben wandered around looking for something to buy that could justify his visit.

Once the bell confirmed the girl had left the store, Jackson said, "Neighbor's daughter. She just inherited her grandpa's Oldsmobile." He shook his head in disbelief, "I was there the day they brought her home from the hospital."

Reuben set down a roll of masking tape and slid it across the counter. Jackson lifted an eyebrow. "You come in here just for that?"

"I'm not going to try to use a credit card if that's what you're concerned about."

"No, I just figure maybe you were looking for some townie perspective on that brawl you started last night." His eyes crinkled at the corners.

"First of all, I need this tape. And second, Dana Van Sykes body-slammed *me*."

"After you threw a rock."

"I did not *throw a rock*. I mean, I did, but not the way you make it sound."

"Oh, I'm familiar. My brother used to do that old trick," Jackson said. "He'd toss up pop flies and then, while my attention was focused on making the catch, he would bean me hard in the stomach. Can't tell you how many times I fell for it."

"I'm pretty sure that's not the same thing."

"Maybe not, but it still bugs the crap out of me." Jackson rang up the tape. "Two dollars and nineteen cents."

Reuben dug exact change from his pocket. "But you're right. I did come in for another reason. Different subject." Reuben tried to look casual as he glanced around to see if there were other customers or employees in the store.

"I'm all ears."

"When I was in here a couple months ago, there were two guys in a pickup truck out front, and one of them, with a thick mustache had just come from the store. They spoke Spanish to each other. My guess is they're probably from Mexico or Latin America—"

"Mexico is generally considered part of Latin America but go on."

"I'm pretty sure they work at the goat farm by my house."

Jackson stood up straighter and folded his thick arms over his chest. "And?"

"Let me back up," Reuben said, pausing to gather his thoughts. "Over the last few days, there have been some sudden changes in my personal life—"

"You mean your girlfriend dumping you?"

Reuben shook his head. He hadn't even told Kip yet. "Is there anything that goes on in this town you don't know about?"

"No, Popple. There is not."

Reuben sighed. "Yes, Adrian and I broke up. And while there were a few reasons for that, one contributing factor was Scarecrow Jesus potentially causing some problems for her business. I don't want to be responsible for that, so I decided I would take it down today—on my terms, just like you suggested. No fanfare, no B3 announcements, just make it gone."

Jackson was focused and listening.

"But then, this morning before dawn, I woke up and found a group of people in the backyard by the garden. I figured they were vandals or one of the Blue Jays up to something. But they were off to the side, just quietly sitting beside the crucifix."

Jackson nodded slowly, then asked, "What happened after you found them?"

"I shouted and scared the hell out of them. It looked like it was three adults and a little kid as they bolted off into the woods. I'm pretty sure one of them was the guy with the mustache from that day. And I think the other guy may work with the goats across the street."

Jackson stood upright again. "So?"

Jackson's patience seemed to be waning, so Reuben decided to get to the point of his visit. "When I went out this morning, I found this on the ground by the woods." He held out a set of rosary beads, polished stones in various earthy shades of light and dark green, yellow and deep burgundy. Dangling from the center was a small silver crucifix. "I think maybe one of them dropped it as they were running."

Jackson's eyes softened a little into a slightly thoughtful expression, but he didn't say anything, and he didn't reach out to inspect the beads, so Reuben continued. "I just wondered, do you think it's possible that maybe they were, I don't know, praying? I had planned to take Scarecrow Jesus down today. But now, I'm wondering if I should leave it up?"

Again, Jackson was pensive a moment. "The answer to your first question is I couldn't say. And I think you know my answer to the second question." Jackson tore the receipt and handed it to Reuben, ending the conversation. "Anything else I can get you today? Lip balm? Birdseed?"

Reuben shook his head, "That's it? That's your input?"

"Here's what I can tell you, Reuben. The guy with the mustache is named Arturo. And he's a good man who wants to keep a low profile. You understand?"

Reuben had heard the disturbing rhetoric in the presidential campaign painting Mexican immigrants as rapists, drug dealers, and killers. At the time, it seemed like outlandish pandering to a small, xenophobic part of the population, but rather than taking a hit in the polls, Donald Trump seemed to be gaining some traction, leaving Reuben to wonder what Jackson might be hearing in his daily dealings with a wider cross section of the community.

"Yeah, I understand."

Evidence of Lou Garoo's displeasure at being stuffed into a cardboard banker's box was all over Reuben's forearms in crisscrossing, bloody claw marks. The cat's howls coming from the passenger seat were an abductee's desperate cry for help.

"You're such a drama queen."

It was a plausible excuse for seeking Maddy out: remembering her stern "suggestion" that Lou Garoo get a rabies vaccination. So he called the vet's office and, trying to disguise his voice, asked to speak to Maddy. When the receptionist said she was with a patient, but could he give her a message, Reuben thanked him but said no. Fifteen minutes later, he called back as if for the first time, asking if he could get an appointment for his cat. As luck would have it, he said, they had a spot at the end of the day.

Reuben's original plan had been to talk to Maddy after the Jays game, wanting to give her a chance to air any grievances, but clearly those plans had been hijacked.

The vet clinic was small, its waiting room barely big enough to hold Reuben with his box of cat and a woman with a nervous Irish setter that kept trying to climb into her lap. Reuben could feel the woman's eyes moving back and forth between him and the box with its growling, yowling contents, now amplified mightily in the presence of a pony-sized dog.

He laughed nervously to the woman. "File this one under pissed off, right?"

The woman shifted her attention away, pulling her dog close to her side.

A voice came from the reception desk. "Reuben?"

It took a moment for Reuben to align the woman in dark-green scrubs with the Maddy he knew from softball. The ponytail was familiar, but she had a faint polish of makeup around her eyes. "Yeah, hi," he said, clearing his throat. "I, uh... there was a raccoon in the yard the other day, and it reminded me that I needed to get this guy a rabies shot. So here we are."

She tilted her head at the filing box and nodded, "I suppose that's one way to get him here."

"I drilled breathing holes in the lid."

"I hope he wasn't inside when you did."

Outwardly, Reuben scoffed, but that was exactly how it went down.

"Come on back, we'll see if I can get this done quickly without stressing him out too much more."

In all, prepping and administering the vaccine took no more than five minutes. Reuben and Maddy worked together as a team, him removing the bungee cord and lifting the lid just enough for her to gently pinch a fold of skin, plunge the syringe, and finish before the cat even knew what was happening. Maddy stroked his fur to offer some comfort.

She handed Reuben two of those tube packets she had with her the day she came out to the house.

"You should give him one of these now and one when you get home as a reward."

"Now? I should I take him out of the box?"

"Oh, heck no. He'll murder us both trying to get him back in." She came over to the other side of the box where the cat's head was positioned. Opening the package, she squeezed a little of the contents to the top and held it out to Reuben.

He hesitated just a moment, his mind rapid-firing that his hand might touch hers, and maybe he should try to avoid that. Or maybe not?

"It's okay, Reuben. He won't bite once he gets a smell of it."

"Maybe you should do it."

"The idea is for you to earn back his trust."

She placed the packet in Reuben's hand with just the slightest brush of her fingertips. Reuben reflexively drew his hand back, but covered his reaction by reaching a little too aggressively into the box, which elicited a swipe and another bloody slash from Lou Garoo. Reuben dropped the packet in with the cat and pulled his hand back.

"I don't want to go back in there to get it," Reuben said, sucking at the fresh wound.

Maddy laughed and gestured to the sink. "Go wash, and I'll get you a Band-Aid."

As he scrubbed his hands, Reuben said over his shoulder, "Hey, do you think maybe we could talk? I know things felt a little off this week and I know it has to do with some of my," he fished for the right word, "actions."

"You mean like sparking a brawl?"

"Come on, admit it. It felt amazing to strike out Dana Van Sykes."

"Maybe. But you probably shouldn't have done it."

"Yeah, well, people have said that about a few things I've done lately."

She handed Reuben a partially opened bandage strip. "We close in thirty minutes, and then I have some cleanup to do. Why don't you take this guy home, get him settled, and I can meet you at the Alewife at seven. If...you think that would be okay with Adrian?"

Adrian's name was a sudden snap in Reuben's brain. He realized that he hadn't really thought about her during his trip to Endicott's and not afterwards when he'd hatched a plan to orchestrate this very meeting with Maddy. Concerned that telling Maddy about the breakup might send the wrong message about why he wanted to talk, he nodded, "Sure, she'll be fine with it."

◆

Maddy, dressed more familiarly in a loose tee and cutoffs, was at a high-top table when Reuben arrived. He saw her wave from the back section near the dart board where he and Kip typically sat. The row of barstools was packed shoulder-to-shoulder with the guys Kip called the "Friday OTs"—old timers—a collection of hardy men in their sixties and seventies sporting belts that sat well below their broad bellies and trucker-style hats loosely perched atop their heads.

"I hope you like Wolcott. I thought we might want a pitcher," Maddy said.

"Not a belly-itcher?" She shook her head at him in comedic disgust. Reuben sidled onto a chair. "Come on, you lobbed that one over the plate." He made a little half bow at his bad joke.

Pouring himself a glass, Reuben wasn't sure how to launch into the conversation he'd worked out in his head, so instead he said, "Have you talked to anyone on the team?"

"Wayne called last night to make sure I got home okay. We chatted a little. He said you defended his honor like a true gentleman."

"It just made me so angry to hear him getting crapped on by that drunk idiot."

"You know who that idiot was, right?"

"I have no idea."

"Pepper Danberry?" Reuben's face showed no recognition of that name. "Wayne's high school nemesis. The guy who may or may not have intentionally sabotaged Wayne's scholarship. You didn't hear that story?"

"Oh, yeah, Donny told me about that a while back. Jeez, why didn't Wayne say something? How did you know that was the guy?"

"I didn't know until our at-bats before the fight. I heard it from Cameron who heard it from Joss who heard it from Donny. I think Wayne wanted to try to keep a lid on things as much as possible."

"And I just kept making things worse." Reuben looked down into his beer. "I bet he wishes I never joined the team."

"Aww gee whiz, Wally, that ain't so."

"Are you making fun of me?"

She bumped his elbow playfully. "You just sounded like one of those sappy, old shows my parents used to make us watch." She flipped a cardboard coaster around in her hands. "Reuben, the bad blood with the Jays has always been there below the surface. Some kind of flare-up was inevitable. You just struck the match."

"I guess knowing it was that guy Pepper, I can feel a little less bad about smacking him. The guy just wouldn't shut up."

"Did you? Feel bad, I mean."

He wasn't sure if she was asking because she thought he should or should not feel bad. "I think I'd like to exercise my fifth amendment rights."

"Fair enough," she said.

In the pause in their conversation, Reuben could hear "Get Off of My Cloud" playing in the background. One of the OTs was singing the chorus loudly, though calling it singing would have been generous.

"So you said you wanted to talk."

No more stalling, he thought. "It didn't pass my notice at practice the other day that you seemed upset, when Donny finished reading the article about the . . . the—"

"Scarecrow Jesus."

"Yes, that."

"I was upset. No, upset isn't the right word." She set the coaster down and leaned back in her chair. "Don't get me wrong, I think it's weird and probably offensive to have a dressed-up depiction of Jesus in your yard, but you're an artist and, whatever, I don't always get art." She took a long swig of her beer. "Maybe it was more that I felt frustrated, or disappointed, that you had nothing to say about it. No explanation of what it meant or why you did it. I get not wanting to talk to a journalist, but we're your team. Your friends. And it seemed like you were just dismissing us."

"No, that wasn't—"

"I was there, at your house, Reuben, the day that lady crashed your backyard. So I know you were trying to keep me from going back there and seeing it."

"But that was because—"

"Granted, you should know I have some personal history that makes me more sensitive to religious stuff than, obviously, everyone else on the team who just kind of shrugged it off."

Instead of trying to interject or defend himself, Reuben topped off his beer and let her talk.

"Not many people know this, but Maddy isn't short for Madison or Madeline. It's Magdalena. My parents were pretty—*are* pretty religious." She picked up the coaster again, keeping her hands busy as she spoke. "It was a big part of my life growing up. My sister and I had this extended family with everyone from the church. There were always picnics and potlucks, kids' clubs, along with all the Sunday school and sermons and whatnot. It was just this insulated little community built around faith and scripture and leading the good life." She put her fingers up in scare quotes around "good." "In summertime, we'd pack up the family van and road trip with a few other church members to do ministry work in poor, rural communities, mostly in the south. The grown-ups would help repair homes and people's cars, set up food gardens, and do a bunch of cooking, while us kids would babysit and teach songs and play games."

It was as if a kind of dam had broken and Maddy just kept talking.

"I won't say it was a perfect childhood. And there were some things that never really sat right with me. When I got older, maybe seventeen or so, I started to pull away. Once I went to college, I moved totally into the outside world. This beer? Forbidden. Sitting here with you would be pretty scandalous, let alone not being married with three kids at this point in my life.

"These days, the only time I'm in church is on Christmas or when I head back for a cousin's wedding." She looked over at the TV screen above the bar. "But some things never leave you, right? I love my parents and I love the people from the church, even if I can't live the way they want me to."

"So when Donny was reading the article, I don't know... I felt protective of them? Of their, you know, devotion. And how hurt they would be if they ever heard about 'Scarecrow Jesus' and even more if they found out I was connected to it, even just by association. I thought, 'He must have some explanation.' Kind of like that pastor in the article said, maybe it was about hoping for a good gardening season. I just wanted to know that you weren't making fun of faith. Of my family and me."

It felt a little like the floor had dropped beneath Reuben.

"It's stupid. I'm fine now, really," Maddy said.

"No, please don't do that. It's not stupid," Reuben said. "And I promise you, I wasn't making fun of anyone. I feel terrible that I left you, of all people, to wonder that. And since you shared your history here. I'll fill you in a little on mine."

He took in a deep breath and held the air in his lungs a moment, as if before plunging into a cold pool. "Did you ever do something that you thought was just you doing something because it was something to do but really it was about doing something else?"

"That's a lot of somethings being done. So I'm not sure?"

Just as he had with Adrian, Reuben told Maddy about Paul. This time, he offered some of the details about their easy friendship in Little League, and then about learning all those years later why Paul had suddenly disappeared without a goodbye or forwarding address.

As he spoke, Maddy's eyes never left him. She seemed to take in his explanation and feel the weight of what had happened with genuine empathy. Without realizing he was going to, Reuben pulled the story back even further, to the beginning. Or what felt like a beginning.

"When people ask me how I got started as an artist, I tell them about the time when I was thirteen and I broke a brand-new boombox."

~

The sheer joy in having received an unexpected gift, when it wasn't even Reuben's birthday, lasted nearly a full day. And not just a regular gift like a new comic book or pair of sneakers. The boombox could play cassettes and compact discs, the latter of which, he only had three, but from now on, CDs would be his only musical purchase.

Reuben's parents presented him with the gift after breakfast on a Sunday morning in June, so he spent almost the entire rainy day in his room playing DJ to an imaginary bar scene for his Star Wars *action figures. Being the only females, original Leia and* The Empire Strikes Back *Leia had a lot of dance partners.*

It hadn't occurred to Reuben that the gift was anything more than a surprise offering by parents who were tired of hearing their son complain loudly that not only did the family's ancient stereo have crappy sound quality, it had devoured three cassettes in the last two months. But then, dinner happened, and with it came some news that made it clear the boombox was a weak attempt to soften the blow.

"So earlier this week, your father learned that his work in Binghamton is just about complete. We're going to be moving to Massachusetts next month. I think you're going to love it, hon. There's so much history there—Bunker Hill. And Salem!"

"War and women getting burned alive. Sounds homey." He said flatly.

What does it matter? *Reuben thought. They'd been in this town since the start of sixth grade, and he'd made no ties. In fact, in some ways, he had been bracing himself for this since the day they moved in, but as the school year started to wind down, and there had been no word of his dad getting transferred, Reuben had been lulled into thinking that this time, they would be staying at least another year.*

The next morning, when Reuben's father was "buttoning things up" at the office, and his mother was spending a day shopping and running errands downtown, Reuben pushed the top of the player and popped in his newest CD, a replacement of the Back In Black *cassette that had been ruined. Halfway through the opening track, it hit him. The packing would begin. A tape gun and the smelly black markers would be left in his room along with a stash of broken-down boxes that had been stored in the attic—some of them dating back two moves ago from Rolling Hills to Albuquerque. Then there would be the drive. The arrival and unpacking. The new streets to learn. Strange new faces with their accents and unfamiliar ways of talking. Fashion trends Reuben's own wardrobe could never keep pace with. And regional foods he would lie and say he liked when he had no idea what they were. As a kid, Reuben was powerless to say no to the constant relocations, so he stopped trying.*

Reuben looked at the boombox. Its round speakers staring at him like giant bug eyes. Like fly eyes, the ones in that eighties horror movie. They were the judging eyes of the kids he faced in the classroom on every first day of school.

Yanking the plug from the wall, he cut off Brian Johnson in midlyric "'Cause if good's on the left, then I'm sticking to the ri—" Reuben carried the player to the hallway, and like Godzilla with a car hoisted over his head, he launched the "gift" from his parents down the flight of stairs where it crashed into the wall and sent pieces flying in all directions.

~

"But that's not the part of the story I tell," Reuben said to Maddy. "I skip past it, saying it was an 'accident' that left the boombox in pieces. And how since I had no hope of rebuilding or repairing it, I turned it into art."

Maddy was all eyes, eagerly taking in the story. "And your parents didn't know?"

"My father would have been ripshit if he knew I did it on purpose, but he left that kind of stuff for my mom to deal with. She, on the other hand, probably suspected I smashed it, but she never let on if she did."

Reuben and Kip's regular waitress came by. "Reuben, can I get you guys another pitcher?"

He gestured to Maddy, figuring she would be ready to head home, but she said, "Can I get a Coke?"

Reuben followed her lead, "Club soda and lime for me."

"First-name basis?" Maddy asked after Janis had left.

"Kip and I come here to play darts sometimes."

Reuben realized he had been going on a long time. "Anyways. It's messy, and it was never one thing but kind of a dense knot of things that got channeled into what became Scarecrow Jesus. That doesn't even account for actually wanting to scare the birds from the garden. Which I swear was the original inspiration."

"I'm not sure scarecrows actually work, anyway," she said and smiled at him. "Thank you. For sharing all that. You really didn't need to, but I'm glad you did. Apparently, I was having a hard time reconciling my impression of you with that of an arrogant artist."

Maddy's implication that he had occupied space in her thoughts gave Reuben a small thrill.

They talked through two more rounds of soft drinks. Reuben asked about her life and experiences. He was keenly interested in hearing about a past that was worlds apart from his own. As she answered, he filed away points of reference in his mind like index cards with imagined pictures of young Magdalena; her little sister, Anna; and parents, Cathy and John. The stray dog they took in and named Pickle for when they found him behind the school gnawing on a whole cucumber. The fact that despite spending a lot of time in a communal environment, Maddy felt awkward and uncomfortable around people, much preferring animals. How learning to pitch for her high school softball team made her the center of attention for the first time in her life, and she both loved and loathed the experience. And that her parents seemed to know that going to a non-Christian college would pull her away from their world and values, but they encouraged her to go anyway because they knew it's what she wanted.

Janis came by to ask about refills, and this time, Maddy declined. Reuben realized he would have happily stayed until closing talking to her. Instead, he paid the tab, telling her it was in thanks for all her help with the cat.

It was close to nine thirty when they left the bar.

"I've been here nearly two years and I'm still not used to there not being streetlights," Reuben said. "When you live in a city, you forget that nighttime is actually really dark."

"Ah, but the stars are brighter," Maddy said. "I actually heard that Saturn and Mars should be visible tonight."

They both looked up, but a thin cloud cover made it hard to see much of anything.

"Hey—" Reuben said, wanting to find a reason to keep Maddy from leaving just yet. "You should come by tomorrow to see it. The crucifix, I mean, given your background. The craftsmanship is rough and rustic, but I think you'd find it really beautiful. Despite the . . . attire."

She looked down at her shoes, seeming unsure how to answer.

"Oh," he said, "I should tell you—and I would have before, but the timing felt weird. Not that now's not weird."

"Just spit it out, Reuben."

"Adrian moved out. We're not together anymore."

She seemed to process the news a moment. "Oh."

Reuben was glad she didn't say: "I'm sorry to hear it" because in the moment, he realized not without a little surprise, that he wasn't sorry it happened. That said, he didn't want to seem like the kind of guy who simply bounces from one woman to the next, and so trying to make it clear he wasn't hitting on Maddy, Reuben improvised. "And also, Kip is coming over for a barbecue so the three of us can hang out."

CHAPTER 22

The weather was perfect for hosting an early dinner on the patio. Reuben had never gotten around to getting outdoor furniture, so he set a trio of kitchen chairs around a card table. Despite a mishmash of place settings and silverware, he tried to make the eclectic style feel intentional, pulling colors and textures together with a cheerful blue, Provence-style tablecloth.

Reuben took a step back to assess the setting, then leaned over and adjusted the placement of a pitcher of sangria so it could catch the late afternoon sunlight in deep jewel tones. The air smelled sweet and smoky from the barbecuing ribs that had been slow cooking on the grill for the last two hours. Reuben nodded, satisfied with the neatly rustic setting he had pulled together.

From behind, he heard flip-flops slapping on the flagstones. "Wow," Kip said. "I feel like I might be underdressed."

Reuben turned and became instantly self-conscious, "Do I look too dressy? Should I change into a t-shirt?"

"Relax, buddy. Everything looks great, especially your crisply ironed, button-up shirt."

The night before, when Reuben asked Kip to come for dinner, Reuben had shared with him the essential updates that had occurred just over the course of the previous two days. First, that he was parting ways with Gallery Fifth. Second, that Adrian had broken things off and moved out. To which Kip responded, "So now you're free to put the moves on Maddy."

"What do you think, I'm a total creep?"

"I'm just saying, take it from someone who knows, the longer it takes to get back in the dating scene, the more feral a guy gets. Last week, I ate an entire pizza by myself. In public. Wearing sweatpants. That had a hole on the right butt cheek. And I fully knew it when I left the house."

"I'm confident I can take a breather before things get that pathetic. But I did have a good long talk with Maddy last night, and we cleared the air about Scarecrow Jesus and the game and everything. For the record, she did not grow up in a cult. It was just a rural, tight-knit religious community."

"That doesn't sound like a cult at all."

It took a little persuading, and a promise to pick up the next two tabs at the Alewife, but Kip agreed to be what he called Reuben's "chastity chaperone" for the dinner with Maddy.

Kip set a white square box down on a side table. "Blueberry pie. From the Erins' farmstand." He strolled around the yard. "Man, the garden's a beast since I last saw it. Those tomato plants are taller than I am. Must be the Son of God shining his light—"

"Get it out of your system now. Maddy's going to be here any minute, and it's going to be awkward enough without your snark."

"Or it could be my snark is exactly what's needed to make it *not* awkward." When Reuben gave him a pointed look, he said, "I'm just saying that guy's no small elephant in the room. And naturally, I'm happy to feed him peanuts."

Reuben didn't have time to answer as he heard a car's engine shut off in the driveway. He gave Kip what he hoped was a "don't be a jerk" look and headed to the front.

Maddy was wearing a sporty navy-blue dress cut just above the knees, her hair pulled back in a wispy low bun. She held a bundle of wildflowers—Queen Anne's lace, chicory, black-eyed Susans, daisies, and some feathery grasses.

She said, "The field across from my apartment is in full bloom."

"They're beautiful." Reuben took the flowers. "Kip is in the back. I hope you like barbecued ribs."

She gave him a pained look, "Not ideal for vegetarians."

Reuben slapped a hand to his forehead. "Of course, you work with animals. I'm so stupid! Don't worry, I also have veggie side dishes, and I can whip up some pasta, no problem. In fact, I'll take away the ribs so you don't even have to see them."

"Relax, I'm just busting you. I'm not vegetarian. And I love ribs."

As they walked back, the barn eclipsed Scarecrow Jesus. Until it didn't. Reuben had gotten used to seeing the structure, but now he imagined seeing it through Maddy's eyes as it drew her like a tractor beam.

"Wow." She turned to look back at Reuben. "It's very . . . present."

"It is a very present presence," Kip said, startling her a little. "Yeah, hey, Maddy."

She gave him a side wave and then went up close to Scarecrow Jesus. Reuben and Kip clasped their hands in front as if conducting a moment of silence as they observed Maddy, whose thoughts seemed to turn inward.

"Do you want me to get a ladder and take off the hat?" Reuben asked her.

Maddy turned to him. He couldn't read her expression. She pressed her lips together in a tight smile as she shook her head. "No."

Tucking her hands in her pockets, she walked over to the table with Reuben trailing behind her.

"You were right keeping me from seeing it that day," she said to Reuben. "If I had wandered back here and stumbled on it, I think I would have reacted terribly. I probably would have quit the team and never spoken to you again."

"And now?" Kip asked, handing her a glass of sangria.

She shrugged and took a sip. "There's no more season, so no reason to quit, right? And I figure Reuben made dinner, so I'm here for at least the next couple hours."

The ribs were better than Reuben could have hoped for, thanks to his having meticulously followed a recipe Rosemary had given him (only after he'd sworn to pass it on to just a single worthy disciple, and even then, only after she was "dead and buried at least six months"). Alongside the barbecue, Reuben served a crumbly jalapeño cornbread and a hand-picked salad medley with juicy tomato wedges, paper-thin sliced radishes, and a sprinkling of snipped herbs.

Over dinner, their conversation wandered from recounts of Thursday's game and brawl with Reuben eventually telling them what really had happened the night Cameron's band was playing.

"I guess I insulted her by trying to buy them a round."

"Reuben, you can spot me a round any time, and I promise to not be insulted," said Kip.

"I don't know, is it possible you came off a bit like an outsider trying to buy them off? I'm not saying it was right for her to get nasty about it, just, you know, sometimes people get weird about others coming into their space and telling them how to act."

When Reuben and Kip both looked at Maddy, processing what she was positing, her face flushed red as if she said something aloud that she hadn't meant to. "In any case, it stinks that the season's over. What are you guys going to do with the extra time?"

Kip replied with surprising enthusiasm about the immersive audio-visual collaboration he and Reuben were working on.

"Wow, Kip, I didn't even know 'sound collector' was an occupation," she said. "I always thought you worked in IT."

"Yeah, that's just my superhero cover." He went on to rattle off a list of some of his favorite recordings including a chittering colony of bats leaving their cave on a full moon night, and the crackling and boom of the ice thaw on Lake Elmore, and how the former was going to be used in an upcoming spy movie starring James Keefner.

It was not a dinner for the delicate as the three gnawed at bones and sucked sticky barbecue sauce from their fingers. But in some ways, that messiness made it an informal, easygoing meal among friends.

Maddy swiped a last smudge of barbecue sauce from the corner of her mouth, then folded her napkin neatly and tucked it under her plate. "That was amazing." She looked out past the slow-bobbing sunflower heads. "And your backyard is so beautiful. How did you find this place?"

"I can't claim credit for it. That was Rosemary. You know, my one-woman fan club in the bleachers."

"Is she your aunt or something?" said Maddy.

"I guess, in a way."

Over dessert, he told them about how he ended up moving to Vermont, starting with the fateful weekend visit to Rosemary's B&B. Turning to Maddy, he said, "You actually met my ex. It was that day she stopped by when you and . . . Adrian were here." He stumbled briefly over her name. "Hannah had come back to apologize for stabbing me."

Kip already knew the story, but Maddy looked at him suddenly as if she'd misheard.

"Not a major stabbing. Just a fork to the hand."

"Just," Maddy echoed.

"Rosemary was so generous when she really had no reason to be." While Reuben knew the words were true, in speaking them, he felt an unexpected swell of emotion recalling how she had been a lifeline in those dim early winter days—a tether, as if he were a helium balloon that would otherwise have simply floated away. Maybe he would paint something for her, Reuben thought, a piece that tried to express the watery intersection of compassion and gratitude.

He held out his hand to show Kip and Maddy the neat line of tine marks, which led to a lively discussion about their respective scars and the injuries that produced them. Kip showed a jagged gash under his chin you could only see when he tipped his head up—a drunken trampoline mishap in his twenties. Reuben rubbed a scar line above his eyebrow he received from an unsanctioned science lab experiment that ended with a beaker explosion and a school suspension. Then, Maddy, blushing bright as a tomato, told them about how when she was fifteen she'd been thrown from a spooked horse and ended up with a piece of rebar impaled just below her left butt cheek.

"I'd be remiss," Kip said, "if I didn't suggest you prove this scar actually exists."

"Dude," Reuben scolded.

"Oh, don't act like you didn't think it, too."

"You're both going to have to take my word for it," Maddy stood abruptly and started collecting the used plates. Kip and Reuben got up to assist, carrying everything to the kitchen.

"I wish I could help with the cleanup, but I've got to tend to Bianca the Basset Hound's biological needs. Plus doing dishes makes my hands chafe."

"You guys are guests. I can totally manage."

"I'll stay and help," Maddy said.

Reuben looked at Kip willing him to stay longer. But Kip just looked plaintively back at him, as if saying, "You're on your own."

So Reuben went on heightened alert to ensure this simple crush did not tip the scales into action, drawing resolve from the fact that even mentioning Adrian earlier that evening made her an invisible presence he couldn't ignore. Plus, Reuben reminded himself, whatever chemistry he felt might be completely one-sided. It wouldn't be the first time. He could rattle off a handful of lopsided relationships from when he was in his twenties. *She's just not that into you*, he recalled friends telling him.

Still, his brain on the hamster wheel would not rest, and it must have shown.

Maddy pulled a serving dish from the drying rack and said, "I feel like I might be making you uncomfortable being here. I'm sure it's weird with Adrian just moving out and all." She looked at him. "I want you to know, I enjoy our friendship. That's all."

What exactly did "That's all" mean? That's all she wanted to say? That's all she considers him: a friend? That's all they'll ever be?

"Yeah," Reuben said. "It's fun talking with you, as a friend. You can't have too many, right?"

She seemed unsure how to respond. "Yeah. Well, no, I think you probably could have too many friends. Or maybe that it's best to just have a few that you're close with. That's more my style. Where should I put this?"

Reuben cursed Kip for leaving. "The cabinet to the left of the refrigerator."

She crossed the kitchen, and Reuben returned to washing the silverware.

"What's this?" she asked.

He turned to see her pointing to the rosary hanging on the key hook. Reuben had left it out at the base of the crucifix the night before in the hope that his neighbors would come back to retrieve it. When it remained untouched in the morning, he brought it inside, meaning to return it later that day. But with all the cooking and cleaning up for the dinner, he'd forgotten. Now, remembering Jackson's words about discretion, Reuben was at a loss for what to say, and so, said nothing.

"For a guy who's not religious, you sure have a lot of religious stuff."

"It's not mine," was all he managed to respond.

She pulled the rosary off the hook and held it up the way a hypnotist would to a patient. "So what kind of religious joke-art is this going to become? Or let me guess, you're going as a nun for Halloween?"

"There's no art or costumes involved. I swear."

She nodded, studying the cross at the base of the rosary. "Reuben, I get that you're pissed—your friend's experience was horrible, really sickening. But maybe you should direct that anger where it belongs." Reuben tried to interject, but her words gained emotional force. "I know to you and lots of other people, these symbols are just tokens to be made fun of. But there are good, kind people who pour their very selves into these artifacts. That devotion is sacred. It should be treated with care. Not smugness. I think it was a mistake coming here."

She tossed the dishtowel on the counter and walked out the back door, the screen sighing shut in her wake. Reuben followed her, hands dripping sudsy water.

"Maddy, that's not what's going on here. I swear."

"Yeah, well, it's getting a little hard to tell what's true," she held her hand out to Scarecrow Jesus as if to prove her point.

"I wish I could explain, but right now, I can't."

"That's fine. It's really not my business. It's fine. I'm fine." But her tone suggested otherwise. She snapped up her purse where she'd left it at the foot of her chair, but the strap got snagged and the bag was slingshot backwards sending the contents spilling all over the ground. "Dammit!"

She squatted down, retrieving her phone, keys, loose change, a packet of tissues, and threw them, one by one, into the maw of her purse. A tube of lip gloss had rolled toward Reuben, and he bent to get it for her. She wouldn't look at him. "I'm sorry," she said. Long strands of her hair had come loose. She closed her eyes. "I get so caught between my old life and this one that sometimes I think I just don't fit anywhere. Not in the church, not out of it."

Reuben understood what she meant. It was the same sense he'd had nearly his whole life as his family would tumbleweed around the country. No sense of belonging, nothing firm and reassuring to lean on.

Reuben and Maddy stood at the same time. The western sky held the sunset's fading orange glow, and the yard had come alive again with bug sounds. Holding the lip gloss out to Maddy, Reuben was suddenly struck by a sweeping feeling. Later, when he rewound the events in his mind, he thought it was like when you're standing in the ocean, and the outgoing wave is pulling the water, pulling you with it, and you know that what comes next is a big wave that's going to knock you over hard, and you can try to beat it to shore but the more you try, the more your ankles sink in the sand, and there's nothing you can do but let it crash over you.

As Maddy came closer to retrieve the lip gloss from him, Reuben felt electric, tingling and hungry to breathe her breath, taste her lips. He moved to kiss her. But Maddy clearly hadn't realized what was happening and angled her head down to retrieve the lip balm at the last second, which caused her forehead to collide painfully with his chin. They both recoiled, hands pressed to their respective injuries.

"Are you kidding me?" she yelled. "Your girlfriend moved out, like, ten minutes ago."

Mortified, Reuben paced in a small circle. "I know. I know. I'm so sorry. I didn't mean it. If Kip had just stayed..."

Maddy slid the purse straps onto her shoulder, turned and walked away. "Maybe you should start thinking before you act."

"Wait, Maddy." Reuben followed her to the front of the house. "Wait. I just have to ask. What if Adrian hadn't just moved out? I mean, what if she wasn't a factor? I feel like there's something, maybe, between you and me that could be..." He was rambling and conscious that he was rambling.

Maddy kept walking, shaking her head. When she got to her car, she opened the door and turned to him, "Reuben, I am a simple person. I lead a quiet life. Between stabbing ex-girlfriends and ballfield brawls and, I can't believe I'm saying this—" she tossed a hand toward the backyard, "bizarre religious things, you've got too much... too much stuff going on around you."

◆

"Smooth," Paul said.

"I'm such an idiot." Reuben hadn't been able to sleep and was glad for the Pacific time zone.

"She's not wrong. Your bed's not even cold. You should probably absorb the end of one relationship before you go head-butting into another."

Paul's dog Joey gave a light woof and entered the camera enthusiastically wagging her entire body. She rested her big snout on Paul's lap and sighed as he stroked her ear.

"Yeah, I know it. You're right. She's right. But somehow this feels different." Reuben thought a moment about his feelings for Adrian, how they hadn't disappeared but they certainly shifted since she'd left. "It's like when I'm working on a painting, and I feel pretty good about what I have. And I think: that's it. I know where I'm going, and it feels solid. That was my life with Adrian. Then I leave the work to settle overnight. I come back and suddenly I see something different that opens a whole new direction. One that's stronger, that feels more right. That's Maddy."

"I think you're putting a little too much faith in a woman you barely know. And speaking of faith..."

"I told you, Maddy's not part of that world anymore."

Paul shook his head. "You're wrong. It's deep to the marrow. She'll never not be part of it."

Reuben knew Paul was thinking about his mother.

"So wait," Paul said. "Can we go back to the rosary beads? What was up with that?"

"Oh. Yeah, then there's that. I suppose you're far enough away that I can fill you in."

"Well then, let me heat up my leftovers and get comfortable."

CHAPTER 23

In the summer, the goats rarely grazed on the roadside stretch of the farm. Their barn was at the far end of the property, and the herd tended to stay in its vicinity. So it was hard to know when someone would be around for Reuben to return the rosary.

He figured if anyone was there when he stopped by, he would do his best to be warm and friendly, not scary. If, as Jackson seemed to imply, the people were not in the country legally, a run-in with the wrong person could be disastrous. To further ensure he didn't come off as a threat, Reuben was carrying a tote bag with some neighborly offerings: a container of still-warm chocolate chip cookies and, for the child, a pack of construction paper plus a big box of crayons he'd bought for Adrian's nephew who showed no interest in them when he visited.

As Reuben walked along the road, he scanned the farm for signs of life. The goats were about a football field away, formless smudges milling about. Closer, but still a short distance from the road, was a small green building. Stretched between it and a thick old sycamore tree was a line of colorful clothes fluttering in the breeze. He took that as a sign that people might be in the vicinity.

There was no break in the length of stone wall, so Reuben slid up and over, landing in the tall grasses on the other side. He walked cautiously, but not secretively, again conscious that his presence could raise alarms. As he approached the building, he saw it was a converted barn with what seemed like a relatively new stoop and front door. To the left of the house was a small vegetable garden with ripening tomatoes, a teepee of pole beans, and a massive tomatillo plant with its pale, lantern blooms.

Reuben stepped up to the door, gently knocking. The glass was covered inside by a curtain, so there was no way to tell if anyone was home. He waited a moment, then knocked again. Hearing no movement, he pulled the items from his tote bag and set them on the stoop, draping the rosary beads over them. He then propped a postcard of Mount Mansfield that he had picked up on his weekend with Hannah. On the back he had sketched a line drawing of Scarecrow Jesus and written the word *Bienvenidos,* below which he printed his name. Reuben stood a moment longer, took one last look around the property, and then retraced his steps to the road.

◆

Though he hoped his message on the postcard conveyed that his neighbors were welcome in his backyard, Reuben was skeptical they would return. Even still, his subconscious nudged him awake right around 4 a.m. just in case they did. For a while he simply lay in bed, mind racing about everything that had happened over the last few weeks. He thought about how Maddy had said there was too much "stuff" in his life. From the day Joy Adams crashed his backyard through everything that followed, it felt to Reuben like his life had become a kind of Rube

Goldberg contraption: one thing colliding with the next, setting it off, and so on in a rapid-fire chain of events.

Unable to fall back asleep, he got up and threw on a sweatshirt. There was just enough moonlight outside to see without turning on the lamp, so he picked up a notebook he kept handy for sketching ideas and jotting down to-do lists and pulled a chair over to the window where he could have a clear view of the backyard.

He doodled for a bit, sharp triangles and curved lines in an abstract landscape, but then, turning the page, he started to sketch a loose portrait of Maddy, her eyes smiling but shyly downcast as if someone had just paid her a compliment. It was a detailed and attentive drawing. Even a stranger could have glanced at the portrait and seen it as an expression of affection, if not outright infatuation.

"Get a grip," he said out loud to the empty room and turned over to another blank page.

By the time the sky behind the barn started to brighten, Reuben had nearly filled the remaining pages of the notebook—not with sketches of Maddy, but a couple ideas for paintings that had enough legs to bring into the studio. During that time, there'd been no movement, no flashlights, no visitors to the backyard.

Despite the lack of sleep, the day had been productive, including a surprisingly easy and enthusiastic conversation with the owner of Gallerie la Genèse. Reuben arranged a visit for the following week during which he would bring a range of paintings and sculptures for Marc Barthelme to choose from. Adrian had been right, it was an important opportunity to take his career to the next level, and Reuben made a note to call and thank her as well as arrange to pick up his pieces from Gallery Fifth. He wondered how she was, if she'd had second thoughts or simply shut the door and moved on. Reuben wondered, too, how he would feel seeing Adrian again. Would there be regret and a bittersweet longing for what he'd lost, or a sense of gratitude that their breakup had been clean and relatively amicable, and how it had given him the chance to get to know Maddy in a way he probably wouldn't have otherwise. And then Reuben felt a pang at how stupid he'd been in making a pass at Maddy, how poor the timing.

Regardless, there was a buoyancy to Reuben's mood that seemed to express itself in a new exploratory work he started, featuring a bright, marshy meadow with thick strokes of red-winged blackbirds swaying on reeds. The style was looser, more relaxed, and though he wasn't sure he liked it, there was a sense that perhaps there was something he could learn from it.

He'd just finished wrapping his brushes when a movement caught his eye. Reuben moved closer to the window and saw what appeared to be an animal huddling near the barn. It was larger than Lou Garoo. Maybe another escaped goat? A dog, more likely. When he realized it wasn't an animal at all, he quietly opened the door and stepped outside.

The child hunkering down in the grass was watching him intently. Reuben waved but saw no acknowledgment back. As he cautiously walked closer, he could see it was a little girl, maybe four or five years old, a red barrette securing her hair away from her round face. It was the same child he'd seen get hoisted onto Arturo's back the other morning.

Reuben approached her like he would a fawn, crouching down when he got close but not too close.

"Hello," he said. The girl was completely still, only her eyes tracking his movements. He tried again, "*Hola. Mi nombre es Reuben.*"

He could see her tightly pressed lips suppress a sudden smile. Though Reuben had done well in high school Spanish, he could only remember the most rudimentary phrases. "*¿Usted vive ahora?*"

The girl tipped her head to the side, again saying nothing, but working hard to stay impassive.

"Not *ahora... aquí.*" He pointed in the direction of the farm. "*¿Vive aquí?*"

At that, she pressed a hand to her lips, but it was no use, a tiny giggle escaped. Reuben laughed, too, knowing he'd made a vocabulary mess of asking her if she lived in the green house up the road. He plucked a little ripe cherry tomato and held it out to the girl, but she stood and ran off toward the woods where the trail was.

Reuben turned a full three-sixty to see if anyone else was around, someone who might have accompanied the little girl, but there was only him. And the ever-present Scarecrow Jesus.

"I never said you could have guests."

Reuben stooped to pick a handful of green beans for lunch. Beside the garden was a piece of paper held in place by a fist-sized rock.

CHAPTER 24

In the days that followed that first visit from Rosario when she'd left the picture, Reuben had kept an eye out for any indication his neighbors had come back. In fact, his brain persisted in instinctively waking around the same predawn hour. He would get up to pee, drink some water, and stop a minute or two to watch out the window to see if there was any movement or flashlights in the garden. It wasn't until a week after he'd given up looking that Reuben found a small, round container, like something left by a garden fairy, on one of the backyard chairs. Beneath the container was another crayon drawing from Rosario, this one was of two animals—maybe dogs or goats—and a tree. Reuben had felt a little pocket of happiness in discovering the secret delivery.

Written on the container lid were the words: "*Arroz con leche.*" He carried it inside and immediately took a spoonful. The rice pudding was lightly sweet with a sprinkling of cinnamon and an unexpected but not unpleasant tang that he thought might have come from goat's rather than cow's milk. He'd intended to just take a taste and save the rest for later, but before Reuben knew it, he'd eaten more than half.

When he went to return the clean container the next morning, he brought along a small watercolor sketch he'd made of the green house, the stone wall in the foreground and a line of colorful, breeze-blown clothes stretching off the edge of the paper. Sliding over the wall again, he had hoped he might see Rosario out playing or one of the others in the garden, but again, no one was around, so he left the container and the painting on the stoop in the same spot where he had returned the rosary beads.

As much as he was enjoying these neighborly exchanges, Reuben felt confounded that, apart from the brief encounter with Rosario in the garden, he hadn't yet personally met Arturo or the others. For the next several days, Reuben set an easel on the porch and worked at painting the jagged tree line along the western edge of his property, all the while keeping a side eye toward the field to catch any movement. The effort paid off a few days later when Reuben suddenly heard the chatter of goats getting closer. Indeed, he could see a few intrepid lead goats making their way closer to the rock wall, their followers not far behind. Reuben tucked into his sneakers and walked briskly down the driveway, scanning the field.

Though the man's back was turned, Reuben recognized the beige baseball cap that he'd seen Arturo wearing at the hardware store.

"Hello! *Hola!*" Reuben waved and yelled, louder and with more enthusiasm than perhaps was called for. It seemed to take a minute for Arturo to turn, perhaps warily, and face Reuben who had already come over the rock wall and was crossing the tall grasses while skirting the herd.

"*Hola,*" Reuben said again once he'd gotten closer, this time a little more reservedly. Arturo nodded to him. "*Gracias,*" Reuben said, "*por el arroz con leche. Esta muy delicioso.*"

Arturo nodded. His hat was pulled low over his eyes. "*Si. Mi esposa es muy buena cocinera.*"

"Oh, no. I don't, *mi español no es bueno.*"

"*Ah, si, si,*" said Arturo, his voice quiet. "I do not English."

"That's okay. *Me llamo Reuben.*" He reached out for a handshake.

Arturo removed a work glove and shook Reuben's hand. "Arturo."

Reuben realized he hadn't given much thought as to what he would say beyond an initial greeting. He wracked his brain trying to remember phrases from high school, but "*Tengo una pluma*" and "*Luis es muy guapo*" were not especially helpful.

"*Yo conocer la niña, Rosario. Ella me,* um brings, *los picturas.*" Reuben was pretty sure he made that last word up, so he mimed drawing a picture.

Arturo seemed displeased that Rosario had visited Reuben. He turned toward the house and said, "*Ella no debería estar deambulando.*" He shook his head soberly. "*Ay, esta niña.*"

One of the goats gently butted its head under Arturo's hand, demanding an ear scratch. Hoping to maintain a friendlier conversation, Reuben said, "*Los animales son . . . bueno.*"

Arturo's mustache lifted upward in a near smile. "*Si, las cabras son muy . . . buenas.*"

"*Las cabras!*" Reuben said pointing to the goats like a five year old at a petting zoo. And then, he attempted to say what he had hoped to convey with the postcard. "*Arturo, a mi casa es Jesus Cristo grande.*" Reuben stretched out his arms crucifixion-like.

"*Si.*"

"*Es okay, bueno, por la familia . . .*" He put his hands together as if in prayer, hoping to demonstrate that they were invited to return to worship.

Arturo seemed to understand. He smiled and nodded his head. "*Gracias.*"

"*Si, de nada,*" Reuben said. The two men stood a moment smiling at each other until finally Reuben said. "I better let you get back to work." He plucked the word from somewhere in his memory: "*¡Trabajo!*"

"*Trabajo, si.*"

"*Yo también. Hasta luego, Arturo.*"

"*Adiós.*"

The family did eventually come back to visit Scarecrow Jesus in the predawn hours. Not every day, but occasionally. Reuben would know they had been there when he went out in the morning and found Rosario's drawings. After that, in the weeks that followed, he strolled over once with an extra loaf of banana bread he'd made, and another time with a packet of stickers for Rosario. That time, she was outside with her mother, whose name was Elena, he learned. They were collecting tomatoes in a basket. Language remained a barrier, and so the visit was short and tentative, but friendly. Before he left, Rosario handed Reuben one of the oblong plum tomatoes she'd just picked.

On his way home, Reuben made a mental note to check out what the library had available for learning Spanish.

HOME

"There's gonna be times when you're a runner, and your third-base coach is telling you to hold up. Ninety-nine percent of the time that's the right call. He's watching the play and has eyes you don't have in that moment. But every once in a while, you're gonna have a little voice pop up in your head that says, 'He's wrong. I can make it.' And you do all those instant calculations about the outfielder's arm, the catcher's skill, your own speed. You gotta make a split-second decision if the potential reward is worth the risk. Including your coach's wrath if you go for it.

"Point is, deciding for yourself and owning whatever comes next is what life is all about. Testing that out on the ball field—mind, only one percent of the time—is not a bad way to start standing in your own shoes."
—Coach Allen Bordo

CHAPTER 25

Levi Hoover was not what you would call a happy man. And after forty-three years, it showed on his face in the deep crease between his brows where he often expressed his displeasure. Chronic sleep deprivation was at least partly to blame. Though he'd worked the early morning shift at the coffee roasting plant for nearly three years, his social schedule never adjusted, and so when the guys showed up several nights a week for cards and general shit-shooting, toting 24-pack boxes of Coors and nacho fixings, he sometimes wouldn't get to sleep until after eleven, only to be painfully awakened by the 4:00 a.m. alarm clock.

The fact that the rest of the town would still be sleeping another couple of hours was always a sour thought as he passed the neighborhood's darkened homes. But today, Levi's mood was downright resentful, having unwittingly hit snooze twice. Stressed and pressed for time, he was just one late punch-in away from getting written up at a time when the gossip in the break room was that layoffs were imminent. More than losing income, getting fired would be one more humiliation added to Becca's checklist of Levi failures. She barely let him spend time with Kaden as it was. Dropping off the monthly check was the one guarantee Levi had for keeping connected to his own son.

He threw himself into a pair of passably clean jeans and t-shirt, stuffed a stale bread roll into his mouth, and tore out the door. He'd have to shave some time off the commute, so he took the dirt backroad route he normally avoided because of the washboard ruts. Foot pressed firmly on the gas pedal, Levi took the curves so tightly, the car's rear fishtailed around one of them.

Just one more turn by the Wilson Woods, and then the road would be straightaway to the main road. Coming over the rise, Levi caught a glance of movement at the edge of the woods. Damn deer, he thought, just a breath before they started to move across the street.

Levi blinked a fast second, realizing that it wasn't a group of deer. It was people. Adrenaline shot through his system as he slammed, nearly stood on the brake pedal. Dirt and rocks flew as the car skidded long into a stop. The group had bolted, almost all making it across the road, but Levi's right bumper just barely clipped one of them, sending him tumbling hard to the ground then into the grass by the rock wall. The others—a man, woman, and a little kid—turned around, horror freezing on their faces.

Levi put the car in park and stumbled out, engine still running. His heart nearly blasted from his chest. "Oh my god, oh my god. What the holy hell . . ."

The man who had been hit was up on one knee by the time the woman reached him. She pulled his right arm over her shoulder as the other man propped him up from the left. None of them saying a word or even looking over.

Levi took in their appearance and said to himself, *Mexicans.*

The little girl was sobbing now, clinging to her mother's leg as the four of them started walking toward the wall.

"Hey!" he shouted to them. But they continued walking away, huddled together like a single organism. "Well fucking fine if you don't want my help!"

By the time he got back in the driver's seat, Levi was shaking and taking large gulping breaths. He slammed his hands hard on the wheel. "Assholes! Ruined my whole fucking day!"

CHAPTER 26

Reuben was in the barn welding a green copper leaf to a beam that he'd carved with pits and striations to look like the trunk of an old maple. A small portable speaker on the workbench was playing *Roller Derby Dame*, the debut EP from Cameron's band. Hippo Campus had built up quite a local following and, according to Kip, according to Donny, according to Joss, the band would be heading out on their first tour around the Northeast, playing small venues and opening for a popular band from Buffalo.

Between the music and the welding, Reuben hadn't heard that someone had entered the barn and was trying to get his attention. So when he glanced up to see a police officer waving full arms at him in the doorway, he nearly burned a scar into the wood. Sliding off his helmet, Reuben went to stop the music.

"Sorry, I didn't quite know how to safely get your attention." It was Officer Lempke, the woman who had taken his statement after the brawl with the Blue Jays.

"Sure, no, I'll just need a moment to put my heart back in my chest." He took a breath. "What brings you here, Officer? I promise I haven't been on a ball field in weeks."

"Good to know, Mr. Downes. I'm here on a different matter." As was the case the last time they met, Officer Lempke was not interested in any talk extraneous to the concern at hand. "There was an incident reported this morning. A driver coming down Popple Hill Road at about 4:30 a.m. seems to have had an accident with a group of people crossing the street just up the road from your house. I'm wondering if you saw or heard anything?"

Reuben's chest wrenched tight. "Car accident? Is everyone all right? What happened?"

"According to the driver," she consulted her notepad, "three of the persons—a man, woman, and child—were unharmed. The fourth, a man, was hit with enough force to send him into the culvert. But, with his friends' help, he was able to stand. The driver tried to assist but the people left the scene very quickly, entering the property across the street."

"Are you kidding? He let them go off injured after he hit them with his car?"

Officer Lempke held her hands up, "I can't say for sure what transpired beyond the facts I was given. I have just conveyed those to you. As soon as the driver reported the incident, I went out to the farm to see if anyone needed help. Now, I've just come from there, and—"

Reuben looked at the clock, "It's 12:49. That's about eight hours after the accident. How could—"

"It seems, Mr. Downes, that you were not aware of this incident before now, so I will take my leave and thank you to keep an eye out."

"You're leaving?"

"There's not much I can do if there's no injured party to be found. If anything, or anyone, needs further attention, please give the station a call." She handed him a business card.

Reuben waited no more than five minutes after Officer Lempke left the driveway before zipping up into his jacket and straight-lining his way across the road to the farm. The tall weeds grabbed at his legs as he walked quickly, closing the distance to the green house. Reuben swore he wouldn't leave the property until someone answered the door and he found out if everyone was okay.

His first set of knocks went unanswered.

"*Arturo! Elena! Soy Reuben.* I heard what happened. *Accidente con el... carro—coche!*" The word was like a dusty relic in the attic of his brain. And then he found other words there. "*Ayuda. Yo puedo ayuda, si necesito.*"

No movement, no noise. Deciding he would cross the field to the goat barn, Reuben turned to go. But then, heard a whisper from inside.

He moved back to the door and said, "*¿Necesitas ayuda?*"

"*No, gracias,*" came Elena's quiet voice.

Was that true? Reuben wondered. "*¿Es la verdad?*"

He heard whispering again. Then footsteps before the door opened a crack. Elena's eyes moved from one side of Reuben to the other to make sure there was no one behind him. She stepped aside to let him in.

It was the first time he'd been inside the house, essentially one large open room with a sink, refrigerator, and stove directly in front of him. To his left was a loveseat and two wooden chairs. A small TV sat on a low table. On the far side were the beds. The man Reuben hadn't officially met yet, the one who'd rescued the goat from Reuben's truck, was lying down but propped up on pillows. At the foot of the bed, Rosario sat holding a doll in her lap. She looked at him with big, serious eyes. Arturo didn't seem to be there.

Elena walked him over to the bed.

"*Este es Tomás,*" Elena said. "*Él fue herido.*"

Reuben wasn't sure what she said but he could see that the blood had seeped through a bandage on Tomás's forehead.

Now what? Reuben thought.

"*Tomás,* are there other injuries? *¿Otro...mal?*" He knew the words weren't right so he continued with ones he could remember. "*¿Los brazos? ¿Las piernas?*" Then he held his stomach like he had a bellyache and then his chest and pretended to cough.

"*No,*" Tomás answered in a quiet voice. "*Solamente la cabeza.*" He pointed to the wound on his head.

"*El corte es profundo,*" Elena said. She reached over to Tomás's bandage. He flinched as she gently peeled the tape and showed a gaping gash with a skin flap that made Reuben's knees wobble. He had to look away to avoid fainting. Reuben had no first aid training but knew enough that with a head injury like that, Tomás might also have concussion.

"I can take you to the hospital. *Hospital?*"

The word seemed to be the same in English and Spanish by virtue of their emphatic response, "*No, no.*"

Healthcare facilities meant admission forms and medical bills.

"*¿Dónde está, Arturo?*"

"*Con las cabras.*"

"No hospital?" Reuben asked again.

"*No hospital.*" Elena said with the tone of a firmly closed door.

He was loath to do it, but Reuben knew he needed to make a call.

"*Mi amiga,* Maddy, *es possible que ella ayuda. ¿Con permiso?*" He pulled his phone from his jacket pocket and held it up with a questioning look on his face.

Elena and Tomás regarded each other. Then Elena reached for a flip phone on the night table and made a call, Reuben thought was probably to Arturo. She spoke so quickly that the only words Reuben caught were the ones he had used *"amiga"* and *"ayuda."*

Elena held the phone aside and asked Reuben, *"¿Ella es una doctora?"*

Reuben said, "Not exactly, but she can help."

Elena seemed to understand him and looked to Tomás who simply nodded once.

◆

Opening the text to Maddy with *You know how in Mafia movies they bring in a vet to treat gunshot wounds to avoid involving the police?* may not have been the most thoughtful strategy, but it did get Maddy to quickly reply: *Please be joking.*

Reuben assured her that no one had been shot but there was a small injury that needed to be looked at by someone with competent first aid skills, and it required discretion. He could picture her face, set and stern, reminding herself this was exactly the kind of "stuff" she had told him she wanted no part of. He quickly followed up saying that if she would let him call her, he would explain what had happened, as well as the rosary beads and why he had been so evasive about them.

"You're lucky my shift just finished," were the first words Maddy said when she picked up on the second ring. In an aside to someone, he heard her say "See you in the morning," then she returned to Reuben, "Mind you, I'm only listening. I'm not promising anything."

"Understood."

Pacing the cement stoop, Reuben told her pretty much everything, as matter-of-factly and efficiently as possible, starting with that first encounter with the migrant family and the dropped rosary beads that Maddy had seen when she was over and finishing with the accident and how Reuben had nearly passed out at the sight of the wound.

She was quiet a moment then said, "I'm not a doctor, Reuben. I'm not even a nurse's assistant."

"I know. They understand, I explained to them. More or less."

"I can't administer—"

"It's just cleaning the wound and probably doing a few stitches."

"*Just.*" She chuffed. "Also, I don't speak Spanish."

"I barely do, either, but we managed to understand each other. Look," Reuben took a breath, "I don't know a lot about their situation, but they're adamant about not going to the hospital. I'm afraid he's going to jump right back into work, and then the wound will get worse, possibly infected."

And so, Maddy reluctantly agreed to come, bringing some supplies with her. Reuben was waiting by his mailbox when she pulled in the driveway. Between the way things were left between them and the strangeness and intensity of the circumstances, their reunion was stiff and strained. Reuben was sure to keep at least a six-foot buffer of space between them to assure her this wasn't an elaborate ruse to make another pass.

"Thank you," Reuben said, trying to break the ice. "I know this is a lot to ask."

"I will get in huge trouble if anyone finds out."

"They won't. I promise."

With softball only happening in spring and summer, Reuben hadn't spent any time with Maddy in the fall.

In the cool late-September weather, she'd traded her leggings and sporty shorts for a pair of faded jeans that were frayed in places on the pockets and cuffs. Her brown hair was pulled back in the familiar ponytail, and he could see the gray collar of a flannel button-down poking out from under her rust-colored fleece, everything perfectly complementing the landscape's seasonal palette.

They walked up the road, chatting benignly about the change in the temperatures and Cameron's band's new album, which they had both listened to that day. Reuben held out a hand to help Maddy slide over the rock wall, but she dismissed the gesture regarding him flatly, "I think I can manage." He lowered his chin deferentially.

Once they'd reached the house, Reuben knocked, saying, "*Soy* Reuben. *Y mi amiga*, Maddy."

It was Arturo who opened the door, having returned from the barn. Reuben could tell he was uneasy letting them into their home. But Maddy seemed to anticipate the need to put them at ease and shifted into warm smiles and a calming voice that she was probably more accustomed to using with concerned pet owners.

"It's okay," she said, putting a gentle hand on Arturo's arm. "I'm here to help." She opened her portable medical kit to show him the supplies inside.

Reuben had brought a different set of supplies in a cloth bag. He gestured for Rosario to join him by the couch. When she hesitated, he took out a sketch pad and some colored pencils, setting them on the small coffee table. She stood watching and waiting, but clearly curious. When Reuben started doodling, she inched her way over.

While Maddy and the grown-ups tended to Tomás, Reuben sketched the head of a horse with a brown pencil and then held it out to Rosario, encouraging her to continue the drawing. Still cautious, she carefully took the pencil in her tiny, dimpled hand. Concentrating fully, she made a wide, flat circle body beneath the head with four stick legs at various angles below as if the horse were running. She handed the pencil back to him. Reuben set it down then picked up a robin's-egg-blue pencil. Rosario crinkled up her nose when she saw he was going to color the body with it. Then, following his lead, she picked up the green pencil and started coloring the head with it. Reuben kept half his awareness tuned to the situation with Tomás and the grown-ups' quiet conversation. The other half he focused on Rosario as the two of them took turns drawing different parts of the scene including a purple sun and an orange tree.

When Reuben heard a shift to a more relaxed tone in the conversation behind him, he turned to see Maddy handing Elena some first aid supplies. Tomás was inspecting his freshly bandaged head in a hand mirror.

"We're all set," Maddy said to Reuben. "The wound is cleaned, and I put in few stitches. Seems like it was a sharp rock that had cut him, not anything metal. Which is lucky because then he probably would have needed a tetanus shot, and there's no way I was going to be able to administer that."

"Any concern about a concussion?" Reuben asked.

"I don't think so. He seems pretty alert, just a little shaken. They all are."

Arturo came over and put a hand on Rosario's head, saying something quietly to her. She gathered up the pencils and put all but one back in the bag. With a steady hand, she signed her name in big block letters in the lower right corner of the drawing before handing it to Reuben to add his own.

He wrote his name just below hers. "Good teamwork," he said, and she beamed.

As Maddy and Reuben moved toward the door, Arturo hurried over to intercept them. He held out a folded set of bills to Maddy. She shook her head and said, "No, no, *gracias.*"

"*Si, si, por favor,*" he said.

"It's okay. No money," she said.

Arturo turned and said something to Elena. She went to the freezer and took out a round container like the one that had held the rice pudding. "*Tomen estas al menos, como agradecimiento.*" She held it out. "*Son albóndigas.*"

"I think that's meatballs?" Reuben said to Maddy.

Arturo nodded, "*Si, albóndigas.*"

"It's okay, you don't need to give me anything," Maddy said.

Elena pushed the container closer.

"I think they want to be able to thank you."

She hesitated and then smiled. "Okay," Maddy said and took the container. "*Muchas gracias.*"

Tomás, walking slowly, had come over with his freshly bandaged head. "*Gracias a ustedes,*" he said reaching his hand to shake Maddy's, then Reuben's.

"*Hasta luego,* Reuben," Rosario shouted after he and Maddy were already out the door and on the stoop.

"See ya later, Rosario," Reuben shouted back.

"See ya later," she repeated.

Sunset was still a couple hours away, but the temperature had started to drop. Maddy zipped her fleece up to her chin, and Reuben stuffed his hands in his jacket pockets.

"They seem like nice people," she said.

"Yes, they really are," Reuben said, then quickly added. "Though obviously, I haven't had a lot of deep conversations with them." He intended it as a light joke, but it fell flat, even to him. "I don't know much about them, really. How long they've been here. Not even where they came from. They were at the farm when I moved in, I'm pretty sure. I sort of met Tomás my first week when a loose goat ended up on my truck. But it took a good year for us to meet, really. And weirdly, I have Scarecrow Jesus to thank for that."

When they reached the stone wall, Maddy offered her hand to help Reuben over it. "Your reverse sexism is noted," he said, resisting the urge to reach for her hand. "Does that mean we're friends again?"

"I don't put my career on the line for just anybody."

Whether she did so for him or for a family in need, he didn't care. She was there walking beside him.

After a moment, Maddy said, "So let me get this straight. You think Tomás was hit crossing the road after they had a prayer service or something in your backyard?"

Reuben was still processing that part. "I can't be sure, but I think that's what happened. There's a deer trail up the road, closer to their house, that leads through the woods to my backyard. They've used it the few times they've come by. It's always super early in the morning. Most of the time I don't even know they've been there, except when Rosario leaves me a picture or a pinecone or something."

"She seems to like you."

"I'm sure I'm more a curiosity than anything. The neighbor who talks funny Spanish and has a giant Jesus in his backyard. I'm not sure if she gets to spend time with other kids."

A breeze had picked up, making the leaves flutter and wave.

"Scarecrow Jesus," Maddy said shaking her head. "A desecration to some. A place to pray for others."

"And then there's Paul—" Reuben said.

"What about you?"

"I don't really know. Seems like it could be all of that. And maybe more." He was thinking about how in some way, Scarecrow Jesus was also what drew him and Maddy closer.

When they reached the driveway, Reuben opened the mailbox and pulled out a handful of envelopes and a grocery circular. Lou Garoo was rolling in the dirt, pausing occasionally on his back, spread-eagled but keeping a wary eye on them as they approached. When they were within a few feet, he righted himself, filthy with dust, and sat hunched like a sphinx, as if he was about to pose a riddle they needed to answer before they could pass. When Maddy tried to deliver a behind-the-ear scratch, the cat swatted at her defensively.

"I get it, Lou. Your driveway, your rules." She gave him a wide berth, shortcutting over to her car, which was parked next to Reuben's truck like it belonged there. She paused and turned to Reuben, holding up the container of *albondigas*. "This is too much for me to eat by myself."

"They actually make great leftovers. You can have it one day with rice, and the next on a crusty baguette with a little chopped cilantro. Like a Mexican *banh mi*."

Maddy looked down at her shoes.

"Or," Reuben said, "We can share. I could defrost them and split into two containers."

"Reuben, do I have to invite myself in?"

He shrugged. "I didn't want to presume. I was clearly not great at reading the room last time you were here."

She smiled. "This meal belongs to both of us. We should enjoy it together."

"It just so happens I have a baguette in the freezer. May I officially invite you to come in for an early dinner?"

"I'm so glad you thought of it," she said.

Maddy followed him up the porch stairs and inside. She must have glanced in the laundry room and seen the cat's litter box tucked in the corner.

"Looks like your barn cat is now a house cat?"

"Sort of. I figured it was going to be getting cold again and decided that training him to come in when it gets dark might be a good thing."

She seemed to approve of this logic. Although it wasn't entirely honest. Rather, the house had felt big and empty and quiet after Adrian left. Bringing Lou Garoo inside for the night gave Reuben a presence to talk to, even if the cat simply regarded him blank faced and unimpressed with whatever idea or insight Reuben had spoken aloud. Gradually, the cat allowed something adjacent to affection, voluntarily curling up beside Reuben on the couch while watching TV, sometimes even offering a contented snore. In the morning, after eating, Lou Garoo would sit by the back door, staring at the handle until Reuben let him outside to do whatever it is a cat does during his day.

As the meatballs heated on the stove, Maddy set the table and Reuben shredded carrots and diced cilantro and parsley together for toppings. The kitchen was filled with the rich aroma of tomatoes and onions and a hint of earthy smoke from the chiles. It was a little after four o'clock when they sat down to eat.

"Oh my gosh, this is amazing," said Maddy. "I should barter services for food more often."

"Better yet, we should ask Elena to teach us how to make them."

"Who's this 'we' you refer to? I am much more partial to eating than I am to cooking." She took a big bite as if to demonstrate. "Don't get me wrong, I know my way around a kitchen. You couldn't grow up in my house without learning how to prepare the meals. Me and my sister were kneading bread before we could walk. I'm a badass seamstress, too."

"I'm sure Tomás can attest to that," Reuben said.

She continued. "All that 'women's work' though, it just didn't fit for me. At the end of a meal, the girls would get a look or a nod that said it was time to clear the table and start the dishwashing. Made me nuts. And I'd get crazy jealous of my boy cousins who learned carpentry and car repair. They got to play soccer and baseball."

"Is that what made you leave?"

"Not primarily. For a long time, I just thought I was a weirdo for not caring about keeping house or learning to be a good wife. I just figured I would get used to it." She pressed a tiny bread crumb on the table with her finger and deposited it on her plate. "It was something different that eventually led me away. Someone, I should say."

She started telling him about the summer she was sixteen, and a few families from the church were on their annual service trip, traveling to a town about thirty miles outside Wheeling, West Virginia. The arrangements were similar to past trips. The group would be doing construction work and home repairs, cooking community meals and then, of course, there were church services in the morning and evening. Being the oldest, Maddy's job was to take care of the kids—keeping them busy with games and races, reading books, and doing crafts.

"I wasn't particularly good with the kids. I mean, you know me, I'm not the most warm and huggable of people." Reuben might debate the latter but didn't dare say so. "Mostly, I set things up and bossed the bigger kids around. They were the ones running the activities. This one day, I was off to the side, watching a kickball game or something, and a girl my age, maybe a little older, comes over and stands next to me, really close, like shoulder-to-shoulder, and says, 'Why don't you go the fuck home?' I had no experience with that kind of talk. I didn't know what to make of it, so I must have just looked at her confused. She said, 'We never asked you people to come here. You just showed up, like you're better than us. Like we don't know how to take care of our own' is what she said. I told her she had us pegged wrong, that we were there to help, to make things easier and better for her and her neighbors. She said something like, 'All those good deeds, though, they come with a catch, don't they? We don't need Jesus,' she said. 'Don't tell us to pray. Praying doesn't give us money or jobs.'"

"That must have felt like a bit of a slap."

"Actually, it was more like she handed me a grenade and walked away." Maddy picked up the empty dishes and carried them to the sink. "Because after that, I couldn't avoid seeing something I hadn't noticed before, which was this tension and ambivalence in the communities we were so certain that we were 'saving.' They tolerated us and they accepted our help, but I think there was this undercurrent of good riddance when we were finally getting in our vans and leaving. Not everyone. For sure, some were genuinely grateful for our help, and a handful who had, at least temporarily, 'found God.' But that girl's words stuck with me. It was like putting on a pair of glasses and seeing the world clearly for the first time. Eventually, all those things—like the sexism—that had nagged at me, that I'd just pushed to the back of my thoughts, I don't know, they kind of elbowed their way to the front. And then the big question landed." She stopped talking.

"The big question?"

"Did I actually believe in God?"

Reuben remembered her words from the last time they talked, about how she didn't fit in the church or outside it anymore. "And?"

"The honest answer was I didn't know, so I figured I should move away and see if God followed." She refilled her glass of water and leaned back against the sink. "He didn't, or at least not in any way that aligned with what I'd been taught. I didn't feel like a bad person when I went on dates or had a drink. I felt different, but also the same. I was still a close part of my family, but also outside of them."

"I get that. I know what it's like to feel adrift. Like there's nothing anchoring you," Reuben said. "You never know, maybe someday we can be that for each other." It was as if someone had distracted his brain long enough to let the words escape of their own accord. Reuben hadn't even really been conscious of the thought until it was mortifyingly out in the space between them. His shoulders sank. "You must think I'm the biggest ass. I wasn't making another pass, I promise."

Maddy shook her head slowly and said, "Well. That's disappointing."

"Oh?" he asked. She gave him an exaggeratedly coy look. "I'm not one to question your change of heart, but why the change of heart?"

"You're not in total rebound mode. That's the easy answer."

"I'm not interested in easy answers."

She heaved a sigh. "I don't know, Reuben. After that night and how we left things, all I could think about was what a long winter it was going to be without talking to you."

"You could have called at any time—"

"It's not that easy." She folded her arms across her chest. "But I will admit, when I saw your name pop up on my phone, I kind of felt this little happy spark."

Reuben felt an electric current run through his body. Maddy's eyes were locked on his as she took a step closer. It took all his restraint to simply stand still, holding back the kind physical momentum that might otherwise have broken the spell. And so, she kept moving toward him. It was that charged breath of a moment before a first kiss, the kind you only get once.

And then, a sudden movement in the backyard caught Reuben's eye. He broke away from their almost-embrace and leaned toward the window.

"Oh my god, Reuben! I thought—" Maddy said.

"There's someone out there."

"In the yard?"

"Yeah. Maybe it's Arturo?" He moved to the door, then stopped and turned back to her, taking both her hands in his. They were smooth and warm. "Please don't go anywhere."

"As long as it's not another ex-girlfriend."

The light was fading fast, leaving the backyard flat with dim shadows. Though the back door wasn't quiet on the close, the figure, who was on the path near the garden, didn't seem to notice and continued to walk around as if wandering other people's yards was nothing unusual. As Reuben got closer, he could see it was a stocky guy with a kind of eighties shoulder-length halo of curls. He wore a thick, hooded jacket, and the various pockets of his cargo pants were stuffed, weighted down with hidden things. He didn't seem to be a threatening presence but was definitely an odd one.

Seeing Reuben, the guy looked over and smiled broadly. "You're taller than I was expecting."

Reuben cocked his head. "Do we know each other?"

The visitor nodded slowly, looking strangely like a bobblehead version of himself. "Not really. But not for lack of trying on my part. I get it though. You're not a big phone person."

"I'm sorry, who are you?"

"Patton. Papadopoulos. *Vermont Weekly*."

"Oh. Oh, yeah, no." Reuben waved his hands dismissively. "No thank you. Not interested."

Patton continued as if he hadn't heard Reuben. "It's still here. Scarecrow Jesus. I had wondered."

"It's an old story, man. People have moved on, and I'd like to keep it that way." Reuben gestured to the path to the driveway, inviting Patton to take it.

"Well, see, there's a fresh angle I'm looking into."

Reuben didn't like the sound of that. "What fresh angle?" He stepped closer to the reporter, but Patton kept moving around, seeming to be making mental notes about the backyard scene.

"What fresh angle?" Reuben repeated.

"Let's just say, I have this idiot brother-in-law. Not a bad guy, just says and does cringey, kind of ill-advised things. A lot. Sometimes it's hard to believe he and my wife were raised in the same household but you never know how that DNA is gonna shake out."

"I actually have company right now, so—"

"Right. Let me cut to the chase. So, Levi was driving into work early this morning, like predawn. Just a tiny bit up the road over there," he pointed off beyond the barn, "And, uh, he ended up hitting someone with his car. Can you believe it?"

Reuben, never a winner in a poker game, did his best to look appalled. "Geez, that sounds terrible."

"He said there were four people crossing the road, actually, three adults and a little kid. Kid was totally fine, thank God. But definitely weird they were walking the road at that hour."

"I'm pretty much guaranteed to be sleeping at that time so I'm not a witness. Sorry you came out here for nothing."

Patton held a hand up. "Well, not nothing. My brother-in-law was pretty sure the people didn't speak English. That they were probably migrant workers. Although, Levi being Levi, he, of course, called them 'illegals.' See what I mean? Cringey."

Maddy, who had been hovering by the door, shouted to Reuben, "Hey, I'm sorry, but I have to head home."

Reuben felt a crush of disappointment. "No, no, stay. This guy was just leaving."

"Actually, I wasn't," Patton said.

"Thanks," she said, "but I think we've concluded our business for the day."

"I see," Reuben said, wondering if she'd overheard the conversation and wanted to be far away from a reporter's questions.

"So you'll drop off that estimate at our office maybe tomorrow?" she asked.

"Yes, I will definitely be in touch about that."

"That sounds wonderful." He couldn't see her expression well, but it seemed to be smiling. "I'll see myself out the front, then," she said.

"Hey Mad...son. Ms. Madson? Thank you for the opportunity to work with you." Reuben watched her go back through the kitchen, longing to follow her.

"Sorry to interrupt your date."

"Not a date. And let's not pretend you're sorry."

Patton shrugged.

"Look," Reuben said. "I really don't have anything to tell you. I wasn't there. So if you don't mind—"

"Don't you want to know what happened? Someone was hit by a car just up the road from your house."

Reuben didn't want to let on that he knew what happened, and clearly more than Patton. "Yeah, of course, I do. Is the person okay?"

"I don't know. Levi said they ran off."

"Seems like a dead end for your story, then."

Patton again did the bobblehead thing. "Do you believe in coincidences, Reuben?"

Reuben felt himself getting impatient. "I don't know, maybe?"

"I don't. It's the reporter in me. In 9.73 times out of ten, there's a reasonable connection, even if you can't spot it right away."

"That's a very specific statistic."

Patton rubbed his arms a little. "It's getting kind of cold out here. Maybe I could come in and just borrow ten minutes of your time, then I swear, I'll get out of your hair tonight?"

It was difficult to imagine this guy could order takeout in ten minutes. But again, Reuben wanted to avoid seeming cagey, so he relented and invited the reporter into the studio.

Patton wandered the space, looking at Reuben's various works in progress: a large-format seascape, two smaller studies of the same scene and a two-foot-tall bristlecone pine tree he was constructing from strands of reclaimed wire. All would be making their way to Gallerie la Genèse once complete.

"Wow, you do some impressive work in here. I've only seen that big landscape piece you did for the Wallington Bank lobby and, no offense, I barely even noticed it."

"It's a bank, Patton. Provocative art isn't really their style."

"Not like Scarecrow Jesus?"

"That wasn't art."

"Be real," Patton said. "It's too controversial. Where did you even get an eight-foot-tall crucifix, anyway?"

"Weren't you here to talk about the car accident?"

"See, that's where this idea of coincidence comes in. But before I get to that, I want you to understand something. I grew up in this county. I know its people. I *am* its people. So more than anyone, I have a deep love for the communities here.

"I also lived in Atlanta for six years and spent ten months traveling throughout Mexico and Central America. You move around the world, and you start to understand there are pockets of the U.S. where perspectives might be a little . . . insulated. And maybe not challenged enough." He picked up a square gum eraser and started fiddling with it. "Frankly, that's why I moved back home. As a journalist, I wanted to share with my community stories that took on a little complexity, that showed the nuance in topics that, on the surface, might simply seem black or white. Maybe I could help people feel like even if they didn't agree, they had a better understanding of why someone might have a different opinion."

He paused, waiting for Reuben to say something.

"I confess, I'm still not connecting the dots here."

"One of those complex topics I've been known to wade into is Vermont's migrant community—working conditions, policy—or lack thereof. Legal issues, those kinds of things. So when my wife told me about her brother's literal run-in today with what seems likely to have been a migrant family on the same road as Scarecrow Jesus, I thought I'd come by and see what's going on in this neighborhood."

As he talked, Patton walked the space like Columbo about to name whodunnit. "Sure enough, there's that goat farm across the way. Now migrant workers tend more toward cow operations, but farms need help, and it seems feasible that this group is working there." He picked up various objects, considered them, and put them down again in exactly the same position from which he lifted them. "Levi said his conscience got the better of him and he went and filed a police report, which I went to check out earlier today. It seems the family was crossing the street from the opposite side of the farm. I parked up that way, just checking around the area. No one was around at the farm, not even the goats."

"They're usually in the far field," Reuben said, not sure why he felt compelled to offer the detail.

"As I was walking around, I discovered there's a bit of a trail on this side of the road, right near where the accident was said to have happened."

Reuben started to break out in a tingly sweat. He leaned his elbow on the worktable and tried hard to strike a casual pose. "Deer come and go from there all the time," he said to Patton. "A lot of deer. Coyote, too. Probably chasing the deer. It's practically a nature highway."

"Well, I followed that trail. Thankfully, it was short. I'm not much of a hiker." He pointed to his white-socked feet showing through a pair of bright orange Crocs. "Surprisingly, it led me to your backyard where I finally came face-to-face with the infamous Scarecrow Jesus. Oh, I also found this in one of low bushes near it."

Patton unbuttoned one of his cargo pockets and took out a rolled piece of construction paper. As he smoothed it out on the worktable, Reuben could see it was one of Rosario's drawings, but it looked dirt smudged and possibly rained on, leaving him to suspect that it had blown away in one of the recent storms. The colors had smeared like a watercolor, but it clearly showed four stick figures gathered two and two on either side of a scarecrow that held colorful bunches of flowers in each its outstretched hands. The top of the picture had the words *FLORS* and *POR RUBIN* written in careful block letters; the bottom was signed, as always, *ROSARIO*.

Reuben's brain couldn't process quickly enough how to navigate this conversation, so he opted to say nothing.

"They were coming from here this morning, weren't they?" Patton asked gently.

Reuben shook his head, "I don't know."

"I swear, Reuben, I'm not here to get anyone in trouble. I just came out to see if there was a story." Then, almost as an aside, he said, "I wasn't expecting it to be this one."

"And what exactly do you think 'this one' is?"

Here Patton veered a little off course again. "During that year when I was traveling out of the country, I can't tell you how often I would encounter these roadside shrines. Have you seen them? You're driving along an empty, dusty road, come over a rise and there's this little holy oasis. Sometimes it's just a simple, unadorned cross surrounded by candles that have been burned down to the glass. Other times, it's an elaborate structure, colorful and covered in garlands of fake flowers. Or maybe it's a memorial to a tragedy that happened there. Sometimes, it's just a remote sanctuary giving travelers who are far from home a place to pray."

Patton's words hung in the air, heavy with implication. Reuben still didn't trust himself to say anything, and so kept his arms folded and lips pressed together to the point where the silence between them felt like a standoff.

"So I have to wonder," Patton said, "if Scarecrow Jesus is a little like those shrines. And maybe, the flannel and the jeans and the hat, they were just camouflage to hide the fact that you set up a makeshift church for your neighbors who can't easily practice their religion in public."

"That's absurd," Reuben said firmly, though he could feel his pulse hammering in his head.

"Is it?"

"I did not create a makeshift church."

"If I've gotten it wrong, then you tell me what's going on. Including why you put it up in the first place." When Reuben didn't answer, Patton said, "Buddy, your name is on this picture of people hanging out by Scarecrow Jesus, drawn by the kid across the street who had a family member hit by a car this morning. Coming from a trail leading to your backyard. See? In 9.73 out of ten. Make that 9.4."

"I need to ask you to leave, Patton."

He made an exasperated noise. "I know. It's a lot to take in, and I don't really know what your relationship to them is. Clearly, it's friendly. My intent is, too." Patton pulled a business card from a pocket and set it down on the workbench. "Just do me a favor. Don't totally shut me out. Go read some of my articles. I think you'll find I'm a fair and thoughtful reporter on the subject."

That evening, a search of the *Vermont Weekly* website revealed over two dozen articles and commentaries by Patton Papadopoulos, including the one on Scarecrow Jesus. Sitting at the kitchen table with a cup of tea, Reuben skimmed the results and found four stories that explored and reported on events within the migrant worker community. The earliest one, from 2013, opened with an analogy in which Patton invited readers to imagine their house was on fire. The choice was to wait for the fire department, which, in this hypothetical, was quite a distance away and would not arrive in time to save the home, or do whatever they could in the moment to put out the fire and minimize the damage. The choice for many self-sufficient Vermonters, he wrote, would be clear—don't wait for help; save the house. Now, he asked readers to imagine they were a third-generation dairy farmer who can't find any workers to help with the care and milking of their 200-head herd of Holsteins, not to mention, the farm is barely surviving financially. "For many farmers," Patton wrote, "the choice is stark: sell off their beloved livestock and land or do whatever they can to keep their family farm on life support." The latter choice meant tapping a ready, willing, and, frankly, cheap migrant labor pool while turning a blind eye to the law.

A follow-up article, presenting the migrant workers' perspective, took a similar tactic, asking readers to think back to the reasons many of their own immigrant ancestors fled their home countries—violence, poverty, hunger, disease, opportunity. The only difference between the great migration of the early twentieth century and today, Patton argued, is policy. "And while the promise of immigration reform is an empty can that gets kicked down the road every political cycle, migrant workers continue to risk dangerous, often deadly journeys in the hope of finding safety or of earning money to send home to families struggling to have enough to eat."

A later piece focused on some of the problems caused by the state's adoption of what was essentially a "Don't ask, don't tell" policy, the worst of which were suffered by migrant workers in the form of physical abuse, unpaid work, and dangerous, unsanitary living conditions. Patton also cited conflicts between local law enforcement and federal immigration agents, pitting communities that were willing to accept the presence of undocumented immigrants versus the feds who were not.

While it was clear Patton's position leaned toward support for the migrant workers and farming community, true to his assertion, he worked hard to honestly articulate the complexity of the situation. After all, the law was the law, and there were consequences for breaking it, including deportation when undocumented workers were caught in the wrong place at the wrong time.

When Patton had finally moved to the door to leave, Reuben was noncommittal, saying only that he might check out an article. It was clear, however, that Patton would remain persistent when later that night, an email came through Reuben's website contact form.

>
> NAME: Patton Papadopoulos
> SUBJECT: Chicory Field Farm
> EMAIL: patton@vtwkly.com
>
> One of my sources tells me that your neighbor, Chicory Field goat farm, is owned by a woman named Claire Meloy. Back in the nineties, she and her husband, Troy, left Silicon Valley to lead a simpler, back-to-the-land life. They started the goat farm, learning how to make their own cheese, which, it turned out, they were pretty good at, so they expanded the herd and sold their chèvre to local specialty and health food stores. Eventually, demand for the cheese

outstripped their interest in making it, and they sold the formula to one of the larger producers. But they kept the goats and sold the milk to bottlers, other cheese makers, and a confectioner that makes a killer caramel sauce.

Fast forward ten years. Troy is tragically killed when his bike is hit by a distracted driver. Claire is understandably devastated. Family and friends tell her sell the goats, get a dog, move away, whatever, because she clearly can't manage the farm on her own. But the goats are her connection to Troy, and she says hell no, just get me some help, which one of her friends does, recruiting three migrant workers — two of them a couple — away from a less-than-scrupulous cow farm operation. Then a couple years ago, Claire developed rheumatoid arthritis. Now she handles all the business transactions, and the people working the farm handle the care and milking of the animals. Arturo Gomez Fernandez and his wife Elena Garcia Juarez are both from Guatemala. Their friend Tomás Navarro Ruiz is from Mexico. Arturo and Elena have a four-year-old daughter, Rosario Gomez Garcia. I know at least that name is familiar to you.

I have an article to write, one that adds yet another human angle to the complex story about illegal immigration: faith. Some of the readers who are most hostile to the idea of migrants being here are, ironically, devout church goers. I want to help them imagine what it would be like to leave behind, not just their homeland, but also their faith community. The migrants may work themselves to the bone every day on the farm, but their spiritual need doesn't just disappear. In fact, it probably just gets bigger. That was what was so clear to me when I found that drawing and put some of the pieces together. You say you didn't intend to create a space for worship but that's what it became, didn't it?

Let me assure you, I will include no identifying information about you, the family, or the farm. I will include no references to Scarecrow Jesus. It'll just be "a neighbor who welcomed the farm workers to his yard to practice their religion."

What the story is missing is the (anonymous) voice and perspective of real people. For that, I'm asking you to share the attached message with the family to see if I can visit or at least talk with them over the phone about their experiences. I don't know what their level of literacy is, so I kept the message very brief, and if they have questions, maybe you can just fill them in as best you can. I know it's a lot to ask, and I will understand if they decline.

> I just have to believe the more we stop trying to pretend stories like these aren't happening, the sooner we'll be able to make change possible. Call me an optimist, but I think local church leaders might read the story and open their doors to those who are missing the spiritual connection a church provides.
> -PP

The attachment was written in Spanish so Reuben could only get the barest gist based on what Patton explained in the body of the email. Reuben sat for a while, ruminating on Patton's arguments. Ultimately, the man was simply asking for help in delivering a message. Had he asked Reuben to give it to Rosemary, he wouldn't have hesitated. Though Reuben knew that wasn't exactly apt comparison, he ultimately decided that he would print the message and bring it over. If Arturo, Elena, or Tomás didn't want to speak with Patton, they wouldn't.

Reuben had already planned on going over to check on Tomás the next morning. And so he replied to Patton that he would give them the message but do nothing more. If they didn't follow up, Reuben insisted that Patton drop the matter or seek different sources. Also, if the story did go forward, and he so much as gave a whiff that it was in any way connected to Scarecrow Jesus or Reuben himself, he would expose Patton for being a liar and an unscrupulous journalist.

CHAPTER 27

Reuben was scheduled to leave town the next day to deliver his latest pieces to the gallery in Montreal. His plan had been to spend a few days restaurant-hopping and exploring some neighborhoods off the tourist path. He considered postponing the trip just so he could see Maddy sooner, but ultimately decided that it wasn't bad to take a pause to make sure their tentative feelings weren't simply from coming down off the day's intensity. Still, the fact that she offered to feed Lou Garoo while he was away seemed encouraging.

Once he arrived in Montreal, he texted her, letting her know that he'd stopped by the farm earlier that morning. Elena had just finished applying a clean bandage, and Tomás was doing well. He then explained as concisely as possible who the unexpected visitor had been and the basic gist of how and why he had shown up. When he'd gone over that morning, Reuben brought along the message from Patton and gave it to Elena. *What she chooses to do from here is up to her.*

Over the course of the next two days, Reuben sent Maddy pictures of things that caught his eye. Random shots of graffiti art, abstract architectural details, the gleeful exchange between a knife-juggling busker and a pair of young twins. In return, Maddy sent a photo of Lou Garoo, looking furious at being "under house arrest" as she captioned it. Plus a few pics of some of her patients: Polly, a long-eared cocker spaniel and a rescued squirrel with a broken leg.

I've secretly named him Wayne. 😂

The delivery and installation at Gallerie went smoothly. As Reuben was setting up the new pieces with one of the staff members, the owner, Marc Barthelme stopped in. They chatted a bit about the talented new artist adjacent to Reuben's area, about what events were coming up at the gallery, and how the changing season was inspiring fresh color palettes in Reuben's current projects.

As he walked back to his truck, Reuben thought about the space and the people, and the eclectic, artsy neighborhood. Everything had an urban warmth and charm that made Reuben thankful, though not without a little wistful ambivalence, that Adrian had given him the boot from Gallery Fifth. And though he would never admit it out loud, Reuben's opinion might even have softened toward John Eastlake, who in fact, had made a really good match for Reuben's work. And so that one door closing, another opening idiom felt particularly apt, in Reuben's case, not just in art, but in relationships as well.

When he returned home three days later, Reuben and Maddy's reunion wasn't the kind of intimate setting he had been hoping for. Instead, it was at a gathering of the Mallards at the local Irish bar/pizza parlor. Donny had invited them all to officially close out the cut-short season and offer a bon voyage to Cameron, whose band would be heading out on their tour the following week.

It was the first time the team had all been together since the night of the brawl, which was now a little over two months ago.

A few of the team members were already seated when Reuben arrived, including Maddy, who was between Patrice on one side and Kip on the other. As Donny arrived carrying a couple pitchers of beer, Kip politely stood up and said, "Hey, I'm going to move to the other side of the table. Nothing personal, Maddy, it's just a little drafty over here by the window."

As he passed, Kip mumbled, "I've been holding the seat for fifteen minutes waiting for you to get here." He gave Reuben a subtle fist bump.

"I don't mind drafts, Maddy," Reuben said, making his way over.

"Me neither," said Wayne, holding up his just-filled mug. "I'd say a toast, but the rock star isn't here yet."

As if simply waiting for his cue, Cameron walked in, Joss right beside him. It took a moment for Reuben to realize they were holding hands. The others around the table noticed, too. Wayne even did a surprised double take.

When the two had settled in their chairs, all the *hellos* and *how's it goings* exchanged, and no one had yet acknowledged this new development between Joss and Cameron, Patrice chimed in, "I cannot help but notice that the two of you seem to be more than friends today?"

Cameron beamed while Joss seemed slightly mortified. Cameron responded, "Yeah. And no one is as surprised as I am."

"Dude, stop it," Joss said quietly, her eyes focused on the silverware roll-up in front of her.

"I thought you were gay," said Donny, loud enough to be heard by the people at the next table who craned their heads.

"She can be bi," Maddy said.

"I dunno," Joss said, exceedingly uncomfortable having her sex life served up as casual conversation. "I'm not gay or bi. I'm just...Cameron. Or whatever."

Kip started with an "Awww," which the rest of the team chorused in.

Cameron waved off the sentiment, "It took a bunch of groupies for her to realize what a catch I am."

Reuben found this role reversal—Cameron's bravado, Joss's bashfulness—unexpectedly charming in the way these two friends becoming a couple had softened each other's hard-wired tendencies.

He wondered if he and Maddy would get that chance to evolve in this way, and in what ways they would grow into each other and beyond themselves. Would her outspokenness and sly sarcasm rub off on him? Would she adopt his...what? What did Reuben bring to the table beyond an artist's eye and decent cooking skills? He was reasonably affectionate, but temperament-wise, he was clumsy and often caught unaware by things others saw coming miles before he did. These were not exactly coveted traits.

He could feel the warmth radiating outward from Maddy's leg, and it suddenly felt like a gift that didn't belong to him, that maybe she deserved more than what Reuben could offer her. That seemed to have been the conclusion Adrian had come to. Stepping outside himself to imagine what Maddy saw in him, Reuben was wary that if she looked too closely, she would find him lacking.

Cameron was mapping for everyone the route of their pending tour, mentioning a stop in Philadelphia, but Reuben's mind was stuck, anxious and looping on this idea that perhaps he had put too much confidence in the likelihood of a romantic relationship with Maddy. Then, miraculously, her hand reached for his under the table. It was cool and dry just as it had been several nights ago. The effect was immediate, like someone lifting the needle on a skipping record, and a warmth in his chest replaced the worry. Gently running his thumb over her knuckles, Reuben kept his eyes forward, now reengaged with the moment.

Maddy leaned over and quietly asked him, "Good trip?"

"Yeah, it really was."

A couple of waitstaff delivered several pizzas to the elevated metal stands on the table.

"Send the pineapple down here," Wayne shouted. "*Maybe* I'll share with the rest of you, but better get in on it fast. I make no *promises*."

The table became a bustling scene with people handing their plates, asking for pepperoni or mushroom and peppers, slices served and passed, making stops along the way for tossed salad.

"So, Wayne," Kip shouted from the opposite end of the table, "what's the plan for next season? Are we going to be allowed to play?"

"What the hell, Kip? Can't we just enjoy some fucking pizza?" Donny asked.

It was such a strong response that several people around the table paused midbite to look at Donny then back at Kip who looked confused.

Wayne patted Donny's shoulder and said something in an aside to him. Then Wayne turned his attention outward toward the table. "Truth is, you guys, I'm hanging up my cleats."

"What?" Joss said setting her mug down hard.

The energy around the table seemed to sag upon hearing the news.

Kip said, "Naw, c'mon, Wayne."

"It's been a good run, but speaking of running... I can't anymore. Everything hurts when I do. And I don't like that feeling one bit. So come next spring, I'll be swinging a set of old man golf clubs instead of a bat."

Reuben looked at Donny who had scrunched up his face and held it there, determined not to show emotion, but he wasn't fooling anyone. He and Wayne had played baseball together since high school. It was their history. While no one could doubt their friendship would stay close, there was something genuinely sad about this long chapter in their lives closing, not just for the two of them, but for everyone around the table who had gotten to play with them.

Donny summed up best what most of the team around the table had yet to register for themselves, "Getting old just sucks ass."

"A toast, then," Patrice stood up, raising his glass of club soda. "To Wayne, with gratitude for all the seasons past and wishes for many happy seasons ahead." Everyone stood and clinked mugs.

"To Wayne."

"Cheers."

"And good luck to you all," Wayne said in return. "I've heard tell that Dana Van Sykes has generously volunteered to take charge of the Coleslaw League."

"It was really good to see everyone," Reuben said to Maddy as he walked her to her car. "I guess that'll be it until spring. If we even have a season next year."

"Do you want to come over?" Maddy asked.

"Oh." Reuben had to pause to make sure he heard her correctly.

"Sorry, I just knew if I didn't put it out there right away, I would chicken out, and we'd keep doing this 'Will they, won't they?' thing."

"So they will?"

"I suppose that's up to us."

Her eyes caught the overhead parking lot light, and he noticed for the first time that they had a darker, nearly black ring around the lighter brown iris. She wore no eyeliner, no mascara. It was just Maddy there, open, honest, inviting. He leaned down and kissed her, tentatively, then fully as she returned the kiss, a spark catching heated fire between them. She leaned back against the car and pulled Reuben, pressing him to her body.

He was nearly lost in his senses, the taste of her infused with a light, sweet vanilla scent from her skin or her hair or both, and their mingling breath tinged with malty beer. His hands were lightly cradling her jawline, hers were on the small of his back.

The sound of voices approaching jolted them out of the moment, and they pulled apart. Thank goodness it was a pair of strangers and not Kip, Wayne, and Donny, who stayed for another round when everyone else peeled away.

"Follow my car," Maddy said, her words somewhere between a question and a command.

Although it was only twenty minutes away, the drive to Maddy's building mostly took back roads, so Reuben wasn't sure he would be able to find his way home without a GPS. In any case, he wasn't concentrating on the road, simply following the leading taillights of her hatchback, his focus hijacked, anticipating her breath and body colliding again with his own.

Maddy was waiting beside her car when Reuben reached her walking from the visitor parking space. As he threaded his fingers into hers, the thrill of contact still fresh, she pointed to their left in the direction of an adjacent field, telling him about a series of mountain biking trails that she liked to ride but it was getting harder to see the trail now that the leaves were coming down.

Inside, they walked a dimly lit hall. Greeting her down-the-hall neighbor, Mr. Pasawan, Maddy slowed Reuben's pace as they passed, perhaps trying not to broadcast how eager they were to get behind closed doors. Reuben toyed with her ponytail as she fit the key in the lock. Then they tumbled inside, clumsily entwined. Lights off, he held onto her, letting her navigate to the bedroom. They exchanged no words, just breath, as they urgently unbuttoned, unzipped, undressed.

The sex with Maddy was beautifully uncomplicated in ways that Reuben's first encounters with other women hadn't been. Maybe there was something in the fact that they'd known each other for well over two years before this moment. Though that familiarity did nothing to diminish the thrill of exploring each other's bodies, all sensual touch and reactive sounds. When Reuben's fingertips felt the scar high on the back of her left hamstring, the one she had told him and Kip about, it felt like a secret unlocked.

"It's real," he said aloud, surprising them both.

Maddy laughed, "Did you think I made it up?"

"No, I mean. We talked about it back then. And now we're here. In this moment. And it's real." He pulled her over on top of him. "I'm not making any sense."

"I understand you."

Later, as Maddy dozed, Reuben crept out of bed for a glass of water. Beyond the bedroom, the space was an open floor plan between the kitchen, a small dining nook, and the living room. Even in the ambient light, he could see her home was neat and clutter-free, but not without warmth. A neatly folded, antique-looking quilt draped the back of the couch. Family photos were scattered around the computer desk, including a framed newspaper clipping of Maddy caught in full windmill pitch—that familiar determined look on her face—with a caption, "*Student Athlete of the Week: Talbot Memorial High's senior Magdalena Frye pitches her second no-hitter of the season.*" Reuben smiled at this tiny window into her past.

He continued quietly exploring the space. The focal point on her living room wall was a wide freestanding shelf with the books arranged in horizontal stacks, the widest spines on the bottom tapering up to the narrowest. In the dim light, the effect was that of a city skyline. A found-art display of sorts, made even more meaningful for the words and layers of information and stories contained within them.

He sipped at the water and retrieved his phone from the pocket of his jacket, which had been hastily dropped by the door. There was a voice mail from his mother, letting him know that it had been a long time since she'd heard from him, and was everything okay? There was also an eye roll-inducing text from Kip saying that he hoped Reuben was having a *Mad-nificent* evening. Reuben's email inbox had a message from Marc Barthelme, letting him know that his *Crow Number Four* sculpture had been purchased earlier that day by a well-known TV weatherman from Ottawa. Then, just below that message, was a reply from Patton. The contents were brief.

NAME: Patton Papadopoulos
SUBJECT: Chicory Field Farm
EMAIL: patton@vtwkly.com

Had a lovely call with Elena Garcia Juarez this morning. She was pretty eager to tell their story. Seems she wants to get involved in some advocacy work. I promised her total anonymity in exchange for her perspectives. She mentioned a friend of yours helped with some stitches — perhaps your date from the other night? I kept that part otr. Attached is the article that's being printed tomorrow. As promised, neither you nor S.J. are referenced in the slightest.
—P

CHAPTER 28

Reuben had to read the article twice before he could stop second-guessing the wisdom of his having introduced Patton to Elena. More commentary than news story, the published piece titled "Losing Their Religion" was, as Patton promised, legitimately anonymous, having withheld nearly all the details that had led him to the story in the first place. Instead, the article's focus was on highlighting yet one more difficult aspect of the migrant worker's experience in Vermont: the inability to practice their religion as part of a congregation. He argued, beyond the obvious risks of exposure he presented, there were also language barriers, transportation issues, and extremely long working hours that left little time for everyday or even holiday-specific rituals.

As for the car accident, there was only a passing mention of a "near-miss road-crossing incident" among some of the hazards migrant workers faced when having to move about the community discreetly, often in the predawn hours. But because the article spoke in broad, statewide terms, thankfully, there was no reason for anyone to try to place the references.

Later in the article, Elena was quoted in translation, her name changed to Ana to protect her identity:

> "Back home, church was a very big part of my life. When I came to Vermont, God felt very far away, and it made me feel sad and lonely. When the neighbor welcomed us to pray at a space in his yard, it was like God had come back to me. I felt some peace in my heart for the first time since coming here."

The words gave Reuben a pang. Until reading the article, it hadn't really hit him that the display in his backyard would have been as deeply meaningful in the way Elena described.

Reuben had to admit, Patton's handling of the topic was thoughtful, and it seemed feasible that his work could, in some measure, engage readers—religious or not—who might not otherwise empathize with the migrants.

In the days following the publication, the article hadn't seemed to cause any obvious ripple effect in the public. And at least from a distance, it appeared that life at the farm quietly continued.

Reuben shifted his focus to two priorities: finishing the components of the sugaring installation so he and Kip could start experimenting with audio set up, and spending as much time with Maddy as was reasonable without tipping the scale into "too much, too soon" territory. They went on their first official date to a new tapas bar located in a cozy converted grist mill. Reuben had to laugh when she asked if it was in "the city," Burlington being a fraction of the size of Hartford, which itself wasn't particularly big, either.

After dinner, they took a stroll along the lake but cut it short due to a biting wind strong enough to make whitecaps on the water. Maddy followed Reuben to his house. They had sex again, unhurried and exploring this time, learning each other's cues, getting to know each other's bodies. She didn't stay overnight, though, not wanting to have to scramble in the morning to get home and shower for an early workday.

"How come you have no pets?" he asked as he watched her dress, shadows shifting over her skin as she moved. He saw her pause a moment before reaching behind and hooking her bra. "I mean because of your work, I just assumed you like animals."

"It's going to sound silly."

"No, it won't."

She came and sat down on the bed to slide on her socks. "I feel like they can tell. Animals. That I'm like this angel of death. You know, when I have to help put them down. It's one thing when I'm in the office, but I feel like if I ever had a dog or even a parakeet that had to live with me coming home afterward, they'd just know, you know?"

Reuben could feel his chest swelling, stretching to reach her.

"You're looking at me funny." She hid her eyes behind her hair, self-consciously.

"No, I think that's really beautiful is all." He didn't want her to leave. "Can I cook you dinner tomorrow?" he asked.

"I was planning on a solo feast of frozen ravioli."

"Pro tip: they're better when you defrost them."

"You cooking types with your fancy ways." She leaned over and kissed him deeply. "I think I'll take a rain check."

"Oh."

"It's nothing bad, I promise. These last two nights have been wonderful. I just think we shouldn't throw ourselves headlong into it. That's how people lose themselves in relationships, y'know?"

Maddy's words reminded Reuben of what Adrian had said before she moved out: that she loved Reuben, but she didn't love who she was with him. The idea that someone would be diminished in a relationship rather than be expanded by it was something he understood. He need only look back at his time with Hannah to realize how he'd made himself small to accommodate her big personality.

"I want this to work, Maddy. If we're going to be 'us', jeez, I hope you'll always feel like you can be you."

She smiled and nodded, kissed him goodbye.

After she left, Reuben stayed in bed feeling the absence of her warmth. He thought back to an interview he had done a few years ago on a podcast about creativity. The host had asked how he approached starting a new piece, essentially making something out of nothing. Reuben explained that he didn't think of a blank canvas as the absence of art. Instead, he believed that every new work already existed somewhere in the world, and that, for him, an artist's job was more like that of an archaeologist uncovering a scene one section at a time, and finessing until the details were honest, clear, and compelling. "It's a revealing," he had said, "Never a creation from nothing."

As Reuben lay there, thinking about Maddy, her multitude of layers and depths yet to be discovered, he thought that love is a little like art, a gradual uncovering of what already exists and simply needs time and attention to discover it.

◆

Winter was a hint in the air later that morning. The countertop space heater in the barn made the workbench tolerably warm to get some soldering done, as Reuben applied thin filigree veins to dozens of cut metal leaves that would serve as the ground cover. Though he tried to focus, his mind kept wandering back to Maddy, imagining her slowly becoming part of his every day in the coming weeks. He pictured her reading a book beside him on the couch, the two of them sharing the big fleece blanket as the first real snow fell outside.

It could all go sideways, he reminded himself. And yet, Reuben couldn't steer his thoughts away from all the experiences he wanted to share with her, things he'd done and places he'd been, things they could discover together. He wanted to sketch her, paint her in shades of blue and gold.

His daydreaming was interrupted as Lou Garoo barreled through the barn's cat door, something outside having spooked him. His ears were angled backward, and his tail flicked back and forth.

It better not be that stupid dog again.

Reuben pulled aside the barn door, blinking against the sunlight. He turned toward the road just as a voice yelled from a car by the mailbox, "Let's go, Levi!" And before Reuben realized what was happening, a guy came bolting from the backyard, right past Reuben and down the driveway.

"Hey!" Reuben yelled.

The runner didn't look back. Someone opened the back door of the car, and the guy tumbled in. The driver barely waited for him to be fully inside before they took off.

"The hell?" Reuben said aloud.

I don't care what Kip says, I have got to put up No Trespassing *signs.* Reuben walked quickly in the direction of where the guy had come from, wondering if he had vandalized something. *Levi*, he thought. *Levi. Why does that name sound familiar?*

He could see nothing amiss in the backyard. The sunflowers were at peak, their big lion heads just starting to become too heavy for their stalks. The two pumpkins he'd managed to grow were still lying fat and happy in the garden, the kale toweringly tall, and presiding over it all, Scarecrow Jesus, flannel shirt just barely riffling in the breeze.

And then Reuben remembered.

Minutes later, he was in the kitchen, pacing and scrolling through several months of voice mail messages, back and back and back until he found the one from Patton Papadopoulos. He called the number, and when it went right to voice mail, Reuben said, "Why the hell would your brother-in-law have been in my backyard just now? Call me ASAP."

He stashed the phone in his back pocket and leaned on the sink, watching out the window. An uneasiness was taking root in Reuben's chest. He made a decision. Sliding back into his jacket, he straight-lined a path to the garden.

Spring and summer had come and gone since he'd first put up Scarecrow Jesus. So much had happened in between. He stood looking at it, realizing how the crucifix's strange presence had become background for him, just another landscape feature. Now, up close, Reuben could see the green flannel was pale and sun-faded, and there appeared to be some moss growing in the folds of the jeans.

He stood a moment thinking about what this space had meant to Elena and the family. But the uneasiness he was now feeling took over. Wrapping his arms around Jesus's knees, Reuben lifted the figure up and off the hooks that held it in place. The effort released a faint smell of mildew, dirt, and damp. Jesus was heavier than Reuben remembered, and as he awkwardly carried the figure to the yard cart, Reuben thought they must have looked like a ridiculous parody of that *Dirty Dancing* scene where Patrick Swayze hoists Jennifer Grey up overhead. After settling Jesus and ensuring the cart wouldn't topple, Reuben grabbed a shovel and loosened the soil around the base of the cross enough to release it with a hard lift. He wheeled both pieces to the back of the barn where he had previously stored them and threw a heavy-duty army tarp on top. What he would do with them from here was not something Reuben was ready to think about. As Jackson Endicott had said: You can't just take something like that to the dump. Maybe there was somewhere on the goat farm it could go.

On the stairs, as he headed up for a shower, Reuben's phone rang. He answered right away.

Patton said, "So, yeah. I think we have a small issue."

◆

 **Levi Hoover**

47m

That "road incident" in @PPapadap's article in @VTWkly about the illegals was me almost accidentally mowing them over with my car. Idiots were hanging out in the middle of Popple Hill at 5 a.m. after doing some voodoo worship over with Scarecrow Jesus. @ReubenDownes, what kind of church you running over there?

There was an ominous quality to the photo of Scarecrow Jesus that Levi had included in the post—the angle looming, a filter applied to heighten the shadows for dramatic effect. Already, there were more than thirty comments. Most were outraged, some horrifyingly telling Levi that, next time, he shouldn't brake. Two posts claimed that Reuben was "literally the Antichrist." The few lone voices urging civility were met with recommendations that they either a) go fuck themselves, or b) leave America to go be with the foreigners they love so much.

"These people are horrible," Reuben said.

"Dude, this is baseline shit. What social media utopia have you been living in?"

"It's never really been my thing."

"I hate to tell you, but it has just become your thing."

And then they both saw it. A new comment posted in real time:

> **Hey@ImmigrationAndCustoms Enforcement (ICE) what R U doing abt this at Chicory goat farm 1722 Orrville Town Rd.**

"Shit."

"Shit."

"Patton, you created this mess."

"Technically, you started it."

"It's your brother-in-law."

"It's your Jesus."

"Elena needs to know what's going on."

"You're right. Yeah. You should go over ASAP and talk to her."

"I. Don't. Speak. Spanish!" In the background, Reuben could hear buttons on a microwave being pressed.

"Listen, Patton, I need you to drop what you're doing, drive over here, and come with me to explain to Elena what is happening."

Patton didn't answer right away. "Man, I don't know if I can face her. How do you explain something like this? I'm the question-asking, typing-on-a-screen guy. I'm not the delivering-alarming-news guy."

Reuben was likewise uneasy about telling Elena, Arturo, and Tomás that not only were people threatening them online, but that they'd been called out to immigration, their location exposed. And what exactly were Reuben and Patton going to suggest they do? Be extra-extra cautious? Don't leave the house? For how long?

"Just get over here. And get your asshole brother-in-law to take that post down!"

As he waited for Patton, Reuben paced the porch to keep warm, warily observing any car that drove by. Every so often, he'd glance at Levi's post to see fresh comments, thumbs-ups, thumbs-downs, and angry emojis. Finally, after about forty minutes, Patton's car arrived trailing a rooster tail of road dirt behind it.

Reuben strode over before Patton had turned off the engine. Their greetings were curt with Reuben getting him up to speed on the latest online vitriol.

"I asked my wife to have Levi take down the post. If he hasn't yet, he will. As someone frequently on the receiving end of her opinions, she can be intensely persuasive."

"Man, if you knew your brother-in-law was an asshole, why didn't you see this coming?"

"I mean, the guy has some anger management issues, but I guess I just underestimated that he'd try to claim his fifteen minutes of fame."

Walking the road to the green house, they discussed how they would open the conversation, being calm but clear in presenting the facts of the situation. It was just about sunset when they got to the front stoop. Reuben knocked lightly on the door, *"Hola, estamos Rueben y Patton – ¿el...journalista?*

"Periodista," corrected Patton loud enough to be heard inside the house.

Tomás opened the door, a friendly but curious look on his face. A square Band-Aid had replaced the gauze on his forehead. Behind him, Reuben could see Elena was in the kitchen filling a pot with water.

"¿Podemos entrar?" Patton asked.

Tomás nodded and pulled the door open wider for them to come inside. Patton introduced himself with a handshake and a small head bow to Elena. Arturo was on the couch watching TV, Rosario by his feet playing with a Barbie doll dressed in a hot-pink ball gown. On the corner table, Reuben could see a copy of the *Vermont Weekly* issue that the article had been published in.

From that point on, Reuben struggled to keep up with the conversation, only getting a sense of the emotional tenor of the room as Patton spoke hesitantly then more rapidly about the day's events. Arturo's eyes flashed, serious and angry between Patton and Elena as Tomás, leaning on the wall by the window, arms folded, shook his head, unsurprised by the news being delivered.

Reuben squatted down, trying to distract Rosario. Though she was making the Barbie move, he could tell her ears and attention were tuned to the adults' discussion. Reuben felt frustrated by the language barrier, knowing that even a child could understand what was being said when he couldn't.

There was a brief, tense exchange between Arturo and Elena. While they were talking, Reuben stood and went over to Patton to get a rough translation.

"They're concerned, but it sounds like they're not unused to these kinds of threats."

"So what happens now?"

Patton shrugged. "Life goes on. They try not to leave the property and hope things die down quickly."

Just then, Tomás whistled lightly to get everyone to stop talking. He had pulled the window curtain aside just a little and was intently looking outside. Arturo joined him, watched a moment, and asked Elena something.

Patton said to Reuben, "Sounds like there's a car coming down the driveway by the main house and barn. Arturo is asking if *doña* Meloy—the farm's owner—was expected back today. Elena says, no, she will be in Pennsylvania through the weekend."

"Who do they think it is, then?" It was a dumb question, Reuben knew, but he felt the need to say something, to be part of what was happening.

The air in the room felt tight as the two men didn't move, just stood silently watching. When a series of shots clapped out, everyone instantly dropped down to the floor and hunkered there, Elena enfolding herself around Rosario.

Tomás peeked out the low corner of the window. *"Ellos están disparándole al camión,"* he said in a hushed voice.

Arturo hit his fist on the floor.

"What did he say?" Reuben asked, his pulse hammering hard in his ears.

"He said they're shooting at the truck."

Tomás said something so fast, Reuben didn't catch a word, but whatever it was set everyone in motion. Arturo scooped Rosario on his back and Elena grabbed jackets.

Patton said, "The flashlights were pointing this way."

"Reuben, *¿podemos ir a su casa?*"

"¿*Su casa?* Reuben repeated not really processing the words.

"*Your* house," Patton said. "Can we go to your house?"

"Yes, *si, si,* of course!" Reuben answered.

They left the house by a back door Reuben had never noticed before. As they approached the stone wall, another two shots rang out followed by the sound of shattering glass. Nobody spoke as they crossed the road. There was barely enough light to see where they were going but they managed to follow the trail to Reuben's backyard easily. With Patton and Reuben bringing up the rear, Tomás was in front, followed by Elena, then Arturo carrying Rosario who, to Reuben's astonishment, had not let out so much as a whimper throughout the mad dash to get away from the house. But when they reached the garden, she whispered something to her father.

Arturo turned to Reuben and whispered. "*Jesús—¿Ya se fue?*"

Reuben wasn't exactly sure what he was asking, but it seemed to relate to the removal of Scarecrow Jesus. Rosario was looking at him over her father's shoulder, her eyes about to spill over with tears.

"*Jesús en el . . . casa,*" Reuben replied, pointing to the barn. This did not change Rosario's expression in the least, so he pantomimed that Jesus was sleeping. He closed his eyes, folded his hands beneath his chin and let out a quiet snore. She nodded, her mouth tucked in a tight pout as she swiped at her eyes with the sleeve of her jacket.

Reuben led them into the house through the kitchen's back door. He kept the lights dim, thinking it would be best to avoid drawing any attention. Pulling over two side chairs, he gestured for everyone to take seats at the table. Then he went to the living room and pulled the blinds down over the big window that overlooked the front yard.

Now what? Reuben thought. He returned to the kitchen where there was a quiet discussion happening.

"I'm calling the police," Reuben said to Patton.

All eyes turned to him. "*Nada de policía,*" said Arturo.

"They were shooting," said Reuben, making a gun gesture.

"Let's just take a minute," Patton said. "They're probably gone by now."

"Doesn't mean they won't come back or that others won't come."

Patton nodded. "And immigration is another concern since they were flagged." While Patton initiated a discussion in Spanish, Reuben took a pitcher from the shelf and filled it with water. He brought it to the table with some glasses.

"You got any snacks, too?" Patton asked. "I didn't get to eat my burrito after you called."

Reuben pulled a bowl of red grapes from the refrigerator and set them down, eliciting a disappointed look from Patton. The group had continued talking.

"It sounds like Elena has a cousin who would normally help them but the dairy he worked at recently closed, and he's filling in at a place across the lake." Patton plucked a couple grapes from the bunch then said, "Hey, do me a favor." He handed Reuben his phone. "Punch in your address?"

"Why?"

"Because without a warrant, ICE can only detain undocumented suspects within a hundred miles of the border and the coastline. I know Orrville is far enough away from the ocean but I'm not sure about Canada."

Reuben typed his address in the search bar. "Shit. It's eighty-two miles from the nearest border crossing."

"Okay, okay, that's not terrible. So maybe we could help them get twenty or more miles south of here just to buy some time." He took his phone back. "Let me talk to them, see what they want to do. But maybe you can come up with an idea of somewhere they could go?"

There was certainly a place that came to mind for Reuben.

He would be taking a big gamble showing up at Rosemary's with a group of undocumented farm workers, but he believed it was the only way she wouldn't outright say no to letting the family stay out of sight overnight. Though, of course, her willingness wasn't guaranteed.

In the breath of pause between conversations, they all heard it. The sound of a car pulling in the driveway. Reuben's adrenaline spiked again. What if it was the gun nuts? Or the police or ICE?

"Wait here."

Reuben went to the darkened laundry room for a view of the driveway. He hadn't realized he was holding his breath until, seeing that it was Maddy's car, his shoulders collapsed on the exhale.

"It's okay! *Esta* Maddy," he shouted, yanking open the front door to quickly usher her inside.

"Oh my gosh, Reuben, you scared me! Why is it so dark?" She was carrying a couple of brown paper bags, folded over at the top.

"What's . . . what are you doing here?" he asked.

"I know I said I wasn't going to come by for dinner, but then I realized, I really wanted to." She stretched up on her toes and kissed him quickly. "We don't need arbitrary boundaries around when we can or can't see each other. We're both adults and—" She stopped, registering what must have been a tense look on his face. "Anyway, I hope it's okay that I just stopped over? Do you like Philly cheesesteaks and fries?" She held up the bags.

"I do. I love them." Reuben wanted nothing more than to grab a couple beers from the fridge, settle on the couch with her to watch a movie while they ate. "But, I have a situation I'm navigating. A pretty serious one."

He saw a tired disappointment in her eyes. "Again?"

Reuben nodded ruefully. He took her hand and walked her to the kitchen where Tomás, Elena, Arturo, Rosario, and Patton sat together in the dark, waiting. Tomás gave a small wave when he saw her.

"Is better," Tomás said, rubbing his fingers over the healed wound to show it no longer hurt. "Elena, she take out." He mimed sewing.

Maddy, nonplussed to see everyone looking at her, took a moment to understand what Tomás was saying, but then she smiled warmly. "I'm so glad you're doing well." She turned to Reuben for an explanation.

He pulled her into the corner of the kitchen. She looked back. "Isn't that the reporter guy?"

"It is. Patton. I don't have much time to go into the details but there was an incident at the farm, some very real threats, and there's a chance immigration could come out. We're hoping to get them away from the farm for a bit until things calm down."

She spoke quietly. "I don't mean to be cold here, but are you sure you want to get involved? If you get caught, you could be in serious trouble."

Reuben rubbed a hand over his face, smoothed his beard before saying out loud what had been constantly running through his head since Levi's post went up. "I was told to let them keep a low profile, and I did just the opposite. I should never have connected them with a reporter, of all people. Hopefully this is all going to blow over quickly. But right now, I have a responsibility to help."

She zipped her jacket up over her chin, "Okay," was all she said.

"But if things work out tonight, and I can buy some time, I should only be gone about an hour." Reuben knew he was being overly optimistic. "Why don't you just hang out here. Eat, listen to music. When I get home, I promise I will tell you everything."

Patton cleared his throat, letting Reuben know they needed him in the discussion.

"Maddy, I swear it won't always be like this—"

She nodded, her lips pressed in a tight line, clearly not convinced.

Maddy handed him the bags of food. "Thanks, but I'm going to go. You guys take the food. We'll talk tomorrow, I guess."

It was decided that while Reuben drove the group to Rosemary's in the hope that they could stay overnight in the garage apartment, Patton would make some calls to better understand the situation.

"Depending on what happens, I may need to get some other entities involved."

"What, like, immigration lawyers?"

"Potentially. But especially Claire Meloy, the farm's owner."

A side thought occurred to Reuben, "So what happens to the goats while they're away?"

"Oh, yeah," Patton said. "I told them you would help with that."

"Help, how?"

Patton snapped at him. "I don't know exactly. I can only solve one problem at a time. I'm focused on the administrative side of things. You'll need to handle the . . . other stuff."

"Goats need to be milked, Patton."

Patton said something quickly in Spanish to Arturo that Reuben didn't catch.

"*Dos veces al día,*" he said. "*Una vez en la mañana y la otra en la tarde.*"

"You are correct," Patton said to Reuben. "They need to be milked once in the morning and then again in the afternoon."

Reuben grabbed Patton's sleeve and pulled him aside. "I barely manage to keep a cat alive, Patton."

"Take it easy. I'll be talking to Claire. I'm sure she'll know someone who can step in to help. But you'll need to head over there—" He turned back to Arturo, "*¿A que hora en la mañana?*"

"*No más tarde que a las cinco en la mañana.*"

Five a.m., Reuben understood. "Not me, Patton. Us."

"I've got my hands full, Downes."

"No, no, no. You want to tell the migrants' story? You're part of it now."

As the crow flies, the Schuyler Inn was twenty-five miles from the farm, but the winding roads made it more like thirty. Tomás was in the passenger seat while the others sat in the back. Reuben looked in the rearview mirror to see Arturo watching warily out the window. Reuben tried to imagine what could be going through their minds. He thought about how fragile their everyday stability was, that at any time, deportation could be just a traffic stop away. He looked at Rosario holding onto her mother's hand. If she was born here, things could get very complicated.

The truck smelled of fries and onions and peppers. "*Quien gusta los* french fries?" Reuben asked trying to sound upbeat.

"*¡A mí, me gustan!*" Rosario shouted louder than Reuben had ever heard her speak.

"*¡Ay, niñita!*" her mother shushed her.

She whisper-spoke to Elena, "*¿Mamá, puedo tener unas papas fritas?*"

Reuben gestured for Tomás to pass around the take-out bags Maddy had brought, a pang of guilt still weighing Reuben's mind about how she had left. But in the moment, navigating the way to Rosemary's, he forced himself to just focus on one thing at a time.

Rosario, happily munching fries, was watching a cartoon on Arturo's phone, the characters' exaggerated, excitable Spanish voices filling the quiet. Keeping an occasional eye in the rearview mirror, Reuben noticed that Arturo and Elena were looking in opposite directions.

Tomás spoke quietly and hesitantly to Reuben, "Arturo, uh, he no happy she talk with the writer."

"I should never have given her his note."

Tomás shrugged a little. "She want that the people, uh... *comprende.*"

"*¿Comprende los migras?*"

"*Los migrantes, si.*"

He seemed to be saying that Elena wants people to understand the migrant experience. Reuben wondered if this was something Patton promised he could do when he asked to interview her. The way things turned out, the effect was the exact opposite.

The inn was brightly lit both inside and outside when they arrived. It was the early side of the busiest tourist season, and Reuben was wary that a full roster of guests would be yet another barrier to Rosemary's willingness to letting the family stay. When he parked and turned off the car, Arturo took the phone from Rosario, silencing the cartoon.

"*Un momento.*" Reuben held up his hand. "Um, stay *aquí. En el coche. Si?*"

Yes, Tomás nodded, they would wait in the car.

Guillaume was outside stuffing a canvas carrier with firewood. He was close to seventy years old but built like a bear and could carry nearly a dozen logs at a time. "Hiya," he said, gesturing Reuben to follow him to the back door.

Rosemary was in the kitchen putting away silverware from the dishwasher rack. Reuben had been rehearsing what he would say to her, but he'd become jittery, not knowing what Plan B would be if she sent them away. She flipped a dishtowel over her shoulder when she saw him.

"Well if it isn't the Antichrist himself," she said. "I would think you'd be home with the shades drawn."

"Oh," Reuben said. "You do social media?"

"Honey, this inn has got over a thousand followers. I'm practically an influencer." She looked at him and shook her head. "And you have got a PR problem."

"It's actually a little more serious than that."

Guillaume, who would ordinarily busy himself with chores in another room, sat down at the kitchen table biting noisily into a piece of toast. He seemed to be listening to the conversation.

Rosemary went back to sorting silverware. "It seems like that could be the case for your farm neighbors. What was happening over in your backyard, anyway?"

"*Ses voisins—les travailleurs migrants—sont dehors, dans la voiture,*" Guillaume said.

Rosemary's focus shifted sharply to Guillaume, a silent exchange happening between them. Then she seemed to understand. "Oh no. Holy heck, no, Reuben. Find somewhere else. They cannot stay here."

This was not how the conversation was supposed to go. Reuben started rapid-firing the points he had hoped to ease into. "If they could just stay in the apartment overnight. Someone came onto the farm property firing a gun. It's not safe right now."

"Have them at your house, then. Or Kip's."

"They're still within immigration's jurisdiction by us. It's just one night while the newspaper guy helps them figure out some things. They're good people, Rosie. They have a little girl named Rosario who thinks I'm funny even when I'm not trying to be. And I'm terrified they're going to be split up. I'll pick them up tomorrow. I promise you won't even know they're there."

"I'd like to help, Reuben, I really would, but I can't. I'm sorry."

"*Ce n'est pas vrai, ma chérie.*"

"It *is* true, Gui," she said.

Guillaume continued speaking in French, gaining volume and speed.

"No," Rosemary interrupted. "It's too much to risk."

In all the times Reuben had been around, he hadn't seen many extended dialogues between them, never noticed how well they understood each other's language but responded to each other in their own.

A boisterous exchange of voices and laughter came from the front door as a group of guests came in and tromped upstairs.

"Just one night," Reuben said. "Your guests won't know they're here. No one will know they're here."

"I don't exactly trust your track record for not attracting attention." She sat down next to Guillaume and reached for his hand. "It's not that I have an issue with them being here, generally or specifically. It's that Gui is not exactly here legally, either."

This was news to Reuben, and it must have shown on his face.

"It's stupid really. He was visiting a friend and stayed at the inn the first year I was open. I didn't want him to leave, and he didn't want to go home. We always figured we would get around to getting him a green card."

"*Nous devrions les aider.*" He took her hand and gave it a squeeze.

"He wants to help, so that's what we'll do." She pulled the familiar four-leaf clover keychain from a drawer. "We're going upstairs and will be completely hands-off. In fact, this conversation never happened. If the bull crap hits the fan, you're on your own. That means you'll have been breaking and entering, in addition to harboring."

Earlier, when Maddy had asked Reuben if he really wanted to get involved, he didn't hesitate. It had been easy to keep moving forward when he was with the family, getting himself deeper into the situation. Real people caught in a situation that he had contributed to. But now, Rosemary's words made it clear: he was committing a crime that could be classified as a felony. What if he had put too much faith in Patton's ability to protect, not just the family, but himself? His hesitation had become an uncomfortable silence in the room.

"Hon, you've got people out in your car depending on you. Seems it might be a little too late for cold feet."

◆

Having gotten the family comfortably settled in the apartment with fresh sheets and some snacks he pulled together from Rosemary's pantry stash, Reuben headed home. On the road, he felt a release of the lock-tight tension he'd been holding for hours. He felt exhausted, flattened like a cartoon character that had collided with a cement wall.

It was nearly ten o'clock by the time Reuben turned into the driveway where the porch light had been turned on, its golden glow a beacon welcoming him home. Off to the side, beside the spot where he usually parked his truck, was Maddy's little blue car.

A sudden warmth filled Reuben's chest as he bounded quickly to the house. She was on the far corner of the couch, the fleece blanket tucked up under her chin. When Maddy saw him, she pulled the remote from under the blanket and turned off the television.

"You're home."

"You're here."

"Is everything okay?"

Reuben dropped his shoes on the mat by the door and went to the living room. "For now."

He sat down heavily beside her. The spare key she'd used for taking care of Lou Garoo when Reuben was in Montreal was lying on the coffee table. The cat himself was perched on the windowsill keeping intense watch over the nighttime yard.

"I didn't think you would come back," he said.

Maddy untucked the blanket from her feet and handed the edge to Reuben who pulled it over himself. He moved closer and she stretched her legs onto his lap.

"I got halfway home," she said. "And realized I was worried. For them. For you. I'm sorry I wasn't more supportive in the moment. I should have helped."

"No, that wasn't on you. You already put yourself on the line last week."

She shrugged off his words. "So can you tell me what happened?"

Reuben took a breath. She listened quietly as he told her about Levi and his post, the comments and the outing of their location. He tried to downplay the shooting, but the nature of guns is that they're inherently violent and, in this case, intended to threaten.

"But," Reuben quickly added, "I just heard from Patton that a neighbor on Orrville Town Road nabbed a photo of the license plate of the guys as they were leaving the farm. She called it in to the police, and the assholes have been taken into custody and charged with reckless endangerment."

"Oh, that's a huge relief."

Reuben explained Patton's plan of moving the family out of immigration's reach at Rosemary's just until they had a better handle on the situation.

"Rosario was fast asleep by the time I left. They're comfortable for tonight. We'll see what happens tomorrow." Reuben collapsed his head to the back of the couch. "Which reminds me, I've got to get to sleep. Patton is meeting me at the barn at 5 a.m."

"Oh gosh, the goats! How are you—"

Reuben shook his head, his voice cracking a little, "I...I don't even know. Patton couldn't find someone to handle the goats in the morning so he's going to get Arturo on a video call and translate what we need to do and..." Maddy looked at him, deeply skeptical. Reuben's exhaustion got the better of him and he sank deep into the couch, "I know. It's a lot. But we'll figure it out. We just need to get through tomorrow."

She reached out and took his hand. "When I get in, I'll ask at the office if anyone is experienced with goats if they still need help in the afternoon."

"No," Reuben said. "I don't want you getting involved any more than you already have. Don't mention goats to anyone. I'm not even sure you should be here."

"Do you want me to go?"

"No."

"Then let's get you to bed. Or those goats will eat you alive tomorrow."

"Wait, are they like pigs? Do goats eat people, too?"

CHAPTER 29

Reuben's mind was disoriented, knocked off-center from arriving home in the dark the night before and leaving the house in the still-dark predawn. The world felt eerily still, muted and wrapped in a chilly fog as he walked, hearing only the crunching of his work boots on the road. Once he cleared the stone wall, he kept the headlamp fixed on the ground, making sure he didn't roll an ankle or trip on a fallen branch.

By the time Reuben had crossed the field, the sky above the tree line was just starting to brighten from black to blue. He had never been to the far side of the farm, which was normally accessed via a driveway off Orrville's main road—the direction the shooters had come in from. The windows in the white clapboard farmhouse, presumably the owner's, were dark, shades pulled, like the house itself were sleeping. Just beyond it was the truck Reuben had seen Arturo driving that day at Endicott's. Seeing the rear window shot out, the shattered glass, and three neat bullet holes in the tailgate made the hairs on Reuben's arm prickle.

"Yo!"

Reuben jumped at the sound of Patton's voice. He was leaning on his car parked in front of a tall, industrial-looking barn.

"Goats are this way!"

Reuben took a calming breath and walked over. Patton was holding a phone in front of his mouth in one hand and a giant travel mug in the other. Speaking rapidly in Spanish, he walked past Reuben and approached the barn's metal door. An overhead floodlight tripped on, covering them in bright, white light. Patton stretched the mug backward, foisting it on Reuben who fumbled to keep it from dropping. Patton punched a code into the security panel; they heard a short hum and a click allowing them access.

Inside, was a cacophony of goat voices, curious and demanding. The air smelled earthy with the tang of hay and manure. Now fully awake, Reuben felt a near panic kick in. What were they thinking trying to attempt this? Nearly anyone else in the world would be better suited to the task.

"This is insane, Patton. How are we even going to—"

Patton held up a hand for Reuben to stop talking so he could hear what was being said through the phone. He then flipped a switch, and the overhead lighting buzzed to life. They were in a small anteroom that held a stainless steel utility sink and an aluminum tank roughly the size of a cement truck. Everything was pristinely clean.

"*Si, si, okay,*" said Patton. He was now facing Reuben with a serious look. "Arturo says before we go in, we need to scrub our shoes in the bleach solution, so we don't track in bacteria." They both looked down at Patton's Crocs, his white socks showing through the holes.

"Why the hell would you wear those?"

"I have wide feet," Patton said, as if that were a sufficient explanation. He slipped off his shoes and left them beside the drain in the floor, backing away toward the door and continuing to talk to Arturo. That left Reuben to fill the bucket in the sink with bleach and water. There was a long-handled brush beside the sink that Reuben assumed he should use to scrub the soles and sides of his boots and the Crocs.

Once Reuben had finished, Patton swigged the last of his coffee and pointed to his shoes, "Can you bring them to me? I don't want to get my socks wet."

Reuben reminded himself they were there to help with a situation they created—that spending time with Patton was part of Reuben's penance. He picked up the orange shoes, drained them, and tossed them one at a time within Patton's reach.

"You didn't dry them."

Reuben snatched a nearby roll of paper towels and threw it at Patton who failed to catch it.

Arturo was now on video, and Patton held his phone up so Reuben could say hello, then he pointed for Reuben to head up a set of short steps to the interior door. The closer Reuben got, the louder the bleating became. He took a deep breath before pushing down the handle and swinging opening the door.

There were easily a hundred goats divided among two pens running along either side of the barn. Most of the goats were white, a few were mottled brown. Their ears flexed and flopped as they turned at once like a single, multiheaded organism, all those eyes staring with eager interest at Reuben and Patton who, likewise, stood in the doorway and stared back.

"That's a lot of goats," Patton said, swiping at the back of his neck.

It was certainly a daunting scene, this barn full of livestock with their swollen udders and demanding cries. But Reuben had been here many times before—not this actual setting, but rather, living through this feeling of encountering the unknown and having to make a choice to either retreat or throw himself headlong into whatever came next. Abandoning the goats—and by extension, Arturo, Elena, Rosario, and Tomás—was not an option. He gathered the kind of deep resolve he'd built up years ago as the "new kid" approaching the crowded playgrounds filled with as many potential enemies as allies, and turned to Patton. "We can do this. What needs to happen first?"

Reuben's manufactured confidence seemed to jolt Patton into action, and he started an animated dialogue with Arturo. "Apparently, timing was on our side yesterday," Patton told Reuben. "Tomás and Arturo had just finished all the clean-up and prep for this morning's milking just before we came over, and the ignoramus brigade started shooting."

"Who were those guys, anyway? Did Levi know them?"

"Nah, just a pair of yokels from Darby. Police pretty much knew who it was when it was called in."

"And ICE?"

"Not sure yet what the risk is, but Claire Meloy, farm's owner, is on her way back so we'll have a better sense then."

Arturo asked something from the video call.

"Let's just try not to make a shitty situation worse," Reuben said.

Patton assumed the role of translator and overseer, while Reuben was laborer and goat wrangler. Arturo painstakingly talked them through the steps. If his patience had started to wear thin, Reuben couldn't hear it in his voice.

The milking process consisted of corralling twenty goats at a time into a holding area where their energy and enthusiasm seemed to suggest they knew food and milking were imminent. Once the animals were secured, Reuben and Patton were instructed to go to the adjacent milking parlor where they would pull a lever that would lift the holding area door from the other side. This allowed the goats to enter in a somewhat orderly manner, situating each in an individual slot with swiveling dividers that kept them separated.

Arturo, communicating through Patton, instructed Reuben to add grain to the large bin, which would then get distributed to each goat. Patton turned the camera outward at Arturo's request so he could explain which buttons needed to be pressed and in what order, eventually starting up the milking equipment.

While the goats chowed on their breakfast, Reuben's job was to walk along their hind side, dipping the teats into a container of iodine and moving down the line before going back to the start with a cloth to wipe the excess, and finally attaching the milking tubes. There was no getting around Reuben's initial squeamishness, that undercurrent of feeling like some kind of pervert. He reminded himself that this kind of intimacy with animals was just part of the job, what Maddy experienced every day at the vet's office. It would be something they could laugh about later that night.

Eventually, once his concerns about being kicked or shat upon had proven overblown, the actions became automatic, almost meditative as the sound of the milking machine filled the room with a steady, industrial rhythm like a layered track in a Nine Inch Nails song...punctuated by goat cries.

"Arturo says it should take about fifteen minutes to milk the group."

"Fifty?" Reuben shouted back, dismayed, realizing he would be standing here milking goats for the next four hours.

Patton held up his fingers: one, five. *Oh*, Reuben nodded with relief, then chided himself, recalling from one of Patton's articles that farm workers typically put in fourteen- to sixteen-hour days. Was that what he was in for if Arturo and Tomás needed to stay away another day? What if they couldn't find some help? And what about tomorrow? And the day after that? Reuben couldn't put his life on hold to be a barely functional goat farmer. So far, there hadn't been a downtime moment to get an update from Patton on what he'd learned about what might happen next.

After the first round of milking was complete, Arturo had Reuben do another pass with the iodine before releasing the goats to spend the day out in the pasture. Patton unlatched the bay door, and he and Reuben lifted it, opening out to the wide pasture. All but a few reluctant straggler goats spilled out into the chilly air. Reuben and Patton did their awkward best, yelling and flailing their arms to encourage the rest to follow their flock, even giving a hard nudge on the rump to a couple. It was fully morning now, and sunshine was lighting up the fog as it slowly rose like a long, slow exhale.

If goat milking had been a P.E. activity, Reuben thought, *he and Patton would have been the last kids picked*. And yet, with the lowest of expectations, they had managed to get their first task done, using technology and, Reuben had to admit, a bit of teamwork. He slapped a congratulatory hand on Patton's shoulder as they watched the goats shuffle and bump in the grass, enjoying their full bellies, empty udders, and the open space.

"Yeah. Alright," Patton said, bobble-heading in his way, expressing a similar sense of satisfaction. He gave Reuben a thumbs up and said, "Let's go hook up the next batch of ladies."

"No, no," Reuben said. "Don't say it like that."

They closed the bay and headed back to the pen area. As they walked, Patton was chatting with Arturo, Reuben hoped, about the next steps for getting the family back to the farm as quickly but safely as possible.

But what Reuben saw through the door's square window made it clear they had a more immediately pressing issue to deal with. About a dozen goats had escaped the left side pen and were wreaking havoc throughout the barn, pulling hay from stored bales, climbing onto stacks of barrels, knocking over tools, nipping and kicking at each other. On the opposite side, the goats that were still secured were pressed up against the gate bleating a frenzied racket like inmates egging on escapees in a prison riot.

"For fuck's sake, Patton, when I asked if you locked the gate, you said yes!"

He came up beside Reuben and looked through the window.

"No, you said, 'Should I lock the gate?' and I said, 'Yes.'"

"Why would I do that when I was leaving the room before you?"

"Because I was the one getting instructions from Arturo."

"¿Hola? ¿Patton, hola?" They could hear Arturo speaking through the phone.

"Uh, le llamo más tarde, Arturo," Patton said, and he hung up, pocketing the phone.

They started with the goats closest to the premilking holding pen, whistling and encouraging them like dogs as Reuben and Patton shepherded them one by one until they had corralled a full twenty. Patton made a show of locking the gate this time, shaking it a few times to ensure it was properly secured.

The remaining goats, clearly relishing their freedom, were harder to wrangle as they climbed out of reach or ran off with what surely sounded like laughter when Patton or Reuben got within a few feet.

During that time, Patton's phone rang and rang. "I need to tell Arturo what's going on."

He left the barn area for quiet, letting Reuben handle the last two goats who had managed to get up into a loft area. He grabbed a bucket full of grain from the milking room bin and set off to coax them back down. By the time Patton returned, all the goats were secured. Though the mess left in their wake was profound, Patton and Reuben just focused on the milking, knowing that it would be easier to clean the disaster in the barn once all the goats were contentedly outside.

So when the farm's owner, Claire Meloy arrived—having been recalled early from a visit with her sister by Patton's news the night before—she was less than pleased.

Her eyes scanned the chaos. She didn't even pause to introduce herself before saying, "Does everything you two touch turn to shit?"

Patton chimed in to offer some positive news. "The first two rounds of goats are done. Arturo's been walking us through—" he held up his phone to show the video call.

She grabbed the phone, and as Patton had done, went off to speak privately with Arturo.

"You've got some iodine on your shirt," Patton said pointing to Reuben. "That'll stain."

Ignoring the comment, Reuben grabbed a janitor-size broom that one of the goats had dragged to the middle of the floor as if to say, "You're gonna need this." He and Patton got to work picking up the things that were obviously now trash, while stepping gingerly around the spilled, partially eaten grain, unsure whether it was still usable.

Claire returned within five minutes. Patton asked, "Hey, what would you like us to do with—"

"Leave it. I need you to go pick up Arturo and the others and drive them back here."

Reuben and Patton looked at one another with concern.

"What did you say to him?" Patton asked.

Claire, who was about a foot shorter than both Reuben and Patton, pointed an authoritative stare at him. "I told Arturo, 'no trabajo means no dinero, no casa, adios.' I will replace them by the end of the day if I need to."

Reuben sucked in a breath.

"Do you have something to say?" she asked him.

"It's just that, isn't that a bit . . . harsh? People came on the property shooting. Did you see what they did to the truck?"

"And those *gentlemen* have been apprehended."

"What about Immigration? They could come by at any point."

"I'm sorry, who are you?"

"Reuben Downes. I live just down the road."

"Right. The artist." She stressed the word, seeming to suggest he leave the important decisions to people who live in the real world.

"I want to be very clear here. The group of people you whisked away are my employees. I house them and pay them—fairly, I might add—for their work. If those goats don't get properly cared for?" She pointed a rigid finger toward the field, "They get sick. If they get sick, I lose my business. My husband is gone, and I have no kids to take me in. This farm business, when I'm ready to sell it, is my retirement fund. That's all I've got. You do not get to fuck around with my life. I've had enough of that in my time."

Registering the cowed look on Reuben's and Patton's faces, her anger softened. When she spoke again, she sounded tired, "I understand last night's situation was scary. And I'm handling that with the police." As an aside, Claire said, "Hate to do it, but I'm going to have to put up a security camera now.

"As for ICE—Arturo, Elena, Tomás, they know the risks. They know their place here is fragile. This isn't a home for them, it's a means to an end on borrowed time."

With Rosario in the picture, Reuben wasn't so sure.

"What I can tell you is this," Claire continued. "ICE won't come onto the property. It's not a good look for the feds to be dragging people from their work and homes, especially if they're just going about their business on the farm."

The ambient noise of a big industrial fan filled the space when she stopped talking. Patton toed some grain into a pile with his Croc. Reuben realized with a kind of mortified shame that things could have gone terribly wrong with their efforts at milking the goats—even worse than the collateral damage they'd caused in simply not locking the pen.

"Don't just stand there looking stupid. Go get my farm hands."

◆

It was just after 9 a.m. when they arrived at the inn. As Patton and Reuben climbed the stairs to the garage apartment, they heard a muffled conversation coming from inside. Reuben tapped lightly on the door, and he was surprised to see Guillaume pulling aside the curtain. He opened the door and invited them in.

Once Reuben's eyes adjusted, he could see everyone was seated around the table. It had been set with a cheery yellow cloth and the same plates Reuben had used when he'd been a tenant in the apartment.

For someone who said she wanted no part of the situation, Rosemary had put together quite a spread of muffins and jam, sausage and toast, a carafe each of orange and cranberry juice, and a large thermos of coffee. It made the paper bag of bagels Reuben was carrying look meager by comparison. Then he remembered the jack-o-lantern sugar cookie he'd bought for Rosario and pulled it from the bag. Still shy around him, she cautiously took it and held it with both hands like it was a small picture book.

Guillaume was saying something through a mouthful of toast in French-tinged Spanish. Though not quite somber, the mood had a tight surface tension. If Reuben was intimidated by Claire, he could only imagine what the conversation felt like for Arturo when she threatened to replace them.

Patton seemed to similarly read the room and approached the table with his hands clasped in front of him. His tone was quiet as he assured everyone that no *oficiales* had been by, and that Claire believed they wouldn't come onto the property. Beyond that, Reuben again struggled to follow the discussion. Arturo asked a couple questions that Patton responded to. Tomás, resting his elbows on the table, listened intently while sipping the rest of his coffee. When there were no more questions, Elena reached over and squeezed Arturo's hand. She said something quietly to him, then she stood and nodded to Rosario to help clear the dishes.

Reuben spoke to Patton, "Did you tell them what happened about the goats escaping?"

Patton looked at him flatly. "Yeah, I believe Claire might have mentioned that to Arturo."

Tomás, confirming what Reuben had suspected—specifically that he understood English more than he let on—leaned forward and squinted a moment. Then, pointing a finger-pistol at Reuben, he said, "You're fired," in a near pitch-perfect imitation of Donald Trump's infamous words from *The Apprentice*.

The moment was so unexpected, neither Reuben nor Patton was sure how to respond until Tomás and Guillaume burst out laughing.

"*Las cabras son assholes,*" Tomás said.

"*¡Ay!*" Elena shouted, snapping a towel at him, and gesturing toward Rosario.

Arturo stood abruptly. "*Bueno. Ya tenemos que ir a trabajar.*"

They had work to do, Reuben understood.

Guillaume waved a hand to Elena, saying, "*Deje los platos, señora.*" She turned off the faucet and thanked him, leaving the breakfast dishes in the sink. Tomás picked up a couple of bags and handed Rosario a purple stuffed unicorn that she squeezed under her arm so she could continue to hold the still-wrapped cookie.

As they headed over to Patton's car, Rosemary came out the back door. She gave the men warm handshakes. When Elena handed over the apartment key and the tea and said, "*Muchas gracias por todo,*" Rosemary pulled her into a grandmotherly hug as she did whenever a favored guest was leaving.

Reuben hung back, waiting to have a quick word.

"That doesn't look very hands-off to me," he said when she reached him.

"Well, you know, I overbake sometimes."

"Thank you."

She shaded her eyes against the sun coming from behind him. "You look tired."

"It was a short night thanks to a very early morning." He watched Rosario climb into the back seat and settle on her mother's lap. "We'll see how things go from here. You know, maybe it was just a blip. A social media much ado about nothing."

Rosemary unrolled the cuffs on her sleeves and buttoned them against the chilly air. "Sure, hon. That can happen, too."

◆

The winding driveway that led back to the farm felt shorter than it had on the way out that morning. Reuben was now paying keen attention to which parts of the property might be able to be seen from the road but there was still good coverage. Had it been a month later, the tall weeds would have been gone and dense sumac trees would have lost their leaves.

When they arrived, Claire was out in the field, wading among the goats, lifting their heads, inspecting their eyes and coats, and scratching their ears affectionately. She didn't look up as Patton parked the car in front of the barn.

Reuben said, "Can you ask if there's anything I can do to help this afternoon? Maybe get them some groceries or other necessities?"

"*Reuben quiere saber si hay algo en que les puede ayudar esta tarde como comprar unos abarrotes o otras necesidades.*"

The response from all three of the adults was quick and unanimous.

"No."

"No, gracias."

"No, hoy no."

Patton didn't need to translate, but he did anyway. "Yeah, no. I think they might not want you to visit for a while."

Reuben bowed his head a little, hurt to think that they might imagine him as a lightning rod. He declined Patton's offer to drop him off at the house, preferring to walk through the back field to the path that led to Reuben's backyard. The absence of Scarecrow Jesus was palpable, as if the entire energy of the landscape had changed, calmed in some way. *Relief* was the word that came to Reuben's mind, having never considered these past months that the tall figure with arms outstretched might have felt in some ways more looming than uplifting.

Squatting down at the pumpkin patch, Reuben poked a fingernail into the skin by the stem, the way Rosemary had taught him, to tell if it was ripe. *Probably needs another week and a half*, he thought. By then, maybe things would settle into normalcy, a simple Saturday morning savoring coffee and just-out-of-the-oven pumpkin bread with Maddy as they talked about what to do with a free and sprawling day ahead.

She had left a note on the kitchen table, *"I hope the goats didn't eat you. Call me with an update."* It was the first time he'd seen her handwriting, angular and slightly masculine, inexplicably sexy. Reuben would call her, but first he would climb the stairs, collapse in bed, and sink into a heavy, impenetrable sleep.

CHAPTER 30

Jackson Endicott had a knack for reading people. It was a skill honed over a lifetime spent in the hardware store, watching customers come in, browse, buy, and leave. As a teen, handling weekend shifts, he would entertain himself and whoever was working in the vicinity by trying to guess the items a customer had come in for, and what extra items they might leave with. Sometimes the guess was informed by what he already knew about them, like Mrs. Deutche, who painted a different room in her house every four or so months. Other times, when a customer swept into the store, irritated and determined to get in and out fast, it was often a plunger or drain snake they needed. If it was summer and there was a kid or two in tow, the checkout would almost always include a bottle of bubbles, which is why they kept a stash right by the checkout counter.

While Jackson knew most of his customers by name, or at least the name of their street, the others could be sorted into three distinct categories along with their distinguishing characteristics. New residents to the area would try to blend in with clothes that helped them look the part of a local. But the clothes were often new or ironed or cut just a little more tailored to fit than was typical.

Parents on their way to or from dropping their out-of-state kids at UVM would remind Jackson of deer, stepping carefully through the aisles, assessing the contents of this new environment, and remaining on high alert for potential threats from the other creatures that approached them.

Then there were the travel writers, most often given away by their comfortable, casual walking shoes. They came in seasonal cycles, either in June or August through early October, to report on the hot spots, hidden gems, and top ten must-dos for summer tourists and autumn leaf peepers. Given its history, genealogy, and obvious country charm, the hardware store was a favorite source, each reporter thinking they were the first to come up with the idea of asking Jackson for his secret stash of off-the-beaten-path tips. He had ready answers, providing locations that were just low popularity enough for him to come across as helpful without giving away anything that would blow up his favorite hikes and swimming holes with tourists, who were more likely than not to get lost or accidentally drown.

So when the unfamiliar twenty-something woman came in, all eyes, scanning the store and stopping to read the history signs, Jackson looked first at her feet: gray mesh athleisure sneakers, as his wife would call them. He teed up his list: the easy, meandering hike up Mount Marla, which paid off with a beautiful panoramic view of Lake Champlain and the Adirondacks; the small but mighty Fleet Museum with its oddball combination of Revolutionary War letters and 1960s hippy commune collectibles; the weekend-only Dough Nut Stop popup in Maysville.

His only other customer at the moment was Sara Werner, picking up bulbs—the lighting and the tulip kind.

As he rang up her purchases, the presumed journalist strolled the store but not too far from the checkout counter.

"That's a nice selection of colors, Sara," Jackson said, wand-scanning the bag of tulip bulbs.

Sara sighed, "I'm planting them in the spot where I buried Willie a few weeks ago. I like to think a part of him will come back and visit every spring."

"For sure, he was good pup. Here's your change, dear." He gently placed a handful of coins and a receipt in her palsied hand. "Why don't you have that lazy neighbor of yours help you with the planting? Get him out of the house and looking at something other than a video game screen."

Sara laughed and slid the bag handle up into the crook of her arm. She waved over her shoulder as she left. Meanwhile, the young woman continued to mill about, so Jackson waited a few beats, restocking the battery display before asking her, "Can I help you find something?"

With that opening, the woman approached the counter. "I wonder if I could ask you a few questions. My name is Lisa Cho, and I am working on a story for *The Boston Globe*—"

"Travel section?"

"Um, no. It's actually, I would say, it's something a friend of mine who lives in Burlington gave me a heads up on . . . a story that's come up on social media about this town and—"

Jackson shifted his weight from leaning in and curious to standing up to his full imposing posture, arms folded across his chest.

"I wouldn't put too much stock in what you read about this town on social media. Most folks here prefer to spend their time in the analog rather than digital world."

Lisa Cho barely waited for him to finish his sentence. "I understand how that would be the case. It's so lovely out here. And also, although this particular story came to light on the internet, it does exist in the, quote, unquote, 'analog world,' and I just... Could I ask you about an artist by the name of Reuben Downes?"

"I'm not sure I know that name," Jackson said flatly.

"Well, you might recall," Lisa continued, "how last spring there was a story in the paper about a display this Reuben Downes put up that people were calling 'Scarecrow Jesus'?"

"Huh, vaguely. I remember the topic came up, but the fuss died down pretty quickly. Haven't heard anything since, so it's probably not even there anymore."

"That's just part of the story, actually. It seems people are now saying it was put up as some kind of makeshift place of worship for some, uh, potentially undocumented, migrant workers that live nearby."

Jackson didn't miss a beat, "That would be a pretty hard secret to keep in a small town like this. Not to mention, it's exactly the kind of urban legend that would get traction on the social medias, the world being what it is today. I suspect you're following a false trail. Now if you're looking for a real trail that's comfortable-shoe friendly and takes you to one of the best views of the lake, I can give you directions to Mount Marla."

◆

Up next, it's Counterpoint *with Tyson Marks. Over to you, Tyson.*

Thanks, Savannah. File this next story under the category: Why am I not surprised?

Tonight, we head over to Vermont, land of Ben & Jerry's Cherry Garcia ice cream, Bernie Sanders socialism, and now... churches for people living in our country illegally.

You heard that right.

It's not enough that in 2014 Vermont decided it was okay to give driver's licenses to illegal immigrants coming here from places like Mexico, Honduras, and Colombia. Oh, you didn't know about that? It's true. It seems that not being able to travel freely throughout the community was an inconvenience for them. Because if nothing else, people who commit a crime need their lives to be easier. Not harder.

Fast forward to just this past week where it's been revealed that a small town in the western part of the state has taken it upon itself to build a sanctuary for the undocumented people living there. And not just any sanctuary, one with a decisively unorthodox take on Christianity.

No, friends, your eyes are not playing tricks on you. That is a photograph of Jesus Christ dressed as a scarecrow. The picture, taken just a few days ago, was found on the property of an artist by the name of Reuben Downes. And apparently, 'Scarecrow Jesus'—as the crucifix has been affectionately named by the locals—has become a bizarre place of worship for the migrants who have made their home on a goat farm just up the road.

You can't make this stuff up, folks.

For a little perspective on just what the heck is going on in the so-called Brave Little State, here is commercial real estate developer and chair of the Burlington mayor's advisory council, Mr. John Eastlake.

Welcome to the program, Mr. Eastlake.

Great to be here, Tyson.

So you were actually the owner of the gallery that fired Mr. Downes when it first came to light that he had installed this, let's just generously call it an interpretation of the most important religious symbol for Christians around the world.

Right. We all know some artists like to push boundaries and challenge the status quo, that's not something we were interested in doing at Gallery Fifth when I was owner. So when the story broke last spring that Mr. Downes had put up this monstrosity, I asked him to provide a statement. He declined. So having no explanation to offer our many disgruntled patrons, I made the hard decision to remove him from our gallery. Now that the rest of the story has come to light, it seems clear what he was hiding.

I understand that now that the details exploded over social media, the installation has been removed. That's certainly a relief. But do you know if anything has been done to address the situation with the undocumented people living, it seems, quite comfortably there?

I have certainly given voice to the issue in my work as part of the mayor's advisory council and with other influential groups. Frankly, it's a travesty when the unemployment rate is what it is, and we're paying decent wages not to our own people but to noncitizens who break the law.

I can't say I disagree with you there, John. Thanks so much for your time tonight.
Next up, achieving fame and fortune from behind bars. How rap culture makes heroes out of murderers.

◆

Hi Reuben, it's Mom. We were just sitting here watching our news program when a story came on that seems like maybe it involves you? Unless there is more than one Reuben Downes in the state of Vermont who happens to be an artist.
I want to know what the hell he was thinking! Ask him that.
Your father and I are concerned. Are you in some kind of trouble? Call us back, please.

◆

Omigod, omigod, omigod! You finally did it! How's it feel to be a pariah? I gotta say, I'm a little jealous. My notoriety was just a Poppets bad-review campaign from Bridezilla. You're a full-on bad boy felling the sensibilities of Christians and racists in a single swoop! It's kind of a turn on. Maybe I should come visit? Call me.

◆

It's Adrian... So John reached out with the latest Scarecrow Jesus plot twist. Something about undocumented farm workers. It was all a bit confusing, and you know John with his bluster. He said he'd been interviewed by Tyson Marks? Seriously? Seems like things might have gotten out of hand? Anyway, I just wanted to check in. Maybe we can meet for coffee, and you can tell me about this latest scandal. I miss our friendship.

Dude. What. The. Fuck. I'm sitting here at a diner in downtown Sacramento, reading the Bee, *and I nearly choked on my toast to see a news roundup with a story about you and your migrant neighbors.*

Sounds like things were not exactly what you said they were. Were you bullshitting?

◆

Allo, Reuben. It's Marc Barthelme from the gallery. I hear you have made quite, eh, the, eh, splash and ripple with a personal installation of the, eh, Scarecrow Jesus. They say he has been taken down. My hope is, eh, that you will bring him to us for an exhibit we can build around the, eh, the controversy? Who was Jesus, if not the protecteur of the vulnerable people such as those who, eh, have come to worship in your sanctuary, yes? We are very excited about this possibility so please call me as quickly as possible.

◆

Mallard Team >
Today 8:36 a.m.

Joss Martin
Is VT Artist a New Patron Saint of Migrant Workers? [link to story]
cliffpost.com

Cameron Davies
!!!

Wayne Radko
Scarecrow Jesus strikes again!

Donny Heiderich
That's one way to get famous

Kip Graaf
Ruby, you have some 'splainin' to do

Maddy Frye
For Pete's sake Mallards don't believe everything you read

Joss Martin
Pretty sure I heard it on the radio too

Reuben ignored all the calls and messages except for Paul's. It had cut deeply, having to imagine Paul questioning whether Reuben had been honest with him.

"It's not true, what they're saying. You know they just spin the story to rile people up for ratings. I swear, the chain of events was exactly as I described them to you."

Behind Paul, the television was playing a good guy-bad guy shootout in an auto scrapyard. Apart from the backlight of the TV and front light of the computer screen, the room was dark, though it still should have been daylight there.

"Yeah, I mean, I guess I kind of figured that. I just..." he took a deep breath. "You know, when you first told me about how you found out your neighbors were coming over to pray, I thought, *Well, that was short-lived.* How you said you put up Scarecrow Jesus in a kind of solidarity with me, and then all of sudden, it was about something else entirely. Something religious, no less."

"Why didn't you say something?"

Paul shrugged. "You were so mortified about how you'd made a pass at Maddy that night, I didn't want to pile on. I figured I'd get the chance to talk to you about it, but it just got harder to bring it up, so I didn't. Until now, seeing it in the freaking national news."

Reuben rubbed the creases in his brow where much of the day's stress had settled. "This thing, it just took on a life of its own, you know? First that Joy lady getting in my face. And then Rosario and her family being here. The threats and media hysteria. It's like the Frankenstein monster out in the world making a mess of things, and I can't corral it back in."

"Damn, that just sucks." Paul's arms were folded tightly across his chest, his expression suggesting it wasn't just religion he was displeased with.

"Oh, man. You just told me how you were feeling, and I put the blame pretty much everywhere else, didn't I?"

"My therapist would call that a classic case of deflection."

"I feel doubly bad now."

"Same therapist would say it's not all about you."

"Right. Let me give this another go." Reuben paused to give genuine thought to his words. "I know there's a lot I screwed up. You don't even know the half of it." He shook his head, still reeling from the events of the past couple of days. But this was about Paul. "I'm sorry I was so clueless about how you were feeling. It kills me to realize that I lost sight of you, of all people, in this. Man, if I could take it all back, starting with putting up that stupid scarecrow, I would."

"Really? Because I just told you how meaningful that was to me. I could be wrong, but maybe what you should have done was own up to why you put it up in the first place. Otherwise, why do it?"

CHAPTER 31

Reuben wanted nothing more than to be in this moment, feeling Maddy's cheek on his chest, her eyelashes fluttering like a moth on his skin every time she blinked. But while his body was warm and settled in her bed, his brain was bouncing between this infuriating publicity, nagging concerns for everyone at the farm, and his conversation with Paul.

"Did you know you smell like fabric softener even when you're naked?" she said.

"That doesn't sound especially manly."

"Oh no, it's very sexy in a Clean Breeze kind of way."

Reuben offered a half-hearted, one-syllable laugh as he watched the lights of a passing car travel the length of the ceiling.

"You're here but you're not here," Maddy said.

"Sorry. I was just thinking that people use the phrase 'going viral' like it's a good thing. But viruses make you sick."

They heard a neighbor down the hall fiddling with their keys in the door, a dog on the other side in a frenzy of yapping to welcome them home. When it was quiet again, Maddy said, "Maybe Paul is right. Maybe you should just make some kind of statement, addressing it all in one fell swoop."

"That sounds like the fastest way to become a human lightning rod."

"True, that could be the outcome. But it could also be that people feed off not knowing where you're coming from." Maddy leaned up on her elbow, her hair messy and spilling over her shoulders. "If you put it out there, maybe it'll be like stealing the oxygen from the flame."

"What would I even say?"

"I don't know. It's your story. Just be honest. People might still not like it or agree with you, but at least you get to explain your side."

◆

> I'm going to try for this to not sound like a nonapology apology. The kind where you say, I'm sorry what I did offended you. I also don't want to simply raise a hand and say, "My bad," and move on the way you do for accidentally blowing through a stop sign.
>
> Here's the truth. Much as I didn't want to admit it at the time, I installed a crucifix in my backyard with Jesus dressed as a scarecrow because I was angry. I had recently learned that my most important childhood friend had been another in the seemingly never-ending cases coming to light about sexual abuse by Catholic priests. He was just a kid. And every day since, he has been wrestling with how that heinous act by someone he trusted

permanently hijacked the course of his life.

Even still, I didn't plot to put up Scarecrow Jesus. It was never a conscious plan. When I was offered the chance to take possession of a discarded eight-foot-tall crucifix, I took it home because I'm an artist. It was a wonderfully strange thing to have in my stash of collected materials, and quite simply, the craftsmanship by this forgotten wood carver—someone who might not have been so different from me—was beautiful. I have never had any religious inclinations, and so that was all it was to me: an artifact made by skilled human hands. Putting it to use would come later.

Looking back, it may have been that my disgust with what had happened to my friend was already on a collision course with Jesus and the cross—that ironically adored depiction of human cruelty and suffering, and, for me at the time, the embodiment of hypocrisy and sickness.

That was the intellectual argument I made to myself. But I now recognize the act was also an emotional catharsis, an outward expression of long-suppressed grief at having lost my best friend at a time when I needed him the most. In this way, the act of installing Scarecrow Jesus was personal. Mocking that symbol felt correct. It felt satisfying.

Would it matter if I said that the public was never meant to encounter the display? That was my stance when the story first broke: what happens in my backyard is my business.

You have to understand, I spent all my formative years moving to different parts of the country every eight to fourteen months. There was never any connection to a place. I had no investment in relationships, let alone friendships. But setting down roots in a town like Orrville, by definition, means you're part of the community. And the boundaries among the people who live here blur. Happily so. Because those who have reached into my life since I moved here are family in ways I never imagined possible. And I do care, more than I would have liked to admit, when my actions rippled outward to affect them.

And they did ripple, reaching my nearest neighbors up the road. Four people who came from Latin America all the way to Vermont, where they now live on the margins because their needs and US laws are incompatible. I'll leave the politics to others who are clearly more inclined to pick up that baton, and keep the focus on the fact that people are just people, everyone doing what they need to live their lives and carry on to the next day for themselves, for their families.

There are people who would have you believe that Scarecrow Jesus was some kind of master strategy to create a beacon that would lure undocumented migrants to Orrville for the purpose of, I don't know what, prayer sessions? Farm worker support groups? The truth is far less interesting. I put up Scarecrow Jesus as a personal protest. I refused to take it down because I didn't like being told what to do. But then I kept it up because it felt good to offer my hard-working, hidden neighbors something that filled just one gap among the many things they left behind.

I know what it feels like to live in a place where you are disconnected from the people around you. And I promise you, it feels so much better to share experiences and care about each other.

Those of you who are inclined to believe in the divine are likely to imagine God's hand in all of this. As indicated, I'm a card-carrying atheist, but I have to believe the answer to what would Jesus do in this case is give this migrant family the space to carry on their lives peacefully.

Lastly, to those of you whose feelings and criticisms I tuned out over the last several months, I'm sorry. If I'd engaged with you instead of putting up defenses, I bet we could have had some meaningful conversations.

Scarecrow Jesus has been taken down and won't be making a return appearance.

CHAPTER 32

Patton helped edit and publish an excerpted version of the letter in the *Weekly's* editorial section. Reuben also posted the full version to the B3 and on his own rarely visited social media accounts. Like the last few pops of popcorn in the microwave, there was a final smattering of responses, most voicing staunch opposition to illegal immigration ("the law is the law is the law") but Maddy's instincts had been right; the letter seemed to take the air out of the controversy, allowing things like bicycling etiquette and an uptick in littering along Molly Babcock Road to fill the space in the community news. And nationally, all eyes and energy were squarely tuned to the gladiator contest between what might be the first woman president and a reality TV star once perfectly parodied by Tomás. It was with no small relief that Scarecrow Jesus and the "church for illegals," as it was described in one tirade, disappeared altogether from the national stage.

The letter didn't erase Reuben's need to return at least some of the phone messages. Reuben found that while his parents listened attentively, and his mother asked a handful of questions about Paul, he sensed the letter would have done a better job explaining than the halting, disordered account he offered them. At the end of the conversation, the only real sticking point for Reuben's mother seemed to be why he would ever have brought home a giant crucifix in the first place.

As it had been politely suggested, Reuben stayed away from the farm the following weeks, though he kept a frequent, curious eye on the property from the vantage point of his porch and when he was out on walks. He rarely saw the goats in the nearby field. Mostly, they stayed in the distance where a couple times he had seen Arturo or Tomás—he couldn't quite tell which one—milling among them, too far away for a wave. All seemed mercifully quiet.

For Reuben, life quickly returned to a satisfyingly unremarkable status quo. Though he was itching to go over to the farm to see how the family was doing, he recalled the emphatic tone in their voices implying Reuben should keep his distance.

He retreated to the studio to finish a wall sculpture featuring a school of scrap metal minnows. Most nights, he and Maddy would have dinner together and spend the night at her apartment when she had an early shift or at his house when she didn't. They were in a kind of beautiful bubble of early romance, telling stories about the past that shaped them, learning how to play to each other's sense of humor. Reuben indoctrinating Maddy in his favorite movies and vice versa with her favorite books, though Reuben admitted to her he wasn't much of a reader.

It was now closing in on the end of October, and Maddy insisted they put up Halloween decorations along Reuben's porch—fake spider webbing and a few rubber bats on strings that swayed when the wind blew. The two pumpkins Reuben had grown, shaped uncannily like the heads of *Sesame Street's* Bert and Ernie, sat on the railing, reminding Reuben as he pulled in the driveway that he needed to plant garlic that day since the weather was about to turn cold for a solid stretch.

He wandered to the back, picking up a hoe he'd left leaning on the side of the barn and got to work loosening the soil so he could mix in some compost. Then he noticed some grass that had grown inside the raised bed frame, and he set to uprooting it. He also figured it was a good time to harvest the rest of the kale. And on and on these small chores presented themselves. This was the way of gardening, he'd learned, a project that was never completed but always demanded more time than you'd originally planned to give it.

Reuben was so focused on all the details of putting the garden to bed for the winter that he didn't notice Rosario had approached from the trail and was standing two feet away from him for who knows how long. When his peripheral vision caught sight of her, he jumped for real and then clowned it out by falling on the ground, holding his heart.

"Happy Halloween to you, too," Reuben said.

"'Appy 'Alloween to you, too," she parroted.

In just a few short weeks, he could see Rosario had grown. Her legs seemed longer, her face a little less round. Hannah had talked about how her niece had grown in this way, first out, then up, alternating between plumping and lengthening, right up until puberty.

"¿Cómo estás, mi amiga?"

"Bien."

"¿Cómo están los cabras?"

"Las cabras."

"Ay, professor. ¿Cómo están las cabras?"

"Profesora."

"Si, si, perdóname."

"*Las cabras son tontas.*"

Reuben didn't know what '*tontas*' meant, so he stuck with the niceties that he knew.

"*Y tu mama y papa, ¿Cómo están ellos?*"

"*Bien.*"

"*Y su tío?*"

"*¿Cuál?*"

¿Cuál? Reuben thought, *Cuál* means 'which.' "*Tu tío Tomás.*"

"*Mi tío ya no está aqui. Tengo un tío nuevo.*"

My uncle is not here. I have a new uncle.

"*¿Dónde está tío Tomás?*"

"*En México. La migra le mandó de regreso. No nos permitieron despedirnos de él. Estábamos tristes.*"

Mexico, the police, goodbye, and sad. These were the only words he understood, but he had an icy feeling that she was saying that Tomás had been deported.

"*¿Tomás es en México...*" Reuben tried to figure out how to ask the right question, "*¿Permanente?*"

Rosario nodded slowly and seriously.

"Oh, Rosario. *Cuando es Tomás... no mas acqui?*" He knew the words were wrong, but she understood.

"*Desde el siete de octubre.*" October seventh, a specific date in her memory. Nearly three weeks ago. "*Pero a mí, me cae muy bien mi tío nuevo. Se llama Pedro Rivera Montenegro. Él es muy alto.*" She shrugged her shoulders quickly up and down trying to seem upbeat about how she liked her new Uncle Pedro, who maybe had a high voice? Reuben wasn't sure about that last word.

She seemed to not want to answer any more questions about Tomás or Pedro, so Reuben stood and walked over to one of the few sunflowers still in bloom. He took out his pocketknife and cut it. "*Para ti, Rosarita,*" he said, and handed her the stiff flower, which was not much smaller than her own face.

"How you say this?" She asked him.

Reuben smiled, "Sunflower."

"Son flaur," Rosario said, and again, "Son flaur."

"*Bueno*. That's good."

"That's good," she repeated. "How you say this?" She pointed to the hoe lying on the ground.

"What is that called?"

"*Si*, what is that colled?"

"It is called a hoe."

"It is called a 'o."

"*Huuhhh, huuhhh, como la...*" Reuben went through a Spanish alphabet song he'd learned in class a million years ago, "*La jota in jalapeño.*"

"Ho. It is called a ho. Son flaur *y* ho."

"*Una buena estudiante.*"

"That's good," she said.

"*Mucho* good."

Rosario beamed. The simple joy of their exchange of words, momentarily distracting Reuben from the news about Tomás. But remembering made Reuben wonder if Rosario's parents knew where she was. It seemed unlikely they would want her wandering over, especially now. "*Ahora, chica, vamos a su casa.*"

Rosario held the sunflower under her chin as they walked side by side along the trail back to the farm. A recent heavy rain had dragged down much of the remaining foliage, so the trail was speckled with wet gold, brown, and red leaves, making the path all but disappear in a few places. The air smelled sweet, musky, and damp. Along the way, she had the same question over and over, "*What is this colled?*" He answered, and she repeated, "A rock." "Moss." "Pine tree." "Cheepmonk."

When they climbed back over the wall together, Arturo took long, fast strides to reach them then took Rosario by the wrist, saying something in a firm tone to her. Like a scolded pup she dropped her chin and nodded slowly. Reuben felt responsible for her getting into trouble despite being the one to bring her back.

Reuben said to Arturo, "*Rosario habla de Tomás*... was it ICE?"

Arturo's face shadowed over. Reuben was unsure if it was because of the situation or because Rosario had spoken to Reuben about it. He simply said, "*Sí.*"

"I'm so sorry. *Lo siento*. Is there anything—"

There were so many questions Reuben wanted to ask, but in this moment, the language barrier simply felt too big to breach. And Arturo was already shepherding Rosario back to the house, ending their encounter.

Before they went inside, he turned to Reuben, "*Gracias por traer a Rosario de vuelta a casa.*" And then he offered a tight but friendly nod.

"Of course," Reuben said.

Patton tapped his sources to piece together what had happened to Tomás. He called Reuben later that night.

"It seems the feds already had their eye on him, his name having been associated with a group that was caught bringing others across the northern border last summer."

Reuben sat down on the couch in his studio. "Why would he have taken that kind of risk?"

"Why does anyone do anything? Money. Or, I don't know, maybe that and he wanted to help others."

Reuben watched a crow pecking around for vegetable remnants in the garden. He thought about October seventh, the date Rosario said Tomás had gone. It was about three weeks after the social post and its aftermath. Reuben would have thought if the feds hadn't made a move at that point, they weren't going to.

"Do you know how it happened?"

"They picked him up at the farm," Patton said.

"Wait, so what Claire said about ICE not coming on the property was bullshit?"

"Technically, they weren't on the property. They just waited, parked on the road, and quietly picked him up when he was setting the garbage out for pickup."

It was a gut punch to imagine. Tomás going about his work, a chore he'd probably done every week for several years.

"How do we know they didn't get the wrong guy?" asked Reuben, still trying to find a way for the story to have a better ending.

"We don't for sure. But..." Patton hesitated.

"But what?"

"It surprised me, is all. When Tomás agreed to leave the farm overnight. Arturo, Elena, and Rosario—they're a family. They don't want to risk getting split apart, so it made sense. But in my experience, the migrants' sense of responsibility to the animals and to a good employer like Claire Meloy is so deeply ingrained, I half expected Tomás to stay with you that night and just get up and work the next day. But when the talk of getting far enough out of ICE jurisdiction came up, and he didn't offer to stay behind... it just caught my attention at the time. And then today when you texted that he'd been deported, it made me wonder if he knew he had something to be concerned about, is all."

Reuben didn't want to believe it was true. Not only because it would recast Tomás in his mind as someone who would break the law at a more serious level, but also because Reuben had a nagging feeling that the attention he and Patton had caused were in some ways responsible for ICE zeroing in on Tomás.

"What's the risk for the family now, Patton? Do they have to do reconnaissance every time they get the mail? Can they even go to the grocery store?"

"I mean, there's always a risk. But I checked and I couldn't find any record of Arturo or Elena on any watch list. So that's on their side. I'm also pretty sure, given the timeline, that Rosario is a US citizen, which might provide some leniency if it ever came to that. But the fact is, I don't really know. I've added it to my list of future reporting topics. And anyway, maybe things will change with a new president coming in."

That night, Reuben wandered the house like a ghost that couldn't remember its purpose. The daylight was nearly gone, though it wasn't even dinnertime yet. Maddy was at a bachelorette "spa evening" for one of her coworkers, and he wouldn't see her until the following night.

He started to fold a load of laundry, but it had been left in the dryer too long and no amount of smoothing would minimize the wrinkles. So as he'd learned from Rosemary, he soaked a towel, put it all back, and set it to dry again. Picking up the thinnest book Maddy had lent him—a collection of letters from a pioneer woman to her brother—Reuben sat down on the couch to read beside Lou Garoo who had decided he liked life better on the inside when the temperature dropped below fifty. But that didn't mean the cat appreciated having company, and he glared, ears back, at the audacity of Reuben's presence.

"Why are you such a dick sometimes?" The empty house fed Reuben's own words back at him.

His conversation with Patton was a continual cloud over his thoughts.

Reuben picked up the phone and texted Rosemary.

You busy?

Almost always. Why do you ask?

Need any help around the inn tonight?

I believe I do. C'mon by.

Reuben pulled one of the bottles of wine Adrian had left behind and headed over.

At this time of year, Guillaume, a former lighting designer for a small theater company in one of the Montreal suburbs, would transform the cheerful inn into a haunted house by creating foreboding shadows that gradually deepened every day until they became full-on menacing the night before Halloween. It had been fun for Reuben to be there when the trick-or-treaters came. Rosemary would dress, quite plausibly, as a witch—not the cliché with the pointed hat and warty nose, but the kind of all-knowing crone that made Puritan men uncomfortable—and Guillaume would put dark circles under his eyes and dress in rags, still going about the yard chores, but now with an axe continually clutched in his hand. It was deliciously terrifying for the older kids, less fun for the little ones that Rosemary would soothe with a special lollipop just for them.

From the entryway, Reuben could smell onions cooking, a hint of bacon, too. There was an older couple on the couch smoothing an old-school paper map in front of them. It immediately brought back memories of sitting in the back seat of Reuben's family's Ford Bronco, the atlas on his lap as he used a thick highlighter to trace a new line from the town they'd just left to the one they were headed to. The yellow marker's path stitched towns and cities together in a zigzag across the country, and in a few cases, back again. He made a note to dig that old memento out from the closet and share it with Maddy or maybe cut it up and use it in a mixed media piece.

As he passed the guest couple, Reuben pointed to the kitchen and said, "Rosemary in there?" The woman nodded while the man shrugged.

When he pushed open the swinging door, Rosemary bustled over, trading a stack of bowls for the bottle of wine he held.

"Soup's on," she said pointing to the steaming pot on the stove. "Potato leek. It'll be good and hot in about ten minutes."

Reuben felt a renewed flush of affection for the woman who knew him well enough to sense when comfort food and company were in order.

"I came by to help, Rosie, not eat."

"Don't you worry, I've got you folding laundry after dinner."

Guillaume came in as Reuben was setting napkins and silverware beside the bowls.

"*Pas de pizza?*" Guillaume asked Rosemary. She shook her head. He turned to Reuben, "*Tout va bien, Reuben?*"

"He's asking how you are," Rosemary said when Reuben floundered for understanding. It was hard enough to muddle through Spanish.

He took a breath and tried to sound upbeat, "Yeah, yeah, all is fine, good."

The old floorboards in the other room groaned as the couple made their way to the room down the hall for the evening. They shouted goodnight to Rosemary, and she hurried to catch them, letting them know that breakfast would be served between seven and nine the next morning.

"*Vin?*" Guillaume held up the bottle in one hand and an opener in the other. Reuben nodded.

The soup was rich and flavorful with layers of smoke and salt infusing the creamy soft potato bites. Rosemary always kept a container of homemade croutons that Reuben suggested they add for a little garlicky crunch.

"My best pupil," Rosemary said, "Culinary, anyway. I had some pretty smart fifth graders."

Reuben acknowledged the joke with a humble head bow. He wasn't sure if in coming over he wanted to talk or just didn't want to be by himself. Either way, Rosemary forced an opening.

"What's got you moping, dear?"

After he'd told them about his exchanges with Rosario and Arturo and the details he'd learned from Patton, Guillaume let out a long, low whistle.

Rosemary said, "Ah, that's a shame."

"*Il avait l'air très gentil. Et drôle, aussi.*"

"Gui says he seemed like a good man. Funny, too."

"Yeah, I think those are both true. But I only barely knew him." Reuben realized they were talking about Tomás as if he had died.

"You know it's entirely possible that he's been happily reunited with family and friends in Mexico," Rosemary said.

Reuben nodded slowly, thinking also that perhaps Tomás wasn't sorry to be missing another dark, cold winter that was just around the corner. But these were optimistic thoughts that couldn't quite ease his own feelings of culpability.

"Jackson Endicott had warned me to leave them to themselves. I didn't listen. Maybe it was selfish. Even though I almost never saw them in the yard, I liked knowing they had been by. It was always a happy surprise when I would find something in the morning that Rosario or Elena left. And then sharing something back with them, it was kind of this really sweet, simple connection between neighbors." Reuben traced clockwise circles in his soup. "But obviously not everyone in the community is interested in having them here. I feel like maybe I gave them a false sense of security."

Rosemary was quick to jump in, "And they didn't deserve that? Feeling that they were safe in their neighborhood?"

"Of course they deserve that. But was it worth it if it meant being exposed? Deported?"

Guillaume, who was chewing a particularly loud crouton, said, *"Seulement Tomás peut répondre à ça."*

"Gui thinks that's not your call to make. Your neighbors are their own people, Reuben. They get to choose the risks they take. And they've taken quite a few to be here, so give them a little credit for being able to decide for themselves how they want to engage—or not—with the people around them."

It was a gentle rebuke that reminded Reuben of what Paul said his therapist would say: it's not all about him. Reuben was quiet as he finished the last few spoonfuls of soup. He recalled Elena's words in the article, how she said she had felt peace in her heart when she visited Scarecrow Jesus. It was true, it wasn't all about him.

"Mind you," Rosemary said pointing with her spoon, "I'm not suggesting you shouldn't always reflect on how your actions impact others and how you might do things differently moving forward. That's the first thing they teach the littles in pre-K."

The mention of pre-K brought Rosario to mind and her new enthusiasm for learning English. Arturo and Elena might not want her coming by but maybe Reuben could go to their house a few times a week to share some vocabulary lessons. Of course, they could decide they want nothing further to do with him. But he hoped it wouldn't be the case.

True to her word, Rosemary put Reuben to work folding soft flannel sheets and still-warm towels. He saw her eyeing his handiwork as she brought in a freshly dried quilt. He took two corners in hand and he and Rosemary met like dancers in the space between them.

"Two years as of last week, right?"

"What is?" Reuben asked.

"I believe you and that nutter were here over Columbus Day weekend two years ago."

"Yeah, let's not call Hannah that anymore. Also, I believe it's Indigenous People's Day now," he said with a smile.

"Fair on both points, my friend. Even an old dog can make reasonable accommodations in her language." She scooped up a tower of towels. "You know, Gui and I made a bet about whether you'd last more than a year here."

"Who lost?"

"I'll never tell. But looks like those roots might be taking hold, what with your garden and your girlfriend?"

It was strange, Reuben realized, the thought of leaving hadn't occurred to him, not once since he'd made the decision to stay. "Might be."

"In that case, I have something for you." Rosemary reached in her back pocket and pulled out a fork.

Reuben let out a surprised chuff. "Oh my god." She held it out to him, and Reuben stepped closer feeling its draw. "You kept it?"

"Thought we might need it as evidence if she went and did something worse. So I set it aside and forgot about it until I came across it about a month ago. Don't worry, I cleaned it."

Reuben took the fork from her. It had some weight but the tines were dull, which meant Hannah had put a hefty force behind it. He could still feel a deep ache when he was gripping a brush for an extended time or lifting a pot from the stove.

"Figured you might have a place for it in one of your sculptures."

He slid the fork into his chest pocket where it sat like a secret friend. "Thanks, Rosie. You never know."

CHAPTER 33

When he first moved into the house on Popple Hill Road, Reuben found the quiet unsettling, especially at night when hardly a car would pass by. With so little background noise, his ears would latch on to the house sounds. The low hum of the refrigerator. Ticks and pops from the wood stove. The steady, percussive rhythm of clothes tumbling in the dryer. Over time, his ears recalibrated to the environment, as did his other senses to the uniformity of sights and perception of space. In fact, the adjustment to a quiet home with a yard and general solitude was physical, a kind of calm ease that settled deep. And now, Reuben was back in the heart of a city, this time feeling overwhelmed just by the walk from the hotel to the gallery on an unseasonably warm Saturday in March, moving briskly among crowds of spring-fever pedestrians. There was so much movement and color, voices weaving together in French and English, shoes scrape-and-clacking on the sidewalk, grumbling trucks, and the howl of a passing fire engine siren. He could feel his pulse ticking up.

Beside him, Kip was taking it all in, his head following every distracting movement, eyes looking up the heights of buildings with such eagerness Reuben wondered if he'd ever been to a city before. Maddy was on Reuben's other side, holding his hand loosely as they walked, dropping it when they needed to make room for someone coming from the other direction and taking it up again after they passed.

It was late afternoon, and the gallery's glass garage door was rolled up, inviting fresh air and passers-by into the space. Mark Barthelme greeted them in the entryway, introducing himself to Kip with a firm handshake, and air kisses on either side of Maddy's cheeks, which made her blush.

This was to be the last walk-through before the opening that evening. While Maddy strolled through the other exhibits, Kip worked on fine tuning sound clarity and speaker angles. Reuben, having learned some tricks of the lighting trade from Guillaume, talked a gallery technician through adjustments to hue and brightness levels. They spent nearly two hours getting every detail just the way they wanted. The result was a surprisingly lifelike outdoor experience, recreated indoors with materials that had metamorphosed from natural to manufactured and back into a facsimile of natural.

As they stood back for a final assessment, Reuben noticed Kip had a tense energy about him, agitated and sharp. "It's weird, isn't it? Gallery openings are always kind of terrifyingly vulnerable."

"I don't think I should come tonight," Kip said. "I don't even like talking to people, let alone up in front of them." He turned to Reuben, wide eyed and unsettled. "You can handle this on your own. You don't need me. Just ask Maddy to record some of it on her phone. That's all I need."

Reuben put a hand on his shoulder. "I can't do it without you. Your work was the seed of this project. It has no reason for being without your recordings. Everything works together beautifully, like we've talked about. There's nothing to be spooked by. You'll do great. And if you don't, so what? The work is its own performance. People will find meaning in it without you. But putting something you created out the world, that's worth taking a moment to savor."

◆

Reuben's own eagerness was less about the evening's opening than meeting up with Paul at the hotel bar beforehand. They had made the plan two months earlier when Paul mentioned he would be traveling to western Maine to scatter his mother's ashes in the lake by her childhood home. When the gallery opening was scheduled for mid-March, Reuben suggested Paul fly into Montreal where he could come to the event, then travel back with Reuben to Vermont and stay for a visit before renting a car and continuing to the ceremony with his cousins. Paul declined the Vermont visit, mostly due to his work schedule, but he did take the flight into Montreal, which proved to be a shorter distance to western Maine than if he had he flown into Boston.

Paul was already seated at a corner table when Reuben arrived a few minutes late. The bar was dim, but he found Paul, thanks to the table's candlelight glinting off the wire frames of his glasses. He stood as Reuben approached.

They both waited a beat, face-to-face, reconciling boyhood memories with the men they had become.

"Last time we were together, neither of us had any facial hair," Paul said, indicating Reuben's closely trimmed beard.

"And you were shorter." Reuben tilted his head, reassessing, "But actually, not by much."

"Yeah, you just grew more than I did."

"Weird, isn't it?"

"Good weird though."

Reuben reached out an arm, and they officially greeted each other with an affectionate back-slap hug.

A waiter came over, and the men sat to order appetizers and drinks. Reuben asked for a Manhattan, and Paul ordered a Coke.

"I mostly try not to drink anymore," he explained.

"Oh, I don't need to—"

"It's really fine. I have no trouble being around other people. Or at least, no more than I do when they're not drinking." He laughed self-deprecatingly.

Small talk about Paul's flight delays and Reuben's slow border crossing quickly gave way to easier, more casual conversation as they settled into the familiar cadence of their video calls. Reuben talked about his project with Kip, how it came about and came together in fits and starts over many months between all the other drama. And how Maddy would be stopping by to meet Paul before they split off for dinner.

"Look at you getting all dewy eyed at the mention of her name," Paul said.

It was true, Reuben couldn't hide a flush of affection whenever he thought or talked about Maddy. "It's been great," he said. "We're taking our first vacation together. Flying out tomorrow night to Mexico City."

"That'll put things to the test as a couple," Paul said. "Do either of you speak Spanish?"

"I've been brushing up on it with the help of a tutor . . . who happens to be a preschooler."

"That makes sense, I'm sure there will be situations where, '*Por favor*, can you tie my shoes?' will come in handy."

The waiter delivered their drinks along with a plate artfully assembled with a round of chèvre, fig chutney, and baguette toasts.

Reuben gave a quick thought of appreciation for goats and their caretakers before digging in.

"What about you? You seeing anyone these days?" Reuben said, unsure whether it was poor form to ask, especially since Paul had never talked about relationships or dating.

"Yeah, sort of. I have a close friend, Marisa, who I've known for years from a support group we met at. Our relationship has just sort of glacially evolved over time. What's nice is that we both understand the occasional need to retreat from the world and just be alone. Other people I dated struggled when I dropped communication for a few days or a week, sometimes more. They got worried or angry, usually one followed by the other, which is understandable. It's nice because Marisa and I enjoy being together when it feels right for both of us, and when it doesn't, we just know to wait it out. Might not work for everyone but it works for us."

"Yeah, of course. That makes sense."

If his time among Hannah, Adrian, and Maddy had taught Reuben anything, it's that every relationship had its own unique fingerprint. The habits and patterns that work well in one are often incompatible in another. And people change, he decided. He had changed. Reuben's attraction to Hannah, he now understood, felt as if his own unsettled state of being had found a compatible frequency with her manic energy; but ultimately, sustaining it was not in his makeup. And with Adrian, it seemed like there was always this space between them—they could lean across and reach each other, but not comfortably, and not for any sustainable amount of time. When she left, she had blamed herself, and he let her, but really, they were both always holding back in their own way.

Paul changed the subject. "So what's the fallout been after your flash of national fame? Are you, like, a resident celebrity now?"

Reuben scoffed, "Thankfully, no. The world has moved on. There were some hard outcomes, you know, but also some positive ones. Patton, the guy who wrote the original feature, did a follow-up story about the rise in harassment against the migrant community. That prompted a few communities to put up ballot measures that allow for more local protection for the migrant workers in their towns."

"Interesting. I haven't a clue how that stuff is handled in California. Of course, California is a bit more of a melting pot than Vermont." He took a bite of the appetizer. "And what about your backyard Jesus?"

Here, Reuben hesitated, knowing how Paul felt about the Church. "It's been, um, repurposed."

"Into actual art?"

"No. A church from one of the neighboring towns reached out and asked if I would give it to them. They wanted to create a safe, welcoming place for the area's migrant community to worship, and I guess Scarecrow Jesus was symbolic in that way. You know, in addition to the regular way."

"Of course they did. Always trying to find more sheep for the flock."

"I know. Your cynicism is fully justified," Reuben said gently. "But I also believe there's a genuinely kind spirit behind the effort to invite people—wherever they're from—to belong, connect."

Paul's words came back fast. "That's a double-edged sword, though, right? People who need to connect and belong are vulnerable. And vulnerable people are sniffed out and preyed on."

Hearing the catch in Paul's voice, seeing a hint of tremor in his hand, it dawned on Reuben that his grasp of Paul's pain had been insufficient, a video transmission that abstracted the depth of the distrust and anger that would always be just below the surface for his friend. And maybe that was Brinkman's greatest crime.

"You know," Reuben's thought wasn't fully formed, but he continued anyway, "I met you at a time when I had decided friendships weren't worth the effort."

"And then I disappeared, confirming that they weren't?"

"We're here, aren't we?"

Paul didn't answer but he smiled and seemed warmed by the question.

Seeing Maddy enter the bar, Reuben waved to her. She weaved through the crowd of bar patrons, which had doubled in the last thirty minutes. She looked simply and elegantly beautiful in a 1920s-style black beaded dress and heels, her narrow face highlighted with a light touch of makeup, a wispy bun secured loosely at the base of her neck. Reuben stood, almost involuntarily, and held out a hand to her as if hastening an understanding to everyone in the room that she was there with him. He kissed her temple. Paul got up and introduced himself.

"Reuben has told me some fun stories about when you guys played baseball together," she said, opening with an easy turn to the conversation.

"Has he?"

"You remember Al D?" Reuben asked.

"Oh my god, that kid couldn't catch a bus."

Reuben said, "The Al D hop."

"So easy, even Al D could field it—holy crap, that's a long time ago." Paul smiled. "Those were sweet days."

"Yeah, they were," Reuben agreed.

The opening had attracted an eclectic mix of art aficionados; hip, urban couples; and a smattering of Americans visiting the city. The immersive exhibit was set in a back corner away from the other sections of the gallery. Kip had suggested having the experience be akin to what the kids in *The Chronicles of Narnia* felt as they wandered from the depths of the wardrobe into the woods. So Marc Barthelme put up tall, textured curtains that allowed visitors to stroll a ways in before sensing the light was changing and hearing subtle nature sounds—wind in the branches, a chickadee. Once in the exhibit, a sign suggested visitors find a place to stand or even sit without speaking, and simply observe the shifting light and audio textures, noting the moment they heard the season's very first droplet of sap ping into the metal bucket. A single moment. A beginning.

They gave visitors forty-five minutes to explore the exhibit and reemerge into a reception area where wine, beer, and light hors d'oeuvres were served as the artists talked about their process. Or at least, Reuben did. Kip, still wildly nervous, struggled to articulately answer audience questions, even the one he had rehearsed over dinner about what had motivated him on his auditory quest. His words came out in a mishmash of thoughts that included a mention of his mother and her illness, the impossibility of holding time, and how sound waves continue long after we no longer detect them. It wasn't until a woman with a pixie haircut and large hoop earrings, who identified herself as a professional DJ, asked about the equipment he used for outdoor versus indoor recording that Kip became less wooden and slid into comparing audio technical specifications like they were his first language.

The question of Scarecrow Jesus came up briefly, and Reuben responded by explaining how even artists don't always have a good sense of where the line between art and life is drawn.

"But that's a topic for another day, a different exhibit," he said.

As the evening wound down, Reuben felt energized, as he always did when people—total strangers, really—interacted with his art, letting it take up space in their minds and circling their impressions back to him.

And it wasn't just the fine art. Lately, he'd come to view his commercial work in a new light, too, when a woman emailed to tell him that a winter landscape he'd painted for a bank client in Boston had provided a moment of calm as she sat in the lobby about to apply for her first mortgage as a newly single woman.

There was something profound about the exchanges, positive or negative, between creator and audience that Reuben knew few people really got to experience. He wondered, now that Kip had participated in the exhibit, if he would be more open to sharing his audio recordings as a new form of art. Reuben hoped so.

The question would have to wait, however, because Kip hurried over, telling Reuben and Maddy they should head out without him. The DJ woman had invited him to the club where she had a regular gig. As he put it, he was interested in doing some "equipment research," a phrasing that normally would have taken on a lewd tone except for Kip seemed completely in earnest.

At nearly 10 p.m., the city had calmed but continued to hum and pulse as cars lined up when the traffic lights turned red, and pedestrians continued to hurry along. In Montreal, even the "WALK" figure on the crossing signals looked pressed for time with its wide stride and arms at purposeful angles. But Reuben and Maddy were in no rush on their stroll back to the hotel.

"How did it feel seeing Paul after all these years?"

"It felt . . ." Reuben resisted the impulse to toss off a simple, *good*. It's what he would have done with Adrian. But Maddy seemed to ask because she was interested in the answer, for what it could tell her about his inner thoughts. After all, they were still in the process of learning each other. "It felt happy. It was good to know that whatever bond we felt in that short time was real. Not just something I clung to because I was a lonely kid. For us being able to pick up again, these decades later, and still feel that easiness, it's really kind of amazing. But sad, too, knowing that we missed out on so much time."

Maddy unclasped his hand and slid her arm into his, so their elbows locked. "Maybe next vacation, we can visit him in California."

There was confidence behind her words. That a future trip together wasn't just expected, it might even be inevitable. He liked hearing it.

As a kid, Reuben hated vacations with his parents. They were almost always tacked on as part of the transition from one home to another, so there was no real relaxation happening, always the hovering cloud of starting over. It didn't matter whether it was a Florida beach town, Washington, D.C., or the Grand Canyon—staying in a strange place with just enough time to recognize landmarks before having to pack up and leave felt too much like regular life.

But now, with their flight leaving the following afternoon, Reuben felt eager to explore new places with Maddy, to taste new foods, meet new people—he was ready to invite the unfamiliar world in. Because when the travel was over, nothing would be as sweet as pulling in the driveway to see the mailbox with its familiar backward lean, the winter-beaten lawn coming into green again, and the wide front porch that would need a fresh coat of paint once spring had fully returned.

EPILOGUE

Though it was early April, the day was raw and windy-cold. Layered in long underwear, pants, shirt, thick hoodie, and fleece, Reuben felt like a walking mummy and wondered how he would manage to squat behind the plate without splitting a seam. As he and Maddy walked toward the field, her perpetually cold hand was like a gentle vampire slowly draining Reuben's body heat.

From behind them came the sound of running footsteps crunching the grass. Reuben turned to see Patrice catching up to them.

"This does not feel like spring!" he said, continuing to jog slowly alongside them. He was wearing a trapper hat with the flaps loosely bouncing over his ears with every step. "Although, I see that love is in the air." Patrice pointed to their clasped hands.

As the three of them approached the field, Reuben saw Donny by the dugout inventorying and inspecting all the gear as Aaron raked the infield, a sleeping, snowsuit-stuffed baby strapped to his back. Joss and Cameron were huddled close, whispering to each other on the bench.

From out of left field, literally, came Wayne and Kip speed-bumping along in a golf cart, the two of them laughing like a couple of delinquent kids. Kip clutched the cart's dashboard with one hand and the roof with the other to keep from getting tossed out.

"Kip, I think you should put a helmet on!" shouted Patrice with a laugh.

Wayne brought the cart to a skidding stop beside third base. The players all gathered around.

"I'm not sure this counts as taking up golf, Wayne." Cameron said.

"Yeah, turns out, I *hated* golf. But I loved the zippy little cars. So I sold the *clubs* and picked up this baby on eBay." He got out of the cart and did a trio of torso twists. "I'm your new outfield *ball* boy, Mallards! Oh, and yeah, I'm still gonna *coach*."

"It's good to have you back, Wayne." Maddy said.

"Well, look at you two," he said, taking in Reuben and Maddy standing close together. "Between you and these other turtledoves," he pointed a chin to Cameron and Joss, "I might just start a softball dating app."

"You can call it, *Great Catch*," said Cameron beaming at Joss who shoved him hard enough to make him stumble.

"Or *Playing the Field*," said Aaron.

"*Swingers!*" said Patrice.

Donny shook his head, "That's a different kind of app."

Kip came over, opening his arms wide to Reuben and Maddy. "Aww, hey you two, how was your wedding?"

All eyes snapped to them.

"Oh, jeez, you guys, not ours!" Maddy said.

Kip smiled sweetly, satisfied he'd elicited the intended response. In fact, Kip had been referring to Rosemary and Guillaume's wedding, which had taken place a week earlier.

Ducks on the Pond

Reuben offered to host the small gathering of friends and siblings, knowing if it were held at the inn that Rosemary would spend the week cooking and cleaning for her own wedding. Guillaume agreed and insisted they take Reuben up on his offer. And so, with some firm input from Rosemary ("No fuss. No DJ. Flowers are acceptable but we'll send them home with the guests. And you'll use my grandmother's table linens."), Reuben and Maddy planned a festive and simple country affair.

Held in a sunset-lit patch of mowed field ("brush-hogged," as Rosemary called it), the ceremony was presided over by Jackson Endicott, who, it came as no surprise to Reuben, happened to also be an ordained minister. His sermon centered on the idea of mature love, the kind that is tempered by reason, wisdom, and an understanding that everything is changing and impermanent.

"But that's all the more reason to cherish this moment, in this place, at this time, and to honor our interconnectedness on a small parcel of land, in the world, within the universe. It's why you've been asked to be here." Jackson held a long pause, looking warmly into the faces of every guest sitting attentively on their folding chairs: Rosemary's twin sister Ellie; Guillaume's three burly brothers, their wives, and a smattering of adult nieces and nephews; Maddy and Reuben, but also Elena, Arturo, Rosario, and "new" Tio Pedro. "Each of you is a thread in the tapestry that embraces Rosemary and Guillaume on their day of union. You are part of them. They are part of you."

When it was time for vows, Rosemary and Guillaume turned to face each other, his hands positively enveloping hers. Their exchanges were very brief and bilingual, but not in the way Reuben was expecting.

"The day when I meet you, *Rosemarie*, I think I don't want to leave the side of this woman," Guillaume said. "So I will not. *Jamais.*"

Then it was Rosemary's turn. "*Mon amour, tu es très doué pour soulever des objets lourds. Et tu es aussi un gentil compagnon, C'est tous ce dont j'ai besoin,*" Rosemary said, which Reuben later learned translated to, "My love, you are very good at lifting heavy things. And you are also a kind companion. That is all I need." The words were classic Rosemary but, in the moment, her eyes betrayed a deep well of emotion threatening to spill over, so she turned to Jackson and said, "Alright, get on with it."

They were pronounced married to loud cheers and applause, and showered with birdseed as they walked, arms locked together, back toward the house where a single long table was draped in Rosemary's grandmother's hand-embroidered tablecloth and set with place settings from the inn. The glasses shined, reflecting the twinkling lights that had been strung around the patio's perimeter.

While Jackson popped bottles of champagne, Reuben, Maddy, Elena, and Rosario all headed to the kitchen where they had spent the last two days preparing a menu that was an eclectic mix of Yankee, Irish, Quebecois, and Guatemalan, the centerpiece of which was a generations-old recipe for a slow cooked stew with chicken, potatoes, tomatoes, chiles, and spices that Elena let Reuben and Rosario apprentice on.

The partygoers celebrated well into the evening. And if communication among the guests wasn't always without confusion, it didn't especially matter, as the food and wine and laughter flowed and ebbed and flowed again.

Once the sun had set and the air became chilly, the party moved inside. A few guests took up places in the kitchen to help with the dishes while others wandered to the living room where one of Guillaume's brothers played tunes on a fiddle he had brought. Pedro picked up a guitar Reuben had kept in a corner of the room—decorative but serviceable—and strummed along. Occasionally, Guillaume, flushed with wine and unabashed affection, and other family members took to singing French folk songs, including what must have been a bawdy serenade to Rosemary who just shook her head, both amused and embarrassed.

Reuben had been to his share of weddings in his late twenties, mostly among college friends. These had been fancy affairs, formal ceremonies, and raucous parties. Rosemary and Guillaume's wedding was something different. It was warm, joyful, sweet, and generous. *And more than all of those*, Reuben thought, *it's beautifully human.*

But to the softball team, whose politeness was just barely masking their impatience to start throwing a ball around, Reuben said, "The wedding was great. Good food, music, and company. The happy couple are in St. Lucia, probably snorkeling as we speak."

Rosemary had sent Reuben a photo of the two of them, transformed into people he hardly recognized, and not just because of the amount of skin they were both revealing (including a faded, inky tattoo covering the expanse of Guillaume's hairy chest), but also because they seemed to radiate pure happiness.

"And that completes the social portion of today's practice," Wayne said. "I'll thank you all to kindly take your warm-up lap so we can get this season started."

But before anyone moved, something behind Reuben had caught people's attention, their necks craning just a little, and Kip shading his eyes to get a clearer view.

Reuben and Maddy turned to see a person walking a straight line over to the group.

"Who's that?" Joss asked what they were all wondering.

"Ah, Jasper!" Patrice yelled, waving his hand high in the air, "Come! Come join!"

Jasper broke into a jog.

"That umpire?" Donny asked.

"Yes, he was graduated last year," Patrice said. "I check, Wayne, he does know the infielder's fly ball rule, so I invited him today to try out for the team."

The kid reached them, a little winded, a mitt secured in his armpit.

"Everybody, this is my friend, Jasper Van Sykes."

The players' attention immediately sharpened, and Jasper noticed, breaking into a grin.

"Yeah, I know. Aunt Dana is kind of intense."

Wayne nodded, a seeming satisfaction on his face. "I think we can *bypass* the tryout *formalities* in this case. Jasper Van Sykes, welcome to the twenty-sixth season of the Coleslaw League."

Ducking back into the golf cart, Wayne squeezed an old-timey ooga horn. "Those softballs aren't going to throw themselves, Mallards! Gotta make the most of the *day*light while we've *got* it."

The cart jolted into motion. As the team jogged to the backstop, Wayne took off, puttering back to the outfield, swooping around, doing precarious grass donuts for the sheer fun of it.

◆

ACKNOWLEGMENTS

It also takes a village to write a book.

Thank you to Lou Aronica, founder and publisher of The Story Plant—your editorial guidance was essential in tightening the nuts and bolts of this story. Thanks also to TSP's associate editor, Allison Maretti, and marketing editorial consultant, Elizabeth Long.

For several years, Suzanne Loring and Benjamin Roesch have been my writing partner rocks, providing wisdom, sharp eyes, and general cheerleading every step of the way as this story grew from a scrap of an idea.

I have so much gratitude for my insightful, enthusiastic beta readers, Heather Schoppmann and Matt Simmons, and especially my former JV high school softball coach, Glen Noto, whose drills, baseball lingo, and stories seamlessly stitched their way into parts of this book. For the record, the Park Ridge Owls were undefeated in my sophomore year.

Speaking of sports, I want to give a nod to the Charlotte Volleyball League who were a source of inspiration in writing about the unique and unexpected bonds that arise from grown-ups getting together to share their love of the game and the occasional barbecue.

The undocumented farm workers situation in Vermont—and indeed, the U.S.—is complex and not easily addressed. But always at the center of it are people. Some of their voices are beautifully, sometimes painfully, captured in a book called *The Most Costly Journey*, a collection of Vermont migrants' personal stories told in translation and illustrated by New England cartoonists. Julia Grand Doucet was an editor of that anthology, and she was an indispensable reader, course-corrector, Spanish translator, and community connector.

Through Julia, I was fortunate to meet a kind and beautiful family within the migrant community who shared their stories and friendship with me. I also received excellent guidance and input from Will Lambek of Migrant Justice.

Because I knew nothing about goat farming, I had an instructive research visit to Ayers Brook Goat Dairy where owner Darryll Breau provided a tour and patiently answered all my questions—right in the heart of kidding season. Oof, those baby goats!

Vance Kiviranna, illustrator and designer of this book's cover, gets a special thanks for pitch-perfectly capturing the spirit (and various plot points) of the story. Thank you also to the crazy-talented team at Bolder & Co. Creative Studio for bearing with me when I disappear from my day job a few times a year to write fiction.

Ducks on the Pond is a book about connection and caring. If these values shine through, it's because I learned them not just from my parents, Bernie and Carol Cohen, but also my wonderful extended family: Arlene and Arthur Cohen; Laura, Rob, Matthew, and Zachary Ciampa; and Mary Ellen, Itzik, and Daniel Yochay.

Last and most, thank you to my extended hearts, my people: Sonya whose fierce determination and creative spark often leave me awed; and Roger, whose "Let's just see what's around the corner" life philosophy always keeps us on the most surprising and enriching paths.

(I'll also add a postscript shout-out to Hades, the barn cat-turned-domestic feline prince whose attitude distinctly resembles that of Lou Garoo.)

ABOUT THE AUTHOR

Amy Klinger lives in Vermont with her husband and daughter. When she's not writing books and creative essays, she is a communications strategy consultant, a hobby baker, gravel biker, and singer for the punk band Violet Crimes. Her first novel, *In Light of Recent Events* was published in 2022. Stop by AmyKlinger.com for blogs and updates.

www.ingramcontent.com/pod-product-compliance
Lightning Source LLC
LaVergne TN
LVHW021650060526
838200LV00050B/2287